"[A] SUPERB COLLECTION."
—*Los Angeles Times Book Review*

"Superbly composed prose . . . Almost every story has a surprising shape that insures its place in the reader's memory."
—*The New Yorker*

"Highly readable . . . These stories . . . reveal fresh paradoxes and connections, deepening our understanding by reminding us that mystery can still be found at the point where limits are battered against and ruefully acknowledged, if not always accepted. . . . [A] memorable collection."

—*San Francisco Chronicle*

"A cast of richly disparate characters . . . *The Night Inspector* was, among many other things, a splendid demonstration of Busch's ability to manipulate the first-person voice. *Don't Tell Anyone* again testifies to this talent."
—*The New York Times Book Review*

"*Don't Tell Anyone* is an intimate book—it concerns intimacy, and it's been written from a zoom lens perspective, though Busch's enlargements of small moments are exquisite in their subtlety."
—ANN BEATTIE

"Fred Busch is the consummate craftsman, but these stories go beyond craft to art. A stunning collection."
—WARD JUST

"How valuable these stories seem to me, how vivid and dead-on about the human condition, how felicitously written. They are, to put it simply, wonderful stories about our stumbling lives."
—PAULA FOX

"Dazzling and true . . . In every story, the dialogue is brisk, funny, and tender . . . always insistently voiced. . . . A strong, affecting denouement closes each tale. . . . Busch's eye and ear are remarkable, and he charts the path of human vulnerability with a sure and steady tread."
—*Publishers Weekly* (starred review)

Don't Tell Anyone

Frederick Busch

Ballantine Books • New York

A Ballantine Book
Published by The Ballantine Publishing Group

Copyright © 2000 by Frederick Busch
Reader's Guide copyright © 2001 by Frederick Busch
and The Ballantine Publishing Group, a division of Random House, Inc.

James Wright, lines from "The Muse" from *Above the River: The Complete Poems* © 1990 by
Anna Wright, Wesleyan University Press, by permission University Press of New England.

www.ballantinebooks.com

A Library of Congress Catalog Card Number can be obtained from the publisher upon request.

ISBN 0-345-44393-4

This edition published by arrangement with W.W. Norton & Company, Inc.

Manufactured in the United States of America

Cover design by Julie Metz
Cover photograph by Frank Hunter

First Ballantine Books Edition: September 2001

10 9 8 7 6 5 4 3 2 1

THESE STORIES have appeared, sometimes in altered form, in the following magazines:

"Heads" in *Harper's;* "Timberline" and "The Ninth, in E Minor" in *The Georgia Review;* "Machias" in *The Threepenny Review;* "Laying the Ghost," "Domicile," and "Are We Pleasing You Tonight?" in *Five Points;* "Still the Same Old Story" and "Bob's Your Uncle" in *The Gettysburg Review;* "Passengers" and "The Baby in the Box" in *Boulevard;* "Vespers" in *The Agni Review;* "The Talking Cure" in *The Missouri Review;* "Malvasia" in *Shenandoah.* Sections of "A Handbook for Spies" in *Iron Horse Literary Review;* "Joy of Cooking" in *Southwest Review.* "Debriefing" appeared in *Writers' Harvest 3.* "The Ninth, in E Minor" was republished in *The 1999 Pushcart Prize XXIII* and "The Talking Cure" in *The 2000 Pushcart Prize XXIV*.

JB

Contents

Heads

Dɪᴅ I ᴛᴇʟʟ ʏᴏᴜ sʜᴇ ᴡᴀs ʀᴀᴘᴇᴅ?

And not by the man she stabbed?

If you could do . . . something—I couldn't remember what—then you'd be able to do something *else*. I couldn't remember that, either. I knew it was the poem they quote at commencements and at civic-awards ceremonies in small upstate communities like mine. I remembered the rhythm of its lines, but I couldn't remember the words.

My head was a hive of half-remembered words, tatters of statement, halves of stories, the litter of alibis, confessions, supplications, and demands, the aftereffects, perhaps, of the time I spent standing beside my grown, or half-grown, ungrown, ingrown child in a courtroom. She trembled, and I tried to situate myself, standing as we were before the clerks' desk, which was before and below the bench of the judge, so that she could lean her thin, shivering body on mine, at least a shoulder or forearm, at least the comfort I could offer with the heft of my hand against the hard, cold, bony fingers of hers. But she would not accept the heat of my flesh or the weight I wished she might prop herself on. The trial for the crime had never taken place, because our lawyer convinced us—Alec, my daughter, and me—that she should plead nolo contendere: guilty, in a word. She had, as they say, copped a plea. She'd bargained down. She and the victim and the Manhattan district attorney's office had agreed to change the shape of events. We would say that Alec did *not* incise three small cuts in the skin of Victor Petrekis's face with a stainless-steel pocket knife brought to her from England by her father when she was small. She and our lawyer, Petrekis and the assistant district attorney, had constructed a language to make her crime the *attempt* of the deed she had in fact done. And we were before the judge to hear the sentence he would pass.

Petrekis and the assistant district attorney stood at our left, the judge's right. The two clerks periodically bent to write on forms. The marshals behind us, their belts creaking with the weight of their guns, their lapel radios hissing static, waited to learn if they would take her to jail. I had been warned that they put your child in handcuffs right there, as she stands beside you, and they take her off. The heavier clerk, her face a kind of mild mask, was the one who swore us in, ending her question—whether we would tell the truth before this court—with the warning that we must remember how on that *great day,* when *all* would be judged, our falsehoods would be weighed against us. It seemed to me she expected us all to lie and was trying, with her impassivity, not to show her disappointment in our dishonesty. But we all said, and in unison, "I do," as if the ceremony were about marriage and not the dissolution of whatever you might name—rest, comfort, household, and, surely, freedom.

Alec wore a suit she had bought for law school. It was too large, like everything she owned, and its eggplant color, once so interesting with her red-gold hair, now seemed to overpower her complexion. It made her look gray. Her hair was thin and muddy-looking, cropped so short I could see, from beside her, the bone of her skull behind her ear. Her head looked vulnerable to the temperature of the air, and of course to the world of cruel surfaces before which her head was naked now. Even the sleeves of the suit seemed too long, as if her body had diminished in length as well as breadth.

The judge had a wattle of chin and a thick, long nose. The flesh of his face was pitted and loose, his scalp very broad and shiny. But his eyes were of a rich, dark blue, and he spoke with an urgency, a sense of concern, in which I believed. He read from sentencing guidelines and asked the assistant district attorney and our lawyer, Sylvia Stern, if they agreed with his understanding of the rules. The ADA, as Sylvia called him, nodded. Sylvia said, "Yes, Judge." I found myself nodding, too, though of course I knew nothing. I knew nothing.

The knife was about three and a half inches long when folded shut. Its single blade was short and thin. Barry had gone to the north of England on a buying trip. He ordered printed cottons to be sold to dressmakers in the States, and he brought home cloth for me and a print of Stonehenge that he said was designed by Turner though etched and inked by someone else, and a little pocket knife for Alec, who was going through a boy phase that year and was pining for a left-handed first baseman's mitt, an aluminum bat, and the kind of knife that guys carried in the pocket of their jeans.

She kept it in her purse during Barry's dying, and through the end of college in the zipper pocket of her rucksack, and in her one semester of law school it was in a compartment of Barry's attaché case, in which she hauled her work between her apartment on 113th Street and the library and classrooms of Columbia Law.

Did I say that she was raped?

The question's rhetorical, of course: the ploy of a woman on a back porch alone, shielded from her neighbors by a waist-high wall, lighting cigarettes and blowing the smoke at blackflies surrounding her head in a cloud, thick as the words in court, as she tries to startle the black night or circumstance itself that hovers about her. She surely, on the other hand, was raped, and by a student she knew, and in the comfort and convenience of her own furnished apartment. He, too, had his time in court, he, too, pleaded guilty after first contesting her claim. He, too, was sentenced, and Alec stood at the left of the bar, the judge's right, and said, once more, her grievance. The man, for whom she was making coffee as they prepared together for a test, had wept, and so had she. She should have howled her rage, though I believe, and so do her doctors, that nothing would have prevented what they came to call the break.

He raped her because he loved her, because he detested her, because he was jealous of her grade in the course, or because, when he was little, it was just this side of possible, his lawyer had claimed at first, that he was abused by a man who led the Cub Scouts. Perhaps each possibility was true. It never mattered to me. I wanted him gelded. I wanted the wound sealed with boiling pitch, with concentrated lime, and bound with barbed wire. It didn't matter to Alec either, though she spoke at first about friendship, and she wondered whether she had led him on. She soon enough stopped.

She soon enough stopped calling home. She soon enough, when I was able to catch her on the phone, spoke with no inflection. Soon, she mostly wept. And of course I should have gone at once, at the first hint of a sign of damage, to the city to rescue her. I should have stolen her. I should have fetched my baby home. But I waited, because I was leading my life, after all. I was teaching high school students how to distinguish between Babylon and Byzantium, Arafat and Attaturk, and I was failing, as were they, but that was how we were required to consume our days, and life was a storm of consequences with which one had to deal, and Alec in New York was only tense about her studies.

"It's the work, Mommy," she said. "I have too much of it."

"Maybe it's the wrong work."

"You sound so *Jewish,* Mommy."

"I think of you in New York, and I remember myself in New York, and I sound *city,*" I said.

"City's Jewish."

"You're in the foothills of Harlem and you can say that?"

"I'm in the foothills of fuck up."

"Alec."

"Gotta go. Gotta go. I'm doing permutations of collateral estoppel, and I can't stop."

"Al, I think maybe you *ought* to stop."

" 'Bill till you drop. Don't stop.' Bye, Mommy."

"Feel good and be careful? Please? Oh, say hello to Coriander," I said, but she'd hung up.

BARRY AND I had lived together in New York for the first few years of our marriage. He was a student at Cooper Union, and I was a dancer, and it's like watching a balloon that leaks while it zips in circles over your head, but in very slow motion, to see how those ambitions were mostly wishes and breath. But we were there when we were young, and on the afternoon of our first married day, in the room-plus-bathroom that we described as *almost* on University Place, I woke up next to my tall, hairy husband with his elegant, long, slender feet, and I didn't know which hunger banged from inside at my ribs—need for food, or need for Barry. Food won, but we hadn't very much. There were crackers and a wad of multipurpose processed cheese on the table seven feet from our bed. But there was a cake, prepared on upper Broadway to the specifications of Barry's mother, and I was assailed by a need for sweets, and the cake was, for reasons we couldn't ever remember, on the little square table from the Workbench that Barry's best man had given us. So I reached out and plucked the three-or-four-inch-high couple, made of sugar in black and white, the bride in her broad white gown, the groom in his morning coat and striped trousers, each with a genderless face of white with periods under black carats for eyes, a dash for a mouth, and I bit—without planning to, and never knowing what I'd meant to signify—at the head of the little groom.

That was how we came to spend our first married afternoon in the office of a dentist named Echaissy on Eighth Street, because the darling couple were made of plaster, and I had cracked a tooth. The groom suffered only a chip to his glossy pompadour. We carried them with us to our next apartment, on Seventeenth Street, and then to Mamaroneck, and then upstate, where Barry took over a factory and I took over a classroom, and where Barry's lungs filled with fibers of cloth, and his body devoured itself. We were married in City Hall, our witnesses had no camera, and the imperfect painted plaster couple are the embodiment and souvenir of what Barry and I and two witnesses had seen. We kept the bride and groom on a bookshelf in our living room, and there they remain, less the same of course, but standing watch over what you might call history.

Coriander was the name we'd given a stuffed tan cat with which Alec had slept since her second or third year. Barry told her stories about Coriander, and the saga had become the subject of Alec's first and only novel, three sheets of paper stapled together, all six sides bearing crayon drawings of adventures about which she had written in thick, tall capitals. I remember one "Aha!" in messy blue letters, and I remember Barry crooning it to Alec months earlier, one week-end night at bedtime. "Aha!" he'd called, "Aha!" she'd echoed, on a Sunday night when, to keep the next morning's class from arriving unmediated, and to demonstrate what I could not adequately say about that father and his child connected by the victorious shout of a make-believe cat, I had seduced him on a little armless rocking chair, outside on our porch, hidden from our neighbors by the porch's waist-high wall. Coriander had been washed, mended, tossed and mauled and embraced in every house we'd lived in, in each of Alec's dormitory rooms, and she had continued to be resident childhood fetish in Alec's place on Broadway and 113th. That was where I went after Alec called to wish me happy birthday.

"Darling," I said. "Al."

"What, Mommy?"

"Al, it isn't my birthday."

"Sure it is. Today's the eleventh, dingbat."

I didn't know what else to say: "But that's Daddy's birthday, re-member? It isn't mine for a month, I'm afraid."

"It isn't?"

"No."

"It's Daddy's birthday? Today? But it can't be his birthday. He's dead."

"Yes," I said. "Where are you, honey? Are you home?"

"What difference could that make? *When* am I is more like it. God. Daddy's dead and you don't even *have* a birthday now. When's mine?"

"Your birthday? Alec, are you in your apartment?"

"Yes. I'm here in the kitchen thing. Ette. Kitchenette. I was look-ing at the ingredients and everything in the cupboard to see if I could make you a cake, you know, or something, but of course that would be so stupid. I can't bake at all, as we both know perfectly well. And the cake I'd have to can't bake would have to be for Daddy, not you, and he's dead. You aren't, right? No. I really meant to ask: Am I?"

"Dead, Al?"

She said, very breezily, "What's your best bet?" Then all I heard was the sound of stoppered crying, someone's mouth and nose cupped shut while they tried not to weep and they failed.

I said, "Al."

"Oh," she said, "I don't think I'm strong enough anymore, Mommy. I don't think I can do this anymore."

"No," I said, "I'm leaving now. I'm coming. Promise me to stay in your apartment. Can you call someone?"

"Sure. What should I call them?" She laughed while she cried.

"Get some friends over, Al. Anyone you trust."

"Well, he's in jail for raping me, actually."

"Someone *else*."

"He's the one who won't see me anymore."

"I don't think I know who you mean."

"Obviously, a man I saw and I don't see him because he refuses to see *me*."

"Is he a—friend?"

"Lover."

"Ah."

"Don't 'ah' me, Mommy, all right? I'm old enough to have a lover."

"Of course. Yes. I don't remember—"

"No," she said. "I never talked about him. We didn't last long enough for me to find a short enough word that could describe how lousy it got so fast. A woman *is* allowed to want a man at the just about end of the twentieth century, may I point out. I keep waiting for a kind of sign or something, but he *will* not stand up for me. He isn't what you'd call a stand-up guy. I tried telling him that. Because *someone* will punish him. *Someone*, of course, is going to demonstrate how you're either a stand-up guy—a man, you know?—the geniune article, or you're hollow. If you're a dummy, I said, don't come around *here*. But I didn't know he'd do what I said to do or not to do. It's pretty clear-cut, though, you know? *You'd* know. You got around a little when you were dancing, right? Man lets you down, you stick a pin in his balloon, right? His name is Victor Petrekis. He's Greek. He's what you would call a classical piece of ass, but hollow. Like those statues they make of the real statues, not in the museum. He can't be there when I need him to be. You know, when it's tough. It's very tough, Mommy."

IT TOOK ME four hours to drive to Manhattan. I double-parked on 113th, and at a very sloppy angle, effectively sealing off the street, I later saw. She sat on the floor, leaning against a wall. The telephone was on the floor beside her. Her legs were crossed at the ankle, and her arms were folded on her chest. She looked as if she were sleeping, but then her eyes opened undramatically, and she said, "How was the drive?" We took her purse and Barry's attaché case filled with law books, I grabbed what mail I could find, and her address book, and she put some clothing in a bag with a carrying strap. She moved slowly, as if her joints were very sore. She was pale and skinny and vacant of expression. Then she seemed to grow angry with me for having come, angry at my insisting she leave.

"Don't blame me if I flunk out," she said, walking down the single flight in front of me. Her bag rasped along the wall of the staircase, and the case clunked on the wrought-iron banister. "They don't make excuses here, understand? A little fruitcake is not an excuse, and anyway no one makes them. Can't you just leave me alone?"

We emerged to the sound of eight kinds of car horn. I set the baggage on the backseat, fastened her belt as if she were very little or very old, and I think that she was both, and I drove us away, pursued by the outraged driver of a yellow cab.

We were on the upper deck of the George Washington Bridge when I thought to say, "Alec? Have you got Coriander?"

"Oh, for Christ's sake, Mommy! Can't you think of something else besides a *doll?*"

"But have you got her?"

"Yes."

We saw a psychologist in the area, and she was worried. She said the word I expected, "depression." She used another word, "psychotic," and I chewed at the inside of my cheek to keep from crying. She referred Alec to a psychiatrist, who referred her to another one, in Cooperstown, and this one, a tall man whose hair was almost the color of Alec's hair, persuaded her to be signed into the psychiatric center. He used the word "medicate," and he said "stabilize." Alec used the word "okay," but I couldn't find one.

Then Alec used the word "no," and we went home. The doctor telephoned her, and then spoke to me, and we struck an agreement: I would bring Alec the next morning to the psychiatric unit of the Imogene Bassett Hospital in Cooperstown, New York, and she would receive "medication" and "stability" and "tests." Alec slept the rest of that day. I didn't. I looked at photographs in our albums, avoiding Barry's face when I could because I missed him when I saw him because when I looked up from the pictures I could never see him again unless I once again looked down. I was trying to find, in photos of Alec as an infant and child and young adult, a clue, in the droop of an eyelid or the tone of her skin, to what all these new words—"depression," "psychosis," "medication"—were about. I saw how often in her pictures she looked serious, or worried, or alert as if to a threat.

So we ought to have known, right?

I had asked this of the doctor, and he'd said, "No, ma'am. No. Forget any words like 'should' and 'ought.' I have astonishing news for you. I want you to memorize what I say. You did not cause this disease and—you ready?—you can't cure it. Didn't cause, can't cure. Hug her when she lets you, and don't get mad at her. It isn't *her* fault, either. Well, you will get mad, but try and not show it."

I said, "But how can you have a problem and it isn't someone's *fault*."

He laughed. "I'm Jewish, too," he said, "but you can get used to it. No-fault disease."

I MADE COFFEE in the early morning, put the photo albums away, found my stomach too upset for coffee, and went upstairs to wake Alec for the drive to Cooperstown. She sat on her bed, her back against the wall, the covers wrapped around her as if she had just been rescued from a wreck at sea. Her face looked almost yellow, and the shadows under her eyes looked brown. She hadn't slept a lot of the night. She had wakened and, sitting before the mirror on her dressing table, she had cut off her hair. It lay on the floor around her chair. She had given herself a crew cut.

"Interesting hair," I said.

"Hair today," she answered, "gone tomorrow. It's tomorrow."

"We need to leave as soon as you shower," I said.

"I'm not going." Her eyes were dark with anger. Looking into them was like looking into the upstairs window of a high, old house. Someone, you suddenly realize with fright, is looking out of the window at you, and their expression has to do with disgust and with mockery.

I tried to say it to myself: *I didn't . . . I can't . . .* But I forgot the doctor's words.

"Sure, Alec. Yes. Absolutely. We have to go."

"Why do we have to go?"

"So you can get better."

"Better," she said.

"It's your *life,* Al. You need to do this."

"Need," she said.

"Al." I remembered his injunction against anger. I thought: Hey, *you* use your tranquillity when it's *your* kid. "Goddamn it, Alec. This is for your *health.*"

She said, as I knew she would, "Health."

Then I realized what I had seen. I went to her dressing table and got down on my hands and knees. Coriander lay among the long, looped shafts and shorter curls of hair, and she lay down there in two pieces. Using her shears, Alec had severed the stuffed head from its stuffed body.

I squatted there, then turned to face her. The terrible face appeared in the window and looked down the length of the room to me.

"Oh, Alec," I said.

She said, "Oh, Mommy. It's only a household pet."

The doctor had given me one more set of instructions, and I remembered them quite well.

I said, "I'm going to call the state police. They'll force you to the hospital, Alec. It'll, I don't know, go on your record. You'll be a lawyer with a note on your record: 'State Police,' it'll say."

"They can't," she said, "and don't pretend they can. You think you can put the whammy over on a *law* student? And *what* record, you Jew-mother jerk."

"I'm going to tell them I feel threatened. They'll do it."

"Threatened," she said. "Only if you're a household pet," she said, "or if you're named Petrekis."

"What about him?"

"You heard me."

"Alec, did you do something to Petrekis?"

"Who?"

"To punish him?"

"For hit-and-run foreplay? It *is* a punishable offense. For hit-and-run *soixante-neuf* compounded by simply yet absolutely Not. Being. A. Stand. Up. Guy."

"Alec, what? What happened?"

"When?"

"Okay. I'm calling the police. Have a happy morning." I went to the foot of the stairs and found the number in the phone book and dialed it. My hand was shaking, and my voice, when I spoke to a woman who called herself sergeant something, wobbled and wavered. I said, "I'm calling from outside of . . . no, it's really in the township . . . Hell. I'm a little nervous. Sorry." Take a breath, ma'am, take your time, are you all right, etc. And I was saying, "My daughter has had what I guess you'd call a nervous breakdown. I need to . . ."

Alec walked downstairs, wearing flannel pajama bottoms, a dirty white T-shirt, and slippers without socks. She shook a blanket out like a cape and wrapped it around her shoulders. She went around the corner into the living room, and I heard noises but closed my eyes and took a breath so I could tell the sergeant what I needed.

Alec reappeared. She was red-faced, and I was grateful for any relief of her pallor, even though she was the color of her anger at me.

"Whore," she said. "Candy-assed Jew whore and your pimp doctor cop friends."

She walked past me and out the back door.

"A second," I said to the sergeant.

I heard my car door slam.

"I'm sorry," I said, swallowing against what I think would have been sobs. "I think it might be all right. I'll call you back if there's a problem. Thank you. I'm very sorry for this."

I didn't and I can't.

I took a jacket and keys and my wallet and went outside to drive her to the hospital. That was where they finally came, a couple of days later, when I was in the visitors' lounge, taking a break from Alec's complaints and her anger at what she called my betrayal. It was a new word to hear from Alec about myself, and I was chewing on it, really tasting its possibilities for me. A man in a wrinkled gray uniform was directed to me in the washed-out light of the beige waiting room, and he presented me with what he called a bench warrant—I had never heard the words—for Alec's arrest, sworn out by a magistrate in Manhattan because she had fled the county to avoid prosecution for stabbing Victor Petrekis in the face.

The information about the face came from the sheriff's deputy who served the warrant. The warrant used the following words: "felonious" and "assault." Neither it nor the deputy conveyed the information that the weapon was the small stainless pocket knife imported by the assailant's father and given to her so she could be, for a little while, one of the fellows. The deputy left, and then I left. I needed to talk to lawyers, and Alec did not need to deal with one more fact served up by the world.

At home, I spent about an hour making chicken salad for a sandwich. I had no bread in the house, so I spent a while longer defrosting some rolls, then slicing and toasting one. I made myself a big sandwich with lots of lettuce, and I carried it into the living room. I wanted to sit with a book and find some language that would do me some good. I drifted along the shelves looking at titles, soon enough coming to the conclusion that I hadn't the energy to read a paragraph of anyone's book. I looked at a stack of CDs. I didn't want music either. I wanted silence, sleep, and somebody, when I woke up, who would manage the claims for health insurance, the bills from the landlord in New York, the conversation with the lawyer I would have to hire to represent Alec in court.

I realized that I was staring not at dust jackets but at the objects in front of them: the bride and groom, who had more or less outlasted Barry and me, despite the nick I'd left on the head of the groom, and who had served to demonstrate, Barry liked to say, how dangerous my appetites had always been. When he spoke about sex, he would leer, I told him, like a peasant in the countryside. And he was pleased to serve as the local life force.

I said, "Barry!"

Their heads were off. She had battered them against the edge of the shelf. Fragments lay there and on the floor, and it came to me then: the poem they recite at you during graduations and the presentation of trophies to injured athletes. It was about how if you could keep your head while all about you were losing theirs and blaming it on you, you'd own the world.

I saw that each figure had a metal rod around which it was molded, so the little couple would probably not crumble further, and would stand, adhering to their little skeletons, for as long as I left them on the shelf. I chewed at my chicken salad sandwich, looking back into their faceless stare.

I let myself pretend that Barry would walk into the living room then and ask me what I was doing.

I let myself pretend I would answer.

"Owning the world," I would say around a mouthful of sandwich.

Bob's Your Uncle

I LOVED HIS MOTHER ONCE. One time, that is, in my marriage to Jillie, I loved this boy's mother, made love to her, once, with gritted teeth, and a wet mouth, and wide eyes. When he came to our house, where his parents years before had brought him to visit with Jillie and me, I thought he carried word of his mother's death. He blinked in my doorway, he smiled with embarrassment as I did. And I started mourning Deborah. And then I was relieved. And then, of course, I grew so guilty about the sorrow and about my almost physical sense of release—freedom from the dream of her, and freedom from the secret—that I was speechless and blushing, a little breathless, while I watched his taxi back down our drive and turn toward Rhinebeck. I nodded to prompt his next words. He nodded back. I felt a tentative relief and I smiled. He smiled in return. I shrugged and held my arms out. He shrugged and we embraced.

Finally, I called, "Kevin Slater's here!"

Kevin nodded his agreement. He carried an expensive leather overnight bag on a shoulder strap, and he wore an unconstructed sportcoat of light brown linen over olive chinos. His shirt was thick, creamy cotton with olive stripes, and his loafers, over bare feet, were of a soft, tan weave. His face had grown long and lean and muscular, but he still, with his peaked eyebrows and big, brown eyes, his tan complexion and his smile you would only call wicked, looked like a boy.

Kevin said, "Hi, Uncle Bob. Hi, Aunt Gillian."

Jillie, arriving behind me, said or sang a long "Oh," and then she shouldered past me to seize Kevin and hug him.

He smiled over her shoulder at me, and I saw in his grin and in his young man's face what I saw, and had told myself I wasn't seeing, when he was a boy: a kind of menace that you call, that I had called, naughty or wicked, but that was maybe threatening—was maybe a sign of something even dangerous. The way certain autistic children can seem ordinary and then, on study, not quite, Kevin seemed in reverse—extraordinary, but then, perhaps, not quite. Maybe he was simply a tall, muscular, *café-au-lait* kid with wicked, call them naughty, eyebrows.

"How's your mother?" I said. "Your folks."

"London still. Dad's a big shot. They send for him in limousines. *American* limousines, the long ones."

Jillie said, "Your mother's all right?"

He shook his head as Jillie released him. His face grew slack and sad. "Mom has a boyfriend. He's a chemist at Glaxo. She says no, but Dad says yes."

I felt as if I'd sucked on a lemon, and as I spoke the pain remained, inside my head, beneath the ears, at the mastoid. "What's your opinion, Kevin?"

"She says no," he answered. "But some nights she doesn't come home and Dad makes breakfast for us."

"You're only as old as you think," Jillie said. Then: "Darling Kevin, come inside and stay for a while. That's why you're here, I think. To stay with us?"

"Could I? I got no place to go, I'm pretty sure. I went to my friend's house in New York, but he moved. I don't know a lot of people, Aunt Gillian." His face wrinkled in horizontal folds, and I thought he was going to cry. She hugged his arm to her, and I watched as he moved it a little to better brush her breast. She tugged him along. When he passed me, as I stood back to hold the door, I smelled again his funk

of airplane travel—unwashed skin, stale air, exhaustion—and I saw
that his swell shirt was dirty, as though he had worn it for a week.
Grit was crushed in the nubbing of his sportcoat, and his trousers
had dark spills of sauce imprinted down the front. I had sat him on
my lap to drive the lawn tractor. I had held him on the dock at our
pond. And here he was, wily and odd-looking, very large and a little
arrested-sounding, and coated with the grime of the world.

When he was four, I remember, they had started visiting doctors
and had begun to send him to private schools. Teachers called him
difficult, one even called him frightening, and that sent his mother to
pediatric psychologists and Kevin to more expensive schools. They
had tried for six years—of taking Deborah's temperature, of consulting fertility cycle charts, of pumping Arthur into test tubes—and
then they had adopted Kevin, a beautiful baby whose birth mother
was Honduran, and Kevin had become the warning bird in Deborah's life. She was like a miner in a coal seam who watched the ca-
nary—a bird's health meant good air, a bird going sick meant
misfortune. Deborah, always extraordinary, with her pale, oval face
and her sad eyes, long pianist's fingers, ebony hair, became brilliant
with Kevin. He was the dream of her life she had dreamed. When he
was well, she shone like his moon. When he was becoming what the
schools called *difficult,* her hair went matte, and her eyes floated over
deep brown, sorrowful semicircles. Arthur, who was erect as a soldier
and who never wanted children, he claimed, was a father dutiful not
to the baby, but to his wife. In serving Kevin, he served her, and I
thought it likely she had never forgiven that disloyalty to Kevin. He
was a sales manager of switches and machine parts for all of western
Europe on behalf of a British firm that also owned paper mills and
bakeries. He'd grown rich and Deborah distant, at least from us, and
their child with Indian and Spanish blood was here, as out of focus—
no: as hard to find a focus for—as an ill-composed snapshot.

Jillie said, "Kevin, how long can you stay?"

From a distance he was a male model, and up close he was a soiled
boy edging toward man. His confused, confusing smile flared, and he
said, "Whatever you say, Aunt Gillian."

"I say you stay as long as you feel like."

He clenched a fist and showed it to me, as if we had both been striving for admission. I nodded back and I guess it was a smile I showed him in return. Jillie took him upstairs and I went, as if casually, to the bookshelves in the living room. I found the book, a collection of poems by Alan Dugan that his mother had given me. There was a poem in it that began, "The curtains belly in the waking room." Deborah had brought it to me, along with a wonderful antique book of flower prints for Jillie, and a bottle of Château Palmer that Arthur analyzed before he let us taste it. They were house gifts she bore, except that I knew which room the curtains had bellied in, and who had wakened with whom, and so did Deborah, and we were the only ones.

Kevin slept off his jet lag, and Jillie and I cast speculations that sank like stones in the sea.

"He might just be a little dopey from travel," she said.

"You know what weariness is, and you know it's something else."

"It couldn't be easy to march into somebody's house after, Jesus, eleven or twelve years, it must be. And say, 'Hello, my mother's sleeping around and my father's too busy, and I'm a little screwed up.' "

"No," I said, "except he didn't say or intimate or even hint *sleeping around*, Jillie."

"She always fancied your ass."

"Oh, come on."

"Didn't she."

"Jillie."

"And you were not, let's say, unalert to that exquisite face or the body that went along with it. Could we say unalert?"

"It isn't even a word, much less a smart idea. No."

"No," she said.

"That is correct."

"No is correct."

"I *said* so."

"And so you did. Except I think she did fancy you, as they say."

"Nobody says fancy you and nobody says unalert."

We were behind the house, in a field that curved like a cheek, and we were walking slowly in the bright six o'clock light of a late-spring sunset. Jillie wore her New York Knicks baseball hat over a new haircut that was so short, she said, the breezes made her cold. She wore the hat, I thought, in mourning for the Knicks, who had once again failed to make progress in the playoffs. I took her hat off and ran my hand through her hair. She held my wrist and pulled my hand down onto her head.

"You are a bit of a frog and a fogey," she said, "but I am not unalert to your cute little paunch and your much-fancied ass."

"You don't know *any* words," I said. "Paunch is out these days."

She looked at my midsection. "Out and over the belt, just about. But we can say belly if you like."

As in what a curtain will do in a bedroom window in the cool air of morning, if you like.

EARLY SUNDAY, KEVIN was up by the time I returned from Rhinebeck with newspapers and German coffee cake. I could smell the shampoo and soap, but I could also smell his clothing—he was wearing what he'd worn the day before—and, for all his scent of soap, there were bands of dirt beneath his nails, and his knuckles seemed dyed a darker brown than his broad hands. Jillie was in her jeans and one of my flannel shirts and she wasn't wearing a brassiere, which I learned by following Kevin's eyes as she walked across the kitchen with coffee and plates for the cake.

"Kevin," I said, "are you all through with school?"

"I'm done with school, Uncle Bob."

"Did you go to prep school?"

"I went to the American school."

"And you graduated?"

"Sure."

"Are you out on your own?"

"Whenever I want."

"No, I mean are you *living* on your own. In an apartment, with a job and a life and all of that."

"Jobs are hard," Kevin said.

Jillie said, "Is there anything in the sports about the Knicks making a deal? So they can *silence* their critics? Bob?"

I finally said, "Ah." She rarely had to do more than hoist a cardboard sign and beat on the congas for five or ten minutes before I understood these signals. Our child had been grown and away long enough for me to have forgotten the need in a household for an alternative language. I passed her the sports section of the *Times* and pretended that I was reading the editorials.

Kevin said, "This is so nice."

I looked over the News of the Week in Review section to watch a giant tear glide out of each eye and down. It was like seeing a toddler in sorrow.

Jillie said, "Kevin, sweetheart. What? Are you homesick?"

He watched her alertly, as if she'd offered a clue. He thought. Then he said, "No, Aunt Gillian. No. We did this when I was a little boy. Remember? Breakfast? Newspapers. Cake. Everybody was happy."

"But it isn't happy at home," Jillie said.

"No more. Dad gets mad. He goes away too much. Mommy does too. I stay with Martha. I go out on Cheyne Walk. I buy things for Martha. I go home. I watch the telly. It's boring! Mostly, it's quite terribly sad."

The last five words came out in a voice that wasn't his. I imagined we were hearing Martha's intonations. He moved his neck as though his collar was tight. He scrubbed at his face with his cupped hands.

"All right, then, Kevin?" Jillie looked up. I had spoken in a kind of echo of the London I heard in his voice.

"Medicine," he said. He smiled, as though divulging something lovely. His beautiful eyes were bright and moist. "I take tablets twice a day." He opened a small gold pill box and removed something smaller than an aspirin, and white. "Once in the morning and once at night, and Bob's your uncle." He pointed at me. "And he is! Bob *is* my uncle!"

So what we had here was a seventeen- or eighteen-year-old boy who was, from time to time, about six years old, I thought. He was built like a goalie for Manchester United and he had been tied to the ground, like Gulliver, but by medicine instead of rope. And he fancied his Aunt Gillian in some fairly obvious ways. He had fled to us, or fled from them, and here he was, a young man charged with the energy of mission, of *errand,* a radiated electric sense that you might as well call purpose. He seemed to me a messenger who tarried, who chatted, who relished our anticipation of what he had come to say. But he didn't, or he wouldn't, or he couldn't, say it. We were waiting, and so, perhaps, was he. Or maybe it was the medicine, or what the medicine held in check.

Gillian asked him if he felt well, and he told her of his stomach troubles on the flight. He proved how well he now felt by eating a large bite of coffee cake. I read in the Travel section that a dollar bought .60 of a pound. I tried to calculate what that meant a pound would cost and, when I arrived at something like twenty-four dollars, I knew what I was going to do. I waggled a finger at Jillie, which meant I'd return in a minute, and, in the extra first-floor bedroom that we shared as an office, I worked out what time it was in London. My answer seemed to be thirteen dollars, so I told the phone to hell with it and dialed the international code. After the hiss and the charge of static, I heard the double ring of an English phone. It went on and on. I thought I felt like Arthur, calling home of an afternoon and wondering why my wife wasn't there to answer.

Kevin was at the sink with Jillie, leaning into her a little as they scraped and washed and dried.

I said, with the tact that won me to the hearts of deponents and courtroom adversaries, "Are you staying long in America, Kevin?"

He turned to me, smiled his smile, shrugged, then turned away and leaned back in against Jillie. He shrugged again. Jillie shrugged, as if in response, but she was signaling me. It meant: *Who knows* what *we've got here? Wait awhile and see.*

I went back to our office and dialed the call again. Thinking as Arthur, I insisted to myself, I wondered what I hadn't for years and years: Where are you now? Whom are you with? What do you feel? And, like Kevin, I was gripped in the stomach, seized that is in the ganglion there, thinking with my belly and probably my balls. Feeling, finally, like no one but me, like a lover gone into the past, I was wounded as I hadn't been for years by the thousands and thousands of miles between upstate New York and the Chelsea Embankment. The telephone chimed the distance. I could feel the hugeness of the surface of the sea between Block Island and Margate. And then the ancient but familiar furtiveness returned, so I hung up.

Kevin, in the kitchen, said, "Bob! Where'd you go?"

"Back there." I pointed with my thumb.

"What'd you do?"

"Nothing much."

"Boring, huh?"

"Kevin, you're not boring. Aunt Gillian isn't boring."

"So *you* must be!"

I said, "Exactly."

In his English voice, he told Jillie, "Bang on right, isn't he?"

She said, "Kevin, in all the years I've spent with this man, and some of them have been lollapaloozas, he has never been boring."

"Lol—"

"Lollapaloozas."

"What's that, Aunt Gillian?"

"It means he is a heavy-duty, full-time, nonstop job."

Kevin looked as though he might glow. "She really likes you, Uncle Bob."

I said, "I hope so."

Kevin gestured at the kitchen or at us. "I'm never going home," he said.

Years before, not long after London, our daughter, Tasha, had told me, "Whenever you lie, Daddy, I know it from your face. You catch yourself. You hear your own lies. I think you hate them or something, because you always look disgusted with yourself."

I'd told her, "No, I can always hedge on the facts, a little, when I'm arguing in court. It's a professional necessity. And I was even a pretty good cardplayer in the Army."

"Well, sure," she'd said, looking like Gillian's younger sister, broad-shouldered and slim-hipped, a fine swimmer, a ferret of fathers. "That's easy, lying to judges and juries and clients and shady lawyers."

"You left out hit men and child molesters."

"But with *us,*" she said, "ha! You're hopeless with us."

Jillie, all those years later, said to Kevin in our kitchen, "You stay as long as you like." She sounded like she meant it.

She was coaching me, and I caught the hint. "As long as you like," I said. It sounded to me like a lie.

"I LOOKED IT up in the big dictionary, and it means you were court-martialed," I said. "Given a dishonorable discharge."

"It means *safe,*" Jillie whispered directly into my ear in bed that night. We were acting like children, I thought, or like a man and woman sneaking some time together in bed. "Bob means safe, it's an old-time English expression. I read it somewhere. I don't remember. Dickens? Thomas Hardy? Arnold Bennett?"

"The turncoat? You'd take his word? It *means* turncoat, maybe."

"No, that's Benedict Arnold." The effect of all this whispering was reminiscent of high school, the wet tongues of girls, the hard, waxy ears of their boyfriends. Her voice, hushing and warm in my ear, was making itself felt on the soles of my feet. They actually tingled. As if a wave of sensation bounced, then, back up through my body, my penis went heavy and hard, and I laid it against her thigh. "Good grief," she said, "I'll keep naming them, if I can remember any more. Oliver Goldsmith. George Gissing. *Thackeray,* oh, yum."

"So the kid's saying to me, Safe as Uncles?"

"He's saying everything's okay. All's well. He's using a piece of old-fashioned slang he heard from his nanny or housekeeper or whatever this Martha person is because she's the only one who hangs around with him now and because he's scared. He's like a child, Bob. He's like that dear little boy he was when they used to bring him here."

"When Deborah used to bring him here. Arthur dropped her off and picked her up because he was too busy in the gadget trade and because we were boring."

"I never cared. She was my friend," Jillie said. "I loved her."

"I used to think you, you know—"

"What?"

"I used to think the two of you—you know."

"Friends?"

"Lesbians?"

"Bob. You sound jealous."

"You know me. I probably was. And there's nothing wrong with—loving each other. However you did it."

"Really?"

I was halfway on top of her now, and my hand was in her pajamas. "I hope I believe it. Would you tell me?"

"What, exactly?"

"If you and she—"

"Deborah."

"Yes."

"Yes."

I said, "*Yes?*"

"I mean, yes, I would tell you. But no. We *loved* each other. We were real friends. *Real* friends. I think that's why I'm all over Kevin. I miss her really a lot. I hurt with missing her when I let myself get into it. Sink down into thinking about it."

My hand was on her stomach, edging down, and she reached in the dark and took hold of my wrist, pushing. *The curtains belly in the waking room.* I said, "Belly," working down with her, our hands moving together from her belly and together on her groin and then our fingers, pressed together, inside her, moving. We were breathing in unison, and the tone of our breathing deepened, but it was still a kind of whisper, a conversation.

Deborah had pointed out the poem for me not only because there had been a heavy white curtain that bellied in the window of the hotel in Marlow. She was also, as the four of us sat together and as Kevin played with a metal reproduction tractor I had bought him, reminding me that I had kneeled before her in the room, beside the bed, and had reached beneath her skirt to take down her pantyhose and underpants and then had climbed up inside the tent of her skirt head-first, kissing her thighs that felt cool to my lips, and working around her groin, biting on her stomach, growling, "Belly," which had made her shriek laughter, as if she were terribly ticklish.

"Idiot," she'd told me, her hand on my head through the skirt. "You're doing Cookie Monster from *Sesame Street*. God. *Coo-kie*. Idiot Bob."

"Belly," I snarled into her, forcing my face where little force was required as she spread her legs to my mouth and fell back on the bed. "Belly," I said, below it.

Jillie was bucking up at our hands, at our fingers, saying, "Bobby, come on," pulling me onto her, replacing our hands with me, filling herself with me as I loved her and cheated again with her friend.

JILLIE CALLED IN, telling them she was away for the day. She was a partner in a letterpress printing company that sold old-fashioned-looking letterhead to the publishers and antiques dealers and artists who lived in our section of Dutchess County, a hundred miles north of New York. I was going to spend the day in the office working on a suit involving an Ethiopian national whose French-owned airplane had fallen into the Mediterranean. I was suing on behalf of the dead man's sister, who had become an American citizen. Jurisdiction wasn't undecipherable, but it was complicated, and I was going to be phoning and faxing all day. But I was also, I told Jillie, going to be worried about her at home with Kevin.

I was leaning over my coffee cup, whispering again, and resenting my need to be secret at home. Although, I reminded myself, I had surely been secret enough before and for a long time. "What if he gets violent?" I roared in a hush. "Didn't he used to get that way when he was a boy? A little boy?"

Jillie said, in less of a whisper than would have made me comfortable, "He got frightened. He got apprehensive. And he's my dear friend's child."

"Your dear friend who hasn't written or called in how long?"

"Well, she's going through some things."

"What?"

"Never *mind*." Jillie rarely sounded stern. I think she learned impatience and cruelty from me. And when she spoke like an angry me to me, I found myself, always, quailed.

"Quelled and quailed," I told her.

"What?"

"The way your eyes get big and your brows go up and your voice gets brittle and mean and your cheeks get pale. You look like a killer."

She nodded, sipped at her coffee, said, "Don't you forget it," and sipped again.

"But call me," I said. "If there's *anything*. You call me."

"And you will ride upstate in a couple of hours, once you get free of the office and out of midtown traffic and off the Henry Hudson Parkway and through the Hawthorne Circle and up the Taconic, and you will rescue me."

I said, "Damned right."

"You're a dope, Bob."

"Damned right," I said.

"A middle-aged dope with delusions of heroism."

"Wrong," I said. "A middle-aged dope with a wife at home alone with a—with a troubled boy."

"Man, nearly."

"Jesus, Jillie. You never called Tasha a *woman* until she was a junior in college."

"It never upset you whether I did or not."

"And this does, so you're doing it?"

She nodded.

"You are really pissed off."

She nodded again.

"I could have sworn we were crazy and all over each other last night."

She nodded.

"And *that* makes you mad?"

She said, "In a way." Then: "No." She shook her head. She took an enormous breath. She said, "This is something to forget. To never mind. I am not pissed off. We *did* have a good time. You know that. I'm thinking, though, we're rolling around in the rack and Debbie's crazy in England and it doesn't seem *fair.*" She took another long breath.

"You'll hyperventilate," I said. "It doesn't seem fair for you to— could I say enjoy? For you to enjoy your marriage? And I suspect she *is* rolling around. In *somebody's* rack."

"If I hyperventilated and fell out of my chair and cracked my head on the floor and died, well-fucked, then that would seem to be a reasonable exchange *and* fair to Debbie. As for her sex life, don't make the mistake of thinking a random screw, or a whole matched set of them, is any substitute for, I don't know—for being happy a little." She watched me. She nodded her head very hard. "Really," she said. "Anything else, and you're dreaming."

At the office, I punched numbers on the phone. I called Deborah and hung up. I called Jillie and disconnected before it could ring. I called Tasha, who was teaching medieval history at the University of Texas in Austin. Her answering machine had no message, only a long pause and then a suddenly burped tone to prompt the speaker, but the caller needed to hear his kid's voice more than tell her anything, so he hung up. I telephoned the retired appellate court judge who was of counsel to the firm handling Air France matters in the States and soon enough was doing the equivalent of starting to try to untie a very tight knot made of soft, wet wool.

The judge and I hung up, issuing the phony quacks of business bonhomie. The telephone rang at once and my secretary, Ms. Seidman, who detested me and all lawyers—everyone, in fact, except the performance artist who pierced his body as part of his art with whom she lived in apparently something of a state of excitation—announced that my wife was on the line.

This time, she was the whisperer. I said, "I can't hear you, Jillie. Is it Kevin?"

She said, very low and muffled, as if her hand was over her lips and the telephone, "He's talking to himself."

"In a menacing way?"

"No, no. It's—it's upsetting. He's so *worried.*"

"*He's* worried. He's in trouble. That's who talks to themselves, people in trouble. Is there any reason to think he's going to act out?"

"Bob, you don't know what in hell act out *means.*"

"No, but I hear it a lot. Do you notice how you're always correcting my words, these days? Jillie: you think—I'm asking this, I guess—do you think he's going to do anything physical to express what's on his mind?"

"That *is* what it means."

"Jillie, for Christ's sake, you're home alone with a kid the size of a goddamned fullback who is *at least* immature and somewhat retarded and worried and frightened and more than likely he's a hell of a lot more screwed up than either of us thought, and you're *teaching* me. Are you—never mind. I'm coming home."

"You can't come home. You have to get rich people out of their responsibilities and obligations, don't you?"

"You're hunting for my *head*, Jillie."

"For your belly."

"My belly?"

In Cookie Monster's voice, she said, "Belly."

"Stay near the door or something," I said. "Go out to Millerton and hang around in crowds."

"Where do they keep them, again, in Millerton?"

I said, "Shit. Goddamn it. Jillie. Take care. I'm coming home."

"Oh, boy," she said.

In the elevator I thought it, and in the car I said it to myself: *"She telephoned you. She picked up the phone and she called you."* Going uptown and west, I said, "And now you're talking to yourself like Kevin, aren't you?" I was doing sixty-five on the Henry Hudson, ignoring the rearview mirror and, frankly, anything to either side. I wasn't driving the car, I was aiming it. I remembered telling clients in ticklish cases to keep their silence. People, you see them and observe their behavior, and you think: nobody talks to *any*one. But you're wrong. They do. Whenever you think they can't, or they won't, then they do. I thought about Jillie and Deborah. Oh, they do, I thought. I said, in a singsong, "She called Kevin's mom-my." Then I said, "Cookie Monster's gonna eat up all of your *ass.*"

I stopped at one of the little places on Route 82 and bought hot dogs and rolls and sodas and a box of chocolate chip cookies. I went seventy miles an hour until I got to our driveway, up which I let the car waddle casually, uncle fellow, daddy guy, coming home with snacks and not a tad concerned about the safety of his wife *or* the menace of her recently discovered rage.

Kevin was outside, splitting kindling. He wore his olive slacks and basket-weave loafers and his cream-and-olive shirt. I watched his back and arms as he swung the ax, and I remembered seeing them, but smaller, and bare, brown in the summer sun, when Deborah and he had come to stay for a week. I had taken him out to our shed and showed him how to split wood. Maybe he was six or seven, broad-backed and strong, and his coordination had been excellent. Once he saw how to stand the chunks upright on the chopping block and swing without fear, letting the momentum of the head of the ax do the work, he became good at it. He was good at it now. As I got out of the car, I heard him grunt as he swung, just as he had a dozen years before. In a way, he was the same boy.

I heard the breath expelled, the woodcrack, the intake of his breath, and then the words. He said, low, *"You* can't go down there! Who ever said *you* could go down there? It isn't allowed, and you know it very well. *Yards* of bother in that, silly boy. You stay up here with me, won't you?" Then he swung, and the wood split, and he stood another piece on the block. "Of course," he said, and in a different, deeper, voice, "this isn't the kind of report we like to get. We don't *blame* you, understand. No one's *blaming* you. All we care about is if you're happy and well. Would you call yourself happy and well? Can you think of anything Mommy and I can do to *make* you happy and well? By God, we would do it, Kev. We'd do anything. You know that." He swung, but the head was canted a little and the ax skipped. He was positioned right, and he was safe. "Look the head right into the wood," he instructed himself. The voice was familiar. Of course. It was mine. He split the piece, took a breath, set up another and, looking at it and saying, "All I love is you," as if Deborah were speaking to her son in our yard, he swung the ax. All he had to do now, I thought, was imitate Jillie divorcing me, and he'd have invoked us all.

Before he could tense for another swing, I said, "Kevin. Hot dogs for lunch."

He turned to watch me walk over from the car. "How come I didn't hear you come here, Uncle Bob?"

"I guess I drove very quietly."

He laughed a little too loudly, watching me with his baby's brown eyes. He was very alert. I wondered what had made him that wary. "I was chopping wood," he said. "In case we need it for the fireplace."

"You did a good job, Kevin. Do you remember how to leave the ax?"

He turned and swung, very hard, and buried the blade in the block.

"Good man," I said with gratitude.

Jillie had been watching us from the kitchen, I thought, because she was at the door before I touched the knob. "Home for lunch, how nice," she said, as if I hadn't driven too quickly. "Kevin's been splitting kindling, and I've been trying to think of something special to eat." I handed her the paper sack, and she said, "My favorite! Hot dogs! My white knight of the sausage casing."

Kevin said, "Yay!"

"Boiled, I think. I have a package of sauerkraut and some yellow mustard and—yes, we'll grill the rolls. It'll be an all Brooklyn hot dog day. Like eating at Nathan's. Kevin—did you ever get to Nathan's at Coney Island?"

He was studying her bottom in her jeans. "No, Aunt Gillian," he told her buttocks.

She said, "We'll go there one day. With Mommy. Kevin? Your mom's coming here."

"Here? How?"

"The same way you did."

"Airplane," he said. "It was a terrible trip. It took for*ever*. They gave me an extra dinner, did I tell you that? When?"

"Jillie," I said, after a while, "Kevin wants to know when she's coming."

"Deborah is coming," Jillie said while looking at me, her brows up and her cheeks pale, "tomorrow. She's going to rent a car and drive up from New York."

"That's an ugly drive if you're jet-lagged."

"No," Jillie said, "she'll take a couple of Valium when she gets on and she'll sleep through. She always does. She'll be fresh for the trip. Will you be glad to see her, Kevin?"

"Yup."

"Will you be glad to see her, Bob?"

"It's been a while, hasn't it? Is Arthur coming?"

Jillie shrugged.

"You called her?"

Jillie, at the stove, nodded.

"How was it? The conversation?"

"Pas devant l'enfant." She added, *"Merde,"* probably because she was pleased with her rediscovered French.

I decided not to be warned off. I really needed to *know.* "I mean, after what? A real while, huh? You guys just clicked right into place and it was like no time lost? Nothing uneasy?"

Jillie said, with conviction, *"Cochon."* You can be cute when you call a man a swine, or you can mean it—the snout, the hairy tail, the four hard hooves.

I decided not to say, in French, Why, what a clever notion you had, making things safe by suggesting he play with the ax. I imagine the idea was to get him outside, away from you. But think how handy it would have been if he'd decided to get back *in* in a hurry. I did say, "I think maybe you want to let us wash your clothes for you, Kevin. I'll give you something of mine, and you let us—"

"That means Aunt Gillian," Jillie said. "Uncle Bob, with his jurisprudence degree and the *summa cum laude* from Cornell never quite got hold of the mystery of the washing machine dial."

"Quel canard," I said. "Jillie, what was Deborah's news? What's up?"

I went to the stoveside counter and took the platter of hot dogs and the basket of rolls. Jillie brought mustard and sauerkraut and glasses of pop on a tray. Kevin seemed to have shrunk in his chair.

Jillie studied him. She said, "Mommy isn't coming because she's angry, Kevin. She's coming because she *misses* you."

He shook his head, and there seemed to be less play to his expression, less life in the muscles of his forehead and jaw. I said, "Hey, Kevin. You take your medicine every day, right?"

"Every day," he said.

"Did you take it *this* day?"

He looked at me and looked at me, and his eyes showed energy for an instant, and he shook his head. "I forgot," he said.

"Let's do it now, Kevin. You go find your medicine, your pills."

"Once in the morning and once with my tea."

"First, you can eat some hot dogs and then you can wash. And *I* will set the left-hand dial at medium, and the right at warm water wash and cold rinse. We'll have you clean as a whistle."

Kevin stuck a finger in each side of his mouth and, from stretched, unnatural-looking lips, he whistled so loudly you'd have thought someone was screaming.

We ate in a silence that wasn't peaceful. I smiled at Jillie and tried to help Kevin tend the sauerkraut that radiated from his plate in a ragged circle on his place mat and the dark wood of the table. I thought of Tasha, and I thought of Deborah. I watched Jillie's shoulders bow down, as she sat, beneath whatever she felt. I had known her for so many years, and I could not have named her feelings. But I felt them gathering. I watched the lines at the sides of her eyes, the shifting muscles of her forearms, the skin of her cheeks, and the flesh at her hairline. Everything moved subtly, in ways I might have claimed once to know, but which now seemed new to me. Birds cackled near the kitchen window, and our mouths made soft noises around our food. It was gathering.

Kevin used the downstairs tub—we could hear him splash like a kid—and I loaded his clothing in the washing machine in the pantry off the kitchen while Jillie cleaned our lunch dishes. It didn't come with violence—an ax, say, wielded by the damaged son, Deborah's hope gone imperfect. It didn't come by surprise. It was the message from my life, and that should always be expected. Later in the day, later that night, alone, I told myself I'd been waiting for it for years.

Jillie came to the pantry with an obvious reluctance. But she couldn't, I saw, have stayed away. She came close to me. I could smell the bright scent of the dishwashing soap and the rich darkness of her perfume on her skin. She reached for my arm, which was poised with detergent above the machine, and she touched the back of my hand. She put her fingers gently around my wrist. She couldn't make her fingers meet although I felt the pressure of her effort. Then she let me go. She took a deep breath. It reminded me of Kevin's breathing outside at the woodpile. I thought of myself in Marlow, years before, panting like a runner.

She said, "What was it, when you were with her, and I was taking Tasha to the British Museum—we were wearing our matching goddamned tan tourist raincoats, Bob, for heaven's sakes! And you and Deborah were laughing and doing everything together that you did. What did you think was coming to you that you deserved so much?"

Kevin stepped into the doorway behind us, a muscular man who wore a towel over grown-up cock and balls, and also a damp, happy child just out of his bath.

Jillie looked from me to Kevin and then again at me. She stood between men gone wrong, or boys who hadn't turned out right. You looked at us, I thought, and we seemed okay. You looked again and we were ruined just a little. We were your dreams come true.

Malvasia

MAL COULDN'T COOK OR CURE, but she could carry. Every weekend she left a patient and generous young man with whom she lived and, as if only Graham's wife had died, and not her mother too, Mal drove her lover's car on what was left of the West Side Highway, and then the Henry Hudson, then the Taconic, bearing her father coffee beans and baguettes from upper Broadway, pasta salads and sundried tomatoes from Greenwich Village, poems from Three Lives.

Graham lived where he had lived with Sarah for twenty of their twenty-seven married years, in what he had told her a year ago was "what's left of Dutchess County." He had snarled to her, and she had not listened to the words, he knew, just his chanting rhythms. "If you're very careful not to look up, and if you don't listen to the goddamned engines everybody is apparently *required* to use all weekend—the goddamned all-terrain vehicles, and the snowmobiles in winter, and the chain saws, those little electric weedcutters that sound like—what? Aluminum *insects,* is what. And if you can filter out the goddamned classic rock 'n' roll radio station that blows down here from Pine Plains like smoke that the *wind* carries—and would you tell me how a band named The Doors gets called *classic?* Anyway." And she had set her chipped coffee mug down on the white metal lawn table and had picked up his hand with both of hers and had kissed it. "Anyway," he'd said.

Graham still commuted. He still went to work. He still came home. He just did less of each, going in on Tuesdays more than Mondays, often sleeping overnight in town and sometimes all day at the Gramercy Park, instead of going to the office or back upstate to the house.

But on weekends he was certain to be there, because that was when Mal, who would have telephoned the office four times during the week to speak with him or leave chipper messages, would unfailingly drive the Taconic, hauling him shopping bags, coming to serve.

Mal, rigged out in clothes left from high school, had insisted that they move the firewood, dumped outside the smokehouse, inside and into rows. They stooped and rose and tossed, then built up stacks. "You know," he said, panting, and noticing that she breathed evenly, "I'm going to burn this wood for nothing but effect."

"For comfort," Mal said. "It smells nice and it feels nice, and—"

"Nice," Graham said. "You're not supposed to burn wood for *nice*. You do it to keep the pipes from bursting. To keep people alive."

"What in hell is *that* supposed to mean, Daddy? Is that a crack about something? Keeping people alive?"

Graham shook his head. He smiled. He knew it was a dreadful smile.

"No. Tell me. Can you?"

"It's nothing lofty or tragic, Mal. I'm glad you got Mom's hair instead of mine. That's all."

"Do I make you think of her?"

He almost said *Hardly.* "I think of her anyway," he did say. "You're not a sign of death to me."

"Jesus," she said. "I never thought I *was.*"

"Good."

"But what a thing to think about."

"The mark of genius," he said, smiling, and seeing in her face that the smile had not improved, "is the willingness of an average man to sound inventive while acting dumb. Bennett Cerf. Or Samuel Johnson."

She stared.

"Anyway," he said, "I was looking at how pretty your hair is, and I was thinking I like it long like that, with those twisty kind of swirls on them, and I was glad you didn't have my Brillo-pad hair."

"Brillo's gray," she said. "Your hair's still black, pretty much. You look younger than you, you know, are."

"Go on," he said, groaning as he bent for more wood, "I don't look a day over eighty."

"You look forty. You are fifty. You act a hundred."

"That's because you make me do things like stacking firewood instead of hiring in some kid from Millerton to do it for me."

"It's good for us to do these things together."

He said, "I know you think so, Mal."

She dropped the split quarters and they clattered on the stone floor. "I'm going in and make us some hot soup and rat poison mixed with deadly amanita," she said. He watched her walk on her stiff legs toward the house. He saw himself, from behind, watching her go.

In the cold smell of old fires, in the dimness of the smokehouse lit by a forty-watt bulb, he studied his wood. The rows were neat and tight—Mal had seen to that. The turrets, made of logs piled, two at a time parallel to each other in alternating directions, which held the long rows hard against the smokehouse wall they stretched to, made him think of pioneer cabins, the way the logs at the corners protruded, like the fingers of hands about to clasp. The wood was a dark orange, sometimes a weathered gray, the birch light in color and heavy-looking, the maple brown with insect trails; the cherry made his mouth water, his jaws ache, as if he'd bitten into sourness. Wood good enough to eat. Eat on. Something. He smiled, and was grateful that Mal didn't see him. He thought of Mal and him and Sarah at their round, claw-legged Victorian dining table. It was made of cherry, and on Saturday afternoons, when he'd caught glimpses of it from the kitchen as he moved about to make their drinks, he'd seen it glow in the unlighted room. The log he'd just kicked, a round piece of limbwood that might be cherry or red oak, had a giant, white, flabby fungus growing on it. His kick had shaken part of it free, and fragments had spattered the smokehouse floor and had clung to the toe of his boot. He heard the side door of the house open out, and he went before Mal had to call him.

They ate standing up in the kitchen. Mal had sat at the set table while Graham had washed his hands. But he'd not been able to sit. He had taken his cup of metallic-tasting canned soup and had slurped from it, standing, looking through the front window at the mailbox across their rural road. So Mal had stood and, sipping, had wandered slowly around him, like a restless dog.

"Good soup," Graham said.

"Mm," she answered, her nose in her cup. He heard her boots scuff the floor; he heard the crunch of something like leaves. "Mommy told me the more garlic and onion leaves you find on a kitchen floor, near the counters—that's how you tell if there's life in a house." He heard things crackle. "I guess there's hope," Mal said.

He said, still facing the window, "You can't save me, Mal. You know that?"

"So can you save me?"

"What?"

"A kid-question," she said. "Daughter-question. Selfish question," she said. "I'm sorry. And I didn't mean to push it, with the leaves."

"No," he said, turning to her, but noticing, just before he did, that his face had been in the window all that time, staring hard. The face was bordered—he had seen its features only faintly—by a huge thicket of untrimmed, unbrushed beard. He blinked and finished turning to Mal, apologizing, but she had gone from the room. He said it anyway: "Yes. I'm sorry. I am." But he knew that his mind was on the window, on the face he thought of as reproachful, and on whether it was still there, watching him look for his daughter.

In the yard, as the clouds banked harder, Mal said, "Early snow."

"Where did you receive the gift," Graham asked, "of knowing all of a sudden how to talk like a laconic farmer instead of a Mount Holyoke graduate? And have I really been looking like *this*? When I go into work?"

She was behind him, fastening the bath towel at his neck and clicking the scissors. I will have to go to barbers from now on, he thought. Sarah had always cut his hair, and now he would go to barbershops. How much do you tip a barber, these days, he wondered. How much do they charge? Where *are* they? He would not permit himself to be clipped and perfumed in some unisexual beauty parlor. "When I was a kid," he said to Mal, who was working on his neck—the Great Artificial Hairline, Sarah had called it, because his neck and back were so hairy, she insisted, the pelt climbed directly up his head—"I used to carry a dollar to Frank's Barbershop. He got seventy-five cents for the haircut, complete with rubbed-in Wildroot from a tapered white bottle, and he kept the change for his tip."

"You can't get mugged on Vanderbilt Avenue for a dollar," Mal said.

"No, but I know a place off East Fourteenth Street where they kill you for half a buck."

The bright autumn light, instead of making the yard look thick and undifferentiated, cast the shadow of every blade of grass, he thought, so that there was too much to see. His eyes ached.

"How come Mommy always cut your hair?"

"I asked her to."

"But why?"

"I don't like those haircutting places, the—you know, the people who put their—"

"—Nah."

"What nah?"

"Nah, I don't believe it," she said, working behind his ears.

"What do you believe, Mal? Ouch."

"Sorry. That you liked her touching you."

"And therefore I asked you to cut my hair because I like *you* touching me?"

She stopped.

"I mean, it's lovely. My big, grown girl is standing up behind me like I'm someone's little kid, and she's trimming me down."

"Are we failing at this, too?"

He let his head fall forward a little. "You're twenty-three. You have a boyfriend in New York. You have a nice job you like. You have a father who's sometimes crazy a little, and he doesn't go in to work all the time, but he can afford to miss a couple of days now and then, and he isn't running around in bars lying dead drunk in the street."

"That doesn't make any sense. You don't run and lie down. You can't be in a bar and on the street. You'll have to decide, Daddy."

"I will. I promise. I think I'll probably just hang around here for a while. Seriously."

"Seriously?"

"Well, you know what I mean. Mal: live your life."

"Aren't you a part of it?"

"Sweetheart, right now I don't have the time."

"I'm edging into your schedule?"

"You're wonderful. You come here and talk your lovely farmer-talk and you chunk wood with me and stack turrets and get the wood in before snow flies, and it's wonderful. All of it."

"All of what?"

"Comfort, I guess."

"Yes," she hissed from behind and above him, pulling back hard on the towel so that his head snapped back. "Yes. Whose comfort, Daddy?"

He tried to turn, and he saw them in the yard, the man rising partway as if to stand and look back at his child. He asked, "Whose?"

"Good question," she said.

He sat back in the white metal lawn chair and heard the side door close. He looked across the yard to the smokehouse and the mound of wood he still had to carry in and stack. The sunset was bleeding brightly onto the underside of the clouds. "Early snow," he said, like a recent widower's daughter who mimicked the farmers upstate.

THE LIVING ROOM was low-ceilinged, dark, decorated with shelves filled with books he'd published and a few he should have. You could put your feet on the coffee table or hang them over the armrests of the sofas in their house. He never came into the room now unless Mal was there to insist, after dinner, that they drink espresso and talk. Tonight she drank espresso and Graham drank grappa. Each time she sipped, she nodded, as if to indicate the quality of the beans she'd brought. He shuddered as he drank.

Mal was talking about Jethro, her boyfriend. His name was Jerry, but she called him Jethro for the sake of complexity, she said. "He had an Italian dictionary," Mal told her father. "The firm is sending somebody over there, for some kind of—I think an Italian client of theirs is buying an American company that's in Rome. I *think*. And Jethro figures, if they're sending somebody, it might as well be him. He. Him."

Graham waved, as if offering dispensation, at her grammatical niceties. He nodded, sipped, and grimaced.

"He looked up everything that started with *mal*. Everything was bad or sick," she said. "I don't remember the words. He read them to me."

"*Malattia*," Graham said, "disease. *Maledetto*, cursed. *Malizia*, vice. Basic *malo*, for bad. That's right. But none of them's you. You're healthy, you're blessed, and you're good." He drank grappa. "You know how you got your name." She lifted her feet from the arm of her loveseat and planted them, in boot socks, on the floor. Her legs were together, her hands were loose on her thighs, and her mouth looked just a little softer. She was a girl, he thought, listening to a story. "You remember," he said.

"The little island. Yes."

"Pantelleria, the little island off Sicily. It's about as big as your apartment. That's right. And on the island they make a wine that we named you after. Malvasia delle Lipari. It's sweet, it's rosy, it's a little peachy, and it's very intense. It's just what you turned out to be." He smiled what he thought was a father's fond smile, and she flinched. "You drink it nicely chilled. Mommy and I drank it in Venice at a restaurant called Pescatore. We ate spider crab there. I think it was early May, it was quite cold. I remember justifying the meal by saying one of our authors was with us. And he would have been. He was supposed to be. He ended up staying back in his room at the Biscanzio with an English editor. She was buying sheets for his new book from us.

"Anyway, Mommy and I drank a lot of wine with dinner, and then the *padrone* brought us a bottle of Malvasia."

"You drank all of it?" He heard in her question not just curiosity, but the displeasure of a generation whose members defended their bodies as those in his had stood guard at their minds.

"Oh, yes," he said. He watched her bright hair spin as she registered her disapproval. He watched Sarah's face in hers as the day's fatigue, and the hypnosis of story, relaxed the muscles at the corners of her mouth, and between her nose and lips, and on her forehead. The slightly broader face and shorter nose—his dubious genetic gift—were less noticeably different from her mother's now. Sarah stared out of Mal at him and waited. So he shut his eyes, he drank off grappa, and then he said, "Yeah. We got lit up on Malvasia. There you were."

"There I was. That was me."

"Somewhat later. Yes."

She and Sarah, taking turns, he thought, regarded the story and its teller in the dim, low room. He saw himself, under their scrutiny, pour with care a few more drops into his glass. I am wholly fine, he demonstrated. He saw the grace with which he silently set the bottle down.

"And then I was there with you and Mommy," she said. When she folded her hands, he noticed how large they were, competent-looking, muscled and veined and roughened by firewood, hands that had seized at the world. "Do you think, Daddy, that we'll ever get to be, you know, the *same?*"

She looked away, as though embarrassed. He set his glass on the coffee table, and grunted as he edged his body forward on the deep sofa set at right angles to the loveseat in which she sat. He walked around the table and sat beside her. He took one of her large, roughened hands. It lay in his like an animal full of trust or recently killed. He raised it to his lips. Her hand stirred, then, and took hold of his, and brought it powerfully to her face. She laid her lips against it, and he pulled his hand away. Then he tried to permit her the kiss, but she moved her head and let him go.

The only face he saw was Mal's, now, and he thought to tell her so, but she had stood, so he stood too, and they did the best they could. "I love you, Mal. Good night," he said.

She said, "Good night."

HE CARRIED HER cup and saucer, his glass and grappa to the kitchen, then found a flashlight that worked—it was in the bread drawer of their cupboard, which Sarah had filled with tools and plumber's tape and matches—and, putting on his canvas chore jacket, he went outside, across the side lawn, to the smokehouse. The stars, when he thought to look for them, were invisible. "Cloud cover," he said. Then he said, "Fuck the clouds. Fuck the stars, while you're at it."

In the smokehouse, in the smell he hated, Graham turned the light on and set his flashlight down, and looked at the rows they had built, and the inchoate heap they still must sort and shape. Wood that was wet from the forest floor stank like unused rooms in old houses. Much of the wood smelled like clotted, dark soil. Lacing it all—the odors and textures, the darkness of the building, the pink-brown or gray of weathered wood—was the high, harsh bite of old smoke, dead fires, the ash of other people's purposes. He felt his face twist. He tore at the light pull and went, without turning his flashlight on, across the lawn, under the *maledetto* sky, to bed.

But he didn't sleep, or let himself try to. He recognized his restlessness, he mistrusted it, he knew that it would keep him awake and moving until he fed what it was, an appetite. He rejected, on behalf of Mal, more grappa. On behalf of Mal, he scooped Balducci's tortellini salad with pesto and halved black olives into a bowl, and he chewed on the bony little pasta shapes and made swilling sounds of satiation, and threw it—soup spoon, pottery bowl, salad—into the garbage pail in the cupboard under the sink. He wiped at his lips and pulled at the mess he had smeared on his beard.

In the little downstairs bathroom, he washed his face and beard. He stayed stooped above the running water in the perfume of soap, washing and rinsing, washing and rinsing, in order not to straighten and see his face in the mirror before him.

With his eyes closed, he saw himself stiffen, then stand erect, then point his face up as if to call. But he said nothing, and only turned off the spigots and replaced the soap in its shell-shaped dish. He took a large bath towel from its hook and draped it around his neck, spreading it across his chest and turning its edge beneath the collar of his shirt. From the kitchen counter, where Mal had tossed them, he took the orange-handled scissors and returned to the bathroom and its mirror, where, like a man who dove into deep cold water with little confidence, he widened his eyes and stared.

He looked at the scissors that he held beside the thickets of beard. Hairs pointed in all directions, curled in disorganization. He studied the tip of the scissors as they touched his whiskers and therefore he didn't have to see his eyes. He simply watched specific hairs as the scissors straddled and closed on them and cut. The snicking sound was a kind of comfort because, he realized, he was cutting with a lively rhythm as if to the beat of a song. There was no song. There was no plan. He didn't want one. He would cut at the beard until he found a shape that he could carry upstairs and present at her bedroom door or hold for the night and bear to breakfast. He could wait, he thought as he cut first at one angle, then at another. He could even wait until later tomorrow, when she waited, impatient, at the smokehouse with its terrible stench of ash. He would bring the face he found tonight. He watched its shape announce itself below his eyes. He would look at them later. She would know what he brought to her.

Him.

He.

Him.

To the memory of Harry Ford

Joy of Cooking

As they chewed at Cheerios in milk and drank unnaturally orange orange juice in the breakfast room off the kitchen of their house, Stephen's daughters studied him through eyes distorted by corrective lenses. Sasha seemed patiently curious, Brigitte apprehensive; neither spoke, and neither looked away. When Rosalie in their bedroom started to sing, not in words, just heavy syllables pounded atop a tune about joy—

Dee duh duh doe
Dee da-da!
Dee duh dee da
Dum da-da!

—Stephen saw his daughters watch him hurry to the kitchen, cocking his head to listen hard. Inside his face, on top of his tongue that rose as if *he* sang, and underneath a brain he thought of as boiling in his blood like an egg in water in a pot on a stove, Stephen supplied the words as Rosalie sang while she packed before leaving him:

Jesus loves me
This I know!
For the Bible
Tells me so!

And we're not even Christians, he thought. We aren't anything.

He had stayed home from work this morning after making sand-wiches for the children's lunches. Sasha liked hard-cooked eggs in slices on mayonnaise smeared over soft white bread. Brigitte ate only smooth peanut butter with grape jelly on the same pulpy bread that Sasha liked. Both girls, nine and eleven, stared at him through dark-framed glasses that reminded him of Rosalie's (as did their eyes), and Stephen bellowed bad jokes, all but screamed *"Sure!"* when Brigitte reminded him about money for milk and an after-school snack. Ros-alie, meanwhile, prowled their bedroom, blowing her nose and slam-ming things.

When the bus came, the children, he knew, were happy to be re-leased. Brigitte had called from the front door, "Bye, Daddy. Bye, Mommy." But Sasha had said nothing. He'd called to them, as if dep-utized, "We love you!" As they fled the tension that ached in the house like flu in muscles, Stephen felt that he, too, had been set free. The feeling didn't last. He heard their bedroom door open as Rosalie marched in her fuzzy, dragging slippers to the bathroom and back. She must have left the door ajar: he heard the brass pulls on their bu-reau jangle, then the *thrap,* four times, of suitcase clasps, and he was certain that Rosalie was packing to leave.

He fetched a mug of coffee from the kitchen to the breakfast room and sat with it as Rosalie hummed, and as the words she didn't say echoed in his inner ear, though not in her voice but in his. She sounded, now, reassured by the song. She sounded young.

When he looked at the tile-topped breakfast table, he understood why his coffee had tasted awful. He had poured not milk but orange juice into his acid third cup. He still held the juice tumbler, which rat-tled on the tabletop to something like the rhythm—*dee* da-da—of Rosalie's song. Stephen kept time.

The tumbler was Sasha's. She had worn too much dark red lipstick, as usual, to counteract what she saw as the scarring effect of her braces. Of course the frame of crimson broadcast her braces, and she looked like the grille of a '49 Buick. Today she'd worn even more than he was used to, and Stephen wondered if, hearing their fight, she had laid the impasto of lipstick on as a rebuke to them. He had locked her out, though, with his porcelain grin, his morning commotion, his all-but-yodeled good cheer. He lifted her juice tumbler, and he kissed the one-lipped print that Sasha's mouth had left on the rim of the glass. It tasted like Crayola.

He left the breakfast room and walked through the kitchen, where the cat was on the counter next to the stove, eating hard-boiled eggs. He went down the small parquet corridor that connected the back of the house to the front, and he stood outside their bedroom door. It had two thin cracks that looked as though someone had tried to draw: they were stick-people, hand-in-hand, made by his kicking at the door when Rosalie had locked him out, years before. He watched her now, and he listened. She was wearing her heavy green plaid bathrobe, with a dark gray bathroom towel around her neck, tucked into the robe, like a scarf. She hummed about Jesus' love.

She looked up from her underwear drawer and her face was sullen, swollen, sliced by her glasses' dark frames. But when she took his stare and countered it with her own, she nearly smiled. He felt his eyebrows rise. "You've got lipstick on your mouth," she said.

He nodded. Leaning against the doorframe, he wiped at his lips, then licked them, then wiped once more. "Sash," he said. "I drank from her glass. She wore lipstick for two today."

Rosalie waited, then looked back into her drawer.

"You shouldn't do this," he said.

"Nope."

"Then don't."

"I shouldn't want to do this," Rosalie said. "I shouldn't feel so bad. Nobody should."

"Then don't feel bad."

"Stephen, we don't need to be as old as we are to talk like this. We could hire a couple of kids. We could get the girls to do it. God knows they hear it enough." After studying her underthings, she plunged both hands into the bureau drawer and drew out what looked like random handsful, then wheeled and went to the suitcases, and tossed some into each. She stood at the suitcases which lay on their bed and, with her back still toward him, she asked, "Why aren't you at work?"

"You really want to know?"

She went back to the bureau and began to examine pantyhose. She didn't answer him.

He said, "Because I'm scared to be. At first I stayed here to fight. But then I heard you singing that goddamned hymn. I thought: she's leaving."

"You're right."

"And I was too frightened."

He watched her shoulders slump. She pulled at the towel, settling it into the robe, around her neck.

"I'd have expected 'Onward, Christian Soldiers,' " he said.

"What was I singing?"

"You didn't know?"

She shook her head, she held up hosiery and shook her head again.

He said, " 'Jesus Loves Me.' "

"I was? Really. I haven't sung that since I was a little girl. It's the song that good little girls like. They're *so* good, Jesus *has* to love them."

"Is this for real, Rosie? With taking the kids, everything? The girls go away, and you go away, and I'm supposed to live here alone?"

"No," she said. "After a while, the girls and I come back, and you've moved out. You're living in an apartment someplace. The girls and I live here. I don't know. Life goes on."

"This is really for real, then."

She slowly nodded.

"No," he said. "Rosie, we *love* each other. That's why we get so mad."

"So? You think love makes you feel better? Who said love makes you feel better? With you and me—and this is thirteen years into the mission, now, long enough for us to be out on the edge of the solar system if we're a rocket ship—"

"Wait a minute."

"Stephen, don't talk like a lawyer now. Don't you dare be smart and logical with me and tell me about facts. That's what got us here."

"No, it isn't, Rosie. What got us here was my wanting you to be my handmaiden. Dedicating your life to the Great Attorney. The thing about you as decoration in my career."

"On your career. You're really trying. You're trying so hard, you sound stupid. Like a kid who studied for a test and he doesn't know what all the memorized answers mean. You've been up half the night—"

"All of it."

"No. I was. I heard you snoring on the sofa."

"Wrong."

"See?"

"See what?"

"Never mind," she said, holding a knot of pantyhose away from her body, as if it were stirring and might strike. She carried it to the bed. "Just, let's say I'm acknowledging that you're really thinking about what we talked about. Except it has so little to do with the damned country club, the damned office dinner, the damned god-damned dance. Those are symptoms. It's all just a cliché. As you pointed out."

"Symptom," he said. "As in disease?"

"As in disease."

"So what's the disease? That you love me?"

She stared at him.

"Yeah," he said. "That's what it is. You love me—lawyer, no lawyer, whatever. That's what bothers the hell out of you: that you love me. *Is* that the disease? How do we treat a thing like that, Rosie?"

"I'm doing it," she said.

"No, you're not. You're taking twice as long to pack as I've ever seen you take to do anything. You could have changed all four tires on your car by now."

She turned to face him. She slowly pulled the towel out of her robe by one end, tugging on it hand over hand until the bath towel was hanging from her hand, and he could see the mottling of blue and red at her throat.

"Jesus! Rosie! I didn't do that!"

She said, "I did."

"Why?"

"Because I can't make you understand, and I can't make *me* understand." Her teeth were clenched as she spoke. "I stood in the bathroom last night, while *you slept,* damn it. You *slept.* And I looked at my stupid round face and my buck teeth—"

"They aren't buck. They're crooked. They're sexy. Your face isn't round the way you say it's round. It's oval. You're a—you're a dish, Rosie."

She shook her head. Her eyes were closed, and she kept them that way as, rolling the towel, squeezing it, she said, "I looked in the bathroom mirror and I grabbed my throat. Like this"—she put one hand around her neck; he saw the thumb slide into its bruised print above her larynx—"and I said, 'Why can't you *learn?*' "

"Rosie," he asked her, "learn what?"

"That you're going to have to keep asking that all the time we're married. That I'm going to choke myself to death or drown the cat. Or you. Choke *you,* drown *you.* Because you see a way of living. Fine. You're entitled to. But it's *yours.* Its teeth are bigger than mine are, even. It could eat me. It could swallow me." She opened her eyes at last. She put the towel around her neck. As she tucked it in, she said, "That's all. It's a goddamned cliché. I know it. Didn't I say that before?"

"I think *I* might have called it that last night. It isn't, Rosie. I really believe that: it isn't."

"No, you were right. All of it's clichés."

"Rosie, but we love each other."

She shrugged.

Stephen slid down with his back against the doorframe. He stuck his legs out so they straddled the wall on which the wide-open door was hinged.

"Are you doing that to keep me in?" Rosalie asked.

"I didn't think of it that way. I'm thinking, just, I don't want you feeling so bad."

"Because I *can* step over you."

"Rosalie, you could step *through* me."

She sat down on the bed, next to the suitcases. She nodded. "I know."

Stephen was thinking that if they made love now he would want to set the suitcases down, not sweep them aside from the bed. He didn't want her to think he was sweeping aside what she'd said. He saw Rosalie watching him, and he knew that she was thinking how aroused he always was when she fought him and told him that she didn't care about love. He didn't smile to her, and when he saw how sad her magnified eyes behind her glasses were, and her mouth, and the brutal bruises on her fragile neck, his eyes filled up.

She said, "What, Stephen?"

"I remembered when I heard that singing before. It wasn't in church."

She lay back on the bed. She pulled her glasses off and held them, folded, in one hand. She drew her legs up and curled herself down toward them so that she wasn't quite a ball, but was lying on her side in a crescent.

"You look like a half-moon," he said.

"You stay there. I don't want this thing ending up in some wild screw and we forget all about it."

"I'll sit right here."

"I mean it, Stephen."

"I was little. I don't know—eight? So my mother was young."

"Your mother was never young, Stephen. She was born old and mean."

"No, she was pretty, and she was young, and my father was gone by then. She was living with Carl Boden."

"The philosopher king."

"He was an interesting guy."

"Smart enough, I'll give him that, to take off on her."

"I think she was one of those people who people leave. I don't know."

"I do. She's mean. She's skinny and mean and she has those thin lips."

"But he was there, then, and for the next ten years or so, huh? And they had a good time together. I remember all those little pats on the ass, and smooching in the kitchen. Nice stuff."

"You would."

Her eyes were closed, and Stephen then closed his. He said, "I remember Carl was wearing this seersucker shirt. And he was sitting in the kitchen, watching her do something. I think she was cooking. I was playing, I guess. Drawing at the table. The radio was on. That was before we moved out to Harrison, so it was up on Eightieth Street, and she was listening to the radio. All of a sudden, Carl says to her, 'You don't sing anymore.' She says *What,* and everybody says *What* a few times, and Carl says, 'I used to love the way you sang when you cooked. It was always so happy.' Something like that—how she sounded happy, and she made him feel happy, and now he's disappointed, something is missing. Do I have to tell you she started to cry?"

He opened his eyes to watch her lift her shoulders. She said, "And?"

"And nothing. She stopped crying. He apologized a lot, she apologized a lot. I shut up and ate my food. Something under sauce, I'm sure. Anyway, the next day's Sunday. We're going to go to Central Park, we're going to hit the streets on Sunday in New York, and the radio's playing. A very dumb, bouncy song. I absolutely cannot remember its name, but I think I still remember what it sounded like. She's making those amazingly thick, brutal flapjacks of hers, and Carl's sitting there reading a book, growling at it the way he always did. And all of a sudden my mother's humming along with the song on the radio. 'Dee duh *duh,*' she sings, all noise, no words, and *heavy,* slamming down on the syllables, as heavy as her pancakes, 'Dee duh *duh!*' She's hitting those off-key notes, she was a terrible singer—and now, because I really don't remember seeing it, but now I imagine how she's looking out of the corner of her eye, right? To see if Carl notices? I didn't figure this out for years, of course."

"You didn't figure it out until this morning."

"Yes. And then Carl leaves the room." He stopped. They were silent.

Rosalie turned onto her side and opened her eyes. "That's the story?"

"That's the story. He throws his book down on the kitchen table, *whammo!,* and he walks out of the room."

"What'd your mother do?"

"I don't remember."

"That's the story. What *she* did, *then."*

Now Stephen lay on his stomach, his feet out in the hall and his torso in the bedroom, and he propped his chin on his forearms. "That's *their* story. My part of it is what I said. How sad she was, trying to show him all of that awful joy I suppose she wasn't feeling. She tried to give him that. I think it was remarkably generous, what she offered."

Rosalie said, "I didn't offer you anything when I was singing. You understand that?"

"I was thinking about how sad it was, somebody who couldn't sing, and who really didn't feel like singing, trying to sing for someone."

"Do not start crying for that woman."

He said, "If I cried, Rosie, it wouldn't be for her."

"Don't you dare and cry for *me."*

"No," he said. He put his head all the way down on his hands.

Rosalie said, "This is impossible. We're impossible."

They lay in silence, he on the floor and she on the bed.

She wakened him by saying, "See? You were sleeping."

"No," he said. He didn't know why. "I wasn't."

He watched her swing her feet over the side of the bed. Her robe was hiked, and he saw her calves and knees, her lower thighs. She pressed them together and pulled the hem of her bathrobe down. She sat on the edge of the bed and said, "Now *I'm* going to sleep. You go someplace else, please."

"Where?"

"I just want to *sleep!"*

He manufactured a dignity with which to climb to his feet and leave. When he was in the kitchen, he heard their bedroom door close. He shooed the cat from the stove, then collected all the dishes and rinsed them, stowed them in the dishwasher. He couldn't remember if you were allowed to wash the iron frying pan in the machine. He scratched at it with a steel pad just in case you weren't. And when the machine was humming and hushing, when the surfaces were wiped down and the wiping rag rinsed in water nearly too hot to touch, he took off his necktie, hung it on the dish towel rack, and telephoned the office.

As he gave instructions and answered questions, he thought of the musical tones he'd punched to reach his secretary. He thought of the clients who pressed those numbers and listened to those tones, waiting for advice. He heard his voice, over so many calls, dispensing wisdoms and assurances, citing statutes, offering precedents. And he knew how he'd concluded so many times that the marital tragedies to which he'd been asked to respond were, finally to him, all alike. It struck him with a kind of disgust how banal he and Rosalie were, how quotidian their sadness would seem to some other lawyer at some other phone number who might hear Stephen complain how his mind was shaken and his heart was sore. He wondered if, when his clients telephoned, his deepest inner parts went to sleep, like an arm pressed into the same position too long, while clients wept descriptions to him of one's suffocation and the other's need for self-expression, and everyone's rage to flee. His secretary waited, and he finally heard the lengthening pause, so he finished and rang off.

Stephen walked from the kitchen to the breakfast room and back. He stood in the kitchen, frightened because he'd no idea what to do. At last, he fetched his briefcase from the hall and set it on the table in the breakfast room. He took from it a yellow ruled pad and the fountain pen that Rosalie had given him when he'd been made a partner. Then he did what he did in the office: he made notes. At the top of the page, he printed PROBLEMS. Halfway down the page he drew a horizontal line and printed SOLUTIONS. It was a letter-size pad, so he had four inches or so for problems—not enough, he thought. He tore the page from the pad and made his dividing line vertical. He headed the left side PROBLEMS. He thought he heard their door slam, and he paused. No one came, he breathed more evenly, and he headed the right-hand side SOLVE. He tore the page away.

On the next clean page, he wrote *Dear Rosalie.* He tore the page out. *Rosie,* he wrote. Looking from the breakfast room to the narrow bookshelves on which stood her cookbooks and his *Encyclopedia of Wines and Spirits,* he saw a very old, blue spine—the *Joy of Cooking* her parents, both dead now, had given them when they married. He set down his pen and went to the kitchen and, singing a song—singing Dee duh *duh!*—and not thinking of its name, he took the book, and he began. The song, he would remember later, was called "If I'd Known You Were Coming, I'd Have Baked a Cake," and his mother, he would then remember, had offered its syllables to her lover, Carl Boden.

But for now, he followed directions. He sifted flour. He found baking powder. He used nine eggs in achieving four separated yolks and whites. He set butter aside to reach room temperature. He found almonds and ground them. He slowly melted chocolate. He whipped up milk and vanilla and egg white without spattering them. And he baked the cake so that a toothpick slid unstained from its core. While it cooled, he mixed the icing, then applied it, maybe a moment too soon. But it was a chocolate fudge cake, made from scratch, and he slugged out the syllables, Dee duh *duh!,* as in the credenza in the living room he found the shoe box labeled BIRTHDAYS and took from it a single pink birthday candle. While he washed the dishes and straightened the kitchen, he thought of Sasha and Brigitte blowing candles out. He was standing near the counter, reading prefatory words on nutrition in the cookbook while the icing hardened, when Rosalie came in. She wore jeans and a soft white cotton shirt that fastened with metal snaps near its floppy collar. In her clean white running shoes she looked springy and competent as she inspected the kitchen, then him. She seemed to him frighteningly older than she'd been. He slid the pink candle into the pocket of his shirt.

She filled the kettle with water and put out instant coffee and one mug.

He heard himself offer, "I was going to do a laundry."

Before the water could be hot enough, she poured it over the coffee and walked past him to the breakfast room. He found a cup and shook some crystals into it and, without stirring the coffee, followed her. He sat and said, "Rosie."

She looked up. Her eyes behind the lenses were red and puffy. Her elbows were on the legal pad and his awful fragment of letter. She had set her cup on his salutation. Her face wasn't angry, it was solemn. She looked to him as she must have looked as a girl in church: sure of what she must do, owlish with her certainty.

He left the table again. He stuck the candle into the cake, and he brought it to her. Setting it on the table, he said, "Here."

"Very nice," she said. "Very well done."

He was going to say, "I made it for you," but then the girls came in. He heard their bus huff away, and he called to them, "Come and get it, ladies! Look at what I made for you!"

Rosalie walked past them, pausing to kiss each daughter on the top of the head. She waved and went toward the other side of the house while Sasha followed her and Brigitte waited. Stephen went to her and stooped, one knee on the floor. "How was school, baby?"

Her face was pale, her eyes narrow. She asked, "Did you make the cake so we wouldn't go away, Daddy?"

He looked down at her pink sneakers. "Yes," he said.

When Rosalie and Sasha returned, he looked up, then stood. Sasha carried two small canvas traveling bags. Rosalie carried two large bags and an over-the-shoulder carryall.

Stephen thought of the advice he gave to shattered men who called. He said something like "Wait," he thought. They came to him with this, and he said, "Wait."

"Daddy," Sasha said. He saw that she'd put lots of fresh lipstick on.

Brigitte said, "Can we have some of the cake?"

That was when Rosalie's face crumpled, but not in tears. She looked as though she fought not to laugh, and Stephen—as the counselor, now, addressing the husband—told himself not to hold that against her.

Stephen told them, "Just a minute, all right?" And he went to the drawer and found the cake server, then tore off several sheets of paper towel. He cut a wedge of chocolate cake with butter cream icing, and he handed it to Brigitte. She held it on her palm. Stephen stepped back to address them all, Sasha and Brigitte and Rosalie, their identical eyes. They paused with their baggage.

Brigitte said, "Thank you, Daddy."

Sasha smiled and shrugged.

Stephen said, "Rosie."

She said, "What?"

He tore off more towels, cut more cake, and came to offer it. He said, "For on the way."

Rosalie shrugged as if echoing Sasha. She looked down at the luggage that occupied her hands. "No room," she apologized.

"Of course," Stephen said. Like three good guests, then, they waited politely. And then, slowly, to show him how reluctantly they left, they left. When the front door closed, he bit a piece of cake and stood in the kitchen and chewed. He heard himself humming the tune he had baked to, and then he remembered its name.

The Talking Cure

LOVE IS UNSPEAKABLE.

Consider the story of the older brother who went off to school, the brilliant, tall mother and wife who hunched herself shorter, curved at her tilted drafting table as if around the buildings she planned for her clients. Consider the husband, son of a bankrupt Hudson Valley apple grower, who made a living as a junior high school principal. And then consider me, fifteen years old and up to my wrists in vomiting dogs and hemorrhaging cats, and the darkening drift and dismay of my parents.

We lived in an old house surrounded by the ruins of the orchards. The air pulsed, in autumn, with the drunken dancing of wasps that had supped on the tan, rotted flesh of English Russets and Chenangos. We walked on the mush of the orchard's decay, and in winter some one of us never failed to be surprised by the glowing red or golden apples which continued to hang, as snow started falling, on the gray-black trunks of dozens of trees. Apple trees aren't peaceful. The trunks and limbs look like tensed or writhing hands.

My mother commuted from the farm to Manhattan in her Karman Ghia, and she designed the structures that held people's lives. And my father continued to fail her, despite what I would have described, if asked, as pretty sizable efforts to win her approval. And my big brother, Edwin, who had escaped, as I saw it, to Ohio, shone over the plains and through the forests, lighting up my mother's face and causing her to say to friends, "Yes, my baby's gone away."

She looked truly sad—and therefore beautiful and fragile—and she looked highly pleased, and both at once. Apparently, she was proud but also bereft. Something had been stolen from her life, and she knew that she would never retrieve it. This is what I thought I learned, spying—younger siblings tend to live sub rosa lives—from around the corners of our rooms, or simply from my place at the kitchen table where I sat in my life and took note of them in theirs while they failed, mercifully often, to notice me. I was like the furniture. I was a shape your eye slid over. You get used to it—to me—and then you say what you wish I hadn't heard. That's how it is with younger brothers when the genius goes to Oberlin and writes home his observations on existentialism and a man my parents referred to as *Sart!* They sneezed or barked it with a powerful emphasis on the final two letters they didn't pronounce.

My father wished to replace her Edwin, and he never could. And, anyway, that led to competition. And who ever heard of a father competing with his son? It was cannibalistic. It was barbaric. It was Freudian.

That was the last word I heard through the screen windows one hot Sunday afternoon, while I was about to use the back door to report in the cool kitchen, shaded by tall, old maples, not runty apple trees, that I had mowed the lawns and could be found in front of our vast, boxy Emerson, watching the New York Yankees stumble and whiff. Freudian. I knew a bit about Freud. He was the specialist in women who wanted penises. I could not imagine my mother ever wanting a penis, nor could I fathom why my father might wish her to develop one. It took several days for further investigation to suggest that Freudian meant having to do with dreams, and with wishes you didn't know you wished. That made sense, given our family. There were a lot of secret wishes flying around.

I was pretty sure that several of them had to do with Dr. Victor Mason, the veterinarian who took care of our terrible cat until she died, and who hired me to work on weekday afternoons and Saturday mornings. My job was to be the big kid who comes into the examination room with the vet and holds your Yorkshire terrier down while Dr. Mason gives him his inoculations. I talked to the animals and rubbed them and made gitchy-goomy noises to keep the animals from realizing what was happening to them, and to keep the owners from realizing what was happening to their animals.

"Court jester of the household pet," my father called me when Dr. Mason was over for dinner on a Sunday night.

"Valuable assistant," Dr. Mason said. "Peter earns his pay. You know what he has to clean up, some days?"

As usual, I sat behind my camouflage screen and the words went over and around me. I ate my cauliflower because it was my policy to attract as little attention as possible, even if the cauliflower was a bit hard to chew. My mother liked to cook, she insisted, and she did it very badly. If she had asked me what I thought of it, I would have told her how colorful the paprika looked on top of the cauliflower stems. I wouldn't have called the paprika pasty or described the stems as wood.

My mother said, "You're talking about Peter behind his front again."

Dr. Mason smiled an enormous grin. He had a broad face in a big square head, and his cheeks and jaws seemed full of muscles. He was taller than my mother, which meant he was bigger by several inches than my father, and he could lift a Great Dane with ease or kneel with some goofy Labrador pup and prod him in the belly with his big head, then kind of jump up to his feet and continue being a vet. Working with him, I felt like the magician's assistant, except I never knew what the trick was going to be. I thought my father was right, the way he described me, and I thought my mother was looking for another nighttime fight.

"That was very clever," Dr. Mason said, " 'talking behind his front.' You managed to say two things at once." Dr. Mason held the patent on telling people what they might have thought they had just finished saying.

"Well, she's a great rhetorician," my father said.

"That's a compliment, Teddy, am I right?" Dr. Mason said.

"Not at all," my mother said.

"Well, of *course* it is," my father said, a little loudly.

So there was a silence that got uncomfortable, and I began to file a flight plan with myself. I needed to get upstairs to my room and do homework, but not only because I had homework to do. When my mother began to wash the dinner pots before she poured their after-dinner coffee, I knew there was more to come than dessert.

"Peter's doing a first-class job for me. You ever think of a career involving medicine, Peter? Some aspect of the biological sciences?" Dr. Mason rubbed his short gray hair as if he were stroking one of his patients. He asked me the question once or twice a week, and I figured it was just another of his routine queries like "Hey, Pete, what're you doing smart these days?" At first I had labored to answer him, describing in some detail a melancholy Hammond Innes book about the wreck of the *Mary Deare,* or the poems I wrote in those days—a *rhyme* to *mime* the *crime* of *time*—or my efforts to bring my grades up by sporadically reading several pages in the dictionary. He didn't listen, I realized, so finally I answered his questions by smiling or shrugging, and then changing into my pale blue veterinarian assistant's laboratory coat and mopping up the latest deposit of a nervous dog.

"Peter?" My mother was reminding me of my manners.

"Yes, sir," I said. "I've been reading about this German guy in World War II. He got to the Forbidden City in Tibet by accident. It's called Lhasa. I've been reading about him, and he got me going to other mountain climbers. This Englishman named Whymper? He tried to climb Mount Everest. He fell off."

"Isn't it funny," my father said. "You could have gotten interested in Tibet. Or Germans. Or foreign languages. Or the way the Communist Chinese took Tibet over. And you ended up interested in mountain climbing. Or is it mountains?"

"I don't know," I said. "Climbing, I guess. But I also read one called *The Rose of Tibet.* There's a lot of all that stuff in it."

"Wonderful," my father said. "I think that's wonderful." He smiled at me as if I had done something noteworthy. That was why he was such a good junior high school principal. He discovered about eleven times a day that people were commendable, and they knew he thought so. He wasn't very good about law and order, and he'd ended up hiring a former state policeman to be in charge of lateness and smoking in the parking lot. He called him an acting assistant principal, but he was the man who chewed your butt if you bothered the seventh-grade girls on school property or even *thought* about fighting.

"Dreaming your way up mountains," my mother said, happy again because she was discovering a possible reflection of Edwin's distant light. "You dream about it, don't you, darling? Or write poems about it. It's a part of your interior life."

Perhaps you could hand out road maps to my interior life, I didn't say. But Dr. Mason was watching me, and I felt as though he had a rough idea of what was on my mind. He nodded once, as if we had finished a discussion. I saw that my father was looking at my mother. As she saw him watching, she tried to keep her smile a second longer, but it shimmered on her face, and you could tell she was making an effort. I didn't know precisely what my father knew about how things were, and I wondered how much of my curiosity was Freudian.

On the job, Dr. Mason was trying to extend my days at school by offering me lessons in nothing less than all of life. He seemed to feel he owed me such advancement. There was a home, of course, though I didn't know where, and there was a wife, I knew, but she was not mentioned by my parents, and only referred to in passing by Dr. Mason. His office was a small white clapboard cabin at the end of a curving dead-end lane, and I walked from school—there wasn't a team or club that sought me, or one to which I could offer a skill—unless we were under a blizzard or a rainstorm, when he came to give me a lift in his scuffed tan, noisy Willys pickup truck. It said *Jeep* on the back and it had four-wheel drive, and I loved it because it made me think of adventures among soldiers on landscapes not to be found in New York state. I was happy in the smell of animal hair and chemicals and disinfectant, pleased to have my hands on so much life, and glad to often enough be the object of its uncomplicated affection. But whether I was mopping or scooping, pinioning to the floor or raising to the stainless-steel examination table, I was made uncomfortable by the weight of Dr. Mason's obligation.

He had to put a golden retriever down. Her master, a bulky man in a dark brown business suit covered with his dying animal's hair, came into the examination room and stood, drifting back and forth over his planted broad feet. He wouldn't set the dog on the table or the floor. You could smell her dying, a kind of sour vegetable odor that came off her scrawny shanks and her motionless tail, her unreflecting eyes, her long, gray, bony muzzle.

"Tony," Dr. Mason said to him, "it's the right time."

"Don't *feel* right, Doc," the owner said. His round, fat face would have been red, I realized, on any other day. But it was a kind of graywhite, and I wondered if his shaky stance meant that he was going to keel over or get sick. I didn't know if I could get through that kind of cleaning up.

"Let's set her on the table, Peter." I stepped closer to the owner and pushed my hands alongside his. "Let Peter take the weight, Tony."

Tony was crying now. He kept shaking his head. I couldn't tell if he was trying to stop the tears or say how sorry he was to let her go. In any case, he didn't let her go, and I stood in front of him, smelling his sad old dog and something spicy, perhaps salami.

"Tony, let Peter take the weight."

"Damn it, Doc."

"Now take it, Peter."

She slid onto me, against my chest, and I braced myself, for though she looked weightless, she was surprisingly heavy. I took another step back, and then I set her on the table and slowly rubbed her behind the ears. She looked at me sideways and her tail moved twice, and then she was still.

"Now what should I do?" Tony asked him.

"You could wait outside," Dr. Mason said. "If you want to. You could wait, and then I could come and talk to you in a minute."

"Just go outside?" Tony said.

"If that's what you want," Dr. Mason said.

"I hate to leave her."

"Yes," Dr. Mason said.

"Doc," Tony said, and he turned to face the door, and then he leaned at it, pulled his shoulders back, and then slammed his forehead on the door. I think he almost knocked himself out, for he slumped against the door a second or two before he started rubbing his head. The dog might have been used to this trick of his because she moved her tail on the table once. Then Tony opened the door. He said, "Bye, darlin.'"

Dr. Mason loaded his syringe, and I waited. He said, "Touch her, Peter."

"You mean pet her?"

"So she isn't alone."

I rubbed her ears and waited.

"She gave that man all the company he ever had. I kind of hoped he would want to stay with her. But it was obvious he couldn't. And do listen to me, sounding ever so slightly like John Fitzgerald Kennedy." Or Billy Graham, I thought. Or Jesus Christ Almighty.

I was rubbing the head of the dog and I was waiting.

"You just make your decision," Dr. Mason said. And, by now, he sounded to me like a slide trombone. He said, "Oh, shit." She breathed a little more, and I rubbed her, and then she stopped. Her tongue slid out, and she looked silly.

I felt his big hand on top of mine. He said, "You don't have to rub her anymore."

That night, my mother stayed late at the office and my father and I made hamburgers and agreed to meet at the Emerson once I'd finished my homework, to see if the Yankees managed to field nine men who could run. I did my assignments, more or less, and I tried to write something about what had happened at Dr. Mason's office. It was an entirely failed poem, I knew, full of words like *sorrow* and *suffering,* and the only rhyme I could find for *suffering* was *Bufferin.* When I surrendered, when I admitted I had slammed, like Tony into the door, against a situation in which my feelings didn't matter and my words had no meaning, I went downstairs to find my father snoring in front of the set, which was full of Yankees disgracing themselves. I was outside before I knew that I wanted to be. And though I wasn't any kind of athlete, I was a boy, and boys run, and so I ran.

It was May, a dark, mild night, and we lived on a hardpan lane, so I had good footing, and I made progress, even if I'd no idea toward what, and soon I began to enjoy myself, growing aware of my location, striking a pace that I could keep with comfort, beginning to think about Tony and his dog, and the way she suddenly was still beneath my hand. I thought of Dr. Mason's little lesson on mortality or decision-making, and I realized I thought of it in two ways. It was pretty piss-poor, I thought. And it was desperate. All of his lessons were. Why did he feel that he had to teach me? He never taught my parents, and he hadn't much of a lesson plan for poor Tony. It was me. The teaching was for *me*.

I ran out of breath and out of isolated road for running. The next turn would take me onto a county highway that went toward the hamlet where we bought our milk and eggs and bread and newspapers. I stopped and panted awhile, and then I began the long walk back. I knew most of the very large old trees I passed, for I had played among them. I knew the giant clumps of brush, the multiple stems of willow near the streams and marshes, and the patches of berries that were good for eating or for collecting in a jar to please your mother. I hadn't pleased her recently, although she approved, apparently, of the fact that I lived more or less inside of my head. My father didn't seem to have pleased her either.

I pretended in those days that our road was the path that Ichabod Crane had taken, pursued by the terrible horseman. Whenever I was alone on that road and I thought of the headless rider, I had to force myself to not look back, to walk instead of run, to inspect the nighttime forest without telling myself, *He is right behind me. He is* HERE.

Dr. Mason, I thought, had pleased her. And as I thought, I realized he had come to mind because I had just now seen him, and only a few hundred feet from me, ghosting by in his truck. Another road ran parallel to ours, but at a considerable distance. You couldn't hear its traffic during the day, and only at night if there wasn't much wind. Because of a pond it had to circle, the road dipped close to ours where a sycamore, blasted by lightning, had taken down several smaller trees and made a clearing. Looking across thoughtlessly, I had seen a truck that might have been Dr. Mason's. But surely I hadn't seen a Karman Ghia too? I stopped and closed my eyes, but I could only see a memory of an empty road. I opened my eyes and took a couple of steps. I waited for an owl to start in terrorizing me with its screeches, or something silent and big to rustle in the brush. But there was only the ten-or-twelve-foot stump of the charred sycamore, and not a vehicle in hearing or sight. Then I closed my eyes and I saw the truck again, and then the little car, and I took off down the road toward home like Ichabod.

My father had gone up to sleep. The house was silent, and I was a fifteen-year-old boy who needed a shower and then was going to bed. I was lying there not reading, because I didn't want to attract attention with my light, when I heard my mother's car slowly roll on the gravel outside our back door. I listened to her footsteps in the kitchen, and then in the living room, and I fell asleep—waking astonished the next morning that I had—as her steps approached my sleeping father, as I imagined him opening his eyes and rising, as she said he always did, to say hello.

The kinds of lessons you get from someone like Dr. Mason, or from people like my parents, are the sort you really can't repeat. If you asked me what I learned from being a vet's assistant, I don't think I could set it out in sentences, although there was plenty going on and, whether it seemed exciting or not, Dr. Mason was of course constantly instructing me. It's like those sessions of show-and-tell we had to endure in elementary school. Edwin always found something profitable in his daily events, and he could bring a shed snakeskin, or sassafras he claimed the Indians used to make tea from, or the history of wonderful events that I had seen as simply the damming of a stream or the spinning off of a hubcap from the Good Humor ice cream truck. Edwin and my mother could live a year and end up with an almanac. I was always left with a headful of worries and words that didn't quite rhyme.

I remember the day Dr. Mason clipped the nails of an excited seven-month-old puppy, a bunchy English setter. He wriggled and then began to yelp—it was a scream, almost—because the clippers nicked the artery behind the claw. There was a jet of blood before Dr. Mason got it under control, and he kept laughing and saying, "You're all right. You're all right." But the dog didn't believe him, and neither did the woman who had brought him in. The dog heaved and slobbered, and I went out for the mop. And when she had gone, before we went into the examination room, Dr. Mason said, "You saw the anger in the owner's face? Did you see how I parried her anger? I understood it, of course. She was frightened, and her fear made her angry. Nine times out of ten, Peter, it's the fear. You understand?"

The Dalai Lama of Dogs and Cats, his heavy head and bloody hands, turned to leave the room, and I was spared having to ask *what* was the fear.

We were about to deal with a combination, I swear it, of some kind of retriever and dachshund. He had a big head with a real grin, and he was close enough to the ground to get his belly wet if it rained. He didn't seem to know that he had an abscessed wound on his flank and that he was going to get lanced, cleaned out, and loaded with antibiotics. Then we were doing a booster distemper shot, and then Dr. Mason changed rooms while I stayed behind to clean up. By the time I came in, the man had set his carton of puppies on the examination table, and he had retreated to the corner. Dr. Mason was leaning on the table, one fist on either side of the box.

"Look at this, Peter. Stick your nose in there and tell me what you see."

There were eight or nine puppies, shifting in their sleep, blind and all but hairless. They whimpered as they slept.

"Mr. Leeth's Irish setter bitch produced these puppies yesterday."

Mr. Leeth was small and sturdy and bald. He had a sad, stubbly face and red nose and cheeks. His pale blue eyes were rimmed in red.

"He needs us to kill them today."

"It's my job," Mr. Leeth told me. I felt myself flush. I was embarrassed that he would think to explain himself to a kid. "They're moving me, and I have to live in a hotel for a month or two while I hunt for a house. The hotel won't let me keep them. I can't even take my old dog with me."

"This is the fruit of an unplanned pregnancy, Peter. Some randy dog crept into the doghouse under the fence and *voilà!* A number of very inconvenient puppies."

"Well, now, just a minute there," Mr. Leeth said. "I don't need a sermon, Doc Mason. I need some service. I know where to go for sermons. If you don't want my business, I imagine I can go look a vet up in the Yellow Pages and then pay *him*. Since when did you start dispensing judgments while you pushed your pills?"

I heard Dr. Mason breathe in, then out. He said, "Have you ever seen me pushing a pill around, Peter? Or bullying a bulldog? Or leaning on a Labrador?" He breathed deeply again. He said, "Tim, you *should* go get your Yellow Pages. If I have a feeling about this, I should keep it to myself. I'm not only a medical man, I'm a business-man, and if I take your money I can damned well keep my mouth shut. I apologize. You're right."

Though Mr. Leeth was about to reply, I knew the little lesson was for me.

He answered, "No, Vic. We both got strung out on this. It's a ter-rible thing to do. Would you— Please take care of it for me." Dr. Mason nodded right away. Mr. Leeth said, "Thank you."

"Do you want to bury them?"

"Oh, Christ," Mr. Leeth said. "Nine little graves?"

"You could do one and tumble them all in. We'll have them in a bag for you later in the day. Just dig yourself a pit and lay the whole deal into it."

Mr. Leeth shook his head. He rubbed and rubbed at his mouth. "Do it for me, Vic?"

"Incineration."

"Please."

"They charge by weight for that. But I can't imagine these little things weigh anything at all. We'll go the minimum fee, and you can pay us later."

Mr. Leeth nodded. He said to me, "What do you think my grand-daughter will say?"

I actually tried to think of what she would say.

Mr. Leeth left, and Dr. Mason went out for a small bottle of clear liquid and he began to load his syringe. He looked down into the box. I didn't.

"I can do this," he said.

I said, inviting him to play the Dalai Lama of Dogs and Cats—no, *needing* him to—"Do you think I should stay here?"

He looked at me and let his head sag, as if he wanted to lay it on his own shoulder and rest. He slumped, then made his chest expand and his head rise slowly on his thick neck. "No," he said, "but that was a good question, and I'm glad you asked it. But no."

I moved very quickly so I wouldn't see him dip his hands into the carton and lift up four or five inches of dog and kill it with a jab of his thumb. I didn't want to hear the boxful snuffling and hear a puppy squeal if the needle woke it for only an instant. They smelled like cereal, like grain, and I wanted to get something else inside my nostrils, I explained to my father that afternoon.

Of course, I did not make it out of the room without instruction.

"Peter," Dr. Mason said.

I stopped at the door.

"I had hard feelings for a man I'd known for years and years. I'd served him, and I'd profited from the service."

"Yes, sir."

"I wasn't supposed to have any feelings about all the dying he requested I dump down into that carton he brought in. He needed me to do my professional work, and I had feelings that weren't wrong, mind you. I think I was right to feel anger. But I was wrong to *express* my feelings. You see? So I forced them away. By the time he left this room, I was purged. I was professional again. Understand?"

I absolutely did not. I heard a whimper from the carton. I said, "Thank you."

His voice was surprised when he said, "Well, sure."

"I think he should have booted the guy in the ass," I told my father.

"Watch your mouth, now."

"*Ass?*"

"Well, you know. Anyway, I'm used to dealing with younger students. It's a habit. And I believe you're wrong. Booting that poor man in the ass would have made no difference in anybody's life."

"But they were little *puppies*. It wasn't their *fault*. And this Leeth guy brings them in so Dr. Mason can swoop down into the box like the Angel of Death because it isn't convenient to let them live."

"That's nice," my father said, "that Angel of Death."

I shrugged modestly.

"How do you think people *my* age feel in their lives, then, Peter?"

I had a vision of a lesson plan, and maybe a poem I would not be able to keep myself from trying to write, about boxes and dead ends and life-and-death and how the carton of puppies could be a lesson to us all. I was afraid that my father would say something about the puppies that would tip me over into that lesson.

So I answered him by saying, "Dad, I wonder if you would do me a favor and not tell me about the older people, and lives and feeling, and all of that? I don't mean to be disrespectful or anything, but I think I just got too many thoughts to deal with today. Would that be all right?"

He looked at me, and he got those dimples around his nose and mouth before he smiled, but he was absolutely wonderful about not letting it get past that. He nodded, he touched me on the leg above my knee and he squeezed, then let me go.

"I'm trimming privet," he said.

"I'll get the mower out in a while."

"Deal," he said. Then he said, "It must have been goddamned tough."

"Language," I tried to joke.

"Seeing the last thing in the world you wanted to see."

I nodded, but he wasn't looking at me. It took me a while, but I did understand that he looked past his kid, and past the night his kid had thought to sneak into, and other nights and afternoons. He was seeing, I understood, the country road along which his tall and sorrowing wife, bereft of her older son and much of motherhood and satisfaction, she might have thought, had driven her Karman Ghia. I figured he saw it follow the Willys pickup truck, and I figured, when I let myself, that he had either witnessed or deduced the last thing in the world he had wanted to see.

For the rest of the years of my life at home, I feared his deciding

to tell me. He mercifully didn't. I feared for him the moment she or
Dr. Mason decided my father was owed what one of them, doubtless,
would describe as the Truth. I don't know whether they did. He out-
lived my mother, and his heart stopped while he was sleeping. Who
is to say what shuts down a heart? I am unable to keep myself from
seeing my mother—on the seat of a pickup truck or in a white clapboard cabin smelling of animal fears and wastes—as she bucks in
her nakedness beneath the man who administers death. *Freudian,*
she'd say. Edwin doesn't know. It's a story I try not to tell.

Passengers

JAMIE REMEMBERED THE MOVIE about murder and sexual violence that he'd watched, too jumpy to sleep, late the night before. Now, Andrea slept and in the soft roar of their passage Jamie watched under his clenched eyelids as the redheaded actress imitated passion with a psychopath in order to save her life. They were on a sailing yacht, and her husband had been lured to inspect a distant, damaged boat. She feigned cooperation and she took off her blouse. The camera stared at her nipples. The killer lay naked before her, and she set herself atop him. Jamie watched her breasts flatten on the killer's chest, and Jamie blinked. Then the killer ripped her shorts away, and she was naked on him. Jamie thought her perfect buttocks clenched in revulsion or embarrassment.

Their flight came into Kennedy, and he smiled, as he always did on returning to New York. Andrea said, "Don't start walking like a gorilla and talking New Yawk. It's a stopover, not a homecoming."

"It's a homecoming," he said. "It always is. Where else do you see that lead-colored air and feel that mugginess and hear that talk?"

"Calcutta," she said. "There's Tim." Their boy was taller than his tall parents, shorter-haired than Jamie remembered, and looking to Jamie almost as he had looked in high school and college. He squinted a little, as if staring into sunlight. His big cheekbones looked possibly larger, his eyes perhaps more tired, and in his hair, at twenty-five, were little flecks that Jamie thought were gray. His big, tired boy, his son who was married and who lived in New York, and who was too unhappy to let them fly on to Europe without a consultation.

Tim said, "You have three hours before you have to line up for the strip search. Don't look at your watch once more, Dad. You eat and drink, *I'll* check *my* watch, and I'll drive you to the terminal on time. Let's get your bags out to the car. I'm double-parked where the limousines double-park. Or maybe I'm towed by now. Or under arrest."

He hadn't smiled except on kissing his mother and then while embracing his father. He'd stopped as he leaned in for the hug, had said, "My voyaging old man!" and had given his familiar, broad grin. Now, he was attentive, energetic, lithe and strong, and miserable.

He drove them in his ancient light blue Datsun to a restaurant in Springfield Gardens. It was called Elan and it looked like a roadhouse in a fifties movie: it was a vast, rectangular brick shed with a long maroon awning and a parking lot on which their plane from San Francisco could have been parked for maintenance. Their table was a reddish banquette, the cuisine was synthetic Chinese. Andrea was promised a special green salad; Jamie and Tim ordered egg rolls and pork lo mein.

Tim was rearranging shapes made of small plastic envelopes containing duck sauce and soy. He bound their slippery surfaces with the more workable paper envelopes of sugar and artificial sweetener. He saw Jamie watching, and he said, "It's nonrepresentational."

Jamie said, "The air-conditioning's good."

"What are you talking about?" Andrea asked.

"We're making conversation, Ma, until I get up the nerve to talk about me and Barbara and how we're—whatever we are."

His mother said, "In a little jam?" She put her hand over Tim's, and Jamie's throat, as ever less sophisticated than the brain it held up, tightened.

"A little jam," Tim said.

Jamie said, "Can I ask how little?"

Tim spread his long arms and then dropped them onto his construction. He began to replace the little envelopes in ceramic ramekins. "Not very little," he finally said.

"What, baby?"

Looking at the remaining envelopes in his hand, Tim answered her: "Sex, I guess you'd call it."

Jamie at once said, "Well, we're not really—"

"No," Tim said, "and neither am I. Barbara thinks I should see a shrink."

"Nothing wrong with getting a little help," Andrea said. "When your car doesn't work, you take it to a garage, don't you?"

Tim shook his head, and then he smiled. Jamie answered for him: "Never. He fixes it himself."

"Always did," Tim said.

Andrea nodded, saying, "Yes, that's right."

"Dysfunction?" Jamie asked.

"Sorry, Dad?"

"Does it—you know: is it something not *working* right?"

Tim blushed, but not for long, and he grinned with what seemed to Jamie was real pleasure. "Dad, it might be worth all of it just to see your eyes get that wise and your mouth do that little thing—like you're tasting sushi for the first time."

"I never did taste it," Jamie said. "Unless it's cooked, it ought to be in the water."

"Good old buccaneer Dad," Tim said. "No. All the parts are there. Everything works, I guess, the way it's supposed to. God. I didn't cut into your trip to make you talk about my seminal vesicles or something."

Andrea said, "You're not cutting in. You're giving us a lift from the domestic to the international terminal. And you're *visiting* with us. We haven't seen you for months. Nothing's a bother. You can have whatever you need, Tim. Tell us."

Barbara, the winter before, had instructed her in-laws that she no longer wished to be known or addressed as Bobbie. It had made Jamie comfortable to use a diminutive, he realized, looking across at his unsettled son. She was redheaded and pale and serious. She never called him Dad. And she'd been more manageable to Jamie, even on the phone, when he could address her with a nickname. He was a little frightened of her, he understood. He wondered if Tim was.

THEY ATE THEIR egg rolls, and Andrea worked her fork through something that was artificially red mixed with green. She demanded her tithe of Jamie's meal, and they all slurped Chinese noodles together and drank the hot, flavorless tea. Tim talked about his work at the Architects' League, and Andrea talked about the agency. Jamie sneaked glances at his watch.

"Tim," he said, before he realized that he would speak, "we really can't stay over, you understand. I mean, Mom's right, of course, and we'll do whatever you need us to. But I don't sense that we're all that much a part of it. Will you tell me if I'm wrong?"

Tim said, "Of course you're not wrong. My marriage is rusty. Or gluey. Or fused. Something's stuck. Something's broken. I don't know. And of course you're not to stay over. I'm sorry if I made you think you'd miss your trip."

"No," Jamie said. "It isn't that I'm *worried* about that. You're not making me think anything. It isn't that." Andrea was staring at him with enormous, angry eyes, and he rushed on. "I don't mean to give you that feeling, any kind of bad feeling, any sense of hurry or anything. As long as it takes. Whatever you need us to do. But tell us, Tim."

"I thought I did."

"No. Can't you be specific?" Jamie said. "Maybe more specific. So we can help. If we *can* help."

"She's pregnant," Tim said.

Jamie felt his face stretch into what he thought might become a smile, but then he saw the sadness on Andrea's face, and he saw that it matched Tim's. He heard himself say, stupidly, "What?"

Andrea answered. "Barbara doesn't want to have it. Am I right?"

"You're right."

Jamie said, "And you?"

Tim shrugged. Jamie had seen him, for so many boyhood years, shrug like that before the lower lip seemed to puff, and his face swelled into pouting.

"No," Jamie said. "Do you want the child?"

Tim said, "Yes. I don't know if we can handle it now, though, the money, the time, what's happening in Barbara's life."

Andrea said, "You can't play cello and travel with a quartet and nurse a baby."

Tim nodded. "I could try and do the taking care of," he said. "You know, mostly on my own. And she would be back for months at a time. Or she could drop out of the quartet for a while, she said at one point. Take what she can get in town for work—fill-ins, mostly. Or we could move someplace where they have a symphony and would want her for steady work. Someplace provincial, Barbara called it."

Jamie said, "What would you do?"

"Public relations?" Tim said. "Fry cook? Janitor someplace? I don't know."

Andrea said, "Everything changes with a baby. It is never the same. Ever."

"I've been guessing that," Tim said. "Are we ready for that?"

His mother said, "Barbara apparently thinks not."

"Barbara thinks not," Tim said.

Jamie said, "And?"

"And that's it, Dad! What *and*? Barbara says, so that's it. It's her body. It's her work. She's gestating, not me. All I supplied, and I quote, was the friction. I believe that's the gist of it."

Jamie said, "She said that?"

Andrea said, "She was upset."

Tim said, "She was mildly upset. She was caterwauling. She was breaking things. She was marching around the apartment like a drill team on speed. Yes. Upset."

"We're sure she's pregnant?" Andrea asked.

"Well, she used one of those U-Test-M kits. She's gone to the doctor." He checked his watch. "Even as we speak. And there *is* time, Dad."

"This is about you, not my schedule," Jamie said, feeling almost truthful. "Do you think she'd talk with Mom? Do you think she would do that, and do you think doing that would help?"

Tim shook his head. "She can get kind of fierce," he said. "She's very independent. She's very private."

Andrea said, "But should we go back and *try* to talk to her?"

"No," Tim said, "you should go on your trip and we'll talk when you get back."

"We haven't done a whole hell of a lot of good," Jamie said.

"I have to decide with her," Tim said. "That's the only good any of us can do." His eyes filled. "The thing is," he said, "the thing I'm hating myself for—I keep thinking she isn't going to see a doctor for a test. She's going to one of those clinics, maybe. She's going—I really keep seeing this. I see her walk in, I see her fill out the forms and put the insurance card down, or the cash, however they do it, and put the papers down on the nurse's desk, and sit down, and then stand up when she's called, and, you know. She goes in and they do it. I can hear what the goddamned doctor says for casual *conversation*. In my mind, you understand. Because, now, all of a sudden, I don't trust her, I suppose she'd say. So how can I claim to love her if I don't trust her? And if I'm right, she's going in there without telling me because *she* doesn't trust *me,* either. So then she can't really love me all that much anymore, right? And what do we have left?"

Andrea wept and put her arms around his neck and pulled him over to her. His teacup went over, a waiter turned, diners looked at them, and Jamie caught himself—*Bastard!* he thought—between his own tears and a furtive sweep of his eyes toward his watch.

"It isn't lost," Andrea said. "You can still be lovers. Like before."

Tim sat back. Andrea did too, but she sat closer to him. Tim said, "I don't know what, precisely, is left. Something broke, though. I felt it."

"You love your wife," Jamie said. He was surprised to hear his voice coarsened by anger. So, he noted, was Andrea.

"Is that a direct order?" Tim asked.

"A guarantee," Jamie said. "You love her. She loves you, and you're going to figure out a compromise."

"Dad, how do you compromise with a baby? The old sword-and-half-a-kid trick?"

"The way you do everything else. You figure out how to do the least damage," Jamie said. "I mean, the days of having what you want, what you need, what you think you'll never live without—gone, Tim. They're gone. Long gone. There's no such thing. Excuse me, I seem to be writing a Miss Lonelyhearts column."

"You sounded almost eloquent," Andrea said.

"Mom sounds surprised," Tim said.

"With good reason, maybe."

Andrea said, "Oh?"

"Well, you never heard as many of my Wise Parent lectures as Tim did, don't forget."

"I see," she said. "That's what you meant."

Tim said, his face confused, "Well, yes. I used to watch him climb out on those limbs when he delivered the late-night advice. I used to see how careful he was not to drop the saw from great heights as he sawed and advised."

"And did he always saw the limb off and go over, onto the ground?"

"Not as often as I thought he would," Tim said.

"Interesting," Andrea said.

"It's like virginity," Jamie said. They looked confused. "Living together, I mean. You know. Once you're in love so much, or you're driven so to be together, and you let's say make love."

"You're blushing," Tim said.

"So be it," Jamie said. "But the point I'm making: time got in when you did. You can't ever be the same. You're part of something so much larger, you see. *Do* you see? Do I, I wonder? I don't know."

Andrea had turned away while he spoke, and she was looking at her son's profile. She said, "Tim? If she does? If she has the procedure? You have to understand it. You have to forgive her."

Tim was shaking his head as his mother spoke. "It's part mine. *She's* part mine. She's supposed to be. I should have a vote."

"If she does it," Andrea said, "it's because she's frightened, perhaps what you're frightened of too."

"She's supposed to be scared along *with* me, not away from me, or in spite of me, or behind my back."

Jamie nodded. Andrea did too, but abruptly stopped, so Jamie did too. They all knew, he thought, that they had each admitted defeat. Tim let his father take care of the bill, and then they walked out of the cold dimness and into the heat and humidity of a late-August afternoon in New York. Tim drove without speaking, and though Andrea gave him their itinerary, and urged him to telephone, and promised that they would call as they could, the atmosphere in the hot little car was of surrender.

Tim helped them carry in their bags. He helped them find the right line. Then he said he ought to leave.

"Absolutely," Andrea said. "I'll cry if you stay here and we wave goodbye."

"I will too," Tim said.

Jamie watched them embrace, and then Tim held Jamie's shoulders and kissed his father on the cheek. He didn't let go, but stood, with his face close to Jamie's, and asked, "How long have you been trying to tell me about sex, Dad?"

Jamie said, "I still keep trying to figure it out. I'm doing a miserable job."

"Me too," Tim said.

"That's probably the secret of it," Jamie said. "We probably figured out the truth of it."

"Lousiness," Tim said, sounding like a little boy. Jamie saw Andrea's face respond as she heard him. She didn't flinch, but her features tightened.

"Unhappiness," Tim said.

Jamie saw Barbara's face, then, saw—he understood this now, watching again as the jump cuts flickered on their television screen— the thighs and lovely buttocks of the red-haired actress lying on the man who menaced her, and to whom she made love at last with what seemed to Jamie like abandon. His son's wife didn't have the actress's freckles, nor the same straight nose. She was fuller in the face, a Polish Rita Hayworth, Jamie had called her. Barbara had replied by claiming never to have seen Rita Hayworth. It had been Barbara: it was she he had recalled, somewhere in the imagery of his dark, sore passage to New York.

"Your basic, middle-class misery," Tim announced. And Jamie knew he ought to have, or pretend to have, if not an antidote he could offer, at least a lie of consolation. His hands were still on Tim's fore-arms, and, clinging to his son, he couldn't move to embrace his wife, whose face, he saw, had grown sad. But he should, he knew, move to comfort her, address the bitterness and loss he found as in a terminal, among the thousand pitched-up passengers, you discover with a shock the long-awaited, the inevitable face. Then everything, sud-denly, was rearranged. All the exhausted faces, dark or pale, had moved several paces along, and his wife was hugging his son again.

The Ninth, in E Minor

THE MORNING AFTER I DROVE to his newest town, I met my father for breakfast. He was wearing hunter's camouflage clothing and looked as if he hadn't slept for a couple of nights. He reminded me of one of those militia clowns you see on television news shows, very watchful and radiating a kind of high seriousness about imminent execution by minions of the state.

I knew he had deeper worries than execution. And I was pleased for him that he wore trousers and T-shirt, a soft, wide-brimmed cap, and hip-length jacket that would help him disappear into the stony landscape of upstate New York. He *needs* the camouflage, I thought, although where we stood—in the lobby of the James Fenimore Cooper Inn—he seemed a little out of place among the college kids and commercial travelers. The inn advertised itself as The Last of the Great Upstate Taverns. My father looked like The Last of the Great Upstate Guerrilla Fighters. Still, I thought, he's got the gear, and one of these days he will blend right in.

"Hi, Baby," he said. He tried to give me one of the old daddy-to-daughter penetrating stares, but his eyes bounced away from mine, and his glance slid down my nose to my chin, then down the front of my shirt to the oval silver belt buckle I had bought in Santa Fe.

"How are you, Daddy?"

He fired off another stare, but it ricocheted. "I have to tell you," he said, "half of the time I'm flat scared."

His shave was smooth, but he'd missed a couple of whiskers, which looked more gray than black. His face had gone all wrinkled and squinty. He looked like my father's older brother, who was shaky and possibly ill and commuting from the farthest suburbs of central mental health. He took his cap off—doffed it, you would have to say. His hair looked soft. You could see how someone would want to reach over and touch it.

"But I don't like to complain," he said.

I got hold of his arm and pulled my way along his brown-and-sand-and-olive-green sleeve until I had his hand, which I held in both of mine. He used enough muscle to keep his arm in that position, but the hand was loose and cool, a kid's.

I asked him, "Do you know what you're scared of?"

He shrugged, and, when he did, I saw a familiar expression inside his tired, frightened face. He made one of those French frowns that suggested not giving a good goddamn, and it pleased me so much, even as it disappeared into his newer face, that I brought his hand up and kissed the backs of his fingers.

"Aw," he said. I thought he was going to cry. I think he thought so too.

"Look," I said, letting go of his hand, "I saw Mommy in New York. That's where I drove up from. We had dinner two days ago. She asked me to remember her to you. She's fine."

He studied my words as if they had formed a complex thought. And then, as if I hadn't said what he was already considering, he asked, "How is she?"

"She's fine. I told you."

"And she asked to be remembered to me."

"Right."

"You're lying, Baby."

"Correct."

"She didn't mention me."

"Oh, she mentioned you."

"Not in a friendly way."

"No."

"She was hostile, then?"

"Hurt, I'd say."

He nodded. "I hate that—I didn't want to hurt anybody," he said. "I just wanted to feel better."

"I know. Do you feel better?"

"Do I look it?"

"Well, with the outfit and all . . ."

"This stuff's practical. You can wear it for weeks before you need to wash it. The rain runs off the coat. You don't need to carry a lot of clothing with you."

"Traveling light, then, is how you would describe yourself?"

"Yes," my father said. "I would say I'm traveling light. But you didn't answer me. How do I look?"

I walked past matching club chairs upholstered in maroon-and-aqua challis, and I looked out a window. A crew had taken down an old, broad maple tree. The sidewalk was buried under branches and bark, and a catwalk of plywood led from the street, around the downed tree, and into the inn. The tree was cut into round sections three or four feet across, and a man in a sweated undershirt was using a long-handled splitting maul to break up one of the sections. Behind him stood another man, who wore a yellow hard hat and an orange shirt and a yellow fluorescent safety vest. He held a long chain saw that shook as it idled. A woman wearing a man's old-fashioned undervest, work gloves, and battered boots watched them both. Occasionally, she directed the man with the splitting maul. Her hair beneath her yellow hard hat looked reddish-gold. The one with the chain saw stared at the front of her shirt. She looked up and saw me. She looked at me through her safety goggles for a while and then she smiled. I couldn't help smiling back.

"You look fine," I said. "It's a beautiful spring morning. Let's eat."

In the Natty Bumppo Room, we were served our juice and coffee by a chunky woman with a happy red face. My father ordered waffles, and I remembered how, when I was in elementary school, he heated frozen waffles in the toaster for me and spread on margarine and syrup. I remembered how broad his hands had seemed. Now, they shook as he spread the margarine. One of his camouflage cuffs had picked up some syrup, and he dripped a little as he worked at his meal. I kept sipping the black coffee, which tasted like my conception of a broth made from long-simmered laundry.

"The hardest part," he said, "it drives me nuts. The thing with the checks."

"Sure," I said, watching the margarine and maple syrup coat his lips. "Mommy has to endorse your checks, then she has to deposit them, then she has to draw a bank check, and then she has to figure out where you are so she can send it along. It's complicated."

"I'm not making it that way on purpose," he said.

"No. But it's complicated." He looked young enough to have been his son, sometimes, and then, suddenly, he looked more like his father. I understood that the man I had thought of as my father, looking like himself, was no longer available. He was several new selves, and I would have to think of him that way.

"I'm just trying to get better," he said.

"Daddy, do you hear from her?"

He went still. He held himself so that—in his camouflage outfit—he suggested a hunter waiting on something skittish, a wild turkey, say, said to be stupid and shy. "I don't see the point of this," he said. "Why not talk about you? That's what fathers want to hear. About their kids. Why not talk about you?"

"All right," I said. "Me. I went to Santa Fe. I had a show in a gallery in Taos, and then I drove down to Santa Fe and I hung out. I walked on the Santa Fe Trail. It goes along the streets there. I ate too much with too much chili in it, and I bought too many pots. Most of the people in the restaurants are important unknown Hollywood celebrities from outside Hollywood."

"Did you sell any pictures?"

"Yes, I did."

"Did you make a lot of money?"

"Some. You want any?"

"Because of how long it takes for your mother to cash my check and send a new one."

"Are you *allowed* to not live at home and still get money from the state?"

"I think you're supposed to stay at home," he said.

"So she's being illegal along with you? To help you out?"

He chewed on the last of his waffle. He nodded.

"Pretty good," I said.

"She's excellent to me."

"Considering," I said. "So how much money could you use?"

"Given the complications of the transmission process," he said.

"Given that," I said. "They sit outside the state office building, the Indians off the pueblos. They hate the people who come, but they all sit there all day long, showing you the silver and the pots all arranged on these beautiful blankets. I bought too much. But I felt embarrassed. One woman with a fly swatter, she kept spanking at the jewelry she was selling. She'd made it. She kept hitting it, and the earrings jumped on the blanket. The rings scattered, and she kept hitting away, pretending she was swatting flies, but she wasn't. She was furious."

"Displacement," my father said.

"It's just a story, Daddy."

"But you told it."

"Yes, but it didn't have a message or anything."

"What did it have?"

"*In situ* Native American displacement, and handmade jewelry. A tourist's usual guilt. Me, on the road, looking around. Me, on my way northeast."

"Did you drive?"

"I did."

"All by yourself?"

"Like you, Daddy."

"No," he said, fitting his mouth to the trembling cup. "We're both together here, so we aren't alone now."

"No." I heard the splitting maul, and I imagined the concussion up his fingers and along his forearm, up through the shoulder and into the top of the spine. It would make your brain shake, I thought.

"A hundred or two?" he said.

"What? Dollars?"

"Is that too much?"

"No," I said, "I have that."

"Thanks, Baby."

"But do you hear from her, Daddy?"

He slumped. He stared at the syrup on his plate. It looked like a pool of sewage where something had drowned.

He said, "Did I tell you I went to Maine?"

I shook my head and signaled for more coffee. When she brought it, I asked if I could smoke in the Natty Bumppo Room, and she said no. I lit a cigarette and when I was done, and had clicked the lighter shut, she took a deep breath of the smoke I exhaled and she grinned.

"What's in Maine?" I asked him.

"Cabins. Very cheap cabins in a place on the coast that nobody knows about. I met a man in New Hampshire—Portsmouth, New Hampshire? He was on the road, like me. He was a former dentist of some special kind. We were very similar. Taking medication, putting the pieces back together, at cetera. And he told me about these cabins. A little smelly with mildew, a little unglamorous, but cheap, and heated if you need, and near the sea. I really wanted to get to the sea."

"So you drove there, and what?"

"I slept for most of the week."

"You still need to sleep a lot."

"Always," he said. "Consciousness," he said, "is very hard work."

"So you slept. You ate lobster."

"A lot."

"And what did you do when you weren't sleeping or eating lobsters or driving?"

"I counted girls in Jeeps."

"There are that many?"

"All over New England," he said, raising a cup that shook. "They're blond, most of them, and they seem very attractive, but I think that's because of the contrast—you know, the elegant, long-legged girl and the stubby, utilitarian vehicle. I found it quite exciting."

"Exciting. Jesus, Daddy, you sound so adolescent. Exciting. Blondes in Jeeps. Well, you're a single man, for the most part. What the hell. Why not. Did you date any?"

"Come on," he said.

"You're not ancient. You could have a date."

"I've had them," he said.

"That's who I was asking you about. Do you hear from her?"

"I'm telling you about the girls in their Jeeps on the coast of Maine, and you keep asking—"

"About the woman you had an affair with who caused you to divorce my mother. Yes."

"That's wrong," he said. "We separated. That's all that I did—I moved away. It was your *mother* sued for divorce."

"I recollect. But you do understand how she felt. There you were, shacking up with a praying mantis from Fort Lee, New Jersey, and not living at home for the better part of two years."

"Do I have to talk about this?"

"Not for *my* two hundred bucks. We're just having an on-the-road visit, and I'm leaving soon enough, and probably you are too."

"I drift around. But that's a little unkind about the money. *And* about the praying mantis thing. Really, to just bring it up."

"Because all you want to do is feel better," I said, lighting another cigarette. By this time, there were several other diners in the Natty Bumppo Room, and one of them was looking over the tops of her gray-tinted lenses to indicate to me her impending death from secondary smoke. *Oh, I'm sorry!* I mouthed to her. I held the cigarette as if I were going to crush it onto my saucer, then I raised it to my mouth and sucked in smoke.

I blew it out as I said to him, "She's the one who led you into your nosedive. She's the reason you crashed in flames when she left you."

"This is not productive for me," he said.

"You're supposed to be productive for *me*," I said. I heard the echo of my voice and, speaking more calmly, I said, "Sorry. I didn't mean to shout. This still fucks me up, though."

"Don't use that kind of language," he said, wiping his eyes.

"No."

"I thought we were going to have a *visit*. A father-and-daughter re-union."

"Well, we are," I said.

"All right. Then tell me about yourself. Tell me what's become of you."

I was working hard to keep his face in focus. He kept looking like somebody else who was related to him, but he was not the him I had known. I was twenty-eight years old, of no fixed abode, and my father, also without his own address, was wearing camouflage clothing in an upstate town a long enough drive from the New York State Thruway to be nothing more than the home of old, rotting trees, a campus in the state's junior college system, and the site of the James Fenimore Cooper Inn.

"What's become of me," I said. "All right. I have two galleries that represent me. One's in Philadelphia and one's in Columbia County, outside New York. I think the owner, who also runs what you would call a big-time gallery on Greene Street, in Manhattan, may be just around the corner from offering me a show in New York City. Which would be very good. I got some attention in Taos, and a lot of New York people were there, along with the usual Hollywood pro-ducer-*manqué* people, both has-beens and would-bes, and the editorial stars who hire agents to get their names in the gossip columns. It was very heady for me to be hit on by such upper-echelon minor lea-guers."

"When you say *hit on*," he said, "what are you telling me?"

"Exactly what you think. A number of men fancied fucking me."

He let his head droop toward his plate. "That's a terrible way to live," he said. "I'm supposed to be protecting you from that."

"But why start now?"

"That's what you came for," he said. "I've been waiting, since you phoned me, to figure out why you would look me up *now*, when you might suspect I'm down on my luck and in unheroic circumstances."

"Unheroic," I said. "But you're wrong. I mean, as far as I *know*, you're wrong. I asked Mommy for your address because I hadn't seen you since I was in graduate school. And you're my father. And I guess I was missing you."

"And because you wanted to tell me the thing about men trying to—you know. Because it would hurt me. And you're angry with me."

"Well, you could say the way you left your wife was a little disappointing to me."

He'd been rubbing at his forehead with the stiffened fingers of his right hand. He stopped, and he looked around his hand, like a kid peeking through a fence, his expression merry and, suddenly, quite demented. Then the merriment left him, and then the craziness, and he looked like a man growing old very quickly. He said, "I have to tell you, the whole thing was disappointing for me as well."

"You mean, leaving your wife for the great adventure and then being dumped."

"And then being dumped," he said.

"Mommy said you were doing drugs when that happened."

"There was nothing we didn't do except heroin," he said. "If we could have bought it safely, I'd have stuffed it up my nose, shot it into my eyeballs, anything."

"Because of the sex?"

He looked right at me. "The best, the most astonishing. I haven't been able to acknowledge a physical sensation since then. Everything I've felt since then is, I don't know—as if it was *reported*. From a long way away."

"Jesus. *And* you loved her?"

"I've dealt with a therapist who says maybe I didn't. Maybe it was the danger. I seem to act self-destructively, from time to time. I seem to possibly not approve of myself. I seem to need to call it love whether that's what I feel or not. I seem to have conflated sex with love."

"A conflatable sex doll," I said. I snickered. He managed to look hurt. "I'm sorry."

"It doesn't matter much. I'm working on my health. It doesn't have to hurt to hear that kind of laughter. I suppose it's good for me. A kind of practice at coping with difficulties."

"No," I said, "I apologize. It just seemed like a very good damned pun, the conflatable sex doll. I am nobody's spokeswoman for reality. I apologize."

"Tell me how your mother is."

"She's fine. She's living a life. I'd feel uncomfortable if I gave you any details. I think she wants to keep that stuff to herself."

"So she's fine, and you've managed to endure the attentions of men with press agents."

"Mostly to evade them, as a matter of fact."

"Mostly?"

"Daddy, if anyone around here's fine, it's me. Nobody has to worry about men, nutrition, the upkeep of my car, or the management of my career. I do my own taxes, I wrote my own will, and I navigate my own cross-country trips."

"Why do you have a will? A legal last will and testament, you're saying? Why?"

"I'm not getting any younger," I said.

"Nonsense. You don't have a family to provide for."

"You know that, do you?"

"You *do?*"

I nodded. I found it difficult to say much.

"What, Baby?"

"A son. His name is Vaughan."

"Vaughan? As in the singer Vaughan Monroe?"

"As in Ralph Vaughan Williams. One of his symphonies was playing when, you know."

"I know nothing," he said. He was pale, and his lips trembled as his hands did, though in a few seconds his mouth calmed down. His fingers didn't.

"He's with Mommy."

"But he lives with you?"

"I'm thinking of living with someone downstate. We would stay together there."

"His father?"

"No. But a man I like. A photographer."

"Criminies," he whispered. "There are all those gaps, all those *facts* I don't know. This is like looking at the family picture album, but most of the pictures aren't in the book. Are you *happy* about this child?"

"Are you happy about me?"

"Sure," he said. "Of course I am."

"Then I'm happy about my boy. Did you really say *criminies?*"

He clasped his hands at the edge of the table, but they upset his breakfast plate. Syrup went into the air, and soggy crumbs, and his stained napkin. The waitress came over to sponge at the mess and remove our dishes. She came back with more coffee and the check.

"Criminies," my father said. "I haven't heard that word for years."

I was counting out money which I slid across the table to him. "I hope this helps," I said, "really."

"I regret needing to accept it," he said. "I regret not seeing you more. I regret your having to leave."

"That's the thing with those family albums, Daddy. People are always leaving them."

"Yes. But I'm a grandfather, right?"

"Yes, you are."

"Could I see him?"

"Ever get downstate?"

"Oh, sure," he said. "I get to plenty of places. I told you, I was all the way up in Maine just a few weeks ago."

"All those girls in Jeeps. I remember. So, sure. Yes. Of course. He's your grandson."

"Big and sloppy like me?"

"His father was a kind of fine-boned man. But he'll have my arms and legs."

"He'll look like a spider monkey."

"You haven't called me a spider monkey for an awfully long time."

"But that's what he look like? I want to think of him with you."

"Very light brown hair, and a long, delicate neck. And great big paws, like a puppy."

"He'll be tall."

We sat, and maybe we were waiting to find some words. But then my father pulled on his camouflage cap, and tugged at the brim. He was ready, I suppose. I left the dining room and then the inn a couple of steps ahead of him. We stopped outside the front doors and watched the man, now shirtless, as he swung, working his way through a chunk of a hundred and fifty years. Splinters flew, and I heard him grunt as the wedge-shaped maul head landed. The woman in the cotton vest was watching it batter the wood.

I put my arms around his neck and hugged him. I kissed his cheek.

"Baby, when does everybody get together again?"

I hugged him again, and then I backed a couple of steps away. I could only shrug.

He said, "I was thinking roughly the same."

I heard the maul. I watched my father zip, then unzip his camouflage hunting coat.

He turned to the woman in the cotton vest and tipped his camouflage cap. She stared at him through her safety goggles.

He was giving a demonstration, I realized. With his helpless, implausible smile, he was showing me his lapsed world of women. He was broken, and he shook with medication, but he dreamed, it was clear, of one more splintered vial of amyl nitrate on the sweaty bedclothes of a praying mantis from Fort Lee, New Jersey. He had confected a ride with a leggy blonde in a black, convertible Jeep on US 1 in Maine. And if the foreman of the forestry crew would talk to him in front of her tired and resentful men, he would chat up that lady and touch, as if by accident, the flesh of her sturdy, tanned arms.

That was why I backed another pace. That was why I turned and went along the duckwalk behind my father, leaving the wreckage of the maple tree and walking toward my car. I wanted to be driving away from him—locked inside with the windows shut and the radio up—before he could tip his cap, and show me his ruined, innocent face, and steal what was left of my life.

Vespers

THIS WAS THE YEAR in which Ronald Reagan thought to honor the S S dead with a wreath in a German graveyard, and when I was in charge of funding grants to sculptors and musicians in both Dakotas, Minnesota, and Wisconsin. We had a dozen proposals on, shall we say, the theme of remembering who, from 1936 to 1945, had died the most and worst. And Bert Wragg, Jr., had brought me with him, for luck and for sex with an older woman, while he interviewed and auditioned in New York.

I rang my brother and missed him at his law firm on Clinton Street. Soon he rang back, chivvying me, at once, to recollect.

"Everything goes in a circle," he said. "Remember? Remember when Daddy said that in Prospect Park when you got lost?"

"Since when did you call him Daddy? We never called him Daddy, did we? And I was six years old, Ira."

Ira said, "Fine. Pop. Fine. Six. You remember calling him Pop?"

"Of course."

"The point is not what I happen to be calling my father in conversation with his daughter," he said.

"This is not a conversation. This is an interborough harangue."

"Now, I believe, you move on to calling it blackmail. Am I right?

As in emotional blackmail, et cetera. Or would that scare the news-boy off? Getting involved with a family where verbal cockfights, in a manner of speaking, are always taking place?"

"You want me to repeat that? So anyone who happens to be stand-ing within six or eight feet could hear me saying newsboy?"

"Up to you," Ira said. "All *I* hear is people objecting to every other word I use."

"You're the one calling names."

"You're making me seduce my own sister."

"That, big fella, is what they call incest. It's illegal. It's immoral. It's disgusting."

" 'At's amore," he sang, in not too bad an imitation of Dean Mar-tin lightly toasted on sixties TV.

It was a routine we had used when we were in one another's com-pany, with dates, during his years in college—Desi and Lucy, but as brother and sister, the ditzy redhead and the serious, clever, somewhat bamboozled guy. He was between Wife Two and a paunchy, sad time of dating widows and the former wives of other cuffed but not quite beaten men. I was going to remain unmarried forever, though I had no interest in solitude. I was back in New York—in Manhattan, to my brother's disappointment—while he was in Park Slope, in Brook-lyn, and determined to take me and Bert Wragg, Jr., from our hotel on Central Park South back to Flatbush, where Ira and I had grown up, sometimes even together.

I said, "We'd have to go tonight. We're really booked."

Bert Wragg, Jr., sat at the foot of the bed and crossed his legs. They were bare, except for navy-blue garters with a red stripe through the center. He was putting on high navy socks that would come over his calf. I had not seen garters on a man since I was a blackboard moni-tor in the sixth-grade class of Miss Fredericks in P.S. 152. The man had been my father, and I had peeked around the corner of my par-ents' bedroom to win a bet: Ira had insisted our father—whom we did call Pop—put his horn-rimmed glasses on before his socks, and I had bet on socks before sight. I won, and I provoked a one-inch rise in my father's bushy brows. We used to wager, too, on who could bring his elastic forehead higher. Ira usually won. He won the baseball cards I bought to cause him to covet them. I didn't care to carry or collect them, though I liked the waxy taste of the gum with which they were packed, and they caused Ira to bet with me, which meant that he had to talk to me as if I was not from the Planet Jerk. So: Pop, the garters, and Bert Wragg, Jr., naked from the waist down, his penis regarding me from the nest of his folded groin, and I thought of the circle Ira said our father had described, and I agreed to subject my anchorman-in-waiting, my boyfriend from the middling market of Minneapolis–St. Paul by way of Ames, Iowa, and Syracuse University to what would at best be a sentimental journey, and to what at the very worst would be a long night with Ira Bloom.

I heard him snort into the phone and whisper, "Myrna, can he really hear you?"

"The newsboy? Yes."

"Are you in love?"

"More than likely."

"A healthy kind of love, or the dark, clammy lust you get yourself into?"

"Latter, no doubt."

"So you call one thing another? Love is lust? Or vicey versey?"

"I think there isn't a y sound, Ira. Just—"

"Could you listen without correcting me? Incorrect as I doubtless am? Could you listen, please? Just, are you coming with the newsboy or without? And I am not being raunchy, I did not *intend* to be raunchy, and don't even begin to correct my raunch. Are you or are you not. Period."

"We will both be downstairs. We will walk outside in, say, forty minutes."

"Half an hour, max," he said.

"We will ride to Brooklyn. We will look. We will then take you to dinner. So you should—wait a minute. Bert? Does Ira need a tie?"

"Not for the Park Bistro," Bert said.

Ira said, "I heard him. How does a talking head on Minnesota TV, good evening, ladies and gentlemen, yawn, know what to wear in my city?"

"Maybe that's why they're trying him out in New York, Ira."

Bert had stood up, and I thought I must look like a mean bit of business in my open, pearly rayon robe to have aroused him so. Of course, I thought, it could also be the thought of his own ruggedly gorgeous face on many millions of TV screens in the greater New York metropolitan area. That's what I liked about Bert Wragg, Jr. He was not above regarding himself in the optimum light, and he was young enough to find his gaze persuasive.

IN THE LONG black car, a Buick, Ira told us, we headed downtown. When we passed Delancey, I knew Ira was taking us over the East River on the Brooklyn Bridge. It was not quite direct, but it would give him a chance to point out to Bert a landmark beloved of hay-seeds.

I'd imagined myself next to Ira, with Bert hidden away from my brother in the shadows of the backseat. But Bert had gone for the front, neglecting to hold my door, almost shouldering me out of the way. His awkward posture reminded me of something I couldn't name, and it wasn't until the end of the afternoon that I remembered: a boy, my date, a Nelson Someone in a workingman's bar in Pough-keepsie, stepping in front of me to fight with someone who had ex-pressed distaste—quite rightly, I thought at the time—for college kids gone slumming.

Bert said, "Ira, I'm curious."

"Speak to me, Bert. I'm here as a—what is it, Myrna, in museums and churches?"

"Docent, dear. Little wives and widows who wear white gloves and show you the stained-glass windows."

"There we are, Ira," Bert said. "It just seemed—still seems, re-ally—we'd have gone a bit more directly by way of the Brooklyn Battery Tunnel, then the Prospect Expressway, then maybe Church Avenue up to your old neighborhood."

"Really?" Ira said. "Really and truly?"

Bert shrugged. I heard the wide wales of his tan corduroy sportcoat rasp. He wore it with jeans, a canvas off-tan shirt from Peterman, and the navy-blue socks held up by the navy-blue-and-red-striped garters.

Ira said, "I thought maybe seeing the bridge was worth the loss of six or eight seconds."

"Absolutely," Bert said. He put his left hand up on the bench seat so that it hung behind Ira. I took it. I leaned forward and put his index finger, very slowly, into my mouth. When I released it and sat back, Ira's eyes were waiting for mine in his rearview mirror.

"Hi," I said.

"Hi," each man replied, one with pleasure and one without.

I watched the back of Ira's head, now that I had seen how familiar his eyes were in their web of lines and folds and the soft flesh in gray-brown crescents beneath that testified to his insomnia. His head had become our pop's, of course, with the same untamed Howdy-Doody wings of wild fringe a few inches above the pointed ears that hung back around his skull like the folded wings of sleeping bats. His head in silhouette was long and slender, and I thought he'd lost weight because the collar of his shirt seemed not to touch his neck. His hands on the steering wheel were long, like Pop's. Unlike our father, he murmured to himself as he steered the car: "Uh-huh," as he turned, "Ah-hm" as he straightened our course again, "Uh-huh" when he checked our location by the street-corner signs. He sang his steering lightly, but with it he confirmed himself to me as a genuine eccentric. I wondered how someone saw me.

I called, "Stop!" We were on Ocean Avenue in middling spring at four o'clock. The air was gathering itself for dusk, perhaps just beginning to take on the weight of reflection of the dirty bricks on the six- and seven-story apartment buildings. Traffic was growing denser with the air that poured invisible yet thick onto Ocean Avenue in a section of Flatbush once called Kensington, the streets of which ran to Midwood, where we'd lived. I'd used to ride my Schwinn on its ticking gears to the gas station to our right.

Ira kept the car in the street, his blinker on, traffic pouring around us. "You don't want to pull in there," he said. "They pump the gas and then they keep the car, the *schwarzim*."

"African-Americans?" Bert apparently felt required to say. His *a,* from his days in Syracuse, had the lag you could hear in Syracuse, Rochester, Buffalo, Cleveland, even Chicago: a flattened gagging that sounded as if the speaker snarled. Bert Wragg would never snarl. But I wondered if his career could be threatened by the bray of the Great Lakes.

"No, mostly Haitians, as a matter of fact," Ira said. "And, probably, most of them not citizens. But you can *call* them African-Americans if you like."

"I used to put air in my tires," I said. "And they had a cooler inside where you could get one of those stubby Cokes in the green glass bottle."

Bert said, "Myrna, those bottles are real antiques."

"So's she," Ira said.

Bert waggled his fingers at me behind Ira's back. I placed nothing in my mouth.

Two short, slender dark-skinned men stood at the office, where I'd used to pay a dime for my soda.

Bert said, "Their hands are behind their backs."

"They don't want you to be frightened," Ira said.

"They're armed," Bert said. "Is that correct?"

"Boy, are they armed," my brother said, in almost a friendly tone.

He pulled out into traffic, and I watched them watch us, alien beings in our time machine. He took a right turn quickly, and then he slowed down because soon—I could feel the car begin to turn, I thought, before Ira murmured at the wheel—we were coming to a left-hand turn, and then the block on which we'd lived. It was as if we had gone across a border, through a checkpoint such as the ones Bert, in his stiff tan correspondent's trench coat, had passed through, once, bringing home the bad news, for the sake of all Minneapolis–St. Paul, on the killings in Herzegovina. If they gave him the job in New York as backup anchor, and if I left my job and came with him, we would have to build him closets no matter where he lived. His raincoats took up more room than my entire wardrobe.

"No more African-Americans," I said.

"Whether of African, American, or otherwise descent," Bert told me.

"Welcome to medieval Poland," Ira said. "Lubavitchers, all you can eat." Tall thin boys in black suits walked with heavy fathers in ditto, while behind them on their broad hips came the girls and women. Everyone seemed pale. No one seemed to be away at work. It felt, on our block, as if we had parked in a village square on a market day. We were paid little attention, although two girls in their late teens, wearing cloth coats that seemed to have belonged to large men, stared at Bert and giggled their embarrassment into their hands.

"They live here?" I heard myself say.

"Some of them live in our *house* here," Ira said, and I heard the sorrow in him for the passage of time, for the dispossession he had suffered. There was the three-story stucco house, in all its broad shelteredness, a fortress of the rising middle class of 1910 who had built it, and then in the 1950s again, so that our mother had once referred to our block, with an immigrant daughter's sense of arrival, as The Suburbs. Ocher-colored paint had been replaced with tan, and the dark brown paint of the screened-in porch had been replaced with forest green. A dogwood tree that Pop had planted after a hurricane took down one of the sycamores had in turn been taken down. The other shade tree, across the walk on its little lawn, had been hacked and trimmed, but was surviving. The prickly hawthorn bushes that had lined the walk to our brick stoop were gone. I had hated them, because whenever I played stoop ball by myself on the walk, the ball would go into the bushes and I would have to wait for Ira to show his invulnerability by plunging his hand into the scratchy hedge. Then I would have to wait while he feinted throwing it to me, and then I would have to chase it when he tossed it over my head.

We were parked next to the fire hydrant outside the house we had lived in for eighteen years of my life, and in the car, between us, it was as if someone were showing those sprockety, ratcheting 8mm silent movies that families like ours used for their grappling with time, capturing in overexposed orange the flesh of children who would one day dissolve into the silt and swamp and thinning memory of what had been East Eighteenth Street, and what had been childhood, and what had been Rasbin's Meat Market on Avenue J, or the fish store with flounder set out on ice, or the elevated tracks of the BMT on Avenue H above the candy store with its wall of ten-cent comic books. Ira, in the front, looked to his right, past Bert, who had turned, politely, to stare at large old houses on little lawns. I, in the back, re-garded them both and I studied my house and waited for clues about what I ought to feel. In the leather cockpit of Ira's car, I felt our mother in her belted orange house dress, our father in his garters and his boxer shorts, our well-furnished childhood rooms, with doors we little people of privilege could shut at will against each other and, crucially, our parents. I did not, however, taste emotions. Perhaps they would come later, I thought, and then I would clutch myself against the ache.

A man had appeared to stand outside the car. He was tall and broad, and I bent to the window to see all of him. He wore a wrin-kled black suit, a rumpled white shirt, and a gray straw fedora with a ribbon that reminded me of Bert's garters. The frames of his glasses were clear plastic. His smooth-shaven face looked responsive to humor. He was someone I would ask for directions in a foreign coun-try, I thought. It was dusk in New York, and he was home from work, I figured, and here we were, parked outside his house. He was the kind of man who came down steps to defend his home. Ira turned his key to send a current through the car, and Bert pushed the switch that rolled his window down.

I waited for a torrent of Yiddish, or Hebrew. I waited for thick, guttural inquiries or demands. The householder bent, straightened, bent again to stare, and muttered.

He bent again and looked in. His face made it clear that unlikeli-hood had descended onto Brooklyn. He said, "Bert Wragg!"

Ira said, "Son of a *bitch.*"

Bert never hesitated. "Hi, hello. Now, where do we know each other from?" As he spoke, he opened the door and stepped out and up. Ira looked at me, and I looked back. We should have laughed, and then, I thought, it would have been all right. As it was, he stared sus-piciously, and I offered my expression of utter innocence, and we locked each other out.

By the time I joined them, Bert was introducing Heschie, short for Herschel I decided, who had rented from a doctor's widow for six years on Cleveland Avenue in St. Paul. Heschie, who then decided we should call him Hesch, had bought the house of our parents from the junior high school science teacher who had bought it from them.

"His wife died," he told us. "Who needs a house without a wife?"

Ira nodded his agreement. "I used to bounce a ball against those steps," he said.

"No, that was me. I'm the girl who used to live here. I used to live here when I was a girl," I said.

Heschie had a wen on his forehead and it seemed to pulse red when he was pleased. Nodding to me, he turned to Bert. He boomed, in a voice that sounded nothing like Bert's but surely was meant to be, " 'Good evening, this is Bert Wragg. And I have news for you.' " He said, "Imagine, in the flesh, with behind him in tow a Jewish girl from the neighborhood, Mr. Bert Wragg, the voice of all Minnesota."

"I grew up other places, Hersch. I'm no more Minnesota than you are."

"Except," Hesch said, pulling at his jacket sleeves as if his body chafed in the dark gabardine, "my boy and my girl, so they wouldn't talk like me or Ada, this of course is the name of my wife, they listened to you when they finished with dinner before I came home. I was in Special Collections at the U: Hebraica. I'm educated, but not so religious, miss, so you're safe. Here is no barbarism or from Luddites or other refusers of progress. We own and operate two word processors, each possessing sixty-four megs of RAM, and I am tenured at Brooklyn College, just a walk from here—well, of course you know where is a walk and isn't. A walk in the jungle, perhaps, if you know what I mean, but nevertheless a walk. But—but—*ah:* the subject at hand. Raised as we were from backward and Orthodox, we could not instruct our children in acclimating to the local mores, the patterns of speech. You understand. But *you,* Mr. Bert Wragg, you were their teacher. Thanks to you, my daughter—*a girl,* and in Minnesota!—became president of her seventh-grade class."

Ira had moved away, but not in concession to Bert. I knew where he'd gone. In 1950 or so, our pop, a Marine, had come home after his outfit had taken terrible losses near Pusan. He had posed for a photograph by our mother, and he had shyly smiled, but I had come, once I knew the story of his war, to not believe the pleasure that his smile suggested. I have chosen, instead, to see sorrow in his eyes. Ira kept the picture on his bureau, at least on any bureau of his that I had seen. Pop had stood in the driveway to be photographed, and Ira had gone there, to the cracked, grainy cement with its grassy stripe down the center that was mostly packed earth and some weeds. I thought of the stripe down Heschie's hatband, and the stripe on Bert's garters and Pop's.

I took Ira's arm and smelled the starch in his shirt and the sweat underneath. He put his arm around my waist. Heschie was leading Bert into my childhood house, and I wanted to be there. It occurred to me that a moment of intimacy with Bert in my girlhood room would be priceless pleasure, or maybe treason, or the combination of both that is the heart of adolescence. But I stayed where I was, held of course by more than Ira's arm.

We stared, side by side, down the driveway toward the garage, as if we looked at someone who smiled back at us.

Ira sighed. I said, "Life biting you, Ira?"

"In the ass," he said. "Hard. But nobody suspects."

"How could they," I asked, "with you so even of temper and low of key? Are you lonely?"

"Yes."

"Sorry for yourself?"

"Of course."

"Any chance of seeing the kids?"

"Weekends," he said.

"Well, it's something. And where does she live with them?"

"Lexington."

"In Kentucky."

"That's the one," Ira said.

"Will you ever see them?"

"From, as they say, time to time." Then he asked, "Myrna, are you guys moving here?"

I pulled his arm tighter around my waist. "If he gets the job. There are a lot of men as good-looking as he is, and several women almost as good-looking, and three or four who are as smart as he is, and it's pretty iffy. He's scared. He doesn't let on."

"But if he gets the job," Ira said.

"If he does, and if we stay together, and if I want to not work for the foundation anymore, and if I can get a job with someone here, and if I want to live with him, and if he wants to live with me. If we can survive the age difference. Then, I'd say, it's a maybe."

"You got so brave," he said. "I'm at the point, now, where I get frightened from waking up frightened."

"I'm callous and cold," I said. "I'm selfish."

"I wonder if Pop was scared. I think about him every day, all of a sudden. I've begun to, I don't know, *study* him in some weird, scary fucking way. He's like a—what's the word?"

"Dead father," I suggested.

BECAUSE WE HAD promised Heschie upon leaving that Mr. Bert Wragg would see where he worked, Ira took us along Eighteenth to J, then up past Ocean to Campus Road. Near where it ran into Flatbush Avenue, we looked at the pretty campus, and at adjacent Midwood, where Ira and I had gone to high school.

"Over there," Ira said, pointing at the little building across from Midwood. I remembered lining up for first or second grade, my legs shaking with fear, outside the entrance marked GIRLS. He told Bert, "We went to grade school, P.S. 152, fully staffed by several dozen virgins over fifty plus Mr. Gottlieb with his big mustache. You had to give Heschie an autograph, right?"

Bert said, "We traded."

"Your signature," Ira said, "for what?"

"He took me up to Myrna's room."

I said, "He did?" I felt myself blush very hard as Ira started us off along Flatbush Avenue in the general direction of the river. Changing lanes, he hummed to himself. I thought of Bert in my girlhood room. It was very exciting, as I'd expected. As I hadn't, it also felt uncomfortable, unhappy, like watching the broad, hairy back of the muscular hand of a grown-up man slide up beneath the party skirt worn by a girl of eight.

"It's his son's room. It smells like old socks, with maybe a trace of sperm."

Ira said, "So it hasn't changed, Myrna, right?"

"I loved it," Bert said, hanging his hand over the back of the seat. I found myself reaching for a finger, and I stopped.

"How'd he know which room was mine?" I heard myself ask him.

"I told him," Bert said.

"How in hell did *you* know?"

"Your stories," he said. "I hear you, Myrna. The room near the stairs before the bathroom, right? I *was* listening."

I said, "I didn't realize I was telling."

"As long as one of us did," Bert said, a martyr to the gathering of news.

At Dorchester Road, humming to himself, Ira turned left, and I knew of course where we were going. A couple of blocks along, he parked, where it said *No Parking,* at the side of the Flatbush-Tompkins Congregational Church.

"I used to walk here every Saturday morning for Cub Scouts," Ira told Bert, "then every Friday night for Boy Scouts. I stayed on into my first year at NYU. I loved it. They let us use the whole upstairs. We had our own basketball court."

We followed him along the walk. Bert said, "Was he an Eagle Scout?"

"Life."

"Sorry?"

"Life Scout. Next to Eagle, but not as good."

"I never belonged to the Scouts."

"You joined the young perverts, though, didn't you?"

"I was born a pervert," he said. "Did you ever do it inside a church?"

"Not with anyone as young as you."

We followed the sound of Ira's feet up two flights of gray-painted iron steps. We came to a couple of locked doors, and one that was open. It led into the tiniest gym I had ever seen—which, when I had seen it a couple of times a year for close to ten years, had seemed no smaller than Madison Square Garden, where we attended the circus.

"Mom and Pop took me here all the time to see you march and shout orders at your little fascist patrol boys in the Alligator Patrol. It used to be so *big*."

Bert said, "The Alligator Patrol. It sounds like St. *Paul*. It's sweet, Ira. What else is worth remembering? The church giving the room over to a bunch of kids, and all those blue-haired ladies dipped in rose water with their shelves of bosom in polka-dotted dresses having coffee and cinnamon-raisin cake and mercy mild downstairs, and there you were, marching back and forth up here. And meaning it."

Ira wasn't listening, though I think Bert thought he was talking to him. Ira was standing at a basket no more than nine feet high set into the wall. Like the floors, the walls were of a treated softwood that gleamed under the ceiling lights protected by metal gridwork. In a far corner that wasn't so very far were five or six dark basketballs. I thought I could smell the electricity in the wiring, and the varnish on the wood. I remembered how on Troop Review night Pop would smile and our mother yawn, and I would inspect the older boys, Explorers they were called. They seemed closer to Pop's age than Ira's, whose bright eyes and hot, flushed face I still could see, whose belief I knew I believed as he clamped his mouth and raised three fingers of his hand to swear his fidelity to courtesy and thrift. And I remembered how they turned these lights off—they went out with a deep *thunk*—and then the boys lit up the darkness of their hall with khaki-colored Army surplus flashlights, pressing a little button to formulate dots and dashes, crying out the Morse code language in which they talked across the blackened gym about great, imagined emergencies for which, I think, Ira believed he was equipped. *Dah! Di-Dit! Dah-Dah! Dit!* they shouted. I took a deep breath, recalling the boys who used to march so grimly in ragged, wheeling failures of geometry, or practice tying knots they'd never need to know. Ira used to call off the names and then, clumsily, but with determination, he would stand before his sweaty, earnest seven-member patrol, his back to the proud, bored families who sat on folding chairs, to illustrate the tying of the sheet bend, sheepshank, bowline, clove. The knots, tied in clothesline, hung with no function from a length of dowel stained brown to represent a tree limb, or from his hand, connecting the dark-knuckled, stumpy fingers to nothing, holding tight to make-believe logs, lead pipes, mountain climbers, or fictitious fallen victims, all accepted on faith, who would one day warrant rescue by a Boy Scout with a length of line.

"We used to play dodge ball," Ira said.

"You throw it as hard as you can at someone on the other side," Bert answered. He took his corduroy sportcoat off and handed it to me.

"I no longer perform dispiriting traditional gestures like holding the guy's coat," I said.

"I wasn't a Boy Scout," Bert said, looking away and letting his coat drop onto the floor at my feet, "but I was a young pervert. We played dodge ball after junior high. They had a recreational center to keep us out of trouble. It didn't. But we did allow them to encourage us to hurt each other with basketballs."

Bert took off his tasseled loafers and trotted out toward the basketballs. He rolled two toward Ira, and then another.

Ira called, "What are the rules?"

"There are never any rules," Bert said.

I asked him. "What will you *pretend* are the rules?"

"No throwing at the head," Ira said, throwing the ball high, missing Bert's head mostly because Bert ducked.

"No throwing at the balls," Bert said, missing Ira's and hitting the wall behind him.

"It's supposed to be you're out if you get hit," I said.

"But there's only you to take somebody's place," Bert said, "and you can't keep taking everybody's place because there isn't enough of you."

"That," Ira said, in Heschie's intonations, "is the voice of all whatever."

He threw the ball and hit Bert on the hip. Bert fired back and Ira caught the ball chest high.

Bert said, "Myrna, you keep pretending you're replacing us both."

He fired the ball at Ira, who giggled in the shrill way boys proclaim their exuberance, and men pretend to be boys.

I left them to it, not so much out of annoyance as because I felt stupid, trying to riddle out who was attacking whom, with what surrogate weapon because of which metaphor we all were supposed to either understand or pretend to not notice. The gym smelled of sweat, probably not theirs, I realized, as I came down into the colder air of the metal stairway, past a door leading to what clearly smelled like a kitchen used a few days before, and then out to the long walk cut through moist and tender-looking lawn. Noises came down the stairs in pursuit—the slamming of leather against wooden walls, the slapping of leather on flesh. It was uncomfortably like hearing someone beaten to the accompaniment of high, psychotic giggles. I went further down the walk, then stopped, before I knew I would, to push my finger at the soft soil. As I stood up, I put it in my mouth up to the second knuckle. I tasted all I could.

Then I went to Ira's car and leaned against the door, some woman strange to the street of high brick or wood-frame houses each behind a wall of hedge, who was wearing a skirt cut a little too short for her age, who looked like a mean bit of business. That was what Pop called me when I was undisciplined or disrespectful in mild-to-somewhat-serious ways. When I really was hard and cruel, and when he suspected me of conduct he could not bear to know about for sure, he called me no names and he listed no rebukes. He grew silent, and he tried to look thoughtful instead of confused. It was then, because I always actually did possess a conscience, I would make for my mother and beg her to interpret us to each other. And of course, since she was as dead as Pop, that was why Ira was now pursuing me.

Because I was their date, and because they were well-bred boys, Bert and Ira came quite promptly from the church where they had settled nothing. They had played a violent and harmless game, and the tails of their shirts hung out of their pants like triangular clubhouse banners. Ira's fringes of hair were aloft, and Bert's thick, glossy hairdo hung in front of his eyes. They stood to regard me. Bert snapped his head back, and his hair sat down in place like a well-

trained, well-groomed dog. Ira pushed at his shirt, which in its white-
ness, now that the sun was down, seemed to glow.

It was the fact of so much darkness, more than the glare of the
lights, that made me blink. I supposed it was an automatic timer that
suddenly lit the stumpy white steeple and the hemlocks that bristled
at the walls. Bert raised an arm. Ira shrugged, then shook his head.
They came along the walk toward me. Or maybe someone inside, I
speculated, some cordial Christian host, with patience for the need-
ful, or the faithless, or the faithful making their return, had thought
to light us on our way.

I waited for the bells in the steeple to ring out the day. Ira came,
winded and disheveled, to stand with me beside his car. Then Bert
Wragg, Jr., joined us, flushed and smiling, perfect and at ease in our
neighborhood, as he had been inside my home, my history, and me.

"Listen," I told them, pointing up.

The man of the world and the man bereft of it looked, expectantly,
while I waited for the bells in the steeple to ring. But none, in another
minute, had sounded. I checked my watch and they, in response, each
looked at theirs. We waited together, looking up and then at each
other.

Often, of course, there are no bells.

Debriefing

I KNEW THE MAN in the elegant gray-black suit who sat in the Windsor chair next to mine because he had recruited me and I had brayed about him and about my service to the security of all the western world to Dr. Ann Paulus while we betrayed her husband and attended seminars about—what else?—the heart. Lipsted, my recruiter, moved his chair so that he sat at an angle to me, I suppose to see my reactions to the questions of his colleague, who sat behind the desk. The colleague, Dennis Schultz, wore a brown sportcoat in Donegal tweed over a tan V-neck sweater, and he consulted, and typed into, a laptop computer. He used his right hand, and his left seemed to me to lie in his lap, although the computer's screen partly blocked my view.

"I know you as Morton Green," Lipsted said.

I said, "That's who I am."

"First-rate," he said. "Now, you broke your glasses in Ireland, I think. You stayed in the Great Western."

"Best Western," Schultz said.

"Great Southern," I told them.

Lipsted raised his eyebrows and nodded. Schultz typed.

"At the airport," Schultz said, looking up.

"They say *on* the airport for some reason," I said.

Lipsted said, "I ought to remind you, I guess, that you agreed to make the courtesy call, and you agreed to be debriefed."

"That's this," I said. "The debriefing, right? Here I am."

"We're grateful for your cooperation," he said, "assuming we can get it."

I said, "I stayed at the Great Southern Hotel, which is on Shannon Airport." I was looking at Lipsted's shoes, which were black and glossy. I wore wide lightweight walking shoes because of the gout, and I wondered if they seemed shabby by comparison. "Oh. And I did break my glasses, yes."

As if I'd praised him, Schultz looked up from the keyboard and smiled a tight, victorious smile. He looked as if he might shave every other day. And his Windsor knot was as large as a young child's fist.

"You arrived on the morning of the ninth?"

I nodded.

"Took a cab to the hotel, I assume."

"Walked," I said. "The hotel is, you know, right on the airport."

"I for one will never forget," Schultz said. Lipsted grinned pretty mirthlessly.

"Then I slept," I said.

"No breakfast?" Lipsted asked. "Nothing else? Shower? Phone call? Talk show on the telly? They do have those, don't they?"

"They have everything we do," Schultz said. "Mr. Green, why wouldn't you have safety glass in them?"

"In my glasses?"

He nodded.

"I guess I should get that. I wear the tinted glass."

"It gets darker in bright light," Lipsted said.

"So they really did break," Schultz said.

"The wing came off the frame."

Schultz said, "Ah. So the *lenses* didn't break. Was it the screw, that little brass screw that goes into the hinge?"

"Right on the money," I said.

"So for that, the screw that holds the wing, you took a cab into—where?"

"The bell captain suggested an optometrist. I took a cab into Ennis, the town's called."

Schultz nodded.

Lipsted asked, "Are you tired? Have we gone on too long? Would you like a break?"

"No," I said, "I just never did one of these before. I'm not sure, in fact, what it is we're actually doing."

"A routine debriefing of a collateral asset," Schultz said.

"Me."

"You."

Lipsted said, "We do this with any number of businessmen and -women, literary people, teachers, students, a broad cross section of Americans who seem to enjoy helping their country."

"They *are* the country," I decided that I had to say.

"A lot of people would consider using a paper clip," Lipsted said. "You straighten one and stick it through the hinge and then you break it off or fold it around the wing. You've probably done that at one time or another."

"I probably have."

"So why, do you think, did you this time *not* do it? And go to the trouble and expense of taking a cab wherever. That's a pain in the ass, if you're jet-lagged and looking for someone to fix your eyeglasses."

"No," I said. "I didn't do it when I was jet-lagged. I did it later in the afternoon, after I slept. And the bell captain gave me an address. Why are we talking about this?"

"Contextualization," Schultz said, typing.

"Humor us," Lipsted said, recrossing his legs and pulling at his trouser pleats. "It's the way we work. Get it all pinned down, then we can understand the entire arc of action as a gestalt. All right? So. We have you sleeping, bell captain, taxi, optometrist. What was the street?"

"No idea," I said.

"Make any phone calls?" Schultz asked. He squinted, as if his eyes were exhausted or as if he'd recently started wearing contact lenses. In a photo on the wall, Schultz shaking hands with the Vice President, he wore wire-framed glasses.

"Besides the bell captain," Lipsted said.

"I called the optometrist's, to make sure they'd be open."

"Number obtained from the bellman," Lipsted added.

"Bell *captain,*" Schultz said.

"I guess concierge, you'd say," I said.

As is so often true with the concierge, he seemed to know about us and not at all to care. He probably knew right away, though I'm sure he heard from the waitress who came to my room with our orders. Long service in the lobbies of hotels, especially a lobby as small as that of the Shannon Great Southern, no doubt trains a man to spot the tall, pale, nervous American leaning over, as if trying to enfold, the small, athletic, nervously alert woman who arrives with the passengers of his plane but who pretends loudly, as he does, that they have, that moment, unexpectedly met. Since they are Americans, they travel in children's clothes—each is wearing soft white sneakers, floppy jeans, shirt hanging out at the waist—and each is certain that the staff of what looks like a long, low, stucco motel will have lost their reservations and canceled their rooms. On the stairs to the second floor, as I hefted her bag as well as my own—"Here," I bellowed, "let me give you a hand, Dr. Paulus!"—I hissed, as we reached the doors, "I'm doing a little job for the Department of State."

Lipsted knew of me through friends, Turkish dissidents at Georgetown, one of whom was an author of mine, and he approached me through them so that I'd feel ashamed of saying no. I was, so I said yes, and I agreed to what Lipsted had called an innocent small run. Hence the braying to Ann, whom I was desperate to impress with a coin of some new denomination. For she knew me, she had known me, and she was determined to give me up. Like a boy who walked on his hands, or who hit a home run, or who chattered loudly of once having done so, I told her about the Department of State between my bouts of nagging.

She lay on her stomach, her face in the pillow, and she submitted to my tracing her vertebrae until I reached the cleft of her buttocks. There, I delicately made the feathery tracks of what I saw, behind my closed eyes, as topographical delineations of her flesh. And then, shifting outside of my interior dark, I traced trails down the back of each thigh. And, instead of permitting our silence to speak, or to save us from speaking, I had, apparently, to tell her, "If your marriage was a huge mistake, this will count as the hugest. We're all that we *have.*" I could hear my presumptiveness dying into a whine, and knew that I deserved what I was bound to hear.

"Morty," she said, half into the pillow, and therefore as if she were far away, and therefore hurting me—permitting me to tell myself that I was hurt—because she was somehow distant, "my marriage was a mistake. Most people's marriage is a mistake. Marriage is where you go to *make* your mistakes. I am raising my children pretty well. I tend to not kill my patients. I am awkward in bed, but not all that bad, I'm told."

"Not by me. *I* tell you you're wonderful. Who tells you different?"

"Thank you."

"No, who do you go to bed with?"

"Morty, stop."

"Ann: who?"

"Charles is who, for godsakes."

"I thought we agreed you'd cut that out."

"Idiot."

"There's no law a woman has to go to bed with her husband. So many women don't, the majority of women in English-speaking countries don't. Women in francophone countries don't. So don't. All right?"

She said, "Fine. I won't."

"How'll I know you aren't anymore?"

"You won't, Morty. And you know why."

"You don't just stop seeing a man if you love him."

"Another Morton Green law of nature," she muttered into the pillow.

"No," I said, "now you have to say you love me. Then I get to badger you about leaving your husband."

"So you can help me raise my kids."

"I'd be all right."

"You'd be terrible. You're selfish, neurotic, and altogether too cute."

"I am cute, aren't I?"

She turned over, and I began to map the rest of her.

Lipsted poured coffee from a white plastic carafe into a cup decorated with the State Department seal. He spilled some into the saucer, and when he tried to wipe the coffee with his thumb, I saw his hand tremble.

"That's fine," I said.

"I can *clean* a little coffee up," he said between his teeth. He used the stiff, luxuriant-looking handkerchief on the saucer, then he wiped his hands dry, then refolded it into his suitcoat pocket. "Like new," he said.

Though I didn't know what he was referring to, I smiled, and Schultz smiled, as if to signal his approval of my cooperation.

"The conference," Schultz began.

"Medico-legal something or other of cardiac bypass procedures," Lipsted said.

"We publish medical texts," I said.

"Textbooks," Schultz said as he typed. Then: "We know this."

"The conference," Lipsted asked, "it was held on the hotel."

"Yes," I said. "At the hotel."

"You're not yanking us around," Schultz said.

"That's correct," I answered. "Why would I do that? How would it work, what would happen, if I got up and left? This isn't a great deal of fun."

"Serving your country can be hard work," Schultz intoned.

"You were kidding," Listed said, "am I right? Because no responsible adult citizen would agree to setting up this kind of a deal and then decide to blindside the government of the United States out of pique."

"What was the name of the woman, Mr. Green?" Schultz was resting his chin in his typing hand, his elbow on the desk. He said, "We have her as Powlus."

"Paulus," I said. "And I'd say pissed off, not pique. You two are a matched set of bullies."

"Not matched," Schultz said. With his right hand, he picked up the sleeve of his left arm and brought it into sight. The hand was shrunken, curled inward at a severe angle, and it looked blue-white. The nails somehow made me think of teeth. "Mr. Lipsted here has two sound hands. I have one. That makes us an unmatched set. Not to mention *his* wife irons his underwear. I acquired this asymmetry in Jerusalem. Car bomb. You read about it. You just didn't know I was there. Just as we didn't know the PLO or the Pan-Arab Jihad, or the Brotherhood of the Martyred Palestinian Children—nobody ever took credit—was there parking the laundry van outside the rare book dealer I used as a drop. I mean, we don't know if it might have been the *Jews,* who can get very freaky about West Bank settlements or the Wall or population purity or anything else. All this is about knowing. Consider this the Office of One-handed Epistemology. And do cut the shit."

I said, "Dr. Ann Paulus, P-A-U-L-U-S. She's a surgeon."

"Thank you," Lipsted said. I heard the saucer rattle at the cup.

"Here it is," I said. "I flew to Shannon from Kennedy on the six-something at night. I got in at dawn. I slept. I guess I flailed around and broke my glasses. I got them fixed in the city. I came back and ate and slept, and the next day I went to the meeting, in the same hotel, on shunts. I was after one of the speakers, a Dr. V. Ramaranda, to do a section on shunts for a revised edition of our cardiac procedures book. I had agreed to have a drink with a man from Turkey if he invited me. He did. I did. He loaned me his pen when I made a note on a napkin, I'd been told he might. After he did, I shook his hand and went up and went to sleep and left for home before lunch."

"And the pen?"

I took it out of my pocket and placed it on Schultz's desk. It was a cheap white plastic pen with a green plastic cap. On its side the pen said *Great Southern*. Schultz stared at it fondly.

Lipsted asked, "What did the gentleman say?"

"That he'd do the article."

"Holy shit," Schultz said.

"I'm sorry. It's my little spy joke. I apologize. The other gentleman talked about the rise of fundamentalism in the academic and gov-

ernmental spheres, and he said he was grateful for the military adopt-
ing a hard line toward the Muslim extremists. He called it an 'infection.' "

Lipsted said, "He used that word."

"Yes."

"It's the kind of word," Lipsted said, "you might expect to hear at
such a conference."

"Of course," I said. "It means something in code?"

"Debriefing," Lipsted said, as if apologizing, "tends to go one way.
We ask, you answer."

It reminded me of Ann, complaining that I demanded much and
told, finally, little. "Morty Green, the sex spy," she'd whispered, when
we were sore, tired, and happier than miserable for a couple of minutes. "What if I made demands? Would we be better off?"

"I'll do anything you say."

"Never," she said. "You're impervious to *say*. I'd have to coerce
you."

"Would you consider coercing me?"

I felt her shake her head. "I will only consider our stopping. No
more talking about it. I'm taking a later plane so I can stay here and
understand how terrible I feel, and then we're not doing it anymore,
anyplace else, no more conferences, no more planned chance meetings
ever again. Nobody ever said you're not supposed to feel lousy in
your life. I think that's a problem with us. We thought we were entitled to feel good. We were acting like patients. From now on, we
have to think like doctors."

"That's why I dropped out of med school."

"Flunked out," she said.

"Why are you kissing me? Why are you—"

"Because I *love* you, stupid."

"Right," I said. "That's right. So leave Charles and let's get, you
know, together."

"Did you say married?"

"I might have."

"We can't."

"But *why?*"

"Because I'm leaving you, Morty. I told you that."

"I give up."

"You never give up."

"You're *counting* on me giving up."

I had swept my arm out, and I knocked the water carafe, the clock radio, and my glasses off the bedside table and against the wall. I heard everything hit.

She put her hand on my throat and gently pressed. I lay back, and she squeezed.

"Ann," I said.

"I feel your voice," she said. "It's pushing up into my hand. I'm holding what you say on my skin. And your pulse: you're a strong, healthy man, Morty. The prognosis is you'll live."

"Sir?"

I suppose I blinked at Lipsted.

He asked, "Are you all right?"

I said, "That's all that I remember."

Lipsted asked, "Did our friend say anything about medical practices?"

"No."

"Social life? Concerts? Art exhibitions?"

"He mentioned rugs," I said. "He called them carpets. He suggested I might want to have him send some kilims to me at home. I said sure. You know, in case it was a password or something about transmitting documents."

Schultz said to Lipsted, "Anything?"

Lipsted shook his head.

"No," Schultz said, "I can tell you we had no paroles established on a carpet theme."

"I'd say you've bought yourself a couple of rugs," Lipsted said. "Give them to your wife as gifts."

"We aren't married anymore," I said.

"Ouch," he said, looking at Schultz.

"We thought there was a trial separation," Schultz said.

"Once upon a time. Then the trial was over."

"Guilty," Schultz said.

I asked, "Of what?"

He smiled as if we were friends.

Lipsted asked, "And Dr. Paulus?"

"Is *she* a government person?" I asked. "Does she do what I did?"

"I can tell you she isn't an asset," Lipsted said. "I can tell you that much. She isn't one of ours. Never employed, never used. You and Dr. Paulus are your own, shall we say, affair. While the other stuff is ours."

Schultz picked up the pen and put it down. "Your government is grateful," he said.

"Couldn't he just have mailed you the pen? Or the information that's in it?"

Lipsted set a file folder on the carpet beside his chair. He said, "No."

"Never," Schultz said. "Epistemology doesn't go through the mails."

Lipsted said, "You don't mail explosives, and you don't mail an international culling. Nor studies of the acquisition thereof. It's a federal law."

"Of nature," she had said. "Laws of nature governing the behavior of men and women in hotels in the Republic of Ireland include the urge to acquire sweets, and that the woman wear the man's striped business shirt so she looks cuddly and innocent and nevertheless piece of ass-y, and that the man reclaim it one slow little button at a time."

"Room service won't deliver this late," I had said. "I'll go downstairs, though, and out to the terminal. I'll bring you something. I'll be back in a little while."

To what I thought of then as her own surprise, she said, and really seemed to mean, "Morty, thank you. Thank you. This is right."

And, to my own astonishment, I went. I watched her lie in bed beneath the duvet while I put on jeans and shoes, no socks, and a dark T-shirt. I didn't kiss her, and I didn't try to preserve the sight of her, wearing my shirt in my bed. I went downstairs and out, across the parking lot and over lawns, under a bright moon and a high gray sky. I heard the harsh coughing of rooks from the flat roof of the hotel. I went through the rows of parked rental cars, lit by green-gray lights on high metal stanchions, and into the arrivals terminal. It wasn't lighted, but was made not dark, with an exhausted-seeming fluorescence. It was a building that took its meaning from what people did inside it, and now it was empty except for a couple of unspeaking women in dark green coveralls who slid wide brooms across the floor. A haggard-looking man in a rumpled shirt and undone necktie stared at me from under his brows while he made a calculator grate and clack under one bright lamp at an auto rental counter. The concessions were closed behind corrugated metal shutters, and, in the thin light, the women pushed their brooms, which made rasping noises on the dark linoleum floor. Papers rattled, and something fell, and I fed coins into brightly lighted machines until I had an armful of sodas and candy bars and crisps.

Now, I saw, men and women in uniform walked silently from the doors at the far end of Arrivals and through a couple of swinging doors. It was a little before four in the morning. Flights would be here in a couple of hours. I waited to see whether the concession stands would open or if someone might deliver early newspapers. One of the cleaning women had stopped working and seemed to be studying me.

I lifted my chin as if to challenge her, but she simply stood a moment more and then went back to pushing her broom, and I left Arrivals, carrying the sweets most adults will buy only for watching films or traveling long distances. As I had a day or so before, I went among the cars, and over flower beds and lawns, toward the Great Southern Hotel. Yellow had poured across the dull gray of the sky, and it seemed to have dropped lower. I had to kick on the door until the night man came, and then I had to ask him if he would hold the sweating cans and crackling packets while I found my key to prove I was a guest. He wore a white shirt and a necktie and a metal pin that said Ethan. He wore striped uniform trousers, and old-fashioned carpet slippers over his socks. His hair seemed combed, but his long, pale face looked rumpled, and I apologized for disturbing him.

"I don't mind at all, sir. It's an aspect of my job, isn't it. Though we'd have had the chars in soon enough on their shift, mind you, and the doors unlocked," he said. "You'd have managed to get in with your snack."

"I was in a little bit of a hurry, I suppose."

"Well, you're American, aren't you? Here you are, then," he told me, "safe as houses. Have a pleasant night or day, sir, as the case may be."

Upstairs, by the light of the corridor, I found what I believe I had suspected I would find, and possibly even what I thought I should want to find—that Ann had left. I considered calling her room. I considered walking along the hall to her door and tapping it, again and again, until she opened. Instead, I stood in my doorway, turned the light switch on, and adjusted my glasses, which, because of their tight-sprung new hinge, squeezed at my ear.

"Mr. Green," Lipsted said, "there are other medical conferences, I bet." He said it with the flippant generosity of minor characters in films and books who reunite the separated lovers.

"She's pretty much married," I said. "She has children. She has a cat and a dog."

"A passion thing," Schultz said. "Passion *and* a little epistemology on the side. That's not bad."

I asked for more coffee. Lipsted suggested a sandwich and a drink. I thought of my armful of chocolates and soft drinks and crisps. I thought of Ann's mouth around a triangle of sandwich.

"And," Schultz reminded me as he placed the pen in a stiff brown envelope and sealed the gummed flap with richly moist repeated licks, "you got the Indian guy to do your chapter." Lipsted poured coffee and the porcelain chattered. One of them spoke about lunch while I thought of how I'd walked into the small, dark room and had switched the lights back on, and then had taken one step backward into the hot, narrow corridor to look at the abandoned bed, the empty room. As I thought of it again, I saw some stiff, exhausted passenger who didn't look like me. He had just walked over from Arrivals, and he didn't want to go inside yet. He waited, perhaps for the Great Southern staff who would make up the room from which Ann, and then I, had already checked out.

Timberline

A MAN RIDES INTO THE NIGHT, he meets a mysterious stranger, his life is changed or it isn't. Nobody tells him which.

For example: when he ran away from home on the eve of his forty-fifth birthday. He was at the Eleventh Street window of their apartment, trying to look through the sycamore trees, and through the nimbus-on-grit glare of the streetlight, toward Greenwich Avenue. He saw what you'd expect. He saw himself, rippling as he moved in the crazy, unclean mirror that the window made. He saw the widow's peak, or thought he did. He saw the pale, shapeless head. But he knew it was him. His guess: he'd know him almost anywhere.

Leslie, behind him in the living room, asked, "What are you looking for?"

He said, "How'd you know I wasn't looking *at?*" Then he said, "You really want to know?"

She said, "I really don't, I suppose. I suppose we're not going up to Madison tomorrow and pick out a print for your birthday."

"Why not?"

"Because you'll have thrown a scene."

"I'm not throwing a scene, Leslie."

"You're getting ready to throw a scene, Hank. And I'll end up crying. My face'll look like you beat me, so you'll be too embarrassed for us to go outside in the morning. You'll spend all Saturday sulking because we didn't get you anything for your birthday. Which you'll decide by Saturday night you do want to celebrate. So we'll go out. We'll go to a new place and you'll fall in love with our waitress, and I'll get surly and we'll hate dinner."

He inspected them in the window glass. He looked for his former lover, stunned wordless, as he had been a number of years before, in a number of borrowed and rented rooms. All he could see of his wife and former graduate student now was her face and brushy haircut floating behind him and to the left, seeming to sit on his shoulder like a second head. He smelled her breath, which was like a spicy vermouth. He smelled her soap, which reminded him of mangos.

A summer wind he thought of as oily moved the plane tree's smaller branches. He thought he could see, through himself and the streetlamp, the lights of a cab turning in toward them from Greenwich. He was thinking about the time he saw his father lifted by winds off the face of Mount Washington. He hadn't known he was recalling it, nor did he know why it should come to mind now. But he couldn't imagine, suddenly, not thinking of it all the time—how his father's dark khaki poncho had filled with the wind that had taken him off.

That had been thirty-six years ago in Franconia, New Hampshire, on the trail from Mizpah Springs up through the boulder fields below the harshest part of the ascent to the hut called Lakes of the Clouds. In the hut there had been an old upright piano, and simple food, and the tall, strong college boys and girls who had carried provisions in pack baskets up to the huts that were run by the Appalachian Mountain Club. The students raced up the trails, he remembered. He remembered hearing the thud of their cleated, heavy boots. He remembered smelling the sweat of a tall, blond woman who had seemed to him then to be almost as old as his father. He had been thrilled by her scent. You heard them coming up the trail, and you stepped aside, feeling lesser than they.

Now, in New York, still a bystander, he was smelling mangos and vermouth. "If you ask me what I was saying," she said, "I'll claim self-defense after I stab you, tonight, while you sleep."

It was time for him to turn around and smile at her and gently take hold of her upper arms, or the back of her neck, and pull her toward him and sink, somehow, through this panic, this utter ignorance of what he ought to be doing, and get to *them*. He wasn't absolutely sure, but he suspected he could always find them in her. And finding them, of course, he'd find himself.

But he kept thinking of himself, the boy at eight, in the sudden summer rainstorm on Mount Washington's lower face, standing alone, blown against a boulder five feet high by the coiling about of the same wind that had taken his father from sight. He stood at the window, and he couldn't turn around until her smeary face had moved from the reflection. Then he turned and looked at the room they had furnished. He walked through it to their little foyer, and he unlocked the door, and he left. He walked to Fourteenth Street, where their car was garaged.

As he drove uptown, proud that he'd remembered in the Seventies how to cut west with Broadway through Columbus to the Henry Hudson, he realized he had no idea how you drive to New Hampshire from New York. He was one of those Manhattanites who understood the subways and made it a matter of honor to use them, despite the hour. He knew the underground map, but he had no sense of direction, and all he understood was that he was driving uptown, the Hudson River on his left, with bunched, dense, unreadable Harlem on his right and the George Washington Bridge beyond it.

As he followed the signs to the bridge, then guessed and took the leftmost ramp that led to it, he accepted that he was driving to New Hampshire. He had believed, on leaving the house, that he was going to take a walk. Now, even while he aimed himself away, he was surprised. He wanted to look at the surface of the river, but he was made anxious by the lights and speed of the traffic. He saw a tugboat, he thought. He thought it was pushing a barge on which a mound—was it garbage?—rode low in the water. Maybe he'd expected to see it. He knew of so many error-laden first-person accounts that historians had banked on, to their grief. People rarely saw what they claimed to.

But he had seen his father on the wind, he thought. It was something he knew. He knew, too, that he would pull over when he could
and telephone Leslie. He would tell her, "Don't worry." She would
swear in the rhythms he knew, and he would grin. "Don't worry,"
he'd say. "I was in some kind of fear fantasy, heading for New England. But it's all right. I'm all right. It was nothing more than dread.
I'll be home soon, and I'll tell you the whole stupid story."

He grinned in the darkness as he headed out on, apparently, the
Palisades Parkway through New Jersey. When he passed a service
station at Ramapo, he thought: The next place I see, I'll turn around.

He saw a sign for Route 17. He was half an hour up the Palisades
Parkway, driving slowly and being steadily passed. He thought he remembered something about 17, that a lot of people he knew had driven it. He wasn't sure it went to New England, he probably should
turn around if he could. He didn't. He followed a sign, after a while,
that took him onto a long, subtle curve, and he had taken a ticket at
a booth, and he was driving upstate on the Thruway. You can always, he thought, get off the Governor Thomas E. Dewey Thruway
and go back in the opposite direction. They can tell you how to do
that. But he didn't ask. He knew he was headed upstate. You could,
he figured, get to New Hampshire from there, or you could always
turn around.

His mother had left them. He didn't know it at the time, of course,
because he was eight. You don't tell an eight-year-old with chubby
legs and prominent teeth and an affection for books and games about
war that his mother every once in a while takes off. Later, he understood that she had left before that summer and would leave again. She
didn't leave permanently until he'd been in college for almost a semester. She kept in touch, thinking he'd need it. And he hadn't the
courage, then, to tell her she was distracting him from the two great
recently discovered programs of his life—falling in love with the his-
torical narrative of anyplace in any age as told by almost anyone at all,
and succumbing to lust with what he later thought of as sagacity.

So Hank's father, in the summer of his boy's ninth year, left alone
with the child by his wife, reread pertinent sections of the Boy Scout
handbook, sought the advice of an outdoorsy friend, and took Hank

by train to New Hampshire. In the motel room that smelled of wax and heat, this man—who had not camped out since basic training—showed Hank every piece of borrowed equipment in each of the borrowed rucksacks.

"We have to be careful up there," his father said. "I don't mean there's anything to be scared of. I mean we have to take precautions. It's what I do in business. It's what you should do in your life. Things are the same, di dum di dum di dum, nothing to worry about"—here, he lit a cigarette—"then all of a sudden they're different. Really changed. Understand? Weather on the mountain changes very suddenly. You feel how hot it is?"

"It's very hot," Hank had answered, eager to be right. This was an important trip, he knew. He didn't know why. "*Very* hot."

"But it still could snow on us once we get up there." His father pointed. "Above timberline. Do you know what that is?"

His father smoked Camels, one after another. His fingers were stained yellow, and Hank loved the harsh, dark smell of the stubby little cigarettes. He heard his father pull the smoke in. Seeing that Hank watched him, he blew a thick, steady smoke ring onto the air. He winked. Hank winked back. His father's gray-brown widow's peak was encircled, after a while, by smoke. It looked the way Mount Washington looked from the front of the motel, hidden at its top by clouds.

That night, on the metal beds with their thin mattress pads, they turned and coughed and slept to waken—Hank because of his father, his father because of one among all the secrets, Hank suspected later, that rose up around him like the smoke of his cigarettes. Early light made his father appear pale and, from the side, vulnerable as he looked through the window. A path that led to the road that would take them to the first of their trails was outside that window. His father, without his wire-rimmed glasses and with his hair pulled up by friction against his pillow, stood at the window and smoked. Seeing his father without glasses felt like seeing him naked. Hank had shut his eyes and, hearing his father taking in smoke and letting it out, he had fallen back to sleep.

They ate what to Hank was an exciting meal because it was composed of food their mother never cooked: sausages and eggs so greasy the oils soaked through the rye bread his father showed him how to fold for sunnyside-up sandwiches.

"You want coffee this morning, Hank?" His father turned a cup of coffee beige with milk and sugar. Hank half expected to be offered a Camel with it and was disappointed when, winking, his thin, sad-faced father frowned around a cigarette and lit it up, but didn't shake the pack to release the tips of one or two and offer it as Hank had seen him do for others at restaurants and parties.

When their waitress brought the check, his father, counting change and squinting against smoke from the cigarette that wobbled between his lips, said, "This man opposite me here is climbing up to Mizpah Springs Hut."

Hank remembered looking into his coffee and blushing, both because of the attention and because he disliked the taste of the coffee which his father had offered with so much sudden good cheer.

"Which one's that again?" she'd asked, taking the money.

"Well, it's just up *there*. It's our first stage. Kind of base camp, on the way to Lakes of the Clouds."

"I know where *that* is," she said, walking away.

"Hurray for you," his father said.

"Hurray for you," Hank said, passing a rest stop and reading the sign that told him he would have to wait for thirty-seven miles before the next. "A man *will* turn around when he's ready to," he said. "He will."

Hank remembered timberline. He remembered their slow, laborious, thirsty climb up a track of dirt and rocks through dense bushes and trees. He remembered the clouds of gnats and blackflies, the stink of citronella and its greasy weight on the skin of his arms and neck and face. His father's lungs made squeaking sounds as he panted, Hank remembered. And he remembered that his father forced a fast, unhappy pace, as if they were driven through discomfort and poor conditioning and the oppressive heat by an obligation that was urgent, undeniable.

When they rested, his father showed him how to sit in the harness of his rucksack with his legs pointing downhill. "Let gravity do the work," his father said. "When you get back up, it'll be easier. The pack'll fall onto your back as you stand. It's an old Boy Scout trick." He smiled as he lit his cigarette and blew the smoke up, at the gnats that hovered about them. "Isn't it great? You show 'em you can take it. You show *you*. I always wanted to do this, Hank. And you. Aren't you something? You're climbing to Mizpah Springs, you're climbing Mount *Washington,* and you're only eight years old. It might be a record. You might be posting a national record."

Hank remembered drinking too much water, and his father's gentle, breathless rebuke when they stood, facing downhill, about an hour later. "The White Mountains make emergencies. That's what I've heard. So you need to make sure there's plenty of water until we get to the Springs."

As they continued to climb, breaking free of the confines of the trail to see the widening white glare of sky unencumbered by brush, his father, struggling for breath, instructed him to note how the trees were lower, the winds steadier. Hank saw, at last, when they made the ridge that would take them to the hut, how entire evergreens, mostly bare of needles (but not dead, his father said), were no higher than his knee.

"It's the cold does it," his father said, "and the winds. They look like miniature trees, but it's all in them—they're just stunted. It's like when you, I don't know, when you just run out of it. This is what it's like." He shielded his face with cupped hands to light a cigarette. "I believe that life is a bivouac, Hank," he said as the wind took his smoke and some of the sound of his words away. "You know what a bivouac is?"

Hank certainly didn't know, but he had shrugged, imitating his father, and he had nodded. When he read the word in college, sitting in the torpor of the library late at night, he had looked up, wide-eyed, feeling in his stomach some of that day: the presence of his father, and his mother's absence.

They ate a sandwich lunch at the small, open hut with its sleeping shelf lined with evergreen branches, and then his father had moved them along, before they could grow too stiff. In the bright, hot midday light, hills below them were black-green under the shadows of clouds that began to mass as they walked. After a couple of hours, as his father complained about the time of day and the changing sky, Hank saw how much darker the hills were, and how clouds thickened above them. Now they were over the timberline. High cairns of rock marked the trail because there were no trees. His father kept the map, in its glassine case, in his hand.

Every January his father solemnly presented him with a wrapped gift, which he in turn gave his mother for her birthday. Every year, she added the scented oil to her bath and presented herself, in her blue silk bathrobe. Hank was aware of the heat of the water and of its perfume. He smelled it through the canvas and dust and wind. He had begun to wonder, as they labored more slowly against the pitch and the difficult, stony footing that made his calves and ankles ache, whether she might greet them, as a surprise, as a reward, when they reached the end of their climb. She came from the bathroom to find him, each year, and she presented herself, smiling, her skin a little damp. "Want a smell, sweetheart?" she would ask.

Hank remembered as he drove how his father made them stop and put on their ponchos, which were very long and which covered their packs and fastened with snaps beneath their arms. His father tugged Hank's into place and then Hank, feeling uneasy, as if he were buttoning his father's shirt, pulled the poncho over his father's rucksack.

Cold winds, then colder winds, drove at them. The field of boulders and cairns and scree, and sudden declines, lay all about him. He couldn't see Mount Washington. Ice-cold mist grew heavier, and the clouds, his father told him, were surrounding them. He thought in the car of his recollection of the night before they climbed—of his father, surrounded by smoke.

Hours into his drive, he saw a sign for Westmoreland. The name of a general whom he associated with the madness of the Vietnam War seemed significant, so he aimed himself there, yawning now and thinking not of a place to call from, or where he might turn around, but of someplace he could sleep.

There were the blue-gray boulders vanishing into the descending clouds, there was the invisible mountain they were partway up, there was timberline below them, and there was his father before him, breathing hard and urging Hank to keep up. "You keep me in sight," his father said, turning clumsily as his poncho was flailed by wind against the hump of his rucksack. "You see me, right?"

Hank, in the car, was going to say, "Right." He rubbed his lips and didn't. He drove the two-lane highway onto which he'd exited from the Thruway. He knew from roadside signs that he wasn't terribly far from where the battle of Oriskany had been fought. With a satisfaction he distrusted, he told himself that he was driving into a footnote.

The Oriskany Falls Hotel was closed, and he drove on for fifteen or twenty miles to Route 20, where he found a motel with an open bar, and with three other cars outside of rooms. The kid who took the imprint of his credit card and gave him a key told him he could get a sandwich and a drink in the bar until half past midnight.

"You close it at twelve-thirty?"

"This here's Oneida County," the crew-cut, harelipped boy of something like twenty intoned, "not Las Vegas, Nevada."

"Damn," Hank said, "I wanted it to be Las Vegas, Nevada."

"But it ain't," the boy said, already looking away.

"It's Oneida County," Hank said. "Am I right?"

The boy didn't answer and Hank didn't blame him.

In the bar, at eleven-fifteen, served—of course—by the harelipped boy, Hank drank bar whiskey and ate two undercooked hot dogs, garnished with yellow mustard, which the boy had purported to roast in a microwave oven on the short counter of the small room. Hank sat at the end of the counter. The red plastic-covered stool to his right was empty, and so was the next one. On the one after that, a man wearing a dirty sling over his suit jacket drank shots with beer. On the stool beside him, a woman with a black hat that was like a turban drank coffee.

He was looking at the hat or at her head, and he didn't know why. Then he did. She was bald, he realized, and she was disguising it with the turban. She looked up, past the man's shoulder, and caught him studying her. She stared back and slowly adjusted her hat, letting it shift enough to confirm her hairlessness. He felt as though she had taken off her shirt.

"Sorry," he had to say.

"Dickie," she said, "I'm going to discuss my life with this man over here, all right?"

The man beside her looked Hank over and shrugged. That says it all, Hank thought: dismissed by a man in a sling who is getting drunk on boilermakers at the outskirts of a footnote.

She was very, very thin, and she was jaundiced-looking. Her mouth, which was broad with a full lower lip, had a jaunty curve despite her pursing it, maybe in pain. She looked like a supporting actress—the one who isn't pursued by Franchot Tone in a movie that Leslie might watch after he had fallen asleep. Hank often woke to find that she'd turned the bedroom TV set low and was sitting on the floor before it, wrapped in a blanket. She reminded him of his father, smoking at the window, studying the White Mountains. Or perhaps he had fashioned the memory of his father after Leslie, he thought. Maybe none of it was true, whatever *true* meant.

She said, "You were looking at me like you knew me." She adjusted her wrinkled ecru shirt in the waistband of her loose cotton slacks, as if expecting him to study her. "But we don't know each other, do we?"

"No, we don't."

"And you're not the kind of man to be rude."

"Not on purpose, usually," he said.

"So you must have been transfixed by my hairdo."

Her eyes were the kind of clear blue that was almost gray. They were large, and so, he realized, was her nose. She was a woman whose bold features could probably compete with even her smooth, broad head for your attention, he thought. He wished he could tell her so.

"I apologize," he said.

She sat beside him. When she leaned closer, he could smell her coffee and a kind of sweetness that he later realized was the corruption in her body. He had come to know that smell in his father, not so many years before. "You're a gentleman, then?" Her voice was low and tired. A couple of hundred miles from home and almost forty-five, he had met someone who made him feel young, someone older than his young wife. He smiled.

"Yeah," she said, accepting the coffee passed over by the boy, "you're a gentleman. You have a gentleman's smile. You're the kind of man who thinks the world is tougher than he is. And you're right. And you smile so maybe it'll be easy on you. Why not?"

"It's my birthday. Thank you. You—"

"What'd I do for you that you're so grateful for? I'm giving you me with cancer so you can enjoy your life while you haven't got it? The cancer, I mean. I don't know if you've got your life. Have you?"

"Like a very, very bad cold," he said.

She shrugged.

He was emboldened to say, "I know. It beats cancer."

She said, "I'll be the judge of that." She looked into his face. He saw the hesitation at the corners of her mouth, and he smiled to signal that he'd laugh if she would, and they both began at once.

After a while he took a pull of his drink and raised his finger to ask for another. The boy looked at the clock, then slowly moved to the shelf of bottles.

"This isn't Las Vegas, Nevada," he told the woman.

"This here's Oneida County," she replied.

He said, "I'm Henry Borden."

"Mine's Lorna Wolf. One *f*—like the animal. The other inmate over there's my brother. We're going to Sayre, Pennsylvania. You know where it is?"

"I don't even know where Oneida County is."

"There's a hospital there," she said.

"Good luck in it, Lorna."

"Oh, no," she said. "We're going there for him. There's a bone guy there. My brother, Dickie, he has to have his arm reset. We did me, in Utica. Now we do him in Sayre. Then we come back and do me. What we do is we drive back and forth. He's got a wonderfully comfortable car—I read a book, and Dickie drives. He's excellent with just the one arm."

He nodded.

"Wait a minute," she said. "Borden? I've heard of you."

He shrugged.

"I heard you on the radio. Henry Borden."

"Hank."

"Hank. I heard you talking about—a crooked President? But which one? A general—was it Grant?"

"Restoring the tomb, yes. It was one of the morning—"

"Sure," she said. "Isn't that something. And we meet up here in the faux Las Vegas of upstate New York. Isn't that something."

She bent to the coffee. The boy poured a shot for Dickie. Lorna took a deep breath, and Hank heard her work to do it. He thought she was going to shout, and he turned to her. She said, looking at her cup, "Oh *God,* I hate decaffeinated coffee." Her voice shook as she straightened to speak. She slowly blew air out between her lips, and it sounded to Hank like his father's cigarette smoke. He sniffed, expecting to smell it.

Then she said, making an effort, letting her anger sink again, "The most powerful stimulant I'm allowed these days is the Prince Valiant cartoon on Sunday. Sometimes, on TV, that fat fascist, what's his name, with the wardrobe. And the occasional cup of decaf." She sipped. "God. So what're you doing in Not Las Vegas?"

"Oh," he said.

"A lecture? Something exciting? Though, if you don't mind my pointing it out, you look—what's the word? You look like you feel a little shady. What's your story, Hank?"

He paid for the drink and her coffee. The boy emphatically snapped switches that shut off outside lights. "You can finish whenever you finish," the boy said, "I don't mind waiting. But I can't sell you no more, 'cause we're closed."

"Closed is closed," Lorna said. "It's apparently twelve-thirty in here when it's not quite midnight in the world."

"This *is* Oneida County," Hank said. Then he said, "I'm sorry, Lorna. I guess I don't really have a story."

"Well, that's all right with me," she said.

He saw his father, who had turned to instruct him about the trail of cairns or the weather, get struck by the wind, which slammed noisily into the mountainside. His father spread his arms for balance and opened his mouth. No sound came out, or the wind suppressed it. In the thick dirty white mist about them, his father, poncho taut with wind, was lifted into the air and taken from sight.

The wind died and the cloud eddied. Rain had made the stones slick and shiny black. A dozen or so feet from the ledge over which his father had flown, Hank had stood in place, his back against rock face. He remembered standing with his legs together, the heels of his boots touching, leaning forward under the weight of his rucksack, his arms folded across his chest for balance or warmth. The wind came up again, and he stood still in it, leaning into the icy rain and waiting.

He didn't know—and he hadn't known then, he was sure—what he might have waited for. But he stood in place and looked at the ledge. Now he wished that this woman, Lorna Wolf, knew about his waiting there. He'd have enjoyed asking her whether she thought he was waiting for instructions.

He suspected she might agree with him—that he was waiting with utterly no hope for his father to reappear and tell him what to do about his father's disappearance. Hank would have stressed, if he'd told her, that he had no confidence at all his father might return. Now it sounded to him like some kind of allegory, and he was almost—almost—grateful that she didn't know.

Slowly, his grinning father, bleeding along one temple and holding his body stiffly, climbed to his feet from the far side of the ledge. He had not been blown off the mountain, only over an apparently undangerous shelf of stone. Holding on to the rock now for balance, his father nodded. Hank wondered whether he had winked. And, walking alongside his son instead of before him, Hank's father told him over and again, until Hank took his turn in telling *him,* how the winds had rolled him over rocks until he'd fetched up hard against some that had broken what would have turned into a fall.

"Only the fall got broken," his father said. "Who'd believe it? Only the fall got broken."

His father held Hank's shoulder, though he didn't lean his weight on him. At one point, they held each other's hands, reaching automatically to balance themselves on a slippery, rounded face.

"I was afraid we'd have to bivouac here," his father said, heaving soon for breath but talking, talking. "You can get benighted and end up frozen dead on this mountain. And this is the *gradual* part. But don't you let anyone tell you it's easy. We'll come back here—I'll get hold of ropes and axes and pitons and whatever else they use, and we'll practice, and we'll come up here another time and climb straight up a different trail. *Route,* they call it. But this is how you start. You start this way, and then you take the more dangerous route."

A few minutes later, his father said, "And my glasses didn't even break."

Hank said, "Only the fall."

His father pounded on his shoulder in response.

They went to the top. His father stopped to light a cigarette where sun broke through the cloud cover. Big athletic hut boys and boyish New England blondes like those he would pursue in college—like Leslie, in fact—worked outside the low wooden building he and his father would enter, making shy, effortful, casual conversation, like people used to adventure.

His mother would not be there to greet them, of course. They would eat and they would listen to a hut boy play the piano, and they would sleep in a dormitory for men. Then they would go home. His mother would have returned. He would become nine and ten and forty-four. And where, in the logs of a thousand centuries' navigation through oceans of blood, would the tiny moment of a father's lifting into the air be entered?

"No story, Lorna," he said. "I wish there was."

She patted his arm.

He thought how, when Leslie slept and he came late to bed, he patted her arm as he lay down. She said she knew in her sleep that he was there, so he did that. She slept with a leg protruding from the comforter, often in the coldest weather. Usually bare, her leg lay on top of the cover, its slender calf and extended foot an elegance he admired.

Lorna leaned over as if she were going to kiss him good night, and he held steady, hoping she would.

"Catch you later," she said, in her hoarse, dark voice.

"Catch you later," he said. "Good luck."

She said, "That's right." Then, louder, she said, "Dickie boy. Early day."

Early day, Hank thought. As soon as he woke, he would telephone Leslie. Lorna's brother slid from the stool, wobbled an instant, braced himself against her with his undamaged arm, and they left. Maybe he would make the call tonight. The glass door closed behind them. Hank looked through it, waiting, but not with hope.

You're right, he told himself. But he heard the words in Leslie's voice, as if his wife were not in Manhattan, as if she were here in Oneida County, bearing all of the rest of his life in her strong hands, in her powerful voice. *You're right,* Leslie said in him: *If you don't have a story, there isn't an end. You don't get punctuation.*

Lorna must have agreed. She did not turn to look at him. She did not wave.

Still the Same Old Story

Once upon a time, I was dissatisfied with how I used my brains and with how Sam used his. He was what they call—and still, in upstate New York, with respect—a banker. I was the banker's wife. And I had grown bored with my candor, weary of my brittleness, bruised by my own dissatisfactions. So, driving from a canal town that since the late nineteenth century had been thrashing about to survive, I went to bed with a man named Max who practiced medicine and who had no heart.

I met him at a party and I met him at the hospital—need I say that I worked for the Auxiliary?—and I met him at a motel outside of Syracuse. He was stocky, and his soft skin gleamed over bunchy muscles. He was the sort of man who exercised not for his health but so that women would admire him. He wasn't, so I'd heard, a good doctor; he wasn't a happy one, and he was close to leaving the area when we met. Perhaps his imminent departure gave us a feeling of license. We made love three times on a Saturday in November, the second time while the Florida–Notre Dame game was showing on the television set. He wasn't so cruel as selfish. He used me hard. I was stimulated by his lack of generosity, I'm sorry to say. And as men must, I've learned, he told his colleagues at the hospital. It seems that doctors, especially, need to talk like boys about sex. Maybe I knew he would. Maybe that foreknowledge was also a stimulant. Maybe I knew when it began that Sam must finally learn of it too.

As is Sam's way, he didn't tell me directly. I knew that something of it was in the wind when he told a story at dinner, after Joanna had gone upstairs to her homework, ending it with these words: "And he said it was the best blow job he ever had."

I knew what Max was saying. I knew that Sam was hearing rumors or reports. I blushed over my chicken with rosemary, and if Max had been at the table instead of Sam, I could not tell—nor can I now—whether I'd have gone around to burrow into his lap or slug him with an herbed paillard.

I said, "Nice language."

Sam looked lean and fit, tired, uninterested in food, and a little dangerous. As he'd aged, as he'd lost hair, his bony forehead and prominent nose made him look like something with keen vision and cruel abilities and the habit of hunting.

He said, "Sharon, a blow job is a blow job. You want to call it, you know—"

"Fellatio?"

"That's right. You want to call it that? It's still what she did with her mouth."

I said, "You know, I think you're right." I cut a square of chicken with considerable care.

"We *agree*," he said to the ceiling. "But I didn't mean"—his smile looked nasty—"to be dis*taste*ful. If you know what I mean." He looked at me with his eyebrows raised, his eyes unblinking. I looked into them. I wanted to find something of our fifteen years together. We watched each other like that, and his eyes filled with tears that ran onto his face. His mouth collapsed, and he said, "Pardon me, please." I remember that I nodded as he left the table. I remember thinking that I should have wept too.

We didn't talk that way again. We meshed our social calendars, as we customarily did, and we attended dinners and cocktail parties at which doctors looked meaningfully over my body and sometimes met my eyes. I suppose they were waiting to be selected for the best-ever sex of their lives. In a provincial big town or small city, sex and thievery and numbers of dollars constitute the curriculum, and apparently reasonable adults grow hypertensive about them. So I was their hot topic. I find it of interest even now that I didn't care.

I knew that Sam and I had foundered. I knew that Joanna could be drowned along with us. I knew, I insisted to myself, that she *might* survive. I worried only about how, I told myself. Everything else, I decided, would take care of itself. I gave up my local newspaper column, slid from the Auxiliary, and signed up for all the substitute teaching of French and Spanish I could, preparing myself for full-time employment as a single parent.

Gene McClatchey telephoned on an April afternoon to say, "This is Gene."

"Gene?"

"At the bank, Sharon? I work for your fucking husband?"

I said, "Not that happily, I guess."

"We need to meet."

And of course I thought he was a tardy quester after the world's best etc. I said, "Why ever, Gene?"

"On account of your husband is dicking my wife? Would that be a good enough why-ever?"

"My husband? Your wife? Valerie?"

He said, "Name someplace, will you? That's private?"

"That's secret, you mean."

He said, "Please?"

We ended up a dozen miles to the north, at a conservation training center run by the state, a little park of nature trails and wooden blinds from which to peer at waterfowl. I don't know why I felt compelled to bring a loaf of bread to feed to the ducks. I tore the pulpy slices into bits and hurled them at mallards while Gene McClatchey, a red-faced man with curly brown hair and a hard, black double-breasted suit, studied the tearing of the bread and its arc toward the water and the wheeling of the ducks as they fed.

He said, impatiently, "You don't seem upset, Sharon."

"I'm not surprised that something happened, Gene. I didn't think of your wife, to tell you the truth. She's so glamorous and Sam's—

well, I don't know, I guess. You want me upset? How upset do you want me?"

"What *I* am," he barked.

"You're jealous," I said. "Or angry. Because the beautiful woman who's supposed to be yours—"

"No! I don't want to hear any of that feminist horseshit about freedom and owning people and whatever. She's my *wife.*"

"And hurt," I said.

"Yeah?"

"Yeah, Gene. Wounded."

"Bitch," he said. He flinched, stepped back from the fence at the duck pond, and scrubbed with his wide hands at his face. He said, "Sorry. I apologize. I'm so *disgusted.* Look at what I found that she left around by accident on purpose. Disgusted'll do it."

He held a small notebook with thick covers. The paper was heavy and the binding looked like the inside covers of a fancy antique book. She had written in aqua ink, of course. She wore mostly pinks and limes and aquas in soft cloth that emphasized her breasts and hips. She was the best-built woman over twenty-five in town. Gene struck her, so they said at our parties. Looking at his big hands and red face, I believed that he might. I recalled her long, solitary walks through a town in which you drove everywhere, in part to show off your car. I remembered marveling at the erectness of her carriage. I remembered watching men who marveled at what she carried with such pride. She might well have enjoyed provoking him, I thought.

"You can borrow it," he said.

"What?"

"You can keep the diary awhile. I have xeroxes. I figured you'd want to see the real thing."

"Oh. Thank you, Gene. But why?"

"They can't get away with it," he said.

"For the sake of argument," I said, "why not?"

"Because it's wrong. That's why I wanted you to know. I want it stopped, Sharon."

"You're asking me to stop Sam from—"

He said, *"Please?"*

I can't believe S! Silly-billy lover! Put the tube of jelly in his hand and he just held it. Asked me what it was for. Looked at me the way he does. I think I got wetter. He said O Boy. My boy lover. O Boy.

———

S says Sh frigid for months. How about those stories about her? Backseats and motels and quickies in cars? S says S wouldn't know where to put a cock without the instruction book. Here's what I told him—Lie down. He knew what I meant.

———

S thinks his daughter smokes pot. Got to talking, asked if he ever tried it, S surprised. Said I heard a good high gives great orgasms. We'll try it together if we can get some. Stay *young*. It's the ticket. Keep your body good and your lover crazy.

———

Gene growling like a dog these days. He smells it. Dogs can smell it on you.

———

You *can't* belong to other people. You have to belong to yourself. You have to love yourself. Then other people.

———

When S comes, his balls jump. Mexican Jumping Balls. S phones up and says Cucaracha! Makes me think of his balls. My lover's balls.

When I showed him the page after page of round, uncertain handwriting, Sam slapped the book from my fingers. I thought of Gene beating on Valerie and wondered if it was my turn. I said, "If you hit me, I might end up killing you, Sam."

He said, "I'll bear that contingency in mind."

"You understand, of course, that she's using you—this thing—affair—relationship—"

"Don't smirk, Sharon. Or I *will* hit you. And then you'll have to kill me, remember. And your mother will raise Joanna in Cleveland while you're a gray-haired convict. And for Christ's sake don't tell me about any *other* woman using adultery against her husband!"

"You think this is about 'adultery,' Sam? Your balls are jumping so high, they're blocking your vision."

"My *balls?*"

I retrieved the diary and painstakingly found the page for him.

Which brings me to Joanna, whom I had to hold and talk to after Sam, that night, took a room at the Valley Rest Motel, which is on the southern end of town. She let me talk, but she had no mercy for my need to hold. She twitched away from me that night. She paced the living room, touched the lampshades, prodded at books, moved records and discs on their shelves. She plucked at her hair and bunched her lips in disgust.

"You know what they'll say about Daddy? Big banker-man Daddy? They'll say, 'Old Sam Edel's been punching the town bag.'" She looked at me pointedly and then she looked away. "You know how humiliating this is?" She looked at me again and cried, "Oh, of *course* you do!" Her pale, imperious face went soft, and she ran to me like a fugitive from *Giselle*. We hugged. By the time I decided it was safe to close my eyes and enjoy what I could, her lean body had gone hard. "That *bitch,*" she whispered.

She endured my rubbing at her hair, and even my kisses. When I explained that her father might really be gone, she simply nodded. "He's angry," I said. "He's not a happy man. But he *adores* you, Joanna."

"That's nice," she said. "A guy'll tell you love all you want. They say it a lot. It's like at a hockey match. They sing 'The Star-Spangled Banner,' they look like nice kids, and then they beat the shit out of each other. It's a guy thing. I'm just not that terribly impressed. I love you. Right. Thanks ever so much."

"Oh, he means it, darling."

"Ma," my fourteen-year-old daughter instructed me, "they all mean it."

"Oh."

"We'll be all right," she said, like an older aunt, embracing me again. It was later, after the buttered popcorn, that she asked me to confirm the requirement under law that her father, once divorced from me, had to help pay her way through college. On behalf of the lawyer I hadn't consulted yet, I guaranteed. It was really then, as I promised Joanna her future, that I began to feel the fractures of our collapse.

S makes me feel worshipped. Says all women before me were girls. Kneels and kisses his way up my legs. Chews at me. I am my lover's food and he is mine. We were starving, but now we nourish each other.

Sam was still away two days later. We spoke coldly on the telephone. I said I'd be out of the house one morning so he could come for clothes. He agreed to a transfer of money from the joint account to my household account. I suggested that we get in touch with lawyers. He was silent for an instant, and then he hung up.

As I walked from the phone, it rang, and I formulated something chilly and not too intimate with which to greet him. But it wasn't Sam. It was the aqua-colored voice.

She said, "Mrs. Edel?"

"This is Sharon, Valerie. I recognize your voice. How are you?"

"Mrs. Edel—"

"Honey," I said, "you're screwing a man who's been married to me for fifteen years, so you can get your nutritious ass down off of your high horse and talk straight a little. You don't want to go around sounding like the district manager for Amway, do you?"

"I want your little snot bitch of a daughter to stop it. Now. And I mean it. That straight enough for you? Honey?"

"If my daughter—you better watch your mouth about her, Valerie. If there is a problem concerning my daughter, please feel as free as possibly only you can feel to tell me all about it."

"You're a possessive, dried-up prude, Sharon. So if he wanders to the warmer climates—"

"I'd call you a tropical rain forest in that case, Valerie. What about my daughter?"

"Tell her to stop stuffing every mailbox she can reach with her letter about *me*. That's what about her."

She hung up. I wondered if she and Sam had decided jointly to hang up on me that day. I went to our empty mailbox and looked across the street, then down our side of the block, and I saw the little white protrusions. As if I were entitled to, I went to my neighbors' house, withdrew the single white page from the box on their porch, and carried it home in clear view, not like a thief but as a citizen bearing the news.

Dear Occupant,
As you may have heard, my father, Mr. Samuel Edel and my mother, Ms. Sharon Hilsinger Edel have separated. Whether that is temporary or permanent, is not yet known. I'm sure the ever reliable town grapevine will let you know as soon as we do.

This is to set the record straight and do away with the rumors and innuendos. My father, Samuel Edel has been having an "affair" with a brainless slut named Ms. Valerie McClatchey. Otherwise known as "The Town Bag." I hear that men of Mr. Edel's age often do things like this e.i. getting oversexed and horny if their wives are getting somewhat mature. That is no excuse. However, I've been hearing vicious gossip that my mother, Ms. Edel pushed him into this type of "activity" by something she did. That is a lie. Mr. Edel went "sex mad" as many men do and broke his sacred marriage vows. He did it on his own e.i. leaving our bed and board. Ms. Edel is a right on woman. She did nothing wrong in this. I gladly put my reputation on the line to say this.

Mr. Edel will have to answer to heaven along with Ms. McClatchey.

Thank you for your time and attention.

Sincerely,
Joanna B. Edel

When I came home, I had Joanna's letter from the Lewis house, from Feimster and Murray and the crazy people on the corner with all the cats. I didn't have it from the Lutheran Home or the Noels'. Mrs. Montemora had beaten me to her mailbox. I had it from Hilsenrath and Boynton and Hendricks. I had turned the corner onto Canal Street, which is also the old north-south highway, and the street had suddenly seemed unnaturally bright, the cars too terribly loud, the people outside the gas-and-electric and the drugstore like a surging mob in a movie—say, *King Kong.* There were too many mail slots in too many doors, too many postboxes, too many streets off Canal, and too many houses on each of the streets. I knew Joanna. Now I knew why I had heard the printer next to our word processor—it had sounded like a little electrical saw during the night. She had printed enough letters for a lot of the boxes in town. And she would have tried to reach them, stalking on her stiff, long legs, her chin up to signify her dignity, her story—Joanna's story about the story—in her backpack and in each of her small hands.

She was late from school. Or maybe her deliveries had taken the entire day. It was almost six, and I was sitting in the perfumed squalor of her room. There were more of the letters in a pile on her desk. Dear Occupant.

I reread one, the line about Ms. Edel, who was a right on woman. Joanna, from her doorway, said, "Why are you in my room? Why are you reading my stuff?"

I said, "I'm an occupant. And how private is a letter you've delivered to every address in the ZIP code? Is that your *hair,* darling?"

It was short, ear-level on one side, a little shorter on the other. It was the color of yellow cough drops, and it looked as though it would glow in the dark. Her lips looked rigid, and her eyes were very wide. She pulled the wiry bunched hair that heaped the top of her head and she flushed as, pulling more hair, she exposed what was a quarter of a shaved scalp. *"This* is my hair," she said.

I thought for an instant that if I dyed my hair the color of hers, she would somehow be less alone in the midst of our lives. But I knew promptly that I wasn't cut out for a cough drop. I said her name a few times.

"It just looked cool when I did it," she said. "Nothing else. It's not the biggest deal in the world. I *like* it like this, Mommy, so don't start, all right?"

I said her name again. And then we were both wailing, and assuring each other that it was only *hair* for Godsakes and, after all, it was going to grow back.

That's the story. It straggles off into Gene McClatchey's swollen, masked, and splinted nose—broken, according to the usual sources, by his wife, who stayed awhile and then left. Sam left, too, to run a bank branch in Sidney, New York, where he lives alone and dates young secretaries and is said to look seedy. Joanna and I came to Cleveland, where her hair grew in as black and thick and springy as before. Everyone in the story thought they were going to die of it, but of course they didn't. Once you're in a story, you must live forever. You must choose again and again. You always do it the same.

Are We Pleasing You Tonight?

WE WERE VERY BUSY, and the rooms were loud. Even the kitchen was loud, though our chef never stood for noise that wasn't necessary. I kept thinking I could hear the barman whistle through his teeth— Comin round the mountain when she *comes*—which he often did when he made mixed drinks. We had two seven-fifteens, a party of three, and a party of two, and the three came early. The old lady led them, then came the son, and then his wife. I looked away from the wife because she was the same bad news I'd been receiving all day.

The old lady was very small, maybe under five feet tall, and her skin was that pale, tender white you only see on the extremely old. Her wraparound skirt and rayon blouse were too large, and I expected her to walk out of her scuffed, low-heeled pumps, like a kid playing Mommy in her parents' bedroom. She didn't shuffle, though. She had a kind of stride, although she wobbled as if the bottoms of her feet were tender. Or maybe it was balance, I remember thinking. The world was spinning a little too fast, or gravity wasn't working right on her, and something kept pulling her slightly sideways. The son walked with his head down, as if she embarrassed him, or as if he embarrassed himself. That's a choice, right there, isn't it? How you call it is who you are.

"How are you?" she asked me before I could say it to her. And she asked as if she knew me. Of course, a lot of people out there thought I was someone to know. It wasn't quite Rick's Place, but it was a good restaurant. I ran it tight, the food was Provençal, we cooked it well and served good wines. I cultivated my tall, tough manner, and my clientele worked to make me smile. People who spend a lot when they dine out consider their money better spent when the people who sell it to them make believe they're friends. As for my famous service, I had learned to run a squad while attached to Graves Registration, and my career had taken me from dishing out the dead to *daube Aixoise*.

"Ah, and *you!*" I said, as if with sudden pleasure.

"Peter," she said, "this is my son, Kent, and his wife, Linda. This is Peter," she said to them. "He owns this lovely place."

It was the way she said Peter. She rounded off the *r* just a little, and I heard New York or New Jersey—she'd say *ah* instead of *are*—and not Southport, Connecticut. I thought I recalled that she'd come, once or twice, with a handsome old man. He was burly the first time, then waxy and thin several months later. I'd forgotten them. Her son was broad and sunburned, his brown hair was bright with highlights of red and light brown from saltwater sailing.

As I seated them, his mother said, "Peter, I wonder if you would instruct our waiter to leave the fourth place setting. It's my husband's birthday. He died."

"I was very sorry to hear about it."

"You heard?"

I bowed my neck and shut my eyes an instant. I didn't want to have to lie again.

She frowned, and her skin, I thought, might crack. Her teeth were dingy with a kind of heavy film. Her dark hair was thinning. And still, she was a pretty thing. She must have been one of those small Austrian cuties with her narrow nose and prominent cheekbones. "Tonight is my husband's birthday," she said. "Kent and Linda and I are having dinner with him." She said it as though the husband had forced his way to dinner with them. He was dead, and she was sorrowful, and he'd been hers, and she was dining in his honor, but he still, according to some definition I hadn't yet heard, was uninvited.

I turned toward the empty chair and nodded deeply. I said, "Happy birthday." I'd fed stranger tables. I had supervised the emptying of cargo planes filled with the horribly dead, the routinely dead, the accidentally dead, and the dead who'd been murdered by people under their command. Service is service.

"Isn't he lovely?" she asked her son and daughter-in-law about me. I tried to avoid the daughter-in-law's eyes. Linda's eyes. She wasn't the twin of the kid in the papers, but she looked enough like her. I had trouble with that. I was having a bad night, and I'd had a bad day.

"He's wonderful," Linda said. Her voice was edgy and entertained at once. It didn't make my night any easier. I refused to meet her eyes.

"I'll take drink orders, and your waiter, Luc, will be over shortly," I said. There was a line at the reservations desk, Luc for Lucien was tripping on something he was managing well enough, but I thought he might be ready to fly, there was a new kid making salads, and it had been a very bad day. In light of which, after taking their orders for Johnnie Walker Black straight up, Beefeater martini rocks, and the house white, a Chalone from Monterey, I turned to the old lady—I thought I could see through the skin of her jaw—and asked her, "Are you going all the way?"

She had brown-green eyes that looked faded, as bleached as her son's thick hair. They smiled when her thin, chapped lips did. "I imagine that I am," she said.

"I meant—" I gestured toward the empty chair.

"No," her son said.

The sound came up as the kitchen opened. My chef was probably getting on the kid. And I needed to get to the desk.

"What a wonderful idea," she said.

Linda, who was tan and not red, and whose blond-brown hair was in those thick, wavy strands, said, "You must have a wonderful imagination, Peter."

That's right. That's right.

"Bourbon?" she asked her son.

"Maker's Mark," he told me, "rocks, water back."

I said, "Thank you. And a happy birthday to—to—" I smiled to finish. I had looked. Now I couldn't stop looking at the daughter-in-law's dark eyes. She was the ghost of the ghost I had seen. It was a terrible night.

By the time I left their drinks order at the service bar and seated people who'd been waiting, the noise level in both rooms was high enough to drown out the shouting in the kitchen. I was on my way there when a yachtsman decided that he and his companion would not wait any longer. He didn't wear socks, and I could see that even his ankles were sunburned. His shirt was open to show the sunburned flesh beneath the coarse gray hair of his chest, though all three of his blazer buttons were fastened. He wanted none of us to miss the golden Bill Blass emblems.

I said, "Let me bring you another round of drinks. I know you and your daughter have been waiting for a while."

"Daughter?" he said.

"Oh," I said, but with a little too much relish in my voice. "Sorry. My mistake."

"You're damned right," he said, taking her hand and aiming them at the door. *"Damned* right."

I smiled at the guests who entered across their bow and told them with the correct hint of regret about their ten-minute wait. I took their order for drinks to the service bar and noted that a tray of cocktails was ready to be delivered. It was the water chaser, in the squat Italian tumbler we used for those purposes, that told me whose order it was. I took the tray to them and apologized for the delay.

The daughter-in-law said nothing, the son thanked me, his mother shrugged as if to signal that, among us working folk, such matters are understood. Definitely a Jew from New York, I thought. We all seemed to fancy ourselves, once in a while, Marxists once removed. When I leaned to set down the bourbon and then the chaser, I saw they'd placed two photographs on the appetizer plate of the fourth place setting.

I looked, I moved a step away, and then, as if to arrange the drinks better, I stepped back. Linda said, "Help yourself." Her voice was as dark as her eyes. Ghost bitch, I thought. I stepped alongside her into the musky cinnamon of her perfume, and I looked down at the pictures. One was of the son, Kent, in happy, animated conversation with a bald, broad-shouldered man an inch or so taller than he. The man, apparently the father who had died, was facing Kent and therefore not the camera. And, in the other, on some path near a lake or pond, carrying a rucksack over one shoulder, this same man was striding from whatever held the camera. When I looked up, his widow was frowning in real distress.

I saw Lucien floating up behind her. Oh, he was on something, I thought. He had a goofy smile on his thin, handsome face, and his lids were flapping as if to keep his eyeballs in his head.

"Luc will take your order. The wine list you see. We have a Domaine du Pesquier Gigondas I like, and it's a good price. The Cahors is inky and full of fruit, unusually good body. The Puligny-Montrachet is *not* a good price, but it's a gorgeous wine. So's the Arneis. If you select the duck special, which Lucien will discuss with you, the Diamond Creek, a fairly dark cabby, would be a happy marriage."

"What a lovely and unusual expression," Linda said. "You really enjoy your work." She said it the way you might tell a child what a big, strong boy he is. Thank you, bitch of a ghost, I didn't say.

"Ladies," I said. And then I couldn't resist it: "Gentlemen. Enjoy." To Luc, bearing down on their table like a fireman on call, I whispered, "A special celebration. A—kind of birthday. You will be alert, please, to their requirements?"

In the kitchen, one of the exhaust fans was faltering. I apologized to Abbie, my chef. She was the tallest person in the room, and that included the kid doing salads, who was over six feet tall. She was also, except for the daughter-in-law in the party of three or, counting dead people, four, the handsomest woman in the restaurant that night. Her long oval face was unhappy now, but not because of the heat. She was orchestrating dinners, and she danced, concentrating. It gave her a displeased expression. Fires flared as she or the sous-chef, Caroline, poured wine into pans. I asked if we had enough duck. Abbie strode like an athlete, spun like a chorus girl, scattered shallots, dipped out gold-green oil and ignored me. Caroline, her deputy, nodded that we did.

To the college boy composing endive, radicchio, scallions, and red-leaf lettuce, I said, "You're doing fine. Don't let the greens get soupy with the vinaigrette. Better to give them too little than too much. In the case of dressing, anyway. *Ça va?*"

He looked up.

"Okay?"

He said, "Sure."

"When it's *your* place, it's sure. In my place, when I ask, you *make* sure and then you tell me, so I *feel* sure. Correct?"

"Yes, sir," he said.

"That's what *ça va* means. Good man."

I went out the kitchen back door, and I stood behind the place, between the stuttering exhaust fan and the one that worked, and I looked down the dark slope of the hill. I lit up and leaned against the wall. At eight in the morning, in the kitchen of my house, four miles away, while mist blew in from the sea and it was chilly enough to make me consider using the fireplace, I'd made the *café filtré* and opened *The New York Times*. It was a stab at discipline, and of course it was a sham, but I never lit the first cigarette until I had read the sports and was ready to look at the business pages. To get there, I turned past the wedding announcements while I lit up, sighing it in, and I saw the face of Tamara Wynn, the girl I had loved in college, and when I was unloading corpses at Dover Air Force Base during the war, and when I was in the first and second graduate schools I'd tried. By the time I was at the Cornell management program, I was past talking about her with the women with whom I tried hard to fall in love, one of whom I'd married.

We'd been the usual story. I was unreconciled to her departure for other men and then marriage to a surgeon. I didn't die of it, but she had died of something about which I hadn't heard. I read in the *Times* how her daughter, Courtney—wasn't there a year when every female born east of the Mississippi received that name?—had been given in marriage by the widowed father, who had been a premed in the class ahead of mine. There was the picture of Courtney, except it looked like her mother. Tamara, with her high brow and wide mouth and reserved, quizzical smile, looked out of the *Times* and up over thirty years.

All I could think to say that morning—I heard my voice; it sounded like a kind of wounded groan—was "Oh. Hello."

Dottie, on her way into the kitchen, said, "Hello to *you*. That was pretty enthusiastic for first thing in the morning."

It wasn't you, Dot. It was the one I loved. It was the daughter of the one I loved. It was dead people. That's my job: meet 'em and greet 'em. Hello.

I put the cigarette out against the wall of my restaurant and stripped it, letting the tobacco and paper fly in the wind. I put the filter in my pocket. I wondered how many ash marks pocked the wall outside the kitchen. I went back in, tucked and groomed in the men's room, wiped the sink clean, and rearranged the white cotton washcloths we folded on a table to be used as towels. Then I went to visit my customers. I managed, by striking off at odd angles, to save until the last the table of three or, depending on how you feel about it, four, one of whom was a woman who could have been the twin of the picture I had seen in the paper. Note this: she was not Courtney or a sister. I could see the differences—a dimpling of chin, a fullness at the neck, the closeness of this woman's eyes compared to Courtney's and Tamara's.

Nevertheless, how *is* that for extracorporeal life? Most nights, you sell food and drink and it's deposited in verifiable flesh. Here, in twelve hours, I had seen two ghosts, and one of them ate a steak of swordfish marinated in oil, white wine, thyme, marjoram, salt, and red pepper flake, accompanied by a scallion risotto and roasted carrots along with a glass of house white at a table one quarter of which was occupied by somebody dead.

The pictures had been moved. The one of the dead fellow walking with his rucksack was, despite the absence of his face, facedown. The other lay near the son, Kent, who was finishing the last of a Black Angus steak we sear on a grill over hardwood and dried grapevines. A good bottle of Châteauneuf-du-Pape, the Vieux Telegraphe, was close to his plate. His mother had given up on her grilled fresh sardines. She was drinking mineral water. Her Scotch was unfinished. She looked to be tasting something spiny and corrosive. As I came up, and Linda's face assumed its look of amusement, I heard the old woman say, "And then, every time, in spite of my best efforts, I remember the dishonesty and disloyalty. How can I forgive them? And I *try*. You compartmentalize your life, and soon you get locked in one of the compartments. And I was locked in another. And guess who'd kept the key?" She raised the mineral water, then put it down. "Still," she said.

Luc hurried past. He was sweating through his shirt and his face ran slick. His eyes were huge, and I couldn't imagine his being able to see for the constant batting of his eyelids. I held a finger in the air, which was normally a sufficient signal for my waiters. It meant they must meet me at the back corner of the service bar *now*.

Linda said, "Is everything all right, Peter?"

"Aren't you kind to ask, madame," I said. "It's a busy night. I must seem preoccupied. Forgive me. Are you pleased? Are we pleasing you tonight?" I had to look at her—I don't know. Yes: I had to look at her encyclopedically. I did. I looked at the way her throat creased when she moved her head. I looked at the folding of flesh at her wrists when she moved her flatware. I looked at the width of her shoulders, the size of her muscled upper arms, the flatness of her barely arched brows.

She said, "What?"

I fled the question. "And you, madame?" I asked her mother-in-law. "Sir?" I said to the son.

Most of a bottle of wine was in his answer: "Ask him."

"Pardon?"

"You didn't ask him." He pointed with his fork at the photographs on the table. Luc went past again, and I raised my finger. He nodded, raised his finger in reply, and all but loped for the kitchen. Tonight, Luc was the amphetamine king, I thought. Tomorrow, he was on probation or canned, I didn't yet know which. I carefully did not look at the woman who smelled so good, who smiled so cruelly, and who bore the face of the woman whose face on her daughter had greeted my day.

The old lady's lips were pursed. It was as if she fought a pain. She looked at her son and then at the photographs. She shook her head. The son gestured again with his fork. I looked at the unused place setting. He was there, of course, though I didn't see him. The son did. So did the widow. I didn't watch to see where the daughter-in-law looked. Though the rest of them couldn't see who sat in Linda's place, I knew, and I didn't want to know, and I stood in silence, my hands clasped before the waist of my lightweight midnight-blue tuxedo, a man of admittedly studied elegance who tried to smile for the clients. Who couldn't, though.

"Cat's got his whatever," the son said.

From out of the kitchen came Luc. He seemed to roll, as if on casters, across the floor. He moved with grace, the burden of his upper body cradled on stiff muscles, while his hips and thighs moved flexibly to cushion his cargo's ride. I saw another waiter, Charles, and the barman, Raymond, as they watched Luc move. They were timing it, as they so often did. I had trained my staff well. By the time he'd arrived behind the old woman, then had moved around her and into her line of sight, the kid from the kitchen, Raymond and Charles had stepped forward.

Luc had listened well to my parting instructions. "We would like, *'sieurs-dames,* to present, for the celebration of your birthday, this token of our absolutely happiest wishes." His voice sounded ever so slightly as if he'd been sucking helium. His eyes goggled as his mouth moved. He bowed, sweating and red-faced, over the small gâteau made with no flour and crushed almonds and imported apricot preserve on which five token candles flared. "And may I ask whose birthday it is?"

The old woman looked at the cake. I saw again how thin and stretched her pale, frayed skin was. Her mouth was open. Her son, lying back in his chair, slowly lifted his soiled white napkin. I thought he might drape it over his face, but he carefully wiped his lips and pointed to the empty chair. I did not look at the daughter-in-law.

Luc strode to stand between the daughter-in-law and the photographs. He looked at me. I shook my head. He didn't know what I meant. Neither did I. He sang, in his drug-enriched tenor, "Happy birthday to you—" And Charles and Raymond joined him, and so did the boy who made the salads, and so did several diners at tables nearby.

Luc mumbled some sounds as he realized he didn't know the birthday celebrant's name. He bestowed the cake on the table, he bowed, and he left to offer service to hungry people who awaited him. The other men went back to their work.

"I am so sorry," I told the old woman. For she had been betrayed again. "It was a misunderstanding."

"Yes," she said. I tried to meet her faded, angry eyes.

The son cleared his throat. He held the photographs. He looked at them with a sorrow I found familiar.

The daughter-in-law's expression was only a little puzzled. I realized she'd seen how susceptible I was to her. She wondered why, but not too much. She didn't mind my appetite. She said to me, "Misunderstanding?"

"Yes," the old woman said, "it always is."

Machias

A CENTURY'S ALMOST OVER, JACK.

Today, I spent my late Saturday morning on the run in that wonderful golden light off the Sound at Lincoln Park. The Fauntleroy-Vashon ferry hooted happily, and I thought, as I outran strollers, that when a front moves in and the sky drops, and everything goes gray and clammy, when you can wipe the water off your face but it isn't raining, the ferries—Southwerth-Vashon, Bremerton-Seattle, the Winslow, the Victoria—sound somber, even sad. I was thinking how what you see and hear depends so much on who you are at the time. I was thinking of a work whistle I used to hear when we spent summers above a small bay in Maine, and the sardine cannery let go its bellow at seven every morning and then at noon, at one and then at five, and your mother and I were still married.

So, with aching shins, resolving once more to give up on the dream of health, yearning for a weekend of sleeping late and marketing unwisely on Pike Place, ogling the impossibly healthy women who might buy eight ounces of yogurt while I bought eight of cholesterol to go with a Pinot Noir, I came back and checked the mail, and there was your wedding invitation.

Now, your love for Melissa, The Marvelous Melissa as you say,

TMM as you called her in your long and wonderfully moving letter to me about "finding the person forever who," came as no surprise. Your plans to marry were clear. Your generation, I might say, in spite of nipples pierced with golden rings, in spite of post-retrofunk clothing and music born of acid tabs, is predictable and even, finally, conservative. But it was the wedding itself that threw me. I read the invitation before and after my shower and, as you can tell from the water stains on the RSVP card that this letter will accompany, I stood and dripped a lot, thinking about you and TMM and your marriage.

I will not bore you with my actually saying, out loud, "My baby's getting married. My *baby* is getting *married.*" Nor will I burden you with the phone call I placed, at eleven-fifteen Pacific Time, to your mother, sleeping beside your stepfather, who that morning was not patrolling the Appalachian Trail. It mightn't displease you to hear that she and I spoke cordially and got choked up, and maybe wept together for an instant, talking about the wedding of which she would be a member and I would be a guest.

And I sat down and thought about Maine again. First I thought about you, and then I thought about us, before you were born, when we were very young and President Kennedy had been dead for five years, and we were five years away from the divorce. We were living in Brookline, then. Your mother designed jackets for books, and I worked cityside for the *Globe*. Your mother's mother left us a little money, and one summer we drove to Maine and cruised the back roads, looking for something nobody else would think of. We found a narrow blacktop road off US 1, and we took it to a little beach of black rocks. From there we took a dirt road that went uphill and we drifted inland a little, since we figured that no one near the ocean would sell at what we could afford. The dirt road became a track, very narrow and stony. It curled back around in the direction of the sea and it took us to an eastward slope that went down past two houses fairly close together, and then steepened, then dropped toward water. The road stopped, above an inlet leading toward the bay, a few hundred yards from the first house, made of shake shingles, its roof falling in, clearly abandoned, with a poster tacked to the side door. The hillside, we learned, was in a place called Machias.

(Say match *eye* us.) Your mother made me stop, and she went to read the sign. I predicted that the sign would warn off trespassers, but it invited them, she shouted, to call a certain realtor. As I stepped outside the car, the whistle on what we'd learn was the sardine cannery sounded. It bellowed like a burly man's welcome.

We were so far north and east, a short drive from Lubec and pretty close to Canada, that we thought we had discovered a new country. Given the arrival of President Nixon, and the word *fascist* everywhere—it was the *real* f-word—and given the sad sense we had, like so many others, of genuine apocalypse, it was precisely a harbor we sought. We wanted someplace very much elsewhere. We were babies in a fallen place, and we were looking for home. Here, self-conscious as maybe you never have been, we were happy under a sky patrolled by nothing more than gulls. We did a few trips between Brookline and the house on weekends, and then we closed on the house and a dozen acres for very little, and we came for our vacation to bring back a place neglected for years. Your mother was talented, I was brawny, and a falling-down house seemed to us merely one more logistical problem to solve: jack the beams, replace some posts and sills, tear some walls down, stud up, lay in plasterboard, hang new doors, tear off shingle and rotted runners, lay down plywood and roofing paper—you know, just *move* things. We were more or less right for a while.

When we bought the place, your mother was worried about the neighbors, whoever lived about twenty yards below us in a house that, like ours, was a basic saltbox with smaller sections added on over the years and covered with creosoted shakes. I vowed to build a six-foot-high fence if the neighbors proved obtrusive. In fact, they lay low. We somehow saw no one for all of the weekends we came up before we closed on the place, and for most of our two-week summer vacation. It was the Saturday near the end, Labor Day approaching, when we would have to pack the car, abandon the tools and building materials, stop sleeping on and eating at the chapped furniture that had come with the house, most of it bought long ago at Montgomery Ward. We were grouchy with each other, but only because we had to leave, and we knew that. We were very good friends for a fairly long time, don't forget. The age of the house, and the tough, taxing work we did, our distance from trafficked roads and any talk about Spiro T. Agnew or the war—we didn't even listen to a radio that first summer—had given us a feeling of removal that we relished. We talked about ourselves as shipwrecked. We lay on the grass out front and listened to the sardine cannery whistle or the unlaboring chug of a fishing boat making for the inlet's neck and then Machias Bay and then the ocean.

Your mother stood above me as I lay with my head under a bathroom sink, trying to connect the trap to new pipe that I'd connect with the waste line. She was wearing Wellingtons, and she pressed a wet, heavy boot against my stomach and she pushed.

"Ease off," I warned her, puffing my belly up at her boot.

I heard a heavy click and then the noise of a spring releasing. She fired, and the staple hit me in the stomach from which she'd taken her foot.

"Okay," she said. "I eased off." She fired again.

"I'm glad we didn't buy a shotgun," I said, trying to turn a screw in a clamp.

She didn't answer. I heard her reload the staple gun and then shoot some more.

"This isn't very satisfactory," your mother said after a while.

"You'd prefer we got a shotgun, then?"

"Jerk," she said. "I don't want to go back."

"We can get a telephone installed for not much more than a million dollars, counting the cost of the poles they'd have to set in, and you could freelance from here," I said. "And I could file copy on, you know, a breaking-and-entering at Dinah's Antique Linen and Chowder Shoppe." In the voice of some guy in a movie wearing a fedora and a thin mustache, I snapped, " 'Hello! *Boston Globe?* Get me Rewrite!' "

She fired a few staples, but at a tired pace: her heart wasn't in the shooting. I wriggled out and lay beneath her, looking up the considerable length of your mother's young legs and her almost flat chest and those big shoulders. I have to tell you, Jack, it was the shoulders, often, that got to me. As a once-married man to an almost-married man, let me say that I reached up for her and got hold of some dungaree and I yanked. I went for her, staple gun and all, and she promptly made it clear that some dusty rolling around in the shattered bathroom of an old house was as much antidote as we would find to our unnamed, wearying dread about the life we were returning to.

And it was just then that a man's voice outside the house, near the bathroom window, said, "Well." We lay still and then pulled at clothing and climbed to our feet.

Your mother whispered, "The city editor?"

I shook my head and whispered back, "Rewrite."

Your mother's lean, long face looked so youthful, then, so fresh in a world we thought of as dangerous, so vulnerable in the damaged little room at which we'd worked, that I put my hands behind my back and, like a boy, leaned over to kiss her smooth cheek.

She whispered, "What?"

"Tribute," I remember telling her.

And I remember how, concentrating on what might wait for us, she simply, silently, nodded, and we went outside.

Charley Kingfield, we would learn his name was, stood and settled his wide-brimmed brown felt hat. He wore the expression of a man who'd been expecting someone who always, disappointingly, came late. He stood in the almost orderly explosion of our lumber, our plumbing supplies, our Sheetrock under tarpaulins, my table saw and boxes of nails, and he said, "Well."

This led to introductions and his volunteering that he was home from recuperating at his widowed sister's, in Searsport, and that he'd been operated on. "For the hernia," he said, tipping his hat to your mother, perhaps because he thought that the surgery, near his loins, suggested intimacy.

He asked, in a slushy voice that always made me want to clear my throat, "What city do you come to us from?"

I answered, and then I asked him the same.

"Shit 'n' goddamn," he said, laughing and showing us his big, yellow teeth, "*no* damn city. I'm from over *there*." He pointed to the house below ours. "Used to be the only person here for eight years after Eleanora died. Me and the goddamn gulls"—he pointed at them, drifting up from their patrol near the cannery. "And Bobo," he said.

"Your son?" your mother asked.

"My goddamn cow," Charley said. "Ate her, finally, two winters ago. She was awful close to indigestible. That was because I'd raised her for the milk, not for eating. Then I went allergic on milk and every other damned thing. 'My son,' " he said derisively.

And, of course, your mother lost her temper. "I forget," she said, "did we *invite* you to come up here and laugh at us, or did you decide it was something you had to do, like a kind of down east welcome wagon?"

" 'Welcome wagon,' " he said, baring his teeth at me and laughing while he pointed at your mother. "That's good," he said.

She probably didn't hear that, because she had already turned and gone to the house, those grand shoulders somehow not swaying as she strode away.

"Piss her off, did I? Didn't mean to," he said. He shyly looked away from my face as he said, "If you can get her to change her mind, you can come down tomorrow. I eat early. Always cook a pot of beans for Sunday night. Brown sugar and fatback, good whiskey, everything the way it's supposed to be. Bring her if you want to."

He wore a navy-blue woolen shirt buttoned to the neck, and his hands were in his pockets, as if because of the cold. It was hot and windless, the sky was the sort that you squinted into but in which you couldn't at first find the sun. He walked slowly and, I realized, with care. He was old, and he seemed to feel fragile. I thought of him, after that, as something that might easily break. When we drove up, after that weekend, I always worried that we'd find him damaged, motionless someplace, his furrowed, broad face as smooth as a sleeping child's. I thought of him at a Sunday-night supper he had eaten with his wife and then alone for eight years. Eleanora, I thought. And I thought—I *knew*—that I would never live above a bay and cook and eat alone and think of a woman who once was my wife.

Your mother relented, though I did have to beg a little, and we went that night to Sunday supper at the old man's home. His house was very dark, and the small dining room, with its sticky table and chairs, its sideboard on which were propped pictures of vessels under sail, was lit by two kerosene lanterns, one on the table and one on a hook near the door.

Your mother said, "Do you have electricity?"

Charley, in the kitchen, called, "I got TV and electric lights and I'm on the goddamn telephone."

"Honey," I whispered, "the lanterns are for *atmosphere*. We're guests."

"God," she said. "You're right. Do we really need this? God."

Charley came in with a bottle of Canadian whiskey and three shot glasses. He opened the sideboard and brought up a bottle of sweet sherry. "For the lady," he said to me. He turned to her and said, "For you." So he and I sipped whiskey and your mother threw down three shot glasses of sherry. Charley watched her with some approval, I thought.

"Oh, yes," he said, as if one of us had asked, "sailed for forty year. Fished for cod halfway up to Russia one year, fished haddock out of Dalhousie. Shit, I pulled net in and out of Campobello until twenty years ago when my joints started in freezing up on me. You get killed, pulling net, and your back don't work right. If the goddamn boom don't come around on you, you being too slow to slip away from the net and duck, then the captain'll kill you for costing him catch. You die either way. I figured, come back up on shore and die slower." He poured whiskey with a very steady hand. He let your mother pour her own sherry. "That's what I've been doing here."

Your mother said, "What?"

He said, "I'd embarrass myself to repeat it, miss."

"Janine," your mother said, and her voice was soft and sad. I remember that, and I remember how his face responded to her, the sweet smile, the yellow teeth.

"That's a beautiful name," he said. "That's an old-fashioned name, sure as shit. Goes back to *my* time." That's when I thought that it wasn't we—playing house, working to bring the house back, but playing, somehow, compared to him—it wasn't we who were ship-wrecked, who stranded ourselves on the coast of Maine. It was

Charley, it was the old sailor, who was all alone in a loud and shift-ing time. I watched him talking to your mother, another man af-fronted and then beguiled by her. He cleaned his glasses on the paper napkin at his place setting, then he stood to walk, sockless in bedroom slippers, to the kitchen and his beans. "Kind of a high-class woman for a hippie boy like you," he said.

"Try and remember that," your mother told me. While he was out of the room, she took my shot glass and drank my whiskey down. Then we ate beans, smoky and pungent, very sweet, boiled so that the skins were off and the liquid was thick on the Wonder Bread we dipped, drinking sherry or Black Velvet whiskey, readily telling Charley, as if we knew so very well, who we were.

On our sagging mattress on the Montgomery Ward bed, in the darkness of the house we'd sought as someplace to escape to, not knowing precisely what we fled, we decided that benign forces had provided him as an adjunct to our house.

"He's the history around here," your mother said.

"He's the father figure," I said.

"Well, that's all right," she said. "If that's what we need, and that's who he is, and nobody minds, then fine."

"Maybe he's just a mascot. People shouldn't be mascots."

"How about Mickey Rooney? He's made a *career* out of being a mascot."

"He gets paid a lot of dough for it," I said.

"Charley can have us for Sunday dinners. He can get to tell us about his life. That's what *he* needs."

"That's what he needs?"

"It's what everyone needs," your mother said.

I said, "I didn't know that."

"Trust me."

"Everyone?"

She said, "Everyone."

"You?"

After a while, she said, "Maybe."

"What? What's *your* story?"

"You already know it," she said,

"No, I mean the real one, the thing that you go around needing all the time to tell. Like Charley."

"You," she said. "You're my story."

"Really?" I heard her head on the old, soft pillow. I couldn't tell whether she nodded or shook it. I said to her, "Then you're *my* story. Is that what you're saying?"

"You tell me," your mother said.

We went back to Brookline, and your mother designed dust jackets while I reported on what seemed to be the news. You've probably never read the books her jackets decorated. A riot on the Boston Common occasioned by a road repair crew assailing four girls carrying posters about murder in Vietnam will be unknown to you. Like those activities at the time, our lives seemed extraordinarily laden, of course. Imagining how my words about them must disappear in your mind, lost in the heavy traffic of thoughts about matters, now, of *real* importance, I suddenly feel as stranded in the nineties as Charley was stranded in your mother's younger days and mine. There. I've made myself feel old enough to have a married son.

We went up to Maine for weekends all autumn and winter. On a snowy night, when we were there to see to the new roof and the pipes we'd drained of water and filled with antifreeze—that weekend, we used the old outhouse: we called it the time machine, since we rode it above the waste of a hundred years—we decided to stay until Monday. That meant a Sunday evening of Canadian whiskey and beans. By then, your mother had convinced Charley that he wasn't betraying her youth, beauty, or sex by serving her the same Black Velvet at which the menfolk sipped.

Years later, we agreed that it was about the time of that winter weekend that we each suspected privately that the trouble we were in was large. I suspected myself first. That is, I noticed how I noticed your mother's pleasure in gently seducing Charley. She cut his hair some fair weekends, carrying a kitchen chair outside into the sun and draping a bath towel around his neck, then slowly, with a lot of soft brushings at his head and neck with her light, long-fingered hands, she groomed him, causing him to shiver and blush. I found it remarkable that I thought cruel her mostly innocent pleasure in making Charley respond. And I saw it as a sign, I remember—as a kind of cat's-paw disturbance in the water that told of a coming, maybe problematic, larger wind. I wasn't much of a sailor, of course. And, even then, I saw myself as judgmental and presumptuous. But I also, somehow, saw that something was on its way. I didn't trust myself, quite, in the matter of your mother's pleasure in making a man respond. But I didn't wholly discount my feelings. And this, while I'm confessing, might round the matter off: when she trimmed my hair, as she usually did, and when she didn't brush her hands against the flesh behind my ears or at the nape of my neck or near my jaw, I felt disappointed, maybe even betrayed. I was jealous—what other word can I use?—of an eighty-year old man.

So: a winter weekend, our stolen extra night, and supper with Charley, who got a little glassy-eyed by the time he served us each a dessert plate with a Hostess Twinkie on it. He'd been silent, often, looking away and squinting, clearly trying to remember something. As he chewed away at his dessert, he smiled—it wasn't a pretty moment, given the yellows of tooth and cake to which we were exposed—because he had obviously recalled what he'd been reaching for.

"It's the goddamn snow brought it back," he said. "But my damned brain, she works slow as molasses some nights, you know, just wouldn't yield it *up."*

"Oh, me too," your mother said.

"Is that an honest fact?" Charley asked her. "It happens to you, too. They just plain damned elude you when you reach for them?"

"Me and old longhair over there," your mother said. It had never escaped Charley that my hair reached my shoulders and almost came to my eyes.

"Actual fact," Charley said. "Shit 'n' goddamn, I don't mind hearing that." He goggled at your mother, and I have to say that in the brown light of those kerosene lanterns, she looked like a slightly too-slender girl in a seventeenth-century painting. I was probably looking at her as goofily as Charley.

"Well," he said, "I remember it now. This had to have happened in the nineteen and thirties. Primitive days around here," he said. "I wasn't married at the time, and I was visiting a girl a good deal younger than me that I didn't like much but was awfully eager to, well, know. To tell you the truth she had a reputation. I believe you understand me and I'd like to let it go pretty delicate at that.

"How was I to know she had a cousin choosing to visit that night, along with her husband and her sister, I believe it was. Full house! Not so far from here—near the boarded-up church where the road narrows down. It was a considerable walk from where I was living at the time. I kept a room ashore, and I was home between a long trip and whatever I'd sign on for. I believe I was considering something to do with freight on the Great Lakes, and I finally turned it down. I liked oceans in those days. Well. I was as they say sparking, and it wasn't hard work. Except for a cousin who happened to be about ten months gone pregnant, and the whimpering, snot-nosed husband of hers, her fat father and fatter mother, and the sister of the pregnant cousin who started in crying when one of us noticed it had snowed, so sudden and heavy, we would all be sleeping there for the night.

"And that, you see, was when the wires broke from the weight of the snow. Not that many people were on the phone, those times, and it was such a treat to have, most folks didn't complain when a wire went down, you understand. What it was happened, though, was the cousin, of course, volunteered she would be delivering her baby in the next couple of hours. Can you hear it? Can you picture it? Labor going on all over the place. Mother and father snarling like hungry dogs and just one bone in the house. Everybody else handing out suggestions you couldn't use no matter what language they said them in.

"Well, we knew we had to call a doctor. We had to get *somebody* in on account of I'd walked there and the other folks had come in a car that couldn't go any further'n we could push it, or the little truck the girl's parents ran. We'd need someone with horses to get a doctor there quick enough, and they'd best be getting started soon. All this is going on in the dark, understand, though I believe they might not have had electricity anyhow. Took 'em long enough to get a big bunch of candles and lamps lit, I remember. And then we all kind of walked

in circles, keeping as far away, most of us, from the poor girl just
about to give birth. Or so she said. She was big enough around, as I
recall."

Can you bear with me through this? I'm really addressing myself
to the RSVP and TMM and most of all to you, Jack. I'm remembering, too, a night you phoned me up, Columbus, Ohio, to Seattle,
Washington, breathing so hard I thought at first you'd run to the
telephone. Your argument with Melissa, or hers with you, sat heavy
on your chest. You were fighting gravity that worked against you
even inside of your ribs. You were beginning to learn to maybe count
on less. Perhaps more than one or two lessons are required. It's nothing any of us want ever to believe.

We talked about Melissa and about your trespass. You had looked
not at a diary she kept but at a note she'd made in a notebook. As I
recall, it was a lesson plan for her history class. It had mentioned you,
had said something about *the same way Jack needs to prove something
matters by* something or other. It mentioned you, and you were drawn
to what you'd looked at idly. And it was Melissa's. That was what really lured you.

I remember this precisely. You said, "Here's why I called. You've
been through being separated."

"A little bit," I told you. I believe I kept the tone light. You were
so focused on Melissa, I realize, you were beyond anything less than
dying declarations or military commands.

You said, "So here's—do you think I have a right? To read her
stuff?"

I told you something like "That's her professional life, Jack."

You said, "That's what she said," or something to that effect. And
then you said you wanted all of her. I can't remember how you
phrased that statement, but I do remember how you ended it: with
"of course." We were men, we loved women, and your assumption
was that we all want, and all are entitled to want, to try possessing all
of whom we love.

I made low and reassuring noises, and I tried to help you convince
yourself through me that you ought to call her up and apologize. I
mentioned appearing in person. I suggested flowers, but you said no

with some heat. So *corny,* you said. We talked a little more, and you thanked me and told me you loved me before you rang off. Remember?

"I was a pretty resourceful man," Charley told us. "I'd sailed a shitways away from the little towns on this coast, and I'd held my own among rough men. Some of them were dangerous, and very few were easy. I lived among them and fought a few of them off in my time. And I was strong. And I was young. And of course, I was stupid as hell, being a strong young man. I told them to wait five or six minutes and then to make their call. I bundled up as good as I could, wrapper at my throat and mittens on my hands, sealskin over my mackinaw, flannel cap pulled down on top of my ears.

"When I went out, I couldn't see for shit. Went around the side of the house by trailing my hands along the clapboard! It was a pure down east blizzard, and I had to fold myself in half and lean into that wind just to not get tossed backwards. I clawed my way to where I needed to be. Which was the dooryard, is all. Thank Christ I didn't have to go no further. The telephone line was just laying there, not all of it on top of the snow. Looked like a dead snake. I never liked snakes, and I had to talk pretty stern to convince myself to bend down, blinded as I was by wind and snow and the cold, of course, and get ahold of the line. One end was easy, I had that, and it didn't hiss or bite me, so I figured I was safe so far. Had to hunt for the other end, which was mostly guessing which way the wind had took her. Found it, finally, and got ahold of her before I could get frightened enough not to.

"Well, this is the part nobody likes. I don't exactly mean that. This is the part nobody I ever told this to believed in. Eleanora told me I lied through my teeth, tongue and lips, but I swear to you I didn't. This is the truest story you ever heard.

"I stood out there in the goddamn blizzard, and it was well past the five minutes I told them inside to wait. So I closed my eyes—now, the wind had froze me already, my face was too numb for me to feel a thing—and I pushed those wires together as hard as I could, and I held 'em there. Stood in the goddamn snow, snow heaping on my face and in my mouth until I must've looked like a goddamn snowman.

I held the wires together, and they made their call. They talked to the goddamn doctor and then they talked to the Navy. There was a small base near Cutler where they have that huge goddamn place now with all the antenna masts. Navy had some kind of vehicle they thought could maybe get through. I don't know, maybe a snowplow of some sort. Doctor said he'd come as fast as he could by horse. See, I held the wires together. Now, I can't swear I heard every word. But I did feel their voices." He leaned his face, eyes rolling with whiskey and fatigue, and pressed closer to your mother. "I felt their voices going through me, you see, from the wire, through my hand, down into my body, and out the other arm and other hand to the other end of the wire.

"You understand, it was just too goddamn cold. I couldn't hold my arms up in the air like that. I kind of looked down, after some time, and I saw that my hands were across my body on account of the cold. I was huddled there, and the wires weren't touching. The voices were going *through* me. And the doctor came a couple of hours later, and she survived all right. So they made the call, you see. The voices were *in* me."

Your mother said, "What about the baby?"

Charley was rewarding himself with a drink. "What's that?"

"The baby?"

"Oh."

"Don't tell me it died," your mother said. "Don't tell me it died."

"No idea," Charley said. "But I think I'd remember if it died, and I don't. So I guess it probably didn't. Anyway, that isn't what the story's about."

"Says you," your mother said.

"What's it about?" I asked him.

Charley finished his drank and banged his glass on the table. He looked at me, and he shook his head, very slowly, and then he put his hand on the table and made his way to his feet. He shook his head again, looked at your mother, waited for her to speak, and then, running his hand over his clipped fringes of hair, he walked into the kitchen, shutting the door behind him.

"We failed the test," I said.

"*He* failed it."

"No," I said, "it's his story."

"Then *everybody* fails the test," your sad, beautiful mother said.

I think it possible, as I look back when I dare, that our conversation in the shabby, lantern-lit dining room of the old man's house in Machias was the largest moment of my life. It went on. It is going on. And I realize now, of course, it's what I fear to provoke, some night, in the souls of you and Melissa. It is absolutely the story I mustn't tell you, and it's therefore in the letter that I know I mustn't send and won't.

I am, of course, returning the RSVP card. For *Number of Persons Attending,* I'll write *One.* I will be at your wedding, Jack. I'll be the character who kissed your mother somewhat seriously. I'll be the guy with hair in need of a trim who brought flowers for the mother of the groom.

The Baby
in the Box

IT WASN'T HIS JOB, it *wasn't* his job, but there he went, in the only vehicle left, a blown-out Suburban with a hundred thousand miles on it and the seat pushed so far forward his belly rubbed against the wheel. He was fighting with the wheel instead of loving it. His father said that when he taught him to drive twenty-five years ago. Love the wheel, be gentle on the wheel, keep your hands on the wheel like you're touching the tits on a girl you're scared that will make you stop.

"Fucking *dwarf*," he shouted as he pushed the truck around the long, uneasy loop of dark, slick county road between the cutoff to Si Bingham Road and the farm track called Cemetery Road in spite of its sign saying Upper Ravine. He was cursing the mechanic, a nephew of the sheriff, who changed the oil and filters on the deputies' cars and who claimed he could change a timing belt and who couldn't. His legs were short. At the station they called him Chicken Man because he walked with his neck stretched and his shoulders back and his knees stiff, thinking it made him look taller. It made him look like a grease-stained, white-faced freak with those dead white eyelashes and knees that didn't work. He pushed the seats all the way up when he test-drove the vehicles so his legs would reach the pedals, and he was a chicken-legged runt.

Pumping the brakes with not much hope because the pedal was almost on the floor to begin with, he remembered the Suburban was in the garage because of a master cylinder leak. So he was going to die, probably burning, when the truck went off the road into trees or those big rocks at the entrance to the snowmobile trail at the mouth of the state forest when the brakes failed and he rolled, and sprayed gas onto the manifold, and exploded.

He didn't pretend that he knew what was happening to the county or his job in it or the world. But he knew nothing much worked right, and on his night shift, often alone at the station, he smoked so much that his tongue felt burned and his chest ached and he recognized he was scared as much as he'd ever been in his life, including his months on patrol in South Korea with an Army platoon of psychopaths, illiterates, and whore dogs.

The rear end of the Suburban swung out as the county road dropped into the valley that ran up to Sheridan Hill Road, where he thought he had to turn. He considered trying to reach someone on the radio. He grabbed the transmitter, then pushed it back hard into its clamp. There wasn't anyone to reach. He was the dispatcher. His chair was empty. His illegal public workplace cigarette was probably just going out, his coffee maybe wasn't quite ice-cold. He had left a note in the station logbook. He had traced over his letters several times with the county ballpoint pen, darkening the words until he'd torn through the page, so there would be no mistaking the emergency that had sent him away from his post. He blinked when he remembered what he had written: *Baby in box*. That was because he couldn't remember whether you spell dumpster with a *p* and it embarrassed him to look uneducated. He snorted and almost blew his nose onto his uniform. He was always finding something, his father pointed out, to get embarrassed by. "You might be better off not thinking," his father had said, making the face he made when he swallowed some of his drink.

"I could follow in your footsteps," he hadn't answered his father.

So they were down to four patrols at night, with the backup emergency vehicle still without a transmission because of course the chicken-legged white-faced son of a bitch was a liar as well as incompetent and he could no sooner change a timing belt than do a hip joint transplant.

And there was no one on overtime clerical work at night to help them catch up because they were cut down on clerical help during *days* as it was. And the sheriff himself was in Albany with a dozen other sheriffs to lobby against the new budget cuts. And the state police were all on call in Oxford, where the deputies had also gone, because a maintenance man laid off by the sheriff's department had been turned down by Wal-Mart for a clerking job and had purchased a rifle at Wal-Mart's excellent discount and had taken hostage several hundred thousand square feet filled with appliances, bright-colored dishes, pet food, plastic toys, and cheap clothes.

"We're biting our tails here," he'd said to the woman on the phone. "We're turned around in a complete circle, three hundred and sixty-five degrees, and we're shooting each other in Oxford, lady. I don't have anyone to *send.*"

"Who is this?" Like she had a right to know and maybe she was going to dock him two weeks' pay or something. "What's your name?"

"My name is not the point, ma'am." He tried to be polite because everything you said on the line was recorded.

She said, "It's three hundred and sixty degrees. You got it mixed up with three hundred and sixty-five days in a year. Anyway, it's really a hundred and *eighty* degrees, if that's what you mean."

"If what's what I mean, ma'am?"

"The turning-around thing. Look. We found a *baby* in the dumpster and you have to send somebody. A nurse. EMTs and the ambulance—"

"You found a baby in a dumpster, you say."

"I don't *say*. I mean, we really found it. We heard it crying."

"Jesus," he had said.

"Amen," she said.

"What I'm telling you, there isn't anybody *here.*"

"How can there not be anybody there? Isn't the sheriff's department one of those places there *is* somebody there? Isn't that—what's it called—government?"

"Restructuring, ma'am. The new budget thing, the contract, I believe they've been calling it?"

"We're doing that here? In this county? *Tonight?*"

"I believe we are, ma'am. We can't even use the copier without permission now."

"This is a very small baby and she doesn't seem to be healthy. Of course, a little time in a dumpster in November can cure you of being healthy."

"Yes, ma'am," he had said. Now, as he turned off, and the Suburban wobbled, and he headed uphill toward where he thought their house might be, he wondered whose baby it could be, and how you threw one away. Did you pitch it up and into the dumpster on the run? Would you climb inside the dumpster's high walls and lay it there? What did you say when the time came to climb back over it and get out and onto the road?

He had said to her, "I'll find you someone."

"I knew you would," she'd said.

"How come?"

"You sounded slightly human is why."

So there he was, slightly human and slightly in control of a huge Suburban that was slightly losing brake fluid and slightly on the way to rescuing a baby that a person had put in a dumpster filled with maybe green garbage and cat vomit or, say, furring strips with nails sticking out and busted Sheetrock and old insulation with mouse turds all over it like raisins in a cake.

He finally did switch the radio on and turn it to the tactical band. He heard the state cops in Oxford and a voice he thought he recognized as the day shift supervisor for the sheriff's department. No one was asleep, and they were all about forty miles south and more than busy. And he was here. They would talk about him failing to man his position. They would talk about the calls coming in that he was not there to answer. Maybe one of the off-duty clerks would decide to come by. Maybe Chicken Man would walk stiff-legged in his sleep and come take the calls. Maybe no one would call.

"My name—you asked me for my name," he'd said.

"All right," she'd said, "but that was when I was going to try and get you fired."

"It's Ivan. It's Ivanhoe, but I don't use it. Ivan Krisp."

"But really Ivanhoe," she'd said. "It's a very unusual name. Do you spell the crispy part with a *c?*"

HE RAN OFF THE road about half a mile away from her house. He'd been driving fast on Sheridan Hill Road when the surface curved and dipped at once. He'd seen moonlight on wet shale and had pushed the brake pedal down to the floor, figuring he wouldn't get much pressure because of the leak. It had been perfectly amateur maneuvering, and he'd slewed right and gone nose down a few dozen yards past the shoulder into a young stand of hardwood, taking some trees down and whacking his chin on the wheel.

"Okay," he said. "You're not hurt."

His knees did hurt, though, and he was afraid he was going to walk like Chicken Man for the rest of his life. His head was beating, and his chin was bleeding, his hands were wet with his own blood from cupping his face and rubbing it. Probably he looked like somebody shot in the brains. Good way to be sure of keeping Ivan Krisp alive, he thought, is you shoot him in the brains.

Bigger-bellied than when he was young, if you said it kindly, and lard-assed and gut-hung if you talked like a sheriff's deputy commenting on the department night dispatcher's physique, he fought his way out of the door and up, on his hands and very sore knees, to Sheridan Hill Road. He continued to answer a sheriff's department emergency call by responding, as it happened, at one A.M. of a very bright night in November, on foot. He called out *Whoooooo!* which was his rendition of a siren, but it hurt his face and he shut up.

He sped on call, a public servant responding to the public's need, by trundling on his banged-up legs so fast his belly wobbled and his chest ached. He couldn't quite catch his breath, and he had to stop and open his coat to bend over, heaving for air. This will be the way we do it in the new restructuring, he thought: chubby men with funny names would go out on foot to answer calls for assistance. They could carry whistles, and every time they panted they could blow the whistle so vehicular traffic would know to pull over and wait on the side of the road until they were past. You call them, and you could lose a family member, convert to a new religion, develop a hobby, move to another county and leave the empty house for sale before the sheriff's department showed up, he thought. He stopped and caught his breath, or some of it, and lit a cigarette, and coughed so hard on the first hard hook of smoke into his lungs he almost threw up. That's government, he thought.

It was almost two by the time he reached the house. It was a low farmhouse with yellow aluminum siding and a dark green dumpster, one of the long ones, outside on the side of the road, hard against the front of the garage. The outside lights on the house and garage lit the road up, along with the pale blue of the moon. Lights were on in the house. He waited at the door to wipe his face and catch his breath. He listened for the cries of an infant.

The woman who came to the door said, "My God, what happened to your face, Deputy?"

He looked at the blood on his hands. "I had a little fender-bender a ways down there, toward County 29? Cracked my chin on the wheel, and it might not have stopped yet."

"I'd say not," she said.

"Chins and foreheads," he said. "They look worse than they feel. Though I have to admit it feels terrible."

She was as tall as he was and a little heavy-thighed in tight, faded blue jeans. Her face was long and bony, though, and she had hollows at the eyes. She looked like she never slept enough. Her skin was dark, and it looked as though it would feel soft if you put your hand out gently and just touched it under the cheekbone or at the corner of the eye.

She said, "Yes?"

"I'm not a deputy, strictly speaking," he said.

"What *are* you, strictly speaking?" She looked at his gray uniform, his black tie, and he knew she'd been hoping for someone a little more capable-looking. Maybe she'd settle for secretly competent, he thought. He knew *he* would. And he knew he wasn't.

"Well, ma'am, I'm what you call the dispatcher."

"Ivanhoe!"

"Yes, ma'am."

"You're all they had left?"

"I'm the entire available people on call and in the station and on the air. It's a terrible night. There isn't anyone. I'm not supposed to be here. I *can't* be here. Because if I am, I'm not manning the telephone and radio. And I am. So I'm not. I'm in really terrible trouble."

"And you racked the squad car up," she said. "Your fender-bender."

"Blew it off the road," he said. "Might have cracked the block or an axle. It wasn't *really* my fault," he said, hearing his voice skid into the beginning of a whine. "The brake cylinder was leaking, and this guy was supposed—"

"It's not your fault."

"Strictly speaking, since I was at the wheel, I guess it was."

"But it wasn't. It *also* wasn't."

"No."

"No," she said. "It isn't anybody's fault. They just ran out of sheriffs and deputies and cars."

He shrugged. "Where's the baby, ma'am?"

She let him in. The heat in the house was high, and he thought he smelled tomatoes and peppery spices and the dampness of gypsum board and old wood. He was dizzy again, and he caught at her shoulder. She stepped away and he stumbled and then she stepped in again, holding his arm and easing him into a kitchen chair.

"Smells good," he said.

"You got hurt, Ivanhoe."

"No," he said, "only my head and my brains." He put his arms on the table and rested his forehead against them. "Just let me catch my whatever here a minute," he told her.

"I sure can't think of anyone else we can call who'd come out," she said.

"Local services are stretched a little thin," he said.

She said, "How nice to know they're keeping busy. Can we—as soon as you get over your concussion and your fractured skull," she said, "do you think we can load the baby into your arms and wave while you speed the little foundling child away on foot to get rescued? Is that how you see the shape of the evening?"

"Is there a car here, ma'am?" He said it into his hands or onto the tabletop.

"There is a car here," she said. "There is a 1989 Chevrolet Blazer with about an eighth of a tank of gas and something wrong with the battery. As in dead."

He decided that he had to sit up. He did it slowly and was horrified when tears filled his eyes. He blinked, looking away from her, and saw the bare ceiling joists they had pried the Sheetrock from. New sheets of it were stacked against a papered wall that someone had started to strip. "I can walk back to where I went off the road and take the battery out," he said. "There'll be jumper cables in my vehicle, and we can start your Blazer right up, if all it is is a weak cell in the battery or something."

"Does that sound complicated to you too?" she asked. She ran water into a kettle and lit a burner on the stove.

"No, ma'am, it's something I believe I can do." Then he asked her, "Is there a young woman here, ma'am?"

"You're thinking of me as old."

He tried to shake his head. "Oh, no. But I meant somebody of child-bearing age."

"I'm thirty-nine years old," she said. "I have an ample pelvis and I still have my fallopian tubes and both my ovaries."

"Yes, ma'am."

"I could have had a baby and dumped it there."

He thought it was time to be something like an officer of the law, so he made his head stay upright, and he felt in his pockets. "I wonder," he said. "Have you got any pencil and paper I could borrow?"

She was making tea. She pointed at the telephone on the counter near the refrigerator. He found a pad beside it, and a ballpoint pen. She gave him the tea. It was very sweet and very hot. He leaned against the counter. "You told me your name," he said, "but I forget."

She was at the stove again, across the room, with her back to him. "Carole Duchesney." She spelled it, and he wrote it down. As he did, he saw how bloody his fingers were.

"Miz Duchesney."

"Miss."

"Oh," he said, "I would have thought you might sooner call yourself Miz."

"My partner calls herself Miz," she said. "I call myself Miss. I'm an antiquarian."

"Yes, ma'am." He looked at the pad as if there were instructions on it. He reached for a cigarette, but stopped because he knew better. Finally, he heard his mouth say, "What's *her* name, please? Your partner?"

"Frances. Frances Leary. She's one of those redheaded, frecklefaced Learys. *She's* only twenty-seven. With a hell of a pelvis and ovaries on her. It could have been her. That would be interesting as all get out."

"Is she around, ma'am?"

"She is around. Upstairs. With the kid."

"You said the baby isn't healthy?"

"I did, but Frances said I was wrong. She said the little girl was just doing what the situation warranted. Crying really hard and turning red. Frances is from a large family."

He was looking at her, at her tan chamois shirt and her jeans tucked into high black rubber farm boots, her small hands and round fingers, the dark skin of her throat and face. He was trying to see what was different about her.

She raised her chin a little and she said, "What?"

"I don't know quite what I should do next," he said.

"Let's get my Blazer started and drive to the hospital and donate the baby."

"I think we have to get social services into it."

"Orphanages," Miss Duchesney said.

He said, "Well—"

A short, skinny woman with a pale face and cropped red hair and freckles on her nose came into the kitchen. She held the baby across her chest and she was smiling, the way a mother smiles when she presents her child.

Miss Duchesney said, "Frances, this is Ivanhoe Krisp. He's all they had left at the station house, and he abandoned his post to come out here and rescue us from the baby someone left off in the dumpster. On the way, he wrecked his car. He forgot his pencil and paper, so he borrowed some. You can tell from the way his teacup shakes that he is somewhat fucked up. He was wondering what to do next."

Frances didn't speak. Her face reddened, and she smiled the widest smile he remembered seeing.

"Yes," Miss Duchesney said. "It's that wonderful."

"The baby's asleep," he said.

"Or dead," Miss Duchesney said.

"Aw, no."

She said, "No." She walked to him and patted his arm and moved him to the chair. When he was in it, she went to the sink and returned with a brown bowl filled with steaming water. She handed him a folded dish towel. "You might clean the blood away," she said.

He looked into the bowl. He could see a dark shape that he thought might be his reflected face. Looking down, he said, "I found out my daughter, she's a little over sixteen, she's having sex with this boyfriend of hers."

"She probably loves him dearly," Miss Duchesney said.

"It isn't funny to *me*," he said.

"Of course not. You're right. But that's what we all of us said, is what I mean. You're making a total mess of everything, and you naturally resort to blaming it on love. It's been known to be the name of almost everything wrong," she said, behind him.

Frances Leary said, "Cue the violins."

"I hit her tonight," he said without meaning to. "Before I went to work. I slapped her face."

"And yours ends up bleeding," Miss Duchesney said.

"It comes around three hundred and sixty-five degrees," he said, nodding at the shape of the bowl.

"Sixty," she said. "I told you, remember?"

"Right," he said. "And supposed to be one-eighty." She took the towel from him and dipped the end in the water. "My wife is very upset," he said. Miss Duchesney worked the warm cloth on his chin and around his mouth. The baby began to cry, and he jumped. Miss Duchesney took hold of his face and kept working the cloth on it. He said, against the warm towel, "And now the baby's crying."

He saw himself, though he didn't carry a weapon, holding one of the big, black Beretta 9mms that were issued to the deputies. He was kicking at the door of a scuffed white trailer on the side of Sheridan Hill Road. Against the cries of the baby he heard his own voice: "Sheriff's department!" He saw the door swing in and he demanded to know if someone on the premises had driven to the Leary-Duchesney farmhouse to leave a baby off in the stink of garbage and the giggle of rats.

He said, "Should I go back and get the battery?"

"I think that's what you ought to do next," Miss Duchesney said.

Frances Leary said, "That's a girl. That's a girl." From the sound of her voice, she was rocking the baby a little.

"Maybe some milk," he said.

"I think they need formula," Frances Leary said. "A special kind of formula. I don't think they can tolerate milk right away."

"You wouldn't have any formula," he said.

"No," Miss Duchesney said, "we don't use it. And, worse luck, neither of us is lactating tonight."

"No, ma'am," he said. Then he said, "Could I look at the baby?"

Miss Duchesney said, "You've been sitting there with your eyes closed."

He opened them. He stood and leaned on the back of the chair. He felt as short as Chicken Man when Frances Leary bent toward him. He saw a crushed and furrowed face inside a harsh-looking gray woolen blanket. She was red, and dark with crying, and her blunt nose and her eyelids looked like they were made of wax. He saw her fists beside her face. He thought the miniature fingers were perfect.

"Everybody looks like that," he said.

"You're too sentimental for your work," Frances Leary told him.

Miss Duchesney said, "How can you tell what he *does?*"

He had something to ask. Before they fetched the cables and battery to start up her Blazer, and before he drove like hell to the hospital where he would summon social workers and doctors, if the hospital could find them, and call the sheriff at his Albany hotel and begin to lose his job, he had to ask someone his question.

He saw himself kicking in another door in a trailer half a mile down on Sheridan Hill Road. Miss Duchesney and Ms. Leary sat in the Blazer with the child, and he was kicking in the doors of trailers, of shake-shingled one-story houses, of shacks with no siding, of clapboard cabins with rusted tin roofs. Doors slammed in and he followed, assuming the shooter's stance, legs planted wide and Beretta cupped in both hands before him, demanding the surrender of whoever had disposed of a baby.

"Who," he needed to ask, "would throw a person away?"

He broke another lock with two powerful kicks and he was inside, menacing the doughy couple at their television set.

No, he wasn't.

He made his eyes open. He stood in the kitchen of these women and he fastened his jacket. His knees were sore, and he must look, he thought, like a wounded rooster among his willful hens. He went toward the front door, and he didn't speak. He was embarrassed by Miss Duchesney. She made him feel incompetent. She reminded him of his father, a little. And he was afraid that if he asked his question she would answer it.

Laying the Ghost

IT WAS THE DAY OUR LPN, Evangeline Jefferson, who was tall and broad and angry, wore her wraparound sunglasses inside the office under its pale, fluorescent light. Lenny Pravda and I were telling the usual childish body jokes in what we called the lounge, which was very dark because we had someone on the staff who was painfully hungover every day and who kept the clinic as shaded as she could. This was the room we napped in when we needed to, and where we dictated notes, and where every now and again we sat with patients.

Lenny and I left the lounge to walk in opposite directions along the hall to see our first patients of the day. We were the internists in the Medical Arts Building, and above us and around us, insulated by corridors and walls, were cardiologists, gynecologists, orthopedists, and pediatricians. The little building seethed with fear and pain, and, inevitably, anger. Some of it was Lenny's and some of it, I guess, was mine. Lenny was battling despair about the profession, which meant that he was once again convinced of his failure to conduct a selfless, tireless, efficient, and humane practice of what one of my teachers at Bellevue had called the healing arts. As befitted the older man in the partnership, I occasionally offered wisecracks or, in a lower, gruffer voice, something I suppose you'd call a tip—about a medical matter, or about the mistakes we are condemned to once in a while commit. We spoke about our cruel, distant relations, the medical insurance firms whose forms our patients and our practice lived and died upon. We spoke about the fluctuations in the marriage of Lenny Pravda. We rarely spoke about Denise, my wife, who had not been my patient but whom I had lost nonetheless.

Evangeline had taken my patient's weight and blood pressure, and I could smell the mouthwash and chewing gum she used to mask her vodka. I took the blood pressure again and got a slightly higher systole, entered it on the chart, and went on to conduct the very same annual physical I would conduct half a dozen times in the day. My second patient was a woman the left side of whose face went numb, though she had full feeling at the time of the consultation. The third of the afternoon was a borderline diabetic. Evangeline had entered on his chart a blood pressure so far from anything I could register that I decided, pumping the cuff for one more attempt, that it was time to let her go.

Fire her ass was how Lenny would say it, I thought.

Later, I was in the lounge, talking notes into the recorder, when Lenny came in and raised his chin, meaning that he wanted to speak.

"Evangeline is so far off the wagon," I said, making sure the machine wasn't recording, "her mouthwash smells like bargain-basement vodka. Old Mohawk is the brand, I believe. And she's making mistakes."

"Old Mohawk? Jesus. That's worse than the mistakes. We have to fire her ass out of here. You want to talk to her?"

"I thought you might want to do this one."

He shook his head and looked away. "I would just as soon not," he said.

"I'll be the bad father?"

"That's why I came into practice with you," he said, "because you said you'd do all the hard stuff. All *I* had to do, as I recall our interview, was heal the sick, rake in the money, and lay the X-ray technicians."

I shook my head. "Mess around with them, and you'll get a radioactive dick."

"Any activity, of any sort, would be welcome."

"You're having problems in the appendage department?"

"Yeah. It's as tired as I am."

"I'll talk to your wife."

"I know that talk you give," he said. "I heard about it."

"My good father talk?"

"Doctor Prosthetics," he said. Then he waved his little hand back and forth. "Listen," he said, "I need to put a patient in here for a while." He made the kind of face a child makes when swallowing something chalky or bitter. "This is kind of a rough one."

"What's the bad news? You look like it's the *worst* news."

"No," he said, "the worst news is telling someone a person they love is going to die. This is next to the worst."

"The patient's terminal?"

"Mr. Philip Santangelo is going to have to undergo a percutaneous biopsy. I see so much density in the right upper lobe, I don't think we can save it."

"Santangelo," I said.

"Nice guy," Lenny said, "apparently a Marxist in college. Once in a while we would talk a little political theory when I gave him his physical."

"He was never a Marxist," I said. "He was a capitalist with an uncle in the garbage collection rackets in New Jersey and a father who wanted him to be a priest. He did a little Marxist chat because there was a girl he had the hots for who went through a phase of socialism-chic. She often steeled herself to go without hair conditioner."

"You knew him? In college?"

"He wanted to marry my wife. Well. Sleep with my girlfriend."

"The one you married?"

"I used to know this guy pretty well," I said.

"He's a nice guy," Lenny said.

I saw the cascade of money in the air. I was always able to picture it, and I often conjured the shower of currency whether I wanted to or not, twenty-five years afterward. And when I did, my knees ached. As Denise, the girlfriend and then the wife, the wife who threw an embolism and died, facedown on what is now the Jacqueline Bouvier Kennedy Walk around the Central Park Reservoir, would tell me: "You forget *nothing,* you *forgive* nothing." It turned out Denise was halfway right.

"No," I said, "not necessarily."

"Bad memories," he said.

I shrugged. "What the hell, Lenny. She's gone. And Phil's gone too, pretty soon, I take it."

"He's on his way," Lenny said. "Are you really a cold-hearted, terrible man?"

"Yes," I said.

"He's got a family. A couple of kids. He runs some kind of business."

"Bet you he's in garbage collection."

Lenny said, "He will be, soon enough."

"You know, you're pretty goddamned cold yourself. And tough enough to fire Evangeline."

"I'm sticking with the X-ray technicians."

"No, I mean it," I said. "You talk to her, you can use the lounge, and I'll talk to your patient."

"I thought you didn't like the guy."

"No," I lied, "it isn't anything like that. Maybe he'd be comforted by knowing it from me, you know, given the acquaintanceship, friendship, whatever you want to call it."

Lenny looked dubious. He understood me well enough to suspect me, but not well enough to know what to suspect me *of.*

"Really," I said. "Go tell him I'm coming in, I'll see him in the examining room. You bring Evangeline in here and tell her we're finding mistakes on the charts, she has to get help again. But we'll see her through, we'll help her file workman's comp, disability, the usual—you know the drill."

"We've done it with her twice before. In a medical office, that's twice too often."

"I have no doubt we're in it for life. One of us will have to walk her through the other one's funeral."

"We're a couple of swell fellows," Lenny said.

"I have always liked that about us. Yes."

I finished my notes while he went back to Phil Santangelo. Then he and Evangeline returned, she looking clammy and Lenny looking very ill indeed. I shut off the machine, collected the charts in their colored file folders, took them out to the office, and retrieved Phil's chart from the plastic holder on the door of his room. I found what I expected to, and then I knocked. I was opening the door when he called, "Come in," as if he had a choice.

He was pale and he looked chilled in the awful gowns we gave them. It had what I think were supposed to be wildflowers, in aqua-blue ink on a white background. Velcro fasteners held it together in back. We shook hands without speaking. We inspected each other and then we looked away.

"Phil, why don't you put your shirt and pants on? Why did you take your pants *off?*"

"Habit," he said, and I remembered the voice so well.

I sat on the stool and droned about years gone by, the coincidence of his being a patient and my not knowing until today, the annual reunions at school I always managed to miss. I looked at his chart to hide from his embarrassment until I sensed that he was pretty nearly dressed.

"Dr. Pravda talked to you about this?" I pointed at the ghostly mass on the black background, which looked like deep space behind a tiny vessel, in the X-ray picture of his upper lung that was clipped to the broad, metal-framed light on the wall. The vessel wasn't life in the midst of infinite space, though. The mass was death, and *it* was infinite, in its power to surge, to grow, to appear one day, as it might, in the darkness of his brain and kill him in the top of his being.

"I didn't get everything he said, but yeah, he talked to me." He stared at the X-ray as if he knew how to read it.

"Would you sit down, Phil? Hey, it's—remarkable, I guess you'd say, to see you. It's been so long for us, hasn't it?"

He awkwardly shifted his hips as he lifted until he was sitting on the examination table, bunching the paper on the thick, salmon-colored plastic pallet, swinging his legs a little, finally crossing his arms in front of his chest and holding his legs against the side of the table. He looked like a soldier, scared but true, sitting on a cannon pulled by frightened horses toward the war.

"You guys just stopped calling me," he said, "you and Denise." His sallow complexion looked yellow to me, and his blunt nose seemed bulbous. His dark eyes, behind rimless glasses, looked wet. Along with his downturned mouth and small chin, they made him seem wounded. And of course, even before the battle, he was. He said, "I sent you postcards, remember?"

"Well, lives get pretty complicated."

He raised his chin. "You came in here to tell me that, did you?"

I shook my head. I tried to read his thinking, but I couldn't. My vision ended at his skin, and for anything else I'd have to use X-rays.

"I was a year behind you in school," he said, "and a year behind you in meeting Denise. I was *always* behind you. I guess I still am."

"Should I get Dr. Pravda back in? Would that be more comfortable?"

He shook his head. The glow of the bright plate on either side of the X-ray lit his lenses as he moved. "No," he said. "What's the bottom line for me?"

"Dr. Pravda told you the posterior anterior and lateral shot—this X-ray up here—shows a lesion in the right upper lobe of your chest?"

"I had a cold," he said. "You know, I was sniffling and coughing, so I bought this—what's it called? Over the counter?"

"Proprietary medicine?"

He shrugged. "Dristan," he said. He smiled, as if the name embarrassed him, and of course I remembered the smile as he raised the brown paper bag above the floor of our apartment. It was 1973, and he'd brought tickets for the three of us to see *The Hot L Baltimore* and he'd brought the money I had told him we needed so we could pay our $84.36 monthly rent on the one-room-plus-bath. I didn't know, that night, nor for all the nights and days since, that he had grinned at me in embarrassment, although I was certain of it now. I'd known only that he coveted and loved Denise and that he'd sent me to my knees. Because I was a stupid, unobservant man, I continued to think that I was very bad at forgetting.

"And you felt a little better," I said, "even if the cough didn't go away."

"That's right," he said. "It's a common story? It's a punishment for smokers, sure as shit. Can we hear *that* one again?"

"Hey, you stopped smoking. A little late, but you stopped. *I'm* not bitching at you."

"I should have stopped sooner," he said.

I looked at his chart, though I didn't read it. I asked, as if what he told me would make a difference, "So you found this chronic cough irritating."

"My *wife* found it irritating."

"What's your wife's name, Phil?"

Before I found it in the folder, he said, "Sandy. Sandra Wise Santangelo." He almost sobbed, then he coughed to cover the sound. "Names get powerful, huh? When you're talking about leaving them—the people who wear them. I mean—"

"No," I said, "you're right. This is rough, and I know it, and that's why I'm here."

"I never thought you cared that much for me, after a while, to tell you the truth."

"No? Really? That's funny."

He said, "It is?"

I was reading the chart, where the typed words spoken by Lenny Pravda told me of *coarse breath sounds and occasional coarse ronchi scattered throughout chest,* for which he had prescribed *Biaxin 500 mg Q 12 H and Phenargan VC 2 tsp Q I D* and which, a week later, seemed to suggest *some increased comfort and a slight decrease in coughing.* But then, of course, Phil had returned because the coughing had increased. *This therapy must be seen as a failure,* Lenny dictated, noting that he had decided to order a *PA and lateral of upper chest* and noting, later, that the radiologist and he agreed that *X-ray reveals lesion in the right upper lobe suggesting small cell carcinoma. Biopsy stat.*

"Excuse me, Phil?"

"I said what's next? Do I just die?"

I thought: Yes.

I said, "Hell, no. We're going to want a biopsy, Phil. I can refer you to the surgeon we tend to advise our patients to see, or I can help you find someone else. I'll work with whoever you want. Or Lenny. Dr. Pravda. Or both of us, really. We'll both be discussing this case."

"This case."

"I'm sorry, Phil."

"Fucking *case,*" he said.

We would actually make some progress, I thought. We'd get a surgical resection, and we'd drag the poor white hairless man through radiation and chemotherapy, and he'd be sick as hell, but then respond. He'd feel all right after, say, a year, a year and a half. He'd think of himself as well, or, anyway, better. And then the symptoms in the lung would return. And then his head would ache unbearably. We'd set him on a bed and keep him there, with intubated air when he needed it, and a drip for the morphine. The mass with its shaggy edges that he'd think we had exiled would have metastasized. It would live in his brain. It would live on his brain. It would eat his brain and grow and be his death.

At the wooden door in the planking wall of our small, old apartment on Grove Street in Greenwich Village, from which Denise leaves to teach elementary school near Irving Place, and from which I travel to NYU, Philip Santangelo, college buddy to my wife and apparently to me, stands grinning. He wears an almost-yellow widewaled corduroy suit, and his tie is wide and painted with a black fist on an off-yellow ground. His sideburns curl along the bones of his broad jaw. In one hand are three theater tickets, and in the other is a wrinkled brown paper bag. He opens the bag, unrolling its tightly wound top, and he grasps it from the bottom, flinging its contents up and out, then sending the bag up into the air after them: the hundred one-dollar bills fly up, drift down. I see them, slow as feathers in the air of our drafty, romantic flat he must resent. At the door, he stands beside the foot of our bed. There's little else to look at: two old low bookshelves we use as cupboards, a little bar refrigerator and a fourburner stove, an oblong porcelain industrial sink with rusted spigots, and a fireplace we use at great risk. The table is from a diner on Eleventh Avenue that went bankrupt, and it cost us eight dollars plus the long, long crosstown walk plus four dollars more for the second-hand children's wagon we balanced it on as we brought home what, along with two folding chairs, would constitute all of our dining room for years.

That's what he sees, looking in: intimate signs of a life he doesn't share. And of course he also sees me, a red-faced second-year medical student, on his knees in stained wool trousers and a tight, faded blue oxford button-down shirt and a resolutely narrow Rooster knit tie. I am picking up the dollars I begged to borrow. I retrieve them one at a time. The humiliation he planned, I think, requires that I not hurry the process. I am to be on my knees for a while. And that is where I stay, paying the interest in advance by taking each bill and turning it, Washington's head up, and setting it onto the stack beside the fallen paper bag. When Denise comes to help me, I say between tightly clenched teeth, "Do *not* get down here on your goddamned knees, please."

The planking of the floor, on which, of course, we have no carpet, is made of very wide boards, and the cracks between them are spacious. Two of the dollar bills have lodged sideways in such cracks. I call to him, "Phil. What are the odds on this, man?" I say it with what I think of as comradely cheer: interest, paid in full.

"What's a biopsy like?"

"It's uncomfortable. I'm not going to pretend otherwise. We're getting into an area now where nothing much is comfortable as we go on."

"So why would *we* decide to go on?"

"You're pretty angry right now," I said unbrilliantly.

"Wow! No wonder people worship their doctors. You're so god-damned insightful. I'm angry? Would you say I have reason to be?"

"Yes. I would."

"Would you say if your Dr. Pravda colleague had done a little doctoring a little sooner we'd maybe have *caught* this thing sooner?"

"No. He couldn't have possibly found it sooner. If he'd detected pneumonia, he might have ordered pictures of the chest, and then we'd have seen the mass. But I doubt it. No. Nobody would have caught it sooner. I can't think of anyone to blame, Phil."

His face collapsed, and he wept, his arms no longer crossed, his hands clasped in his lap. "I love my wife," he said. "I love my wife."

I didn't tell him about Denise. I was going to keep her, whose pointy elbows and hoarse voice I had lost, at least that much to myself. I looked at his X-ray. I looked at his creased, wet face, blotched but pale. I saw pictures of organs, I saw the man sealed in his skin. But I was also, suddenly, seeing something she had never known. I wanted her to hear what I'd forgotten, what Pete had just brought back without knowing it, the way a wind brings rain.

"I love her so much," he whispered.

I nodded.

What something in his voice, like a cruel, sharp musical note in the laboring of a rusted machine, had returned to me was the evening a child died. It was a cold Manhattan night, and we were in our thirties, living by then on the Upper West Side, not too far from the place we would one day buy. I slept in a sad, uncomfortable state because I had lost a patient, a teenage girl, whose lung collapsed. I felt disgraced because I had had to attempt three times before I got the tube into her lung, and I felt disgust because I had worried about my ineptitude and my reputation as much as I had mourned the loss of a thirteen-year old, not particularly pleasant or winning, but a life in its envelope of flesh that I had failed to keep intact.

I dreamed that I called Denise, I called and called her, but she didn't answer. I knew she was on the telephone line as I howled her name, and I knew she heard me. She did not respond. I thought, in my dream, that she couldn't. I grew terrified for her danger, and I shouted, again and again, "Dennie!"

I cried aloud, I think, and wakened her. What she did was comfort me, shaking my shoulder, touching my face. But she needed comforting too. Our faces were close, and her breath on my skin excited me. Something about our proximity—no, our sudden, surprising, intimacy, our sensual collision—told me we would make love.

My hand was on her belly, which was cold under her pajamas, and my face—my lips—lay at her throat. She said, "Thank God you shouted."

"Thank God you woke me."

"I had the most horrible dream," she said. "It was—I was trying to talk to you, we were on the phone, and I couldn't say a word. I was in big trouble, and I needed you, and nothing worked—I couldn't talk."

I said nothing. I wanted her. I didn't care to delay with talk of a dream we seemed to have shared. I worked my hand on her, and in her, I appeased my hunger for the lost life of the child, I drove at Denise and drove myself through her at what had diminished me in the operating room, and I was heated but cold, and we made love, I guess you could call it, for we were wet with each other, the taste of her flesh was in my mouth and on my lips. And I was sad, I remember, as I fell asleep, because for all our laboring upon each other's bodies, we had achieved nothing, I thought, like the intimacy of that mutual dream. I knew it, and then I didn't know, and then I lived the rest of her life with Denise, and then I lived without her.

But I should have told her, I thought.

Pete raised his chin, like an animal sniffing, and he looked at me hard, as if he'd felt the pressure of my emotions.

"We'll do everything we can," I said.

He nodded. He looked down at his hands.

I thought of the money raining in our little Greenwich Village room. I thought of us, in a larger apartment, miles uptown, when we were together in the nightmare.

His glasses caught the light again as he moved his head, first to look at the glowing X-ray, then to focus on me. He waited. I looked at the chart because I could think of nothing to offer him. When I looked up, he was taking his glasses off to set them on the rustling paper beside him. He wiped at his eyes with his cuffs, like a kid. Then he very deliberately set his face inside his cupped hands and sat that way.

Dennie, I could hear myself calling when I entered the place on West Eighty-eighth where we had only partway consumed our marriage, our friendship, our youth. *Dennie, I saw Pete Santangelo today. Remember him?*

And she would ask me if I still nourished, still *cherished,* my grudge.

And I would tell her.

No, I'd say. *God, no.* And then I'd say, *Yes.* I would watch her face light up as she shook her head like a parent.

I did want to tell her.

Pete lowered his hands: though dressed, he was naked. He no longer hid—he had no way to hide—his comprehension. He knew where he'd come to. He knew that what he wanted in his life was not of consequence, nor would it be.

Dennie! I called.

The door opened in with a noisy rattle of the knob, and Evangeline, as smeared and shocked as Pete, stepped into the room. "Bastards," she said. "Smug, sober, upright hypocrites. It's because I'm not a slender woman, isn't it? It's a form of persecution," she said to Pete, as if she knew him. "I'm an ample-size woman, and I never had a hope here. And you knew it, you pious citizen bastards."

Lenny came in behind her to seize her shoulders, but she shrugged through the grasp of his gentle, small hands. He said, "This is so dreadful."

Pete got down from the table and stood beside it, his fingers touching the top, as if he wanted to be sure of his balance. He turned to look at his X-ray. He stared at the picture about the end of his life, and then he faced me, grinning as he had on Grove Street.

And if Denise could return somehow to ask me what I thought of Phil Santangelo's reappearance in my doorway, I would not recite, I swear it, how he came here bearing his broken self instead of a sack of dollar bills. I would tell her that he brought a story stolen because withheld, and kept for no reason but lust and then some failure of feeling, and then forgotten.

"It is so true," Evangeline said. "Some fat-assed Baptist lady with a lower lip this thick didn't ever stand a chance here. And what in hell are *you* smiling about?"

I would tell Denise my portion of the nightmare, if my failure to be an honest man, if the stony rules of chemistry, if all the bylaws of the flesh, could be reversed. I would tell her we'd been rare together, we had dreamed the same dream. I would woo her with the secret that we did and did not share.

Domicile

IT MADE ME THINK OF FAIRY TALES—stories of children who drop from the sky or roll from the cupped petals of a silky flower—because he simply appeared one morning and was picked up by a yellow van, a small school bus, which meant that an actual adult had made arrangements for him, and that school authorities acknowledged his existence, and that he was an authentic child, not a product of my second-rate education or of what I considered then, with what I'll now call theatrics, as my third-rate mind.

Wearing a blue hip-length jacket that was streaked with a faded white or yellow stain along both arms and down its back, from underneath the fleece-lined hood to its hem, he did this every day: walked out the door of the white wood motel cabin, pulled the door shut with both hands, then climbed down two steps and walked around to the side of the cabin that faced the direction from which the little bus came. He stood very still, always, as if his khaki knapsack were heavy and pinned him in place. When the bus appeared, he hiked with long, measured steps to the edge of the road, cutting across the ice and snow over the gravel drive that led to the closed offices of the shut-down motel. He arrived as the bus did, and he climbed into it as he had walked, with a nonchalance that seemed important to project.

He was gone until around four o'clock in the afternoon, when the bus paused to let him emerge, and he hiked to the cabin, climbed its steps, and, using a bright, brass-colored key attached to a long, oval tag—the sort you're issued as you sign the register and show them a credit card or dare them to turn down cash—opened the door of the cabin, the one closest of all eight to the one with OFFICE on its door, and he went inside. He had been doing this for a week, since the February thaw had hardened back into mud frozen in twists and ruts and permanent pockmarks into which new snow had fallen in a thin, icy crust through which the mud glared up in weak sunlight like sewage.

The bus, then, would move from view, and so would the kid. Except for the usual squirrels and the usual birds, and the usual March winds that came up the Hudson Valley bearing moisture, all that was left on the one-lane blacktop county road was me, moving snow and ice off stones with a stiff brown whisk broom and my canvas-gloved fingers, sorting the ones I would use to repair the roadside wall which, among other chores, provided me with cramped shelter and, sometimes, food. I was in a good deal of trouble that year, and I knew it, though I didn't worry. I think that I did not. I was fit, and too stupid to be frightened for long, and more concerned about the kid of eight or nine who lived at the nameless motel—its square sign was missing from a rusted roadside frame on top of two scuffed four-by-fours—than I was about the long-range prospect. I actually didn't have one, I now believe. I had decided, as I remember it, to think a couple of hours ahead—the next few pages of a book I tried to read, the next few lines of a sketch I tried to make, the next meal of the day.

I had broken my last dollar to buy a can of supermarket-brand creamed corn, and when I wasn't speculating about the kid, as I built my pile of fieldstones, I was tantalizing myself with alternate visions of dinner cooked on the two-burner gas stove in the trailer: corn chowder made with water and some frozen potatoes I had found in their garden, or plain creamed corn spooned hot onto slices of stiff but not yet moldy Wonder Bread, and with potatoes reserved for the next night's meal.

The light in the window of the cabin across the road was a yellow that verged on palest amber, and it wavered almost as a candle would. I'd have bet that he was using kerosene, and I worried for him, thinking of the fumes, thinking of the flame. I had seen a car there once, its long, scarred hood half hidden behind the cabin, but I had never seen who drove it, nor had I never witnessed an adult who waved him goodbye or who greeted him. There he was at his place, and there I was at mine—a graduated senior who had spent an extra semester making up credits, living in a trailer I had to hunch in unless I sat in my canvas director's chair of glossy red wood and black cloth that I had salvaged from behind a dorm. I could of course lie in the built-in bed too short for me. The toilet wasn't hooked up to a septic system, though my landladies had assured me that flushing would come with spring. I cooked with bottled water they supplied, and I took showers at the main house. I used the pine forest behind the trailer for my john unless I made it to town and the burger palace bathrooms. The battery in my Datsun was absolutely dead now, so I stayed at home and I shat in the woods like a bear.

I probably looked like one. I had a lot of dark hair in those days, and no mirror. I shaved and combed myself in the fugitive reflections of the few framed pictures I owned, one of them—an etching of a woman's footprint, long and narrow and perfect (you could tell) in its arch, pressed into bright sand—by a person named Julia, the owner of the foot, who had left the area and me and who had not looked, nor written, nor telephoned, back. I had no phone, but the landladies did, and they'd have come for me if she had called the house. She knew where it was, and where the trailer was. She had wakened in it with me, had answered its small door when one of them—the mother, Mrs. Peete—had knocked, on an autumn morning, with a chore for me. Julia was now in Central America, and she wasn't alone, while I was here, cutting knobby, icy potatoes into an aluminum saucepan, slashing in some onion to fry with them, opening a can of creamed corn, pouring in water, and pronouncing myself competent as I bent in the trailer, shuffled in my crouch, and worried about the temperature—it was diving again—and about my landladies, and about the boy across the road.

Not a night to be a kid and living alone, I thought.

It did not take a genius like Julia to make the point. I knew which kid I was feeling sorrier for. And the night would get worse. It was the night I broke my policy and, as my father had asked me to, I did, on a trial basis, consider the future. I stood at the stove and fanned my fingers out, one at a time, to indicate to myself that I was being concrete and realistic.

No Julia now, nor tomorrow, nor ever: one.

Given my academic record, no vocation-with-coat-and-tie plus prospects of a sleek-apartment-in-a-bigtime-city: two.

Noplace to live except here, in trade for too much work, or at home, in exchange for enduring desperate lessons about life plus the long, silent evenings of a faltering marriage that ought to have died some time ago: three.

Present prospects had dimmed for me with the rise, you would have to say, in immediate pleasures—landlady problems, you could call them: four.

I apparently could not paint a picture unless I worked in a bright, heated studio, supplied like a locker room for the gifted and talented children of the managerial class, by a high-tuition college, and that was a kind of truth you had to face, I was beginning to think, or you might end up teaching design in community colleges and overdosing on whatever it was you could—now that you had some kind of salary—afford: five.

She knocked five times, it seemed to me, and I am not kidding. I knew who it was, and I was spooked because she was there and because it felt as though she was reading my mind.

She came in, as I expected her to, and, as I expected her to, she said, "Oh, Jesus Christ. How can we let you live like this?" I wasn't surprised that she was a little tipsy.

She wore a red wool mackinaw with black designs, the kind of hunting coat somebody would have used twenty-five years before. She wore a long-billed red woolen hat with earflaps, and old black woolen gloves. Her face was shiny and flushed, her crinkly, bright brown hair had bits of ice in it, and her eyes were wide and light. When she took the hat off and beat it against the side of her leg, ice flew up into the light and disappeared, and her hair sprang out, giving her face a wild look, as if she reacted with shock to something nobody else could see. I smelled the sweetness of the Manhattans she drank, and the smoke from their kitchen woodstove and from her cigarettes.

"You mind if I drop in?" she said, unbuttoning the coat.

"Want some soup?"

"Is *that* what that is."

"I dug the potatoes up in your garden," I said, staring into the pot. "You don't mind, right?"

"You must be strong as an ox to get to them. Well, you are. The ground's so damned hard, David. You know, we'd have given you potatoes. And—whatever. Soup. Dinner whenever you want it. I keep telling you that."

I nodded. "Would you like some?"

She kept her coat on. "It's awfully damned cold in here."

"There isn't any heat."

"We'll get electric baseboard heating installed. Come spring. The land will sell by then. Property sells better in the spring. We'll have some money, and we'll make you comfortable. We promised that."

I nodded.

"But you'll have left by then, you're saying."

I said, "You know, Rebecca, I don't have any idea. I don't have plans for anything except the wall, and maybe building you some raised beds for the garden."

She was standing closer, then, directly behind me, and then she was leaning in on me, first against my back and then against the rest, holding on from behind with an arm around my waist. It made me uncomfortable that a woman who once had been married and who wore an antique coat like that would feel the need to hug me. I guess you would say I felt unworthy.

"Tell me more about raised beds. They sound fascinating," she said, running her hand up under my shirt. I felt her cold nose at the back of my neck and I felt the words against my nape as she said them. "Whatever they are," she said, "you build us some."

"Your mother won't shell out for the lumber. She won't ever fix this place. She hates me. She thinks I'm a wastrel and the last of the hippies and the seducer of her kid," I said.

"Don't be insulting," she said. "You never seduced me. Yes, you did. But I knew you didn't mean to. You were respectful. You pay your respects, and you stand there being shaggy and a little shy, and people sometimes, anyway, no matter their intentions or any of that, they fall in—whatchamacallit."

"Did you ever think of that as scary?"

"It's the word you're scared of," she said. "You're saving it for Miss Plexiglas Maidenhead of the Short Attention Span. But that's fine. Really. Let's say fall into . . . flesh. That's what happens when people get to be postgraduates."

"You always talk about how old you are," I said.

"Postgraduate, I said. Who said anything about old?"

"No, you're afraid that you're the scary older woman."

"I'd just as soon you do not predict my intentions or supply me with meanings. What happens," she said against the back of my neck, "is that people fall into flesh."

I turned off the stove. She was pulling on me and my leg went back for support, and she pushed her groin against it as she dragged me by the waist, and I started to fall. She straightened and caught me, big as I was, because she was a strong woman and she liked to prove her strength. I pushed off, turned, and we were standing straight again. I put my hands inside her jacket.

She hissed because I had touched bare skin. I said, "No wonder you're cold." She pulled me toward the built-in bed a few feet from the stove.

"You aren't resisting," she asked. "We could cancel the rest of the badinage and just enjoy ourselves. Do you think?"

"I'm not resisting," I said.

"I'm not resisting either," she said.

I tried to say how grateful I was, and how worried about my gratitude, and how she turned my temperature up like an oven. But the idea of saying it and of knowing she had heard it would make me sad. What happened a lot, that year, was that I worried about making myself sad and then about permitting myself too much pleasure. It was like taking care of a sick roommate, or a patient, except that he was me. The lights were on, but we closed our eyes. You always want a little darkness when you go to bed with someone who's a stranger you will probably never know much better but who you like a lot. You end up watching yourself and each other, which is what you need, together, to get past. And I knew her well enough to know that the end of anything at all could make her sad—of her marriage some years ago, of her father's life last year, of her twenties this year, of her mother's money, of whatever she and I were caught in, and probably, I thought, of what she would describe as the end of her happiness or sanity or something immense and dreadful to conclude.

"You don't need to call Julia those Miss Whatever names," I said, "do you?"

"Yes," she said. "Very much. Absolutely very much. She's got training-bra spring in her tits, and she's got you forlorn. Yes, I do."

"You don't even need a bra, Rebecca. Look at you."

When she looked down at herself, as I looked up her chest, beneath me, where we lay, her eyes nearly crossed. She put her hands on herself and said, "They're hard as ice."

"It's the cold."

"So, David," she said, "let's be practical. Get me warm here, will you?"

It was Rebecca in the darkness I wanted, so I pulled the covers up over us, and I also closed my eyes. I lay inside her, and she lay beneath me inside her dead father's hunting coat. Later on, I thought that we hadn't solved very much between us, and then, still later, after she had gone to the house, as I stood at the stove in the smell of natural gas and of her whiskey and vermouth and cigarettes and soap while the soup slowly cooked, I thought that we hadn't done so badly at what it is you do when the weather is bad, and prospects are slim, and it is best to not be wholly on your own.

The next morning, there was some kind of dazzle in the sky. The clouds were milky and low in a blanket, and little flecks of sun broke through. They made me think of the flecks of ice in Rebecca's hair as she shook them off in the dull light of the trailer. They also made me think of the gray-white plastic walls of the trailer, which were flecked with a gold-colored paint. I noticed the sky, and then the low gray car that was parked behind the kid's cabin at the motel. It looked as though it had been in a fire, or as though whitewash had been dumped all over it and badly cleaned off. I wondered if the stains on his jacket had something to do with the charred look of the car, an old Pontiac with busted springing in the back which suggested that someone had used it for hauling heavy freight over long distances.

I lugged and wrestled a long, flat rock that would serve as a kind of keystone for the wall, at what was once, years before, the beginning of their driveway, when they kept it paved and when anyone drove on it to visit them. The wall would be about three feet high and would separate their land from the road for a hundred feet, ending at the other end of their former driveway, near the stone house where Rebecca and Mrs. Josephine Peete managed a very small estate, mostly by selling off parcels of their property. They were in a corner of what had been hundreds of acres. They were the only year-round residents, and in winter, without the protection of foliage and brush, they could see the A-frames and faux-Victorian cottages of their neighbors.

The kid backed from the door of his cabin as I loaded a wheelbarrow with rocks to set out in a bottom layer leading from the keystone. He didn't come down the steps to wait for the bus, and he didn't wear his backpack. That was how I knew it was Saturday morning.

"Hey," I called across the road.

He looked at me, but his face showed no expression and he didn't reply.

"I live over here," I said. "In the little trailer in there." I pointed in the general direction of the pine trees. "How's it going?" I asked, trying to sound like an all-right person.

He studied me, and then he took his hands out of his coat pockets and lifted them a little way into the air before him and, with no expression, shrugged. He looked like a miniature man who indicated that fate would have its say.

"I'm David," I said. "I work at this place."

His hands were back in his pockets and his pointed, pale face gave me nothing.

"Okay," I said. "It's time to work."

I fitted the stones together right. I knew how to do that because all I ever did right as a kid was build. I'd constructed a fortress near my parents' place in South Jersey, narrow but tall, maybe fourteen feet high, made of wood on a stone foundation—not drypoint, like this one, but made solid with mortar—and it still was there. My mother reported on it when she and my father came to see me, after I had finally graduated. She'd been kneeling at the little refrigerator in my trailer, putting packets of food inside, and she had just told me how my fort still stood, when she began to cry. I thought she was crying about the size of the trailer, the smell of it, the pretty powerful sense it radiated that, living in it, you had given up on acquiring a future. I didn't ask her, though. I sat back at the little fold-up table and let her pretend not to cry while she, down at the refrigerator, pretended not to know that I observed her weeping. Giving that kind of privacy to each other can be almost as good as a set of walls, or a door you can close behind you. My father had never learned about it, and pretty soon he was standing behind her, almost shouting down onto her head. "Lily! What? What's wrong?" He turned to look at me, and something about my face—maybe the nothing I tried to compose on it—made him think about shooting me, or slugging me, or shouting. "Lil," he said, "*tell* me."

When I looked up from the second barrow load, the kid was on the Peetes' side of the county road, and he was watching me.

"I guess you're allowed to cross the road," I said. "Your mother lets you do that? Your father?"

He said, "Traffic here is surprisingly light."

"Yes, it is."

"Surprisingly light."

"Yes. There isn't very much of it at all."

"No," he said, moving his arms, "and you don't see a great deal of commercial traffic, do you? I would say it's mostly residential."

"That's what I would say too," I said. I was on my knees, and they were growing cold, but I was afraid that I would startle him if I rose. "So how's school?"

"School is a responsibility," he said. "Some things—you just soldier on. Do you know that expression?"

"I think I've heard it used," I said. "And that's what you do on schooldays? You soldier on?"

He nodded.

"You don't like it, though."

"Oh, I don't mind," he said. "It's what I'm supposed to do, so I do it. School's all right. Are you a college student?"

"No," I said, "but I used to be."

"What exactly are you?"

"I'm the handyman," I said. "I do the chores for Mrs. Peete."

"Like building a fence," he said.

"This is going to be a wall, actually. You can *use* it as a fence, but it's a wall."

"How do you know the difference?"

"Well, *I* know because I'm building it. You'll know because I told you."

"And I might tell someone else," he said. "So *they* would know." His lips looked swollen, his skin seemed almost blue beneath its pallor. His hands were broad, with long fingers, and he kept returning them to the pockets of his coat. "So if it keeps a person out, it acts like a fence. But it's a wall."

"This baby is nothing but wall," I said. "So I told you, right? And I told you my name?"

"David."

"So now you can tell me yours."

"All right." He looked at the ground before him, and I wondered if he was making one up. Finally, he said, "Artie."

"Artie what?"

"Artie Arthur."

"Glad to meet you, Artie."

He said, "Hi."

"I hope you don't mind my noticing," I said, "but I really couldn't help it. There being so little traffic around here to look at. I've seen you leave for school."

"Bus 26."

"And I've seen you come home on it."

"Well, it's my bus," he said. "Number 26."

"Yeah. No, I was wondering, when you get home from school is there anyone around to say hello? Or goodbye when you, you know, start to soldier on?"

His face was almost purple, the blush coming in over that milky skin with blue beneath it. "Nobody's neglecting me," he said.

"No," I said, "I didn't think so. Absolutely not. I don't need to hear *anything,*" I said. "Zero is good enough for me."

"Zero probability," he said.

"Pardon?"

"Zero as a base."

"All right." But he had nothing more to say except, after a while, "I have to go."

"I'll cross you," I said.

"The traffic here is surprisingly light," he said, "so there's no need to bother."

"Surprisingly light," I said. "Catch you later."

He removed his right hand from his pocket and he waved it as an infant would, holding it before him and opening and closing his fist.

"Bye-bye," I said.

He looked to his right, then to his left, and he dashed for the motel grounds and his cabin, admitting himself with the brass key on the oval tag. At the door, he turned to look across the road. "Domicile," he called, sweeping his arm about him, and then he went in.

I arranged a few more barrow loads, and Mrs. Peete drove past as I worked, her face set and her eyes wide with panic. She would not have agreed with Artie Arthur about the traffic on our road. Even the memory of traffic was enough to undo her. And my presence didn't help. I worked for a while longer, then got myself away from the vicinity of the house, now that Mrs. Peete was gone. If I didn't, I would drift up the driveway and finally I would knock at the door, hoping that Rebecca would be in. And then I would have to admit to myself what I had done, and I would be forced to guess why, and then I would be stuck with my answer, either making up lies to contradict it, or agreeing with myself about my needs. At that time of my life, I was bent on the conquest of many of my needs, among them the falling into anything, even, sometimes, what Rebecca referred to as the flesh. It was what I had decided to aim for—speaking of fences and walls—after Julia secured her passport and cried the night before she left, and didn't cry in the morning, and then was gone.

I took myself down the road, away from their house, and into the hummocky field, through which I walked to the swamp behind it. Hundreds of trees had come down over the years, leaving only dozens standing, and most of them dying or dead. Everything there was a kind of icy gray—the surface of the water, the vegetation on top of and around it; even the gigantic flying dinosaur, the blue heron who roosted in one of the trees, was gray. The air coming over the water was steady and cold. I had never been to Central America, but when I thought of Julia living with some kind of not-quite-royal person who was dedicated to aiding the orphans of war-torn states, I thought of this kind of damp wind and this kind of desolate countryside. She would be brave and beautiful in it, and he would be earnest, and at night they would drink some kind of brandy and list their good deeds and then devour each other's body in some bullet-pocked hotel room. The heron was at the far side of the swamp now, in the top limbs of a dead aspen. He looked to be about a million years old.

I went a little closer to the swamp, ducking under evergreen branches and the leafless branches of oaks. Closer, I could see something green in the water, and I wondered if spring was really so close. I was very tired, I realized, of clenching myself against the cold. It was not vegetation, though I thought I could smell some. It seemed to be cloth. I went as close as I could, with the toes of my boots almost in water, and I saw that the cloth was in layers, green and bright blue, red and white stripes, a good deal of white. Near a tamarack still without needles, but with black-green buds on it, I saw a large oblong green garbage pail. I squatted at the edge and studied the cloth. It might be clothing. It might be someone *wearing* it. I thought, of course, about Artie Arthur and whoever he might no longer live with. I thought, too, of the burnt car that had parked near his cabin. Julia would lead me to the cabin and knock on the door and make inquiries. Rebecca would insist on our conferring in bed, or at least in a clinch. I would have done either, I suspected, with either of them.

I squatted there, looking at the cloth, most of which was underwater, though some of it lay along the surface. I saw myself returning to the Peetes' garage and fetching a long square-headed rake and returning to the swamp. I saw myself dragging at the offshore cloth, pulling it in to me, and then seeing how, very slowly, the corpse beneath it rolled over and came to the surface to bob there, swollen and eaten away, with maybe no nose or lips or fingers.

Of course I was seeing only cloth, no corpse, and even if there *were* a corpse it did not have to be Artie Arthur's mother, or some young aunt, his mother's kid sister, say, who had tried to rescue him or who had been the only relative left in the world to take care of him on a daily basis. I had no idea why he might require rescuing, or why he had ended up in the mortgage-vortex motel. And I could not account, bloated body in the swamp or none, for the car behind his cabin this morning or its absence on the other mornings.

Otherwise, I thought, I had pretty much caught up on events at the swamp. I stood, and the great blue heron, in all his leathery grayness, jumped slowly into the air and flapped away on wings I would have sworn I heard creaking. I looked at the cloth again and thought again about the rake. This is what can happen, I thought in my father's tones, when you succumb. You let yourself fall into flesh, and then you see what you get.

After Mrs. Peete's car had lurched past, returning from the market, I brushed and brushed at my hair with the set of military brushes my father had given me when I went away to school. He had bought me a gray three-piece suit at Brooks in Manhattan, and a leather toilet kit he'd called a Dopp bag, and a set of stubby, wood-handled hairbrushes. He dressed very well, if your taste runs to clean shirts and shined shoes and good suits. He ran his own consulting firm, and he was brilliant, my mother said, and I knew him to be very sharp about numbers and strategy. He was always making plans with me, over the phone, when I was in school, to come up with strategies for dealing with my teachers. I remember how during one of those calls I insisted that all they wanted was for me to read my fucking *textbooks*. I was almost in tears. After quite a long silence, he breathed out hard, and the noise flooded the receiver and my head. "Strange, how I never thought of that," he said. "I kept thinking you'd gone stupid," he said, "but all we're confronted with here is you're lazy. Is that right? Or you're busy curing cancer, and you don't have time to waste on what the mortals are supposed to do?"

I took a towel and my toilet kit, and I walked across the frozen but softening ruts and wrinkles to the Peetes'. Rebecca's very old Saab wasn't parked beside her mother's sedan, and I was relieved and disappointed. Mrs. Peete, in fawn-colored slacks and a black turtleneck, her slacks tucked into high, black boots—a kind of joke about country manors and those who struggled to maintain them—seemed not to be relieved, and, actually, she appeared to be very disappointed when she opened her door to find me on the old stone stoop.

"Oh," is all she said.

"Hi. I was wondering if I could use the shower today. Now, actually. If that would be all right."

"You look like you could use one."

So much for the military brush.

"I thought you were here for your wages," she said.

"You don't pay me wages, Mrs. Peete."

"Yes," she said, "that's right."

"Though you *could,* if you really wanted to."

Her glare was not what you would call the expression of someone receptive to humor. The only time I saw her face in a friendly expression is when she reminded Rebecca, in front of me, of a habit of Rebecca's former husband, a viola player in Albany. He seemed to like to crack his knuckles, and Mrs. Peete's square face, with its bulging blue eyes, framed by a coppery color so fake it made the color of Rebecca's hair look phony, had broken into three sections: the creased forehead notched vertically above the nose, and then the cheeks which dimpled and went red, and then the mouth, lips parted to show her thick yellow teeth in a glaze of saliva.

She waddled ahead of me, as small and chunky as Rebecca was tall and thin. She led me upstairs, on creaking steps, although she knew I knew the way. She pointed to the guest room, where I would change, and from which I would walk, in only a towel, to the adjacent bathroom. She would sit in her own bedroom, down the hall, and would listen. I assumed that's what she did—listen to the pad of my bare feet, to the sound of the shower or the flushing of the toilet or the scratching of the towel against my back as I dried off. When I was done, she would listen to my return to the guest room and, when she heard my boots on the floor, she would emerge from her room to frown at my cleatmarks—though she'd never asked me to take off my boots—and then she would lead me down the stairs.

The guest room was painted pink, with white woodwork. The bathroom was tiled in white with pink woodwork. The soap was pink, and so was the bath mat, and so were the towels that I was not allowed to use. I tried to think of Mrs. Peete's pink skin, yards of it, against pink sheets, beneath a pink Mr. Peete, employed, to the moment of his death, as an insurance adjuster. Talk about falling into flesh, I thought. I realized that I'd been singing in the shower about how I was going to board a passenger plane and not come back again. Suspecting that it might be true, and living in hope that it was, Mrs. Peete would have the three-story smile on her face again, I figured.

Downstairs, she led me into the kitchen. I caught a glimpse of the living room, its dark antique furniture, its maroon sofa long enough to use as a lifeboat, and I could see the signs of them both—the scattered magazines and papers of Rebecca, and the basket filled with twine balls on a neat stack of what I knew to be *Reader's Digest* condensed novels (all of William Gaddis's *The Recognitions,* I thought, but in seven pages). I sat at the kitchen table as she expected me to, with my damp towel and toilet kit on the floor beside my feet, hands folded on the table's edge, and Mrs. Peete served out—not once engaging my eyes or, so far as I could tell, looking directly at me—a plate of homemade beans and little pork chunks, all of it baked in molasses, and a large glass of milk. I despised milk, but I always drank it at her table.

"I got the wall started," I said.

"I saw it."

"It's a good idea. You'll like it. You get a feeling of separation, but you still can see what's going on."

"Yes. That's how Rebecca said it. Just exactly like that."

So she had found a way to make it clear precisely why she hated me. Not only did I look a little alien to her—not quite Martian, but not assuredly not, either—but I was her daughter's choice of recreational drug. Which was not entirely true, since Rebecca also brought with her, from time to time, for recreational purposes, a little packet of grass that she purchased in Poughkeepsie. At those times, looking at it from Mrs. Peete's point of view, Rebecca was compounding the crime.

She always poured me a second glass of milk and gave me a plate of her buttery cookies to eat with it. In silence, then, I finished the cookies as she watched me. As she always did when I said my thanks, she replied, "You're entirely welcome." This time, she added, "Have a nice week."

I said, "You can feel a little spring out there."

"I'm not so sure," she said.

I nodded, as if to signal that I'd reconsider, and I gathered my bag and towel, and she walked me to the door, perhaps to make certain that I left.

I paused in the foyer and said, "Could I ask you something about the neighborhood?"

"Neighborhood? There's this and there's that, across the road."

"That's the that I wanted to know about, Mrs. Peete."

"That's the that. You went to college to learn how to talk this way?"

I hung my head, because she was gifted in her production of the sound of sneering and facial furrows of disgust. I could not imagine anyone whose pride she wouldn't erode.

"You know the way to Poughkeepsie? When your car is working?"

"It needs a new battery. It can't hold a charge."

"What does that say about you?" she asked.

"I'm afraid to guess."

Her face writhed and then composed. "This little road, once upon a time, could get you to Poughkeepsie. Parts they don't keep up any-more, and parts they shut down. But in the 1930s, the 1940s, this was a good road. The motel people lived in this house. One of them's a ghost. I have seen him, but never mind. I don't argue about ghosts."

"A little boy?"

She looked pale now, and I understood how much of an effort she was making to be civil, much less give her knowledge away to the hired man. I was stealing her magic and, because of her daughter, she was abetting the theft.

"A man," she said.

"The motel owner?"

She said, "Enough. Enough. Shower, lunch, the guided tour . . . enough. Have a nice week."

"Just—do you remember his name, Mrs. Peete?"

But she had closed the door as I stepped across the threshold. My mouth tasted gluey, and I smelled the heavy, sour smell of milk drift-ing up my face as I sang the song about leaving while I walked. Be-fore I forced myself back into the trailer, I went around to the front and looked across the road at the motel: eight cabins, empty sign frame, and no charred car.

Inside the trailer, I took my jacket off and put a sweater on. It might have been close to spring, but it was very cold, and I was quite sorry for myself.

"Give us a smile, ducky," I said, looking at my reflection on the glass that sealed in Julia's print. "Oh, I see. You're just *not* gonna smile, are you?" I said to the bushy, shape.

"Eat my ass," the shape replied. I did hate cheerleaders. I also hated my poverty and almost any exchange with Mrs. Peete. I detested my insistence on living here the way I did. In addition, I was violently al-lergic to feeling that I had no choice. And I was down to only one, which I despised: go to my parents' home, watch my mother weep, listen to my father, sounding like a badly played slide trombone, per-form his solo from The Lost Time But Lesson Learned Don't Stray Again Now Get Back Prodigal Blues.

Fortunately, the beans began to have their effect, and I was driven from my profitless metaphysics to considerations of the actual: the state of my digestive system, and the cold winds in the woods. I lay down on the little bed and closed my eyes and, every once in a while, sent up a hiss of gastric distress. I actually fell asleep. It was the only other place I knew to go, this side of suicide or military service. I woke with a little stirring of pleasure, for I had come to realize that I had three choices instead of one. Though in truth I could not imagine myself shouting in unison with a bunch of eighteen-year-olds and then running in step for miles to the cadences called by a drill instructor. I think it never occurred to me that I might try to be an officer. Officer Bear. So, I thought, waking, beginning to lose what had passed, an instant before, as an insight, there is always suicide. But maybe this *is* suicide, I thought. It seemed pretty likely. On the other hand, I thought, if you aren't killing yourself tonight, you had better head for the woods.

So I put my jacket on, took toilet paper and flashlight, and went from the trailer in what was now a porous darkness, and I walked into the woods. The winds had died, and I could hear creatures in the underbrush—voles and mice and rats, I thought—and stirrings in the high branches of trees—maybe owls beginning to hunt. I also heard a car gear down, then crunch its way along the gravel of their drive. I cut toward the house and got closer, then stopped behind a Norway maple to listen to Rebecca in the dark. I heard her turn the radio off, and saw the lights go out, before she turned off the motor, which meant that she was sober. When she was drunk enough, she'd leave the Saab in the driveway, engine running, radio loud, and all lit up. I backed away and headed for a far corner of the pine plantation, where I was as useful as I'd been for weeks. Rebecca would eat supper with her mother, and her mother would doubtless describe my provocations. Rebecca would smile her nervous smile—it came and went, like a tic—and I would crouch in the trailer, as I was doing at that moment, and, rather than try to make a sketch or read a book, I would lie in my clothing on the bed, waiting to sleep and, as usual, waking the next day with a kind of alarm as I noted that I had slept the deep, easy sleep of a man possessed of reason who was weary from his many accomplishments.

I was out and working on the wall by seven on Sunday morning, hauling stones, cleaning them off, setting them in. I used the back of a hatchet I had found in their garage for chipping off lumps so the stones would fit together. I whistled a medley of tunes from musicals that had flopped. I was working my way through *Anyone Can Whistle,* which was about crazy people being the only ones who are sane. The sun wasn't strong, but I could feel it, and I sensed the turning of the seasons as, all of a sudden, a fact. I was getting ready. I was going to make a move. I had no idea what it would be, but a move, I would have sworn to you, was forthcoming. I got pretty loud and sparky as I chirped a number that Harry Guardino had bellowed, and then the toes of Rebecca's tan work shoes were between me and the rocks at which I worked.

"Well," I said. "You caught me."

"Working?"

"Whistling."

"Working and whistling," she said. "Isn't this where Sneezy and Dopey and Sleepy come in?"

I did a few bars of "Whistle While You Work" and then stood up. She was hatless, but she wore her father's old mackinaw. I reached for the part where the lapels crossed and I looked inside.

"You have clothes on," I said.

She went red. "Sorry," she said.

"For having, or for not having had?"

She shook her head, looked away, into the sunlight, then back to me. "I need to leave here," she said.

"Me too, Rebecca."

"I can't live with my mother."

"I'm pretty sure that no one can live with your mother. If you don't mind my saying so."

"Nobody can," she said, "you're right. Anyway, *I* can't. I'm signing a lease on a place in Hudson. It's just off the main drag, near all those antique stores. I figure my mother and I might know each other longer if we don't live in the same house. But I *am*—" She closed her mouth and pressed her lips together before she said, "I was about to make one of those miss-your-good-company declamations," she said, looking away again, then looking back. "But I am. What's your thinking on it—about missing me and all?"

I stood there with her, feeling shaggier, and dirtier, and less than familiar with English-language conversations, apprehensive, light-headed, proud as well as embarrassed.

"I will guaranteed be missing you," I said.

She nodded. She looked across at the motel, she looked down the road, as if she thought of crossing it. "So come along," she said.

"To Hudson?"

"To my *place* in Hudson."

I mustered an "Oh!"

"It wouldn't be the same as, you know, moving *in* with me," she said, as the first car of the day passed, an immense Land Rover inhabited by three yellow Labradors and their driver. "You could rent a room from me," she said. "I have a guest bedroom. You could rent it, or you could have it for nothing. You could also use the nonguest bedroom. You know I'm a good copywriter. You know that I write okay ad copy for the third-rate news shows up here. And you know that I'm the voice of upstate HMO. I can afford it. I don't need to take money from you."

"You and your mother need every dime for this place," I said. "You can't even afford to keep it up, much less renovate. And I'd be uncomfortable, staying home while you went to work."

"You could get a job," she said, spreading her legs as if to set herself for warding off my excuses. Her frizzy hair was lit from behind by the sun, and she looked as if she glowed.

"Let's see," I said. "A job, an apartment. Rebecca, I'd be a—excuse me for this. I'd be a husband, wouldn't I?"

"The last of the pagans," she said. She shook her head, though she didn't smile her fast, flickering smile, and I knew for certain that the invitation had been a great deal more serious than I'd guessed. "I am trusting you to *not* bring up the age thing, all right?"

There was nothing else to do, so I stepped up and put my hands on her shoulders and I leaned in and kissed her. It was a long kiss, and at the end she gently bit my lip.

"Pack your things," she said.

"They're in my pockets. There isn't much to pack."

"No," she said. "Charcoal, pencils, brushes, paint, your sketch-books—you know. You can even bring Miss Patootie's etching."

It seemed to me that we were both too embarrassed to understand what we were doing. When you get to that point, I knew then and know better now, you will take steps or draw conclusions you end up regretting. I could offer my four and a half years of college and much of my life with my parents as examples. We stood at the wheelbarrow filled with stones, and then Rebecca turned, the way you do when you're dancing, and she went back toward the house. Then she stopped herself and slowly walked back.

"Look," she said, and her face was full of sorrow for me, "nobody's forcing you to live inside that terrible trailer. Or my apartment. Or anyplace else." Her voice was thick with feeling. "It's pretty much you, David. Whatever place you're inside of, you're the one who turned the lock."

She looked at me very directly, and she nodded her head. She wanted me to know how certain she was of what she had said, and I nodded back with respect. She walked toward the house again, and this time she kept going, waving goodbye over her shoulder. The movement of her fingers reminded me of Artie Arthur's wave. When Rebecca was out of sight, I looked at Artie's cabin: still no car. When, I wondered, would someone come and rescue us?

I finished several yards of wall, and it was a shape now. There were chickadees buzzing back and forth, and there were a few more cars. Surprisingly light traffic, Artie. The sun had a little weight. And to all of it I could now add the stone wall along the edge of Mrs. Peete and Rebecca's property. I had made something pretty true, I thought, looking at the brilliant flecks of mica, the voluptuous white-ness of limestone veins, the hundred shadows and hollows, the sense of bulk and permanence, the undeniable function it served of tying down their land and holding it in place.

Julia would not have hung around even if she knew I was going to build this wall so well. I knew that. And she had seen me at work be-fore. I trusted that she remembered I could build with stone or stud up a house or put up wallboard so well you'd not find the seams. I knew that, and I knew that a sudden reminder would not sweep her back to me. Still, I did wish I could show her what I'd made. I thought of tracking her down by telephone by using a fudged pidgin Spanish, calling with the announcement that I had built another good wall. I thought of hearing, from behind her, around her, the wails of wounded children she was tending as the sniper fire sang off packed earthen streets outside the clinic. I propped the wheelbarrow, standing it on the nose of its wooden frame, against the wall. I collected the discarded stones in a mound. I had been preparing to do it, though I hadn't suspected I was. I know it now. I had awakened with a sense of purpose and, though working on the wall had satisfied much of it, the need to cross the road remained strong.

So I went—across the road, and across the dead lawn, across the pebble walk, directly to Artie Arthur's cabin. I knocked, too driven to be frightened, though I had no idea what to say or do when someone opened the door. But no one did. And the key, its oval tag hanging down from it, was in the lock. So I knew I could turn the knob and go inside, and I did.

I smelled something that reminded me of the milky, pyramidal bottle that Frank the barber would tip over my head when I was a kid. It helped keep my hair in place for a while, though, soon enough, it sprang back up. I realized that I was running my fingers through my hair. I sometimes did that when I was upset. I did it for all three months that Julia and I were together. "It's like you're petting an animal," she had said, "except the animal is you."

There weren't any towels in the bathroom and there weren't sheets on the large bed. Nor was there a television set, a radio, or a clock. The rug was covered with dried mud. An open bureau drawer was stuffed with plastic and cellophane and cardboard wrappers of snack food. Someone had eaten most of two pizzas and a little bit of Chinese food. The wrappers and the top of the bureau were sprinkled with mouse turds. Near the small window, on an oval table, I found burnt matches, perhaps from lighting the lantern by which he had done his homework. The matches were in a neat grouping in a stained, slimy-looking soapdish. The one piece of paper on the table, from a

two-ring looseleaf notebook, had numbers written in an adult hand.
Someone had added the same set of figures about a dozen times.
They always started out with 39,000 of something and then concluded
with a meticulous minus sign, and a final 1,100. On the other side of
the page was handwriting practice, or practice in remembering a
name: ARTIE ARTHUR ARTIE ARTHUR ARTIE ARTHUR ARTIE ARTHUR.
The big characters filled up the page. He was there, but noplace else.
Although there was one more place to look.

When I went outside, I walked around to the back of the cabin and
saw the tracks of the long, charred car pressed into the wet soil. I was
pleased to learn that the vehicle in Artie Arthur's life was actual, and
that I had truly seen it. But I was not pleased with where I had to
look. I crossed the road and went back to their garage, walking along
the side of the stone colonial house, and I fetched the long-handled
rake, which I carried on my shoulder like a man a long time ago off
to rake hay. It was damper and cooler in the field I cut through, and
it was outright cold at the swamp. Little sun seemed to get through
to warm the water, and it radiated cold like a freezer left open. I
squatted at the edge, listening to ducks squabble, and then I straightened and walked to the water, took a breath, and went in up to my
knees. The deep chill went up my legs and through my chest, and my
head suddenly ached as if I'd eaten ice cream too quickly.

I cried out and the ducks, several dozen yards away, took off, making their wheezy noises. I waded further in, balancing myself with the
rake, and then I began to look for the horrible news behind Artie
Arthur's story. I let the rake, which I held at the end of its haft, flop
down, and then I pulled it back to me as if it were a rope, and most
of the time something came with it: bath towels, horribly smeared,
and then a big green towel such as you'd use at the beach, I thought,
and then a shower curtain with figures of seagulls on it. I let the cloth
eddy about me where I stood, and I went back with the rake to free
whatever was trapped beneath the remaining clothes. The reds and
oranges of T-shirts and underwear came up, and then fancy-looking
pajamas that perhaps a small woman had worn. Up, too, came bub-
bles of gas, the broccoli smell of trapped vegetation, and the cheap
white dress shirt of a man with unusually long arms.

I was prepared, or I thought I was, for little Artie, blue and open-eyed, to come rocking up. And I suspected that his mother or aunt might be down there with him. It would be a sudden surfacing, I thought, and then the vandalized body would arrive to float before me, and I would have to figure a way of getting it on shore. But no one came up from exile back to the world. I was surrounded by cheap clothing and filthy towels. I heard his wings before I saw him as the heron clumsily angled for the top of the tree across the swamp. He saw or heard me, then, and he curved off and out of sight. Wading in further, so that the water was above my waist, balancing myself with the rake, I tried once more, but I drew up only weeds and a bit of rotted tree that caught between the tines of the rake.

It was difficult to lift my feet from the floor of the swamp, and it was tricky to escape from its edge. But I finally stood in the field, a failure at rescue and disinterment. I was the robber of graves, and I was the rescuer, with nothing to show for the work and with no evidence of my good intentions except for the odor of rot that I wore.

I went back to their garage and replaced the rake. Rebecca was looking out their kitchen window and when she saw me—I figure I was green from the swamp and red with shame because of my failure—her eyebrows rose. I shrugged in reply. We had slept together a couple of dozen times. We knew each other, I guessed, but I thought then of my parents and I doubted I was right. I didn't know whether to want to know someone or not. I had a suspicion that it was good for the loneliness, but maybe after that you knew in ways you'd rather not.

I went back to the trailer and used some bottled water for a sponge bath at my sink. Then I changed into khakis I ought to have washed some weeks before and a dark green sweatshirt that I rarely wore because it said, across the front, CAMP NOK-A-MIX-ON, which was where I'd worked as a waiter in the summer between my freshman and sophomore years. I put on sneakers and went out to continue at the wall. I kept seeing the door swing in at the motel cabin. I kept thinking of the little kid who wrote his name so many times. And of course I thought about the car. Someone had come to take care of him, I thought—I wished—who wasn't always able to. They were broke and fleeing creditors, I thought. Or they were fleeing the Cosa Nostra, to which the driver of the car owed an allegiance he had violated. Or the father robbed banks. It really didn't matter to me, except that they not be captured, and that Artie have somebody on the other side of his door as he went off to school and returned.

I hauled the stones and cleaned them and set them in. I could feel the cold of them as well as their weight through my rawhide work gloves, and I didn't mind, because what I felt was the first reward of this kind of work. The second was that it stood and you had made it. I caught my breath and stood beside the wall when Rebecca came out to me, wearing her father's coat open. I went back to work as she approached, and she stood there awhile. I felt suddenly very shy with her, and I focused on the wall and on the quality of my work. I was acutely conscious of her bright, crinkly hair, and of her small mouth, her large, smart eyes, and of her body too, hidden within the jeans and coat, but familiar to me—a hipbone I had held to, a breast at which I'd nuzzled. I admired the urgency with which she dived into bed, and with which she drank cocktails made of bourbon and sweet vermouth, and with which she pulled on her cigarettes, or drove the narrow roads, or argued about politics or the cost of hotels in Monopoly. She watched me admire her, and she gestured me up and onto my feet. She had a canvas bag with her, and it contained steaks and the makings of Manhattans. We had a long, drunken evening in the trailer, and we were so far gone, so fervent in pursuit of our anesthetic stupor, that I cannot remember much of what we said, or what we did together, but I remember our saying a lot, and doing a lot. If we were valedictory or sentimental, I have gratefully managed to forget.

A few days later, she moved away, returning irregularly on weekends, when she remained with her mother in the house. On a Saturday in April, when Rebecca hadn't come home, I went over for my shower and my meal. Instead of her beans, Mrs. Peete served up casserole of potatoes and cheese.

I didn't drink the glass of milk that came with it, and she said, "You hate that milk, huh?"

"I'm afraid so," I said. "I never liked it, even when I was a kid."

224 Don't Tell Anyone

"You are still a kid," she said, "but you should have told me. I wouldn't have wasted good milk. It's money down the drain, you understand." She looked at me with a kind of softness I was unaccustomed to. Her face went into those three parts I rarely saw, and I understood that she was relenting. I wondered if Rebecca had put in a good word on my behalf. "You were trying to be polite," she said.

I nodded, tried a smile, didn't get one in return, and kept a serious face on.

"That is what I would call a good sign," she said.

"Mrs. Peete"—I was flooded with courage, desperate with a need to escape, and very glad to feel, and to act on, the need—"would you say you're pleased with what I've built around here? With the repairs I did?"

"You want wages," she said. "They are not a part of our arrangement."

"If you could lend me enough for a new battery," I said, "and maybe a battery cable, I could be on the road. I'd mail you the money. Really. I would."

"Leave?" she said. Her eyes were wet. "You are leaving too? But for where? Doing what?" She paused briefly for the answer I could not begin to give her, and then, moving as her daughter did, she turned to leave the room. I thought of taking a sip of milk to please her, but I couldn't. She came back in with a large brown reptile-hide purse, and she searched in it for her wallet and counted out what I told her I thought a battery would cost.

She nodded in agreement. "Rebecca said about that much."

"She knew I would ask you for this?"

"Oh," she said, "David. You are not as much of a mystery as you would like to think."

A Handbook
for Spies

A Novella

Come Up to Me, Love

In Buddha's Ear

WILLIE THOUGHT OF his parents' life together as an inverted pyramid, a vast funnel, a tornado that stood still. At the wide end was Europe, the world in its war, the Jews in their decimation. His parents in Paris, adolescents already in love, the children of a knotted skein of family friendships, were intended to marry and were happy, they had told him in his boyhood, to oblige their fate. And then the flight with their aunts, the shining vans soon thereafter at the families' doors to transport them to the cattle cars, and the voyage of his parents to England and America, to money and a restless suburban ease, to Willie's years at the Friends school and Columbia University and what he saw as the pyramid's point, the funnel's small mouth, the roar of the whirlwind. His parents, together so long, by now were crushed together in their lives, he decided; the heat of their unannounced friction made him sweat, and their Gallic *sang-froid,* what he saw as a matter-of-fact acceptance of the end of their long, joint adventure, chilled him.

They were a family in fever, he thought, and they were caught in a narrow time. He and his classmates wore narrow-shouldered Harris tweed sportcoats with narrow lapels. They sought to look narrow of shoulder and narrow of hip, their narrow trousers were hung from them by narrow belts, and their neckties—fastened with the old, fat high school Windsor knot pulled tight to their rolled blue oxford cloth button-down collars—were woven in red or yellow or orange, like coded signals from hidden selves they knew they secretly were, slyly crazy with sex or drink or reefer, and the ties were as lean as their options, which some of them thought to be broad.

Willie Bernstein signed a loyalty oath. A tall woman with a long, pale face and a smile filled with teeth and merry intelligence asked the secretary to the assistant dean of faculty if their signatures were required. Willie had already signed because a payday at the end of his first month's teaching was contingent on having sworn to never betray the United States of America, the people of the State of New York, or the colleagues of the profession, as well as having sworn to revile the menace of Communism, rolling in upon the universities even as one debated signing. The tall new assistant professor of classics, still smiling, but no longer merry, wrote, then crossed out her name, then, looking at Willie and shrugging, signed again.

"They'll know I hesitated," she said.

"Yes, but they'll know it wasn't easy."

She held up a blue leather handbag and shook it, as if to signify its emptiness. "It was too easy," she said. The assistant dean's secretary eyed her.

At the end of the first day of classes, he believed that he'd impressed them with Sir Thomas Browne, reading to them that ancient burial urns "contained not single ashes; Without confused burnings they affectionately compounded their bones; passionately endeavoring to continue their living Unions." He said something affectedly coy about everlasting love and then he mentioned long engagements, waited for a laugh and, getting none, nevertheless stumbled on into what he tried to think might become a career. As he did, he thought of the only long union he knew, his parents', and how, while he pawed his high school dates or whinnied like a badly ridden horse with girls in his lean, hard college bed, he was thinking of how to fall in love, how to become youthfully middle-aged and the visibly satisfied inhabitant of a long and reassuring love. He handed out, reproduced in purple ink, the first stanza of John Donne's "The Relique":

> When my grave is broke up again
> Some second guest to entertain,
> (For graves have learned that womanhead
> To be more than one a bed)
>   And he that digs it, spies
> A bracelet of bright hair about the bone,
>   Will he not let us alone,
> And think that there a loving couple lies,
> Who thought that this device might be some way
> To make their souls, at the last busy day,
> Meet at this grave, and make a little stay?

They were not as impressed as Willie with the woman's hair around the dead man's bone. "It makes you shudder," Willie suggested. One kid nodded. One wrote something in his notes. The rest of them waited for Willie to say what the words *really* meant.

In the mail in his department's offices, late that afternoon, he found a notice from the Syracuse draft board, demanding his body for inspection. They called him in every few months to see whether some magic had restored the cartilage in his knees, its early disappearance attested to by the doctor who had cared for him all his childhood years, and who declared his knees to be insufficient for bearing the weight of the realities confronted by the U.S. expeditionary forces in the Republic of Vietnam. Even he considered that they ought to send him over as a typist or clerk. But they classified him, each time, as unwanted unless war was declared. They sneered at him, and he wheezed with relief, while kids without his family doctor, without families who could afford doctors who would write on their behalf, went to war and, more and more of them, died.

Tant pis, he said with his father's native accent, each time he accused himself: so much the worse or, in American, tough shit. Willie Bernstein lived. He imagined himself, as he said it, looking like his tough French father; he knew that he looked like a soft American, nearly still a boy and still in search of the man he had decided he must be.

Because of the draft board letter, he began as a teacher in college by parading naked with a number of his students in the cold upstate halls leased by the U.S. Armed Forces, each of them gripping a sock in which they carried their watch, wallet, and other personal effects, while, in the other hand, they carried the large brown envelope containing their file. As was his habit at these meat parades, he kept a stub of pencil in his wallet and, while hauling his future along from an Army physician who'd taken his blood pressure to a Navy doctor in charge of X-rays, he sneaked the pencil into play and crossed out or changed any numbers the previous doctor had entered. He knew nothing of what the numbers meant. He simply saw himself as a man, undercover, working in ignorance, as if in the dark, at saving his life. Give the machine data it can't use, and it just might spit you out. At home in America, starting a job, once a loyal, oath-reciting Boy Scout who had attained badges of merit, he was also a guerrilla, he thought, as he bent at the trough with a dozen others who filled their specimen bottles so that a laboratory could find them sufficient for the state to send east; his mission was to not be sent.

He was a *sub rosa* man of twenty-six in a country at war—at several wars he realized, reminded of the older one by an angry, tall, lean man with *café au lait* skin who wore a white medical coat in a pocket of which was a coiled stethoscope that looked alive and fangy. He took Willie's envelope, read some file entries, said, "You have the blood pressure, I would say, of a hippo in heat. Go lie down."

A number of them lay on military cots on the military's assumption that their pressure would drop as they relaxed, enabling them to be classified healthy enough to lose their health for the cause. The stink of the urine of hundreds was still in Willie's nose. A boy on a cot beside him lay facing the wall. Blood seeped from something just inside the waistband at the back of his dirty briefs. His skin was gray-white, his blond hair greasy, and he had raised his knees toward his chest against the cold of the room or, Willie thought, the cold inside him; he was feeling that inner chill himself. Willie tried to think professionally. He tried to think of classroom goals, and of articles he ought

to write. He must post office hours, he thought, and buy some sec-
ondhand lamps for his apartment. He wished he still lived in his
apartment on Great Jones Street, over the meat market. He had attended a different meat market at the MLA in Chicago, and now he
was inches from the abattoir.

The doctor returned to them, towering in the small room of mint-
green walls and khaki cots on wooden legs. "You," he said to the
back of the bleeding man, "have a pilonidal cyst on which your Uncle
is going to operate—don't look up at me like I didn't talk English! I
mean your Uncle *Sam,* asshole. More yours than mine. And never
mind how to spell it. It's a cyst, it's infected, and we'll cut it out of you,
free of charge, and you can come and play with us." Willie heard the
kid snuffle in his fear and Willie tried to look away so he could find
a little privacy.

"You"—the doctor was talking to Willie—"stand right up here so
I can give you a little medicine."

In his boxer shorts and goose bumps, he stood barefooted while the
doctor looked down with distaste. He took Willie's blood pressure
with an instrument on noisy wheels rolled in by a sailor. He said,
"You'll do." He then looked at Willie's knees and at the chart, then
back to his knees. "Poor little white guy," he said. He leaned toward
Willie and turned the chart so that Willie could watch him cross out
the old classification and write in *1-A.* "You're going to Vietnam, son.
You'll get to do your part." He smiled with no friendship, but surely
with pleasure. "Maybe you won't have to shoot off your gun. Maybe
you can carry supplies up the line to the bloods."

Willie returned to his apartment to drink a lot of beer and write an
angry letter to his draft board in New York about unbounded racism
in the military health service. He had always fought, Willie thought,
without asking himself about wounds, high risks, or deep scars, for
the rights of the American Negro. Here he was, now, complaining
about one to a Mrs. Doherty of the New York City draft board. He
felt as though he were filing a complaint not against his own beliefs
but in fact against himself. Still, he was writing for his life, he
thought, and he typed the letter, he stamped it and carried it to the
box outside the post office. Then he drank more beer.

When he telephoned his parents and reported that he was on the verge of extinction on account of racial enmity and Presidential lies about peace with honor—"Peace with murder," he all but whimpered—his father, a man who after all had survived the Nazi invasion of his nation, city, and apartment building, was unreassuringly silent.

"That is difficult, eh? I mean that I understand it is difficult for you," his father finally said. "Perhaps you will go to someplace restful—peaceful, of course, is what I mean. Perhaps they will not murder you."

"There's always that," Willie said, blushing.

His father said, "Let me put your mother on."

So he had disappointed his nation, he had disappointed himself, and he had clearly let his father down. He was just twenty-six, he owned a doctorate in seventeenth-century literature, he had a very much used Corvair convertible, a handful of Rooster ties, two sportcoats and some khaki pants, he was beginning a beard, and he occupied the three rooms of a furnished apartment in a pretty college town near the Canadian border, across which, he decided while listening to his mother's consolations, he had every intention of racing in his little blue Corvair toward Tuktoyaktuk, which his atlas showed to be a tiny port on the Beaufort Sea, just east of the Arctic Ocean.

But first he had to attend what the college called a tunk. It was held, in a small Victorian mansion on the campus, to welcome a dozen new teachers. A tunk seemed to be a cocktail party mostly for fraternity boys who had grown up to be teachers. There was much loud laughter, many knowing jokes about deans and faculty meetings and the maneuverings of the local chapter of the American Association of University Professors. There was much eating of boiled shrimp, which apparently were a rarity and around the large bowl of which several dozen men had gathered to drink sweet, acidic wine and, with nervous haste, to dip the shrimp, on toothpicks, into a sauce best described, Willie thought, as red. The only dark face in the room belonged to Dr. Vivek, who was an exchange scholar. Dr. Vivek spoke with frequency of his interest in the novel of the expression of universal love. Dr. Clendinnin, a psychologist, small and slight, bald and very bucktoothed, who wore a bold plaid sportcoat, took pictures of the new faculty, blinding them with the flash of his bulbs. The big, sexy woman of the loyalty oath was there, moving about the room in an effort, Willie would have said, to evade the tall, redheaded senior professor who followed her. He had a leering look which, Willie would learn, was his expression of love for himself. The president of the college was a small round man whose faculty dean was a large round man. They spoke often—no, they listened often—among the dark mahogany bookshelves and worn oriental carpets and yellow-white lace antimacassars and plump crimson chaise-longues to a trim, handsome old man in a rich brown suit cut to flatter his slenderness. He was pointed out as Dr. Wherry, a professor of comparative religion and a man who raised a lot of money for the school. Willie should have guessed his field of study, he thought, drinking the stinging white wine and eating a lot of shrimp dipped in red, as he watched him lean against a huge head of the Buddha which occupied the end of a long cherry table with legs that were thick, four-toed claws. Buddha faced out, Dr. Wherry leaned in, so that his torso lay against the enigmatic eyes. As he spoke to the president and dean, who were stiff with attention, the professor very slowly, keeping pace with the rhythm of his speech, and clearly listening to his own every word with great interest, ran his finger around and around the inside of the Buddha's left ear.

This was a man who knew his work, Willie told himself before he abandoned shrimp and whiskey for an evening during which he planned to consider his early death in a place he knew from Walter Cronkite's television reports to have a sky always crowded with moisture, mine fragments, and the venom of serpents. Putting on his single-breasted tan raincoat and his crushable tan hat—there was lightning and thunder, which he took as a meteorological underlining of his recent brush with intimations of military combat—he went out into the warm rain, holding the door for a woman whose own tan raincoat was open and whose dress was dark with rain. She bit her lip and looked at him with very pale blue eyes. Her arms stayed at her sides and she stood in place, though Willie held the door.

"How is it in there?" she asked. "I'm guessing at something like, say, dead?"

"Are you new here too?"

She shook her head. "Not anywhere," she said.

"You're not—"

"One of the elect? I am not, no. My father is. Fevler? Russian lit? Big schnoz like mine but not as pretty?"

"What would you say is the sound made by the Buddha when he's tickled in the ear by a very confident professor?"

Her face lit up, and she nodded, and her braid swung. She stuck her hand out to shake, and he took it. "He goes *tunk*," she said.

Alien Sperm

"Pull it."

"I don't want to hurt you, Tony."

"Oh, my smarty professor. Could we—just don't *talk* so much about it, will you? Let's just fuckin *fuck*."

When he came, he was to pull on her thick, dark-blond braid, which hung to the small of her back and which emphasized her long, athletic torso, her swimmer's shoulders and chest. Her legs were long, longer than Willie's, but they were so muscular that she never appeared as tall as she was. She called herself Tony, though her parents called her Tanya, and she was here, near the campus and near the border, in her parents' house, because she was in flight from her husband of twenty-two months. She was two years younger than Willie, and a century more experienced. Her nose was curved and regal and it gave her face a look of cruelty which he found galvanizing. Her eyes were the coldest pale blue. He should have been able to see through them, they were so icily clear, but instead, he felt, they saw through his skin into the moving wet organs the metabolism of which raced when she worked him over, which she liked to do, in his bed, and in beds in her parents' home, and against surfaces she clearly chose for their public location.

As he leaned against a low obelisk of gravestone in the faculty cemetery on the grounds of the campus, as the chiseled name of a dead natural sciences doctor pressed their deep serifs against his back,

Tony Fevler thumped him hard. He could feel her pelvic bone like a fist as she slugged him with her groin. This was possibly not about sexual pleasure, Willie thought, wincing and looking up, in the grave-yard, at the evergreens that nearly screened them from the benches and the elms which lined a crescent, planted in lilies, favored by students and teachers for evening walks. It was dark and it was late, but they were nearly in view. He cupped her buttocks and she ground herself against him, feeling suddenly more soft than hard to him, though he grew suddenly harder.

"Did you ever get a blow job in public, Willie?" Her whisper was urgent, and her hands were too. The air poured over him, and its announcement of his nakedness, and her breath on him, were the excitement she had probably intended.

He put his hands on her lovely, thick hair and his hands rode her head as she galloped in place. "You taste like soap and sperm together," she said, kissing the end of his penis, which he waggled at her. It brushed her cheek as she leaned to embrace him, her hands around the backs of his thighs. Then she sighed and slid him slowly into her mouth and slowly moved back and forth. He did his part, and promptly, and he seized her braid and pulled as he bucked.

She stayed there, holding up her open mouth for Willie to inspect.

"Now you just taste like sperm," she said. She licked her lips. She licked her fingers. She made a happy child's tasting noise and, cupping his balls, gently nipped his penis and said, "I have a mouthful of Jewish sperm."

"Is that what does it? The alien in your mouth?"

"Maybe," she said. "I don't know. But it's you." She assumed the expression of a serious little girl. "Is that all right?"

Willie nodded.

"Would you say it?"

He asked, "Say what?"

"Please?"

"I love it."

"No, it's *what* do you love?"

"You, Tony."

"But what'd I *do*?"

"I loved coming in your mouth. I love it when you take me in your mouth."

"When I blow you," she said.

"Yes."

She frowned.

"When you blow me," he said.

"And get a mouthful of Jewish sperm," she said. She was unbuttoning her yellow sleeveless blouse, unfastening her brassiere. She moved closer on her knees, and he wondered why the soil and pebbles didn't hurt them. Then he realized that they did, and she wished them to. She moved up against him and climbed his legs, brushing her nipples against him. She pressed them against his penis, saying, "This is how I clean you off. My mouth and my breasts. I'm wearing you home. I'm still swallowing you."

Willie tugged very gently at her braid.

She said, "I'm not a puppy dog, Willie. I'm not your little girl. I'm the woman you're fucking. I'm the woman who blows you. When you pull the braid is when you *come*. Remember?"

He said, "Yes," feeling a reluctant thrill at his obedient tone.

She kissed him on the stomach, then slid down him, put his penis in her mouth again, then released him and began to fasten her clothes.

"My father thinks we're at a movie."

"What movie did we see?"

"We'll make it up. He wouldn't know a movie if he was in one."

"I think the thing tomorrow might be a movie he'll be in."

"The Fevlers for wine and cheese. You're right. It's a horror movie. I've been to too many of them. She pours out awful wines—I remember this hideous California white port, like maple syrup without the maple. She buys these frightening cheeses, you know, sheep's eyeball in fontana, just awful things. She goes shopping over the weekend and brings home these cheeses that get all overheated in the car, and she puts them out hours ahead of time so they can get overheated again, and all of your faculty sheep come baa-baa around the table in the dining room. 'Ooh! Ah! Look, darling, a real horseshit-with-mildew domestic whatsit! Ooh!' And everybody sips at their gasoline in a goblet, and they spread the horseshit-with-mildew on slightly damp crackers and she asks you questions. 'Where did you do your work? Oh, really? I understand that some of the land grant universities are very satisfactory.' And of course her Serge, she announces, has just finished reading proof of his newest memoir of something that might not have happened, but who can prove it, or a study of Vladimir Nabokov's fictional images of Serge Fevler, his lifelong friend, who is somehow instrumental in the formulation of *Lolita*. Have you read it?"

"You're a lot sexier than she is."

"No, what it is: I *want* to be in bed with you. Lolita needed just to be wanted. I seem to have this need to be fucked a lot by *you*."

"You're the only person I ever talked to who thought about what *Lolita* was feeling," he said. "You're amazing."

"I am a little amazing, I think. Thank you."

"But why are you here with them? If it's that terrible, I mean, and, frankly, I can see how it could get a little . . . cheesy."

They were walking by then, and she leaned over to kiss his cheek. She nipped it, and Willie sprang up hard right away. He adjusted his pants and she brushed the front of them, whispering, "Oh, how lovely. He's joining us again. And I'm here because I don't have a job because I don't have any skills. I didn't finish Skidmore. I can't bring myself to start in selling Revlon compacts in small-town pharmacies yet, though I suppose I will. If Jeff doesn't ride up here and steal me back and rape me until I submit."

"So it's not a divorce."

"It's a me running away. I took a bus until I started to cry, and then I got off and called my mother, and she drove down to Syracuse to get me. Did that do anything for you? About me being raped until I gave in?"

"Tony, I don't think you *do* give in. Even if you're on your knees and I'm the one standing, it's really mostly me on mine."

This time she simply clutched him through his pants, then kissed his mouth very slowly and moistly. "I knew you'd know me, Willie. That's why I picked you out and picked you up. I knew you'd be the one."

"I'm the one?"

"Until I tell you different, big fella, you're the one." She stopped their walking and kissed his face, then bit his upper lip. Willie bit her back. She told him, "Oh, you are."

An older couple, walking the campus, stood a dozen yards from them, each offering a weak smile, as if to demonstrate that they, too, were in favor of seizing the instant when passion drove. Tony fondled, Willie fought back, and they watched.

He made a throat-clearing noise about the watchers and she stopped kissing him long enough to say, "I know."

Names

WILLIE TAUGHT FOUR classes, three of them exercises in torture-by-essay. He assigned the essays, they tortured themselves to write them, and he plucked out his hair, his eyes, his fingernails to grade them every week. The fourth was his reward for teaching freshman comp, a class for sophomores in what the English Department thought of as his specialty: Seventeenth-Century Literature. By now, late October, he thought of Tony Fevler as his specialty. He was waiting to be drafted, now that he was 1-A, and he often lamented to her about his impending death. She took it as a goad, or she felt he ought to be rewarded, or she was truly saddened that he soon would die: one reason was as good as another, and they made risky love in public places, and they celebrated the Jew among—within—them, and they reviled her Jeff, although she said nothing more about him, and Willie pulled at her braid as if he had learned right behavior and must ring a bell to secure his treat.

The only black kid in his class, Daniel Bobson, who always sat in the back, near the windows, got up as Willie read from *The Anatomy of Melancholy* and sauntered across the rear of the classroom toward the door. "Standing waters, thick and ill-coloured," he was reciting, in love with the prose and unalert to his students, "such as come forth of pools and moats where hemp hath been steeped or slimy fishes live, are most unwholesome, putrefied, and full of mites, creepers, slimy, muddy, unclean, corrupt, impure, by reason of the sun's heat and still standing." He looked up to see Bobson go, and to watch the class as they watched him. "Dan," he said, appealing like the novice he was to the student's goodwill, which he should have known the student was not feeling, "this is good stuff."

Bobson didn't stop. He went to the door and walked out, letting the door slam behind him.

"Dan disagrees," Willie said, wishing that he didn't blush so promptly, so thoroughly.

A really bright and happy boy, Riefsnyder, who seemed to enjoy the material, shrugged and, blushing himself, said, "It's Vietnam Memorial Day."

"That's a holiday?"

"We voted it in," one of the other boys said. The school would not admit women until several years after Willie had left the college, the profession, and the country.

Riefsnyder said, "It's a protest, Professor. Against the war?"

"And against college," Willie said.

"No," Riefsnyder said, "but you sometimes wonder what you go to college for if they take you, right after graduation, and send you over and you die."

"Right on," Willie said, surprising them and himself. So he dismissed them, and they drifted, not quite as a group, to the quadrangle. At a microphone on the chapel steps, teachers and students took turns, announcing without inflection the names of Americans dead in Vietnam:

Breshears, Kenneth Lester
Breshears, Ronald Chris
Britten, Lawrence Alan
Broadbeck, John Gilbert
Brockington, Curtis
Brotman, Michael Ray
Brown, Michael Gregory
Brown, Michael R.
Brown, Richard Tyrone

Riefsnyder, short and compact, acned, nearsighted, heavy pageboy bob a curtain to his nearsighted eyes behind thick glasses in wire rims, told Willie that they had begun calling the names as that morning's classes started, standing at the wide, white-fronted, plain chapel. The quadrangle was, there, shaped like an oval, and the chapel marked its top. Classroom buildings lined the right-hand edge while dormitories, all of the same stone, lined the left. Students clustered on the lawn before the chapel as the students on the steps, unpretty in shaggy hair and insufficient washing and beat-up clothes, many of them having spent the night on the quad, Riefsnyder said, called, with a tone of impersonal near-righteousness that Willie only partly trusted, the names which were listed in the *Congressional Register*. The names echoed against the buildings and what was left of the early chill and the wetness of the quadrangle grass. He heard them through the cry of ducks and geese going away. And they clattered at him, as if a child were slamming a toy. The students looked so serious and at once so young—hardly that much younger than Willie— that he felt a great affection for them, and for what they did, and of course he thought they might one day be listing Willie Bernstein on some campus under the wild crying of geese as a man who had been killed. He could always count on himself to direct the focus of a moment to him, he thought.

Then the bells of the chapel began to toll. Slowly and singly, they rang the bells so that the names of the dead and the cries of the geese were audible through what Willie thought of as heartbeats, or a pulse. He had come down the stairs and along the campus with Burton's *Anatomy* in mind, so he wasn't surprised to think of the bells as a heartbeat in something not quite dead.

The students and teachers who read the names did so in large alphabetical sections, but each reader chose someplace new to begin, a disorder which made the death knells somehow harder to bear.

Jones, Clifford Alan
Jones, James Robert
Jones, Jimmie Wayne
Jones, John Wallace
Jones, Robert Emmett
Jordan, Jimmy Dale
Joys, John William

Judge, Mark Warren

They read the deaths alphabetically by service—Air Force, Army, Marine Crops, Navy—and in the order of alphabetically listed states. The dead stood on the pages in their ranks, and the students stood at the chapel and brought them onto the campus.

Profesor Fevler appeared, saying, "This was once called agitprop."

"I'm sorry? You said—"

"Agitprop. Agitation and propaganda. Agents were trained in Moscow to spread dissension and disorder and dismay—all the dises!—in European and American cities. It was how the Comintern would do its work. Advance the day of terminal unrest: revolution, don't you know. What do you think will come of your seeing my daughter, Mr. Bernstein?"

"Sir, I actually haven't thought that far ahead."

"You are seizing what? The day, of course. As well as my daughter."

A professor with a very deep voice, the sort of man, Willie thought, who had to show it off in civic little theater, called names:

McCann, Cecil Darrell

McClain, James Harry

McClurg, Charles D.

McComb, Terry Russell

McCurry, Andreas

McGinnis, William E.

McIlvoy, James Lee

McIntire, Walter Edwin

McKee, Kenneth Dale

"How they expect us to hear these names clearly, assuming that we must hear them, while those bells keep bonging, is beyond me. Can you hear them, quite?"

Willie said, "I suppose that's the idea, maybe."

"Not hearing?"

"Well. Maybe hearing them both at once."

"Ah. 'Send not to know for whom the bell tolls'? That sort of sentimentality?"

Willie tried to smile.

McKellard, Dennis Alvin
McLean, Terry R.
McLennan, Gary Alfred

"She tells me that you're, oh, 'going together.' Ha! I can see from your expression that the going is a departure on which you had not counted. Are you serious about my married young daughter? Isn't it a Victorian question? Alas, I'm a Victorian man."

"Am I serious—"

"You were hired after a committee of responsible, tenured professors inspected your credentials, and you come to us with a degree from a good, if not exactly great, university, and yet I have the feeling that you cannot always quite understand *English*. Are you adverting in a slightly subtle way to my origins in Petersburg, now barbarically named by the brutes in power Leningrad? Is it *my* English rather than your English?" In his shiny blue trench coat and matching blue porkpie hat, grinning without pleasure, like a dog about to bite, from above his bright silk tie, he breathed onto Willie's face, and Willie thought of Fevler's daughter, lips slicked with Willie, running her tongue back and forth on her lips, and then his.

In the sound of the names of stunted lives, therefore, and breathing, he thought, to the rhythm of the bells, he said, "Look."

"Yes," Fevler said, "at what?"

"What would you like me to say? What do you think you really want from me?"

"Respect, which is due an older man, a world traveler, a somewhat well-known author and the father of a woman to whom you pay court. A *married* woman, I must remind myself and you."

"We're friends, Professor Fevler."

"I have tenure for life, and I occupy an endowed chair."

"Yes, sir, I know you do. When I was offered the job, your presence on the faculty was recited as an inducement to accept the offer."

"That was very nice of them. Who was it?"

"Assistant Dean Rice."

"Decent man. I was not parading my accomplishments—well, yes I was. Ridiculous, wasn't I? A man fawning all over himself. That's what daughters do to you, Mr. Bernstein. You get desperate. You pull rank. You become a bully. I cannot believe what I have heard myself say. Is Bernstein a Jewish name?"

"In my case."

"Yes. Well, it was about time the English Department hired someone of your, oh, origin. So many of the good grad students these days are, oh, not to put too fine a point on it, Jews. Mr. Bernstein, will you remember that she is a troubled woman? The bad patch in the marriage, his immaturity and her own and so forth, and of course his military experience. I know you to be a gentleman because Rice, who is a gentleman, hired you. Does this sound antediluvian?"

"Sir?"

"Old-fashioned?"

"No, I knew what you meant. Except, does *what* sound—"

"My insistence upon, and my presumption of, your honor."

"Oh! Yes. My honor. Of course."

"Exactly. I promise to not subject you to the third degree again. My wife, you know, she has certain, I don't know, *concerns*. I promised we would speak, you and I."

"It's fine that we did," Willie said, as if they both were idiots.

"Exactly." He gestured at the students, hunched as if beneath a rain, before the chapel steps. "You know, they have feelings, but little information. Ask them about the domino effect, beginning in Southeast Asia and running around the world, like little ivory dominoes clacking and clicking as they fall. You could end up with Communists in Mexico City. And that," he said, smiling with no affection, pulling at his tie, "is at America's door. They know nothing of such a clear and present danger. While I, I have to say, am acquainted with Mr. Dean Rusk. One speaks with him from time to time."

"A whole generation knows him," Willie couldn't believe he heard himself say. He administered the *coup de grâce* to himself by saying, "*He* talks to *them*. 'Go East,' he says. 'Go East.' So many of them go."

"Yes, it is a pity. War is always a pity. But soldiers must go. Citizens must be soldiers. The domino theory is salient, Mr. Bernstein." Fevler's long, sallow face with its beaked nose, an exaggeration of

Tony's but more expressive in its many foldings—his flesh looked like thick paper, wrinkled many times—was pulsing with the excitement that comes from knowing the truth. "The nations *will* fall."

Willie thought of dominoes going over, then of these boys going over, then of himself going over and down like a figure in a throw-the-darts concession at Coney Island.

"May I return to a topic, Mr. Bernstein? My daughter. In reality, I spoke for myself as well as for my wife."

"Yes, sir, I thought that might have been the case. She's your daughter, too."

"In many ways, in terms of temperament, she's mostly mine. We share a number of traits. I know her very well. She is a damaged girl, poor thing. You know this?"

Willie moved his head, not quite lying Yes, the way he'd learned, in graduate school, to pretend to have read Waugh's *A Handful of Dust,* or *Diana of the Crossways,* or an uncollected article by Rosemond Tuve.

"You know, then, that she married a soldier, or a boy who quickly became one. He is more wounded than she, but only in the flesh. He was in California, on leave, and she flew to visit with him. She reports his face to have burst open. He hadn't the luck to die where he fell. They saved him, they thought. So he and Tony are now luckless. It is why she's home. According to Tony, he is a monster who pines for her when he's stable, which is not, I fear, all of the time. She cannot accept it." Sounding like Willie's mother, he said, "That is not the word. What do I mean?"

"Reconcile herself," Willie suggested.

"Exactly, perhaps. You must, Mr. Bernstein, be careful. No. You must be *worried,* always. She is fragile, in any event. That at least."

Yes, absolutely, he could be worried, Willie knew. Worried wasn't difficult. Jewish boys from New York, raised by witty, powerful, hysterical French mothers, knew to be worried when sticky, steamy sex was offered—when it was flown like a flag. The proof of God's existence for them was twofold: One, the roundup of Jews taken from his parents' neighborhood to Drancy, from where they were transported to Auschwitz. Two, an adult woman who offered her body

and who never spoke a word of rue. God came and got you for accepting her, Willie thought. His draft physical proved that this
dreamy sex was a form of suicide.

"Yes, sir."

"Have you served, already, in the military?"

"Just awaiting the call, Professor Fevler."

"Good man," he said. "I'm off to the library. We're put here to
work, I think, not watch."

McKeague, Gregory Dean

Medley, Michael Milton

Meek, Thomas Wesley

McPhail, Morris Gene

Willie wasn't thinking of them. He was thinking of a Lord God of
Anguish who, according to his ancestors, kept choosing them. Willie
thought, or possibly prayed to this god, *So let go already.*

A Father Stolen or Strayed

THE AGITPROP KEPT him looking at the chapel steps, at the students who appeared to really believe in what propelled their drama,
their melodrama, their sense of the importance of their intonations to
the accompaniment of the harsh, flat clanking of the bells. The professors with them, most of whom Willie didn't know, seemed even
more overcome than their students by the size of the occasion. Perhaps it was their own importance that so taxed them and flattened
their expression, bled out their faces, darkened their eyes. He was
becoming used to professors who believed in their own importance,
and, on any day, as he strutted in his classroom and lit his Luckies
with slow care, holding the match aflame before him to compel their
attention as he spoke of the Metaphysicals, while the cigarette hung
in his lips, he could have matched their every pomp.

More students had gathered, and they'd brought wood and plastic, buckets, electrical gear, and, as the names were read, these students worked with silence and efficiency, a corps of scary engineers
each dressed in black, to build a great wooden box near the middle of

the quadrangle lawn. Willie and the others turned to face them after a while, to see them paint big black circles—tuning knobs, he realized—on the wooden frame. They tacked a sheet of clear plastic that covered the frame from side to side. The names were spoken, but these workers didn't speak. Students sat to study them, and many of the crowd about Willie sat too, and he realized that they saw an audience watching television while, behind them, the pale students and teachers stood and read the names.

What his mother had said the night before, her voice high with a kind of panic, slurred, as if she'd taken tranquilizers, or a lot to drink, was this: "Your father is gone."

"He *died?*"

"God, I don't know. I mean: disappeared."

"Since when?"

"Since this afternoon. He went into the office, he telephoned me in the afternoon, and now they can't find him."

"His office?"

"His office. Not at any hospitals. Nor at police stations."

"Mom, what time did you make all those calls?"

"Just now. Then I called you. I'm sorry, I know you have many papers to grade."

"No, but he's been 'missing' for a couple of—well, it's nine o'clock, right?"

"Nine-eleven."

"So he isn't missing, Mom, he's late."

"Willie, somebody's late when you know where they're being late at. Your father doesn't just disappear. Well. He doesn't usually disappear."

"Which means he does, sometimes."

"You're angry with me," she said. "I'm a nuisance, and you're a college professor. You'll have to forgive me."

"I'm not angry. I'm not busy. I'm barely an assistant professor. I don't need to forgive you: you've done nothing wrong. Mom, why are we talking about me or you if we're looking for a missing father who's only somewhat late?"

"Somewhat." She snorted. "You might say very."

"You're right. I'll say it. Very. How come the hospitals and cops?"

"I have a feeling."

"Mom."

"My mother had the feeling and ten minutes after we left the house, the van to take us to Drancy pulled up at the door. Do not belittle feelings. Not that it helped my parents or our neighbors, God bless them, or any other Jews on the block."

"What is the feeling? I mean, the one now, about Dad?"

"He doesn't love us the same."

Willie sensed that she was right, but of course he was required to say, "He seemed the same to me last time we talked. Busy in his work, disgusted I wouldn't volunteer for the service, into which, by the way, I expect to very shortly be called."

"You'll get the call, you'll hop in your car and drive to Canada. I thought we arranged this, finished, no need for further discussion. I will join you there, or, anyway, smuggle up what you need: food, clothing, certain scholarly books, adequate funds. Of course, you could get married in America. You'll find love, you'll find a safe haven, two for the price of one. You could consider this."

"No more deferments for married men. The way they're going, they need so many bodies, they'll send everyone. Soon they'll send the mothers."

"Never the mothers! Don't joke about mothers, Willie. Who would protect the little children?"

"Mom. Do you want me to call someone?"

"Me."

"I mean to help find Dad."

"I'm going to call his office again, first thing in the morning. Even if he was dead, God forbid, he would still crawl into the office. If he isn't there, I will phone you and ask you, if you could, to come home. If he *is* in the office, then I will murder him for putting me through this and then demand some answers to some questions. Then, also, if you don't mind so terribly, I will phone you and report."

"You're a good agent, Mom. I'll wait for your report. But call me anyway if you get bad news, or scared or something."

"Agent shmagent. I'm not Bing Crosby and life is not *I Spy.*"

"Cosby. Bill Cosby."

"The cute *schwartze,* yes?"

"Black man."

"You'll excuse me, I don't keep up. The words I think of are *homme de couleur,* but we don't say that here, nor do we say *les neiges.* So I change languages in what is left of my brain, and it comes out Yiddish because so many of our friends . . . you understand."

"Mom. *Exacte.* Never mind. Call me. Good luck with what you find."

After a pause, she said, "You think I need it?"

"Nah. Or: we all need it."

"This I can believe."

His student Daniel Bobson was playing an electric, wired blues that drew a feedback scream from the amplifiers and Willie thought of *waging the peace,* and of men and women with their families who watched the news, hunched like these students under the music, the names, the sounding of the bell, to hear the body count and see the usual brief footage of men under fire, or dead. The blues stopped, the names continued, and the silence of the missing blues surrounded the names like the white spaces on a page. Behind the screen, now, a dozen figures dressed in black who wore painted white faces, stark as bone, looked out at the students who watched them.

Bobson gave them the theme song from *Bonanza,* the story about men who lived without a woman and preached loyalty, the love of gold, and excellent table manners. The students with bone-white faces stood erect, like officers. They danced about, they threw up their hands, then they pointed, shouting a knot of noises, only some of which came through with clarity: "Saturation!" "DMZ!" "Hearts and Minds!" "The body count!" "The peace!"

It was crude, and the students laughed like an audience before a jolly farce. They heard, he thought, what they needed to hear. They knew what they knew, and they were told it again. He thought of Professor Fevler and his agitprop. As the names were called, the actors fell silent and moved into a tighter and then a closer cluster, facing outward, not moving, simply watching those who watched them while the names were intoned and the bells were rung.

Smith, Bennie Allen
Smith, Henry Fonzo
Smith, Hubert Ray
Smith, Ralph Nathaniel
Smith, Ralph R.
Smith, Robert Lind
Smith, Robert Louis

The audience watched, the players watched, and the tension grew. A short, thin boy who sat at the front of the audience moved as the names came. He turned to look behind him at the chapel, and the people around him stared as he stood up. He faced the chapel, he smiled, he stopped smiling, he shook his head. The names came on. He held his arms out and opened his mouth and he bellowed, "You called my name!"

He moved through the crowd toward the chapel. The audience turned as he went, and the actors, Willie noted, stayed still. He shouted, "Hey! Hey, listen! Yo! Wait a minute. Hey! You called my *name!*"

The names stopped, and the silence poured in. A student in the center of the crowd—and Willie could not decide whether he was an actor or simply battered by the occasion—began to cough soft cries. He wept, saying, "Oh God. Oh God. Oh God. Oh God."

Et cetera. *Tant pis.*

Willie stepped back, then away, and then he moved as quickly as he could from the quadrangle to the classroom building and the dark, narrow privacy of his underfurnished office. He felt at one with many of his students: there's just so much learning you can brook. The last words he heard from the shouting boy was what he'd expected: his ostensibly ironic "I'm not dead!"

It struck Willie as noteworthy, while he sat in his office, that he was possessed of, or by, an erection as large, and all but independent of him, as any he could remember. He waited to see if it decided to leave the office without him, or write a letter on the desktop Royal. He supposed that he had been thinking of Tony without real awareness, for no one affected his body in such a way as she. He *thought* he'd been thinking of the deaths of children, of desperate Asian people and scared, goofy American boy-men, of himself in particular, and of course his father, dead in the streets, or stolen, or strayed.

Eventually, he subsided, though it took long minutes. Each time he wondered at his body's alertness to the main chance, he thought of Tony, and it stood right up to attend. When he did, at last, get down the hall, mumbling to students, smiling at senior professors as a small dog wags its tail near the very large, ferocious, and local, he found a letter from his New York draft board. All tumescence vanished, he sat in his office with the door closed, and he slowly opened up what he assumed was the notice of his execution by redneck drill instructor or the variety of land mine called, according to *The New York Times,* the Bouncing Betty.

Dear Mrs. Doherty of his draft board reminded him that no one could override the decision of an armed forces doctor. She did not address the question of racial enmity. But she did point out that he had written on the letterhead of a college. Had he not heard that college teachers were deferred?

Had he not? Yes, Mrs. Doherty, he very much had not.

In a high, hoarse voice he last had heard from himself when Tony had him where she wanted him, which was how he wanted her, Willie called—he screeched—and mostly to himself, "I am not dead!"

He sat at his desk and he panted. Outside his plaster walls and wooden door, a student in the hallway said, "Big fuckin deal."

Goodbye, Philip Roth

THEY WERE IN his Sears, Roebuck bed—a wheeled aluminum platform on which a mattress sat—at something like the dinner hour. It had begun with a phone call, his invitation to dinner, and her reply: "Why don't you just eat *me?*"

Instead of celebrating, with candles and an overpriced wine, his liberation from a servitude that hadn't occurred, they had met at his front door and marched, like the rowdy soldiers of an occupying army, up to his bedroom—the bed, a stained veneer bureau, a chair on which the telephone sat—and they had proved Tony's expertise at improving his. She had stood barefoot on the bed and had lifted her short orange-and-black skirt to show him her idea of dinner.

In the sixth grade, Willie's girlfriend was the tall, boyish, Catholic, brown-haired Flora Brown. She was intelligent and cool, composed, only flustered when he tried, with her, to imitate the handsome boys and beautiful girls of Brooklyn College, who strolled a street called Campus Road while holding or smooching or fondling each other. Flora wanted only to grip his hand with hers that never seemed to sweat and to discuss their science project for Miss Frederick's class (a baking soda volcano eruption). And since that twelfth year of his life, because of Flora, Willie had always thought of her serene, long face when he considered the notion and the consequences of chastity. And, unreasonably, she came to mind as he lay head to toe with Tony Fevler. He thought of Flora Brown, and he was wondering what he would one day pay as penalty for such pleasures as these—was he not a Jewish boy?—when the telephone rang in his mother's accent, and he thought of his maybe-missing father. Willie speculated, while he went for the phone, whether the penalties arrived as promptly as this.

And it was, in fact, his mother. Willie sat in the chair, and he covered his wet nakedness with the phone.

"He isn't dead," she said.

"That's great. Is he well?"

"If you mean alive, yes. In adequate health, probably. Everything else, however, is very bad."

"First tell me where you found him, Mom."

"As I guessed. At his office."

"And where had he been?"

"With his control."

"Control?" Tony stood before him, and he pressed forward to butt his head against the smallest swelling of stomach. He raised his face enough to nibble her, and then sat back. "Mom? Control of what?"

Tony whipped her head back, and the braid snaked out and down. She sat on the edge of the bed, opposite him, and she slowly, looking into his eyes, spread her legs.

"Spies, apparently, are instructed—he said 'run'—by a control.

He's a spy, so he has a control. A lawyer. A Cuban lawyer, famous in the intelligence community for ferocious anti-Castro sentiments. Do you believe I suddenly know this information? Cubans and Castro. I always thought Castro was very formidable. An appealing man, I always thought. Your father, who tells me he is a spy, is run by a control who opposes Fidel Castro. For who?"

"There's only one who."

"You guessed?"

"The CIA," he said. "*Dad?* The CIA? A Cuban control? Jesus *God.*"

"Now you know how I feel," his mother said. But Willie was watching as Tony spread her legs apart farther and reached to stroke herself. She slid her finger into her mouth and kept it there an instant, smiling into him with her challenging, sometimes frightening, clear blue eyes. "Willie?"

"Yes," he was able to say. He closed his eyes. "Mom, what do you know about the control?"

"Provided by the CIA, he said."

"Male or female?"

"It makes a difference? Listen to what makes a difference, Willie, never mind he's living a secret life apart from ours. He said, 'Any further questions about this from you will result in great danger to you and Willie.' He sounded sorry, but he also sounded—you can tell after so many years together—like the danger was terrible, and it was right around the corner. Understand? We ask, they hear, finished." She made a whistling sound she must have heard on the streets in Paris when she was a girl. Mom, the *flâneuse.*

"What's his control's name, Mom?"

"He didn't say. Who needs the name? They're 'running' him. Willie, that was his own word. Your father, and someone's running him. It's blackmail, of course."

"Of course."

She had turned to lean on the bed, her buttocks to him, and she was tracing her fingers in the cleft, far down, far back, far in, moving her hips as if a man stood behind her driving slowly in and out.

"Willie?"

"Yes! Mom. What?"

"Listen to this. From when he was an innocent young lawyer, a sweet idealist. He represented Hollywood characters, mostly writers, who were blacklisted. Proscribed, you understand? For years, these people had no work, or little work. In the 1960s, still, no work. Who comes to this country with an English accent on top of his French accent and studies for the bar examination and passes and learns to be American and represents these people for so little money? Him. The same him. He fought for these people who never paid bills, mostly. Communists, of course, and why not? At least until '37, you could see why not. Even after, if you closed your eyes or squinted, you could say, 'Who else stands against Hitler?' Though your father was not in the Party. He did what a man should do. He protected these people. For this, they blackmail him: they'll tell his clients, they warned him. Already, he's a Jew. Now he's a Communist Jew? Forget the law business."

"You wouldn't think of him as scared by that. By much of anything. I thought I was the one who was scared."

"Willie, pay attention! Your father! He travels for the firm, yes? This is a man, your father, who goes to Germany, Italy, Switzerland, France, of course. He drops off, he picks up, people listen, people tell. Then, Willie, what happens, do you think, when he comes back to America?"

"I'm not getting the part about Cuba yet." He reached forward. He had to touch her cold, pale flesh. Where he touched her, though, she was warm.

"In Washington, D.C., and sometimes in an office in New York, they do something called debriefing. You know what this is?"

"I've heard of it. You sound proud."

"I'm—maybe. And confused. And *I'm* frightened. And the lawyer, Willie, she's a woman. Perlita something. The Cuban against Castro. Perlita, I don't know, maybe that was her last name."

"Goddamn," he groaned.

"Willie!"

"Excuse me, Mom. So what do you think about the spy thing with him?"

"At first, I was reluctant. He's a vigorous man, you understand? It sounds like the alibi of someone who steps in, steps out—what's the American?"

"Out."

"But he sounded so upset when he heard how upset I was. And I have to tell you, it does feel real. When something feels real—"

"It might as well be real," he said.

"No, it *is*."

He knew the three-book omnibus volume of Eric Ambler stories his father had purchased from the Book-of-the-Month Club. He knew about a cover story when he heard one. So did his father.

"And then it is," he said.

"Soon he'll be home for dinner, and we'll talk. I have to tell you, I don't know if I'm permitted to say anything else about, you know, the control and debriefing, whatever. Maybe he'll shout if I ask."

"Not at you, Mom."

"I can't tell you how serious he sounded."

"I can imagine."

"You're a good boy, Willie."

That was when Tony moved the phone aside and replaced it with herself, sliding down around him to rest on his lap.

"Oh. Good luck tonight, Mom."

"I'll call you, darling."

"Oh, I know."

"Then *à la prochaine fois,* yes? All right, Willie?"

"Very," he said, blowing a kiss, hanging up, reaching for Tony Fevler. This led to a protracted thrash, which led to them, at around nine that night, eating cheeseburgers in bed and sipping at a green quart bottle of Ballantine's Ale.

Tony had her braid around her neck and resting at her breasts, which had lost their lovemaking flush. He tickled one with the end of her braid and she gently slapped him away. "You're a good cheeseburger maker," she said.

"You're good at everything else."

"Sex?" she said. "You bet your ass."

"Tony, did you ever read a book called *When She Was Good* by Philip Roth?"

"Why?"

"There's a . . . relationship in it. She's a WASP, he's this Jewish guy, and he's very exotic to her."

"Oh," she said, "and I get to play the horny, blond *shikse*. So she fucks him because he's got those cute little Jew horns on his curly head, and then he lights up a Lucky just the way you do and she says, 'Take me away from all this normalcy.' "

"Normality," he couldn't help saying.

"Prick," she said.

"I'm sorry."

"Willie, do you know why I'm just a little nutsy in the sack? Do you know why? Do you think I'm this way just with you?"

He said, and he meant it, "I wish."

"Grow older, sonny," she said. "You do not know why, do you?"

"I do not," he said, sighing the smoke out.

"Then don't quote dirty books at me. I read it. I think he's careless about his characters' lives. You know? He's supposed to consider *their* well-being too. He's—he's frivolous about them. He thinks he's God. This one can have some happiness, this one can't." Her forehead was furrowed, and she looked a lot like her father. She wasn't seeing Willie, he thought, she was seeing Roth as he conducted the cosmos. And then the furrows relaxed and she smiled her sweet, wicked smile. "And what does he *know*? Saying a girl gets turned on by a boy on account of his sweet Jewish sperm on her lips." She set her food on the floor beside the bed and moved down underneath the blankets. "What writers don't know," she said around him.

God missed, he thought. Willie was supposed to go to Southeast Asia and die because of Tony. But God's aim was off. God had struck his *mother*. God had stripped his father's cover and was running him against his own wife, and she knew it, he thought, or she'd know it soon enough. Cuban lawyer, he thought. Anti-Castro, he thought. My sweet ass, he thought, squeezing through the blankets at Tony's, then tearing the blankets away to seize her more directly. She was licking his penis up and down, and when she felt his hands on her, she raised her rump, and he thought *Her* sweet ass. She opened her mouth around him, and he lifted himself to her. Pulling at Tony's braid, cursing the ancient dream of God, regretting his mother's fate, feeling grotesque for having thought of her exactly now, he lost his train of thought.

Flag

A STUDENT-DRIVEN OFF-BLUE SAAB, as high and gawky on its stiff springs as a long-legged teenager, took the curve behind the back door of the theater too quickly and drove halfway up and over a bright yellow Volkswagen Beetle. Glass sprayed up and out, the chromium ring from a headlight assembly rolled along the walk and out of sight, fluids poured, and onlookers talked and called so loudly, and with such simultaneity, that it sounded to Willie as if they cheered. His student, Riefsnyder, stood very still, then pulled a rubber band from his pocket, slung his hair back and forced it through to make a loose ponytail, and, with hair flopping before his eyes, took off his dungaree jacket and waded into the mess.

Tony said, "It'll burn."

In the dull green lights mounted above the theater doors, she looked unwell. When campus security arrived in a waddling Dodge with a flashing red gumball on top, the blinking colors flattered her less.

"No," he said, "Riefsnyder looks like he knows what he's doing. He'd be one of those kids who smokes dope and does beer binges, but who also belongs to the volunteer fire department at home. He likes being central. He'll turn the ignition off. He'll take care."

Tony took Willie's arm. "You like your students," she said. He felt her shiver with excitement or cold or fright.

"Some."

"Some of them like you."

He waited.

"Daddy said. He talks to them."

"He spies on me, you mean."

"You *are* dating his daughter."

"His married daughter. His little girl."

"I won't be married for long."

"That must be so goddamned rough on you."

"No," she said. "On him."

"Your father told me about him."

"He didn't."

"I'm telling you, the guy is an operator. He checks up on me, he interrogates me about my intentions toward you—"

"Your words."

"Sorry. His."

"Intentions toward? The nineteenth-century intentions-toward?"

The driver of the Saab fell backward from his seat into the arms of Riefsnyder and a campus cop. Students ringing the vehicles applauded. Willie noticed, for the first time, that two boys wearing T-shirts and shorts, despite the October weather, had been playing tennis at night while *The Bald Soprano,* with girls borrowed from the community college, had made the audience wriggle and itch in their seats. The tennis players raised their rackets as the students clapped. In the Beetle, the driver didn't move.

"You know," Willie said, "I'm developing some."

"Intentions?"

He nodded. He realized that he had made the grim, single movement he so often had seen his father make, acknowledging what couldn't be helped. It was what remained of a Gallic shrug, and it signified to Willie, he understood, an absolute surrender to circumstance. Bernstein *père* must have hated to give in like that, but he was driven to show his defeat—they none of the three could entertain a concept, feel the *cafard,* be staggered by a circumstance without finding words or, at least, a gesture; they all found flags to raise, even in disgrace.

"Feelings," Willie said. He felt his frown, his ducking and then raising of his chin, were imitations, intentional or not, of his father. If it was not someone's notion of God that drove him, he thought, then it was some genetic twitch. Which meant that he would have to become enslaved to Tony Fevler, hand-in-hand dodge death with her, and then find a bourgeois method of betraying her: the family tradition. His mouth gabbled on, as if it were a drunk, and separate from his brain, so close and so unheeded; it staggered onward, slamming into obstacles, telling her nevertheless, "You know I have deep feelings for you."

She smiled. She said, "Shh." They were talking like a movie now, and she put her fingers against his mouth and he raised his lips so that her fingertips were in his mouth. "Willie," she said.

"Am I in love with you?"

Her hand went still, and then she withdrew it. He expected her to wipe her fingers on her leather jacket, but she put them against her lips, speaking through them as if through a grating. "You are not in love with me. I am not in love with you. You're foggy with sex. You can't believe this thing you lucked into with me, and you're such a puritan, you think you need to marry me or something to rescue your doomed soul. Are those the feelings you think you have?"

She was still pale, almost greenish in the awful lights, and her forehead looked sweaty.

"They're the feelings *you* think I have. I don't know. I don't think it's only sex and games, or—what? Sex and shames. Whatever you're saying."

"It?" she said.

"Sorry?"

"What's the *it* you're saying isn't only sex and thingy?"

She looked at him with what he would later describe to himself as sadness. He would also think, when he did, of Flora Brown, and her sweet, serious face, and he would think of *her* as sad whenever she came to mind. *I am the man,* he would say to no one but himself, years later, *who makes women sad.* And, hearing his self-pity, he would grow sorry for himself, and mourn the women he had lost to sorrow.

"I don't know, Tony. Us is the it. We. No, or what we want to find in each other. No. What we want to find in us. Is that it?"

"*What*'s it?" she shouted.

A number of men in narrow neckties and women on wobbly high heels looked them over, and Willie knew that they had given the

largest gift a member of a faculty can offer to his colleagues: specula-
tion, a secret not unraveled but revealed.

He bent toward her, and he did it slowly for the sake of those who
watched. He kissed her forehead, which was clammy, and he said, "I
know about your husband's terrible disfigurement. I think you fled
it and I took advantage of you. And I'm sorry. And maybe I love you,
I think."

The ambulance backed past the tennis courts, where the boys were
tripping as they swatted the bright balls back and forth in the shadows cast by headlights and emergency lights and the green service
lights on the buildings. Two security men tore the VW's door from
its hinges, one of them keening like a weight lifter coming up against
the bar.

Tony said, "Don't call me anymore. Don't talk to me. You've been
so fucking generous, Willie, I just couldn't bear a minute more of
charity. Which is wonderful to hear about. See, I thought I was doing
you the occasional favor. Next thing you know, someone like you is
telling me these kids crashed their cars because of me."

"Tony," he said, assuming his lecturer's position.

"Next thing, Willie. So no more next things, please. Please?"

He watched the attendants set the slender, terribly loose-limbed
boy on the gurney. His mouth was open and bloody. Willie wanted
to turn his head toward Tony, but he couldn't. He stepped forward
and to his right, then went closer to the ambulance and then around
it, so that she was blocked from his view. He raised his father's chin,
then let it come down.

Debriefing

THE MANSION AT WHICH he learned the ways of the tunk was also
the faculty club, and Willie sat with another young man in tweed
who wore a bold tie, as fat as Willie's was thin, and decorated, in per-
simmon and black and yellow, with gryphons, baxters, and pyramids.
From the pleasure his lunch partner took in smoothing the tie, Willie
inferred with regret that wide ties were about to become the fashion.

He felt pallid and inhibited because of his narrow Rooster, and he went for an extra beer to wash down the steak tips.

"What do you think these really are the tips *of?*" he asked, his effortful wit about something so marginal making him sound to himself like a joke about professors. He looked at the sets of books—big, leather-bound, gleaming translations of Balzac, a 1912 *Encyclopaedia Britannica* in pale green, several varieties of Tennyson, and, wonderfully, a paperbound Dashiell Hammett, *The Glass Key*. The air smelled of thickened gravy and potatoes, and he recognized it: the day when he had been left off by his mother to become a kindergartner and he'd been unable to make the mashed potatoes go down his throat.

His lunch partner shook his head and nervously smiled as gravy seeped from between his lips.

"Good, huh?" Willie said.

Finally swallowing, Instructor in Chemistry Norton Gold said, "Did you say"—he leaned closer to Willie—"tits?"

"Oh! Sorry, no, I wouldn't have had to *ask* about steak tits. We all know what *they* are."

Norton looked at him as though he'd spoken in another language.

"A joke," Willie said. "I didn't say tits, but I also have no idea what steak tits would be. A kind of a joke, anyway. You know?"

"I have a preparation to do," Norton said. "We do labs this afternoon for all the sophomores. The premed grind, right?"

"Right," Willie said. "Good talking to you."

"Ditto," Norton said. *"Ciao."*

"That's *La Dolce Vita,* right?"

"I guess."

"I guess," Willie said.

He'd been looking past Norton to a circular table at the far end of what they all seemed to call the library. It was Fevler and the fellow he'd seen with his finger in the Buddha's ear, Wherry. Buddha wasn't to be seen these days, and Willie assumed that he was brought out only for nighttime social events. Fevler had been beckoning, and Willie had been trying to develop a strategy for going to ground.

Fevler held his hands, palm out, at the height of his chest: They were signaling an impatient *Well?*

Not so well, Willie thought. But, carrying a cup of coffee over, he went, and he was introduced to Wherry, who wore a wonderfully rich suit of darkest blue sharkskin with a faint red stripe in the weave. His shirt was striped in blue with a white collar, and his necktie, dark blue silk, had a thread of red that picked up the red in the suit. His cufflinks were gold buttons that appeared to weigh twenty or thirty pounds each. They, in turn, picked up the gold of the very thin watch on its gold expansion band.

"I was saying," Wherry said, in a drawling, creaky voice he seemed certain would receive attention, "that this time back from Thailand, I had a frightful wait in Paris because of some guerrilla tactic or other. They telephoned and *claimed* to have put a bomb on board, and of course they hadn't, though you don't—do you?—want to take the matter for granted. And then, what I was getting at, then, from Paris, I had of course to fly to *Washington,* instead of New York thence home, because—" he dropped his voice and bent, very slightly, forward, nibbling on a little smudge of cherry cobbler in his teaspoon, and telling them—"there was the debriefing."

"I don't know if Mr. Bernstein knows what you mean," Fevler told him. "I did introduce you, did I not? Wilbur Bernstein?"

"William," he said. "Willie, I suppose. That's what I'm called."

"Willie Loman," Professor Wherry said. "Another Jewish William, though he was, as they like to say, in retail."

"They," he said.

"Whoever," Wherry said. "I'm happy to welcome you, if at this late date, William. Willie? Welcome. Good luck here. Now, I was, oh, it's the sort of thing you'd call 'war stories.' We each travel in our areas of expertise—he in Europe, I in Asia and points south, he in the service of continental literature, I for comparative religion. We are, neither Serge nor I, unknown in the State Department."

"Professor Fevler told me about Secretary Rusk."

"Oh, Dean," Wherry said. "Good God, yes. Though of course one doesn't see him for a routine post-journey debriefing. It's one of the junior boys, very respectful, of course, and not stupid, mind you. These fellows are always Ivy. Nicely bred and nicely trained. It's a matter of what did you see, what did you hear, did anyone attempt to make contact in any intensive, interesting way—that sort of thing. You tell them, and they take a few notes, though I've always wondered if they mustn't record it as well."

"I think not," Fevler said. "The Sovs do that."

"Soviets," Wherry said in response to Willie's expression. "It was Fevler of Petersburg, once upon a time. And the son of the whitest of white Russians. He is not enamored of the Soviets."

"My friend Nabokov," Fevler said, "watched his father assassinated by the mouth-breathing barbarians. In Paris."

"My parents are from Paris," Willie said, having nothing else to say.

"What district?" Fevler asked.

"The Marais."

Wherry said, "A lot of Ashkenazi settled there, as I recall."

"Actually, it was the Vichy listmakers who recalled it. They moved them out, in '41, quite smartly, sir." He knew that his "sir" lacked every intimation the word was meant to convey.

Wherry said, "Our young colleague has a chip on his shoulder."

"Mr. Bernstein speaks his mind," Fevler said. "That needn't be bad."

Willie thought he ought to mention that he was the son of a man who was also debriefed. Unless the word meant for them, as well as for his father, that they got laid by someone to whom they weren't married. Unless, he thought—as he knew his mother could not help hoping—his father's cover story was the truth, and he was blackmailed into serving this government and they, these three men of the world whom Washington debriefed, were warriors in disguise. It, and they, gave Willie a headache.

What, she had asked him, *is It?*

"Sometimes," Willie lectured his elders, "the world is instructive in the carrying of what you call a chip."

"An entire stick," Wherry said. "A log. The trunk of a Sequoia redwood." He checked his watch and shot his cuffs. "I've enjoyed meeting you. Let me say: I have found it instructive to meet you. I hope that you can permit yourself to feel welcome here."

"I thank you for your wholesale hospitality, Professor Wherry."

Fevler made a little giggling noise.

"Ah," Wherry said. "The mercantile matter. Wholesale, retail. How appropriate."

"To what, sir?" Willie knew his teeth showed above his jutting jaw.

"Why," Wherry said, standing slowly and buttoning his jacket, "to sales, of course. Off I go. There are pearls—this is a pork metaphor, and I beg your pardon—to hurl before my swine before the day is done: My one-thirty waits. Gentlemen."

Fevler and Willie watched him move across the room like a yacht. "Legendary man," Fevler said. "He's a man, as you might know, of the upper crust. His people built a good bit of Manhattan. On land they'd always owned. And, admittedly, he's prone to a few of the more vulgar ostentations—pretentiously named single malts, wine by the cellar instead of the case, and a certain narrow, oh, purview where one might wish to see something more democratic. . . ."

"He doesn't like Jews," Willie said.

"We don't have a great many," Fevler said. "It's unrealistic, and we know it. And that is going to change. Meanwhile—"

"I'll bet you counsel patience," Willie said.

Fevler folded his hands and contemplated the result. "Should we address the matter of Tanya?"

"Tony?"

"You know we named her Tanya. Tony is what she named herself."

"Is she all right?"

Fevler focused on his hands, then shook his head. It seemed to Willie that her father was wordless about her, and it seemed to him that each of them was moved by the fact. Finally, Fevler whispered, "I have grave concerns. She is fragile. She is unreconciled."

"To the husband's wound."

"So it would seem."

"Maybe it's time for a doctor to see her. A psychiatrist?"

"My daughter is not crazy, Mr. Bernstein."

"Fragile, you said."

"Not reconciled."

"That's what psychiatrists are for. People like that. With what Tony has."

Fevler shook his head. Willie, with his father's gesture, raised and dropped his chin. "Got a class to bone up for," he said. "I'm talking about the recusant poets. The secret Catholics, Catholics on the run. They made their poems in priest holes. They hid out in barns. Gotta go, Professor Fevler. I hope she's all right."

The it, he heard, in Tony's voice, as he walked across the campus. The flag outside the administration building flew at half-mast for the boy who had died behind the theater. Willie noticed a man to his rear and his right, not directly in sight but not out of it, who looked too old to be a student, but who seemed not to be on the staff. He was wearing a khaki fatigue jacket and jeans and highly polished military boots. He had been on the lawn near Willie in the morning, and had been standing on the walk outside the faculty club when he'd arrived. His face was very red, as if from someplace sunny or as if from strong emotions. When Willie thought of emotions, he thought of Tony, and he wondered if this could be her husband. But, of course, he could not, for his face was unpuckered, unfolded, unscarred, entire. He looked like the kind of tough man in tough bars by whom Willie was always intimidated.

He's a messenger from my *maman's* God, Willie thought. He's here in disguise to tell me that I'm unprepared for class and my mother is being done a cruel turn. So, he thought, was Tony.

They'd been speaking of the famous carriage scene in *Madame Bovary,* of its subtle sexiness—all but a required conversation in graduate school, he'd complained—when Tony had said that the carriage scene, to her, was about despair.

"Flaubert raped her," Willie said.

"Oh," she said. "Oh, well."

She lay with her thigh across his, her pointy elbow painful and pleasant on his chest as she watched him lie against the pillows and smoke. She was considering what he had said, he knew. She pretended to be thoughtless, and she worked at what she heard and saw with a secret seriousness—sometimes, he thought, a kind of desperation—that made her appear unmasked, suddenly quite vulnerable. Her eyes had crossed slightly as they followed the cigarette and the smoke, and the effect had been to make her beaky face less cruel. He'd been immensely moved and on the verge of saying sentimental words when Tony had said, "Well, of course she's treated unfairly. Women generally are. That's how come they end *up* in so many books, Willie. What the hell else are you going to do with them?"

Office Hours

HE WAS IN HIS long, narrow office with its single window and, curiously, beside the door to the hall, its porcelain sink and its tall mirror. He thought of his father's relatives after a death, sitting *shiva,* covering the mirrors of the house with sheets. His father never worshiped nor spoke of a God. It was as if they had quarreled and his father had determined to say nothing of his enemy. He never spoke of how his parents had sent him off to hide with the family with whose daughter and spinster aunts he escaped, nor of how he and the daughter grew up in the tiny town of Winterslow, in the south of England, working with the aunts in their tea and pastry shop, marrying in Southampton, emigrating to Philadelphia, settling in New York. Willie walked to the mirror and hung his sportcoat over the frame so that he was shielded from the sight of himself. The coat slid into the sink, so he forsook further gestures. He read in Johnson's life of Cowley that "the reader commonly thinks his improvement dearly bought, and, though he sometimes admires, is seldom pleased." Go be a poet, he thought, and that's what you get. Then: Ah, the old bought-and-sold motif. Wherry would think Dr. Johnson a Jew.

Oddly, though, it was Fevler who troubled him, and he didn't know why. It was as if he'd decided that Willie was acceptable, now that he and Tony were done. John Donne, Anne Donne, undone, Willie thought in Donne's own words. Fevler *liked* him, Willie understood. Something waved to Willie from the country out behind

Serge Fevler's eyes, which were blue though not the cold, empty color of Tony's. Tanya's. She had a cover, and so of course did Fevler, and so did Willie's father, who never spoke to him of the roundups, or the vacant apartments soon occupied by middling SS bureaucrats, or the families who disappeared. Willie wondered if Perlita Someone or Someone Perlita now heard from him about the end of the world in Paris or the sense, Willie suspected, of being always, even now, on the verge of catastrophe. His father kept a drawerful of chocolate bars in his study. Willie took one as a boy, and his father knew. Instead of speaking, as he surveyed his drawer while Willie ran metal bulldozers into the legs of a cherrywood chair, his father, pale and licking his lips, stood above him and whispered, "These are for just in case. You comprehend what is just in case? Not to touch." He waved his hand from side to side, and he thundered, *"Jamais!"*

Willie realized that the look on Tony's face, at her parents' wine and cheese party which started the semester, was what he imagined his own face had looked like when his father stared down like the God of Suchard Chocolate and roared his injunction. There were three new married couples plus Willie, who was matched to the woman who resigned the loyalty oath and who kindly enough introduced the name and doctoral field of her fiancé. It was a room with wall-to-wall carpeting in beige and Scandinavian birchwood furniture. On the walls were maps of old Russia, prints of Chekhov and Tolstoy, a nineteenth-century photo of the college, and bookcases along which Willie managed to stand, often, and read the titles, and hide from the grinding, slow conversations led by Pamela Fevler, who reminded Willie, in build and facial appearance, very much of Emily Dickinson but without the poems or the Massachusetts. She had an accent imported from the Carolinas and preserved, Willie thought, with much effort. She expostulated on the virtues of *The Pawnbroker,* though, finally, it was too grim. She adored *Juliet of the Spirits. Doctor Zhivago* had broken her heart, she said in a high, girlish voice from the grim narrow lips of her expressionless face. Her language smiled, but she did not.

"Now," she said, "who has read poor Miss O'Connor's last stories? *Everything Rising* . . . I forget. Serge? Serge!" she called across the room to Fevler, who was showing a woman in a red print dress she had sewed—it puffed and drifted in unplanned places, Willie thought—where, as a boy, he had lived in Belorussia.

He shook his head.

"Well, we *are* a group of faculty. One of us must have read them— all those stories about Negroes and white trash and the Holy Ghost?"

Willie, from the end of the bookshelves, was looking down the carpeted corridor that went toward the dining room and kitchen. Tony stood at the kitchen door, her arms at her sides as they had been the night she'd stood at the door of the faculty club, when her soaked dress had fallen against her because, Willie thought, she had worn her coat open so that it would. She had looked like an offering, a surrender, he later told her. And now, in her parents' home, she stood that way again, but wearing Bermuda shorts and no shoes or socks and a ribbed sleeveless T-shirt under which was only her.

"Stay away from the wine," she said. "Anything else you want, you probably can have."

Fevler had said, over his shoulder, "You've met my baby girl!"

Tony's face took on the look that Willie remembered feeling from inside his skin when his father declaimed about chocolates.

"*Converge!*" Mrs. Fevler announced. "All right," she said, "who's seen interesting shows? We saw *Man of La Mancha,*" she called, and Willie imagined those words in the mouth of Emily Dickinson. "Which is as good a way as any to call your attention to a *wonderful* sherry we found. It actually *isn't* Spanish. It comes from California, but you'd never know it. There are bottles and bottles, so you better begin! It's nutty enough for the cheeses, but quite deliciously sweet. Did anyone see *Baker Street?*"

The red-faced man in polished boots was at his office door, knocking. Willie stood, and the man walked in and shut the door. Willie sat down. He lay back in his swivel chair, then thought he'd better stand up. The man was in front of him, his face very red, his mouth twisted.

Willie said, "Yes?"

The man smacked him and Willie went backward in his chair, which slid at the wall. The front of his face was numb, but his ear hurt very much.

Willie rejected all the words that occurred to him, from *What?* to *Hey!* He balled his fists and made himself stand up.

He felt but didn't see the hand that struck him again. He heard a popping noise and, from the pain that pressed at his eyes and upper lip, then nose, he assumed that his nose was broken.

"You pathetic egghead prick," the man said, raising a fist and watching Willie flinch. "Open those hands," he said.

Willie looked at his hands and found them fisted. The pain in his face made him raise his head again, and he opened his hands.

"You're bleeding all over your uniform," the man said.

Willie tried to speak but only could cough.

"You know who I am," the man said.

Willie shook his head very slowly.

"Oh. All right. Sorry. Here's who I am. I'm the guy that isn't killing you with his hands. I'm the one that's giving you a break. And *fuck* your nose. Everybody gets a broken nose. The break I'm giving you is I don't tear out your voicebox. I know how to do that. I can reach into your face and take your tongue. I can get your fucking *heart* in my hands and squeeze it into a glass and make you drink it before I let you fall down. Are we communicating now? Stand over there."

Tony moved inside the mask that crushed against his face, and he stood with his back to the wall of bookshelves. The man sat down in his chair.

"I saw slants that were bad. I saw a sniper we brought down after he made six kills. He was so skinny he looked like slant-colored leather. He was nothing but fingers and an eye. I saw a mother hold her baby out for us to help, and there are armed grenades on the little boy's belly under his shirt. Whango. Goodbye GI. Man, they'd eat their own. But you're the worst one of the ones I saw. On account of *you* are taking advantage of a fucked-up wife of a combat dogface man who has to hear about you doing the kama *what*ever when it's too late to douche her out and clean her up. You reading me? You polluted my wife. You sewered up my fucking *life*. So I feel like it's reasonable I bag you up and ship you home to Israel."

He couldn't sit. He had to stand, and he had to come after Willie again, and he did. Willie backed toward the door, outside of which, he heard, people stood to listen and watch as he was broken apart. The husband pulled Willie in by his necktie and he planted some kind of combat blow to the chest. Willie's breastbone expanded and lit up, he felt the heat come up through his chest, and then the pain, and his heart stopped. He knew it had stopped, and he suspected that he looked like a fish after food in a tank. His mouth moved toward air, but his chest would not work and his heart would not beat. He was on his back, bleeding into his mouth and not breathing. Then he heard someone whoop for air, and he knew it was he. In the hallway, people spoke. The soldier's foot came up between his thighs and Willie tightened them in time to slow but not undo the blow. He heard himself retching. He was mostly pain now, and he was surprised that he wasn't weeping. He was very pleased to not be weeping until the shuddering that poured up pain to his nose informed him that he was, in fact, crying like a kid.

"You were inside her body. Why you get major league payback is: you were inside of the body of my *wife*. Now. Why you still breathe is also her. Son of a bitch motherfuck dogshit. Because she picked you out. This is how a man honors his woman. She ran away and picked you out and did you. She went after your slack, pathetic dogshit body, then I am gonna let it live."

To her, this handsome, raging man was maimed. He was defaced, for her. The dream she'd dreamed was ugly, the argument she'd made for marriage, or escape from her father, or her flight from the upstate, unpoetical Emily Dickinson, was real. The young husband was a festering scar because the young wife was. Or so Willie's life-long training in guilt, fear, displacement, and metaphor had taught him.

And he felt a thrill of pride fire through his terrified nervous system as his mouth said, "She is a very good person. Please don't hurt her."

" 'Please.' Jesus. God. You people," the soldier said. "You kiss what takes you down. Don't you tell me *please*. Don't you tell me what my

wife is and what I can do with her. It's *me* telling *you.* I *served* my
country. You stayed home and you put the meat to my wife. Four-eff
Ho Chi Minh boy."

She had struck her husband with Willie, and now, Willie thought
reasonably, the husband was returning the blows to what he saw as
their source. Unfortunately, Willie had to receive them, but maybe,
he thought, he could be serviceable. Maybe his ancestors' God, so
often unreliable, was punishing with some accuracy. So maybe, now
that Willie was justly punished for his cornucopian sex with Tony, his
fiery, brimming emotions, maybe the cranky, maniac God would
leave his mother alone.

Hey, God, Willie thought. Some wound. Fuck you. And leave my
mother out of it.

Tony's husband, as if he had been waiting for Willie to finish his
final prayer, stepped around Willie and then stepped in. Willie
watched as he coiled himself. He heard the man say, "Jew." Then
Willie watched the boot come.

I'll Be Home for Christmas

FOR A WHILE, THE exploded capillaries around his eyes had made
him resemble a raccoon. His students stared at his face while he
spoke, but he was glad not to be wearing cotton packed into his nostrils and a splint along his nose. The splint hadn't helped, and he
looked a little like a broken-down boxer, and that seemed fine to
him. He shaved his beard, he gave up smoking, and he dated no one.
He took to driving out into the countryside with a bottle of red wine,
and country was most of what this New York borderland offered—
snow-covered fields, mountains of drift, salt on the windshield, and
winds that seemed to wind themselves up in Vancouver before they
roared east over Canada and then came south to spill their snow. He
made notes about the landscape that he didn't reread. He did not
have sex. He did not see Tony. He did not press charges, though this
gesture—towards a vicious God, not towards his assailant—had done
his mother little good. His father continued to work late, to travel

wide, and of course to be debriefed by his control. His mother said she asked no questions, and Willie, sad as he was for her, admired his father's inventiveness. It was a superb cover story, since its imperviousness to questions was built in. To protect herself and Willie, to honor her husband of so many years, and to support his service to the demands of their adopted nation, she would have to cooperate in her own betrayal.

He remembered his boyhood house, its many rooms, its privacies, and the three of them withdrawing behind gently shut doors, and then his mother's peering in at him in his room, and his parents' peering out at him as he played in the yard or the street, his own searching around corners, under beds, in bureau drawers—though never in the chocolate drawer again. All those investigating eyes, he thought, the spying on each other out of—what else could you call it? what else would they claim?—love. Truly, he thought on one of his icy drives, Kafka is the patron saint of families. He had impressed a woman in graduate school with this observation. She had dated him, and it was not impossible, he thought, that Franz Kafka, snug as a bug in a bed, was the reason. To love, Kafka taught, was to be suspicious of all generosity.

He wound up his courses, he graded exams. Riefsnyder flunked the final, but Willie passed him anyway. At the Christmastime tunk, Professor Wherry had sat at the piano, elegant in a camel-hair sportcoat with silver buttons, and had played Christmas carols. Fevler, with his eyebrows and a few nods, had indicated to Willie that they were expected to gather at the piano as the great man played.

"This one," Wherry said, smiling in appreciation of himself, "was Bing Crosby's great hit. I've always favored it because it tells the truth—that the soldier will be home only in his dreams—while it offers the allure of the wish to rejoin his family for the holiday. Quite a complex bit of song. And so many soldiers were away at the time. Quite sad, really, while still celebrating the season. I know a Laotian scholar who sings it not because he understands the lyrics, but because he heard the recording and he knew it to be sad. I've been privileged, I should add, to sing this song *with* Mr. Crosby in his house. Mr. Bernstein, you don't mind a song of Christmas?"

Willie, in what he thought of as a Christmas gift to the gentiles, did not announce that Mr. Bing Crosby was a Jew.

The following Friday, Mrs. Fevler, sounding puzzled, invited Willie for after-dinner coffee and pie. When he arrived, Mrs. Fevler, looking like Emily Dickinson's older aunt, took his coat and brought him to the living room. He smelled the coffee but didn't see it, and there wasn't any pie in sight. There was Tony, however, looking unwell, both thin and pregnant. He felt only a little like the man on the floor of his office, kicked into submission.

"He isn't here," Tony said. "He reenlisted. It's only me." She walked to him and stood before him with her head down. "And the baby," she said.

"His baby."

She smiled as if he were, perhaps, her very young nephew. "Yes," she said. "He had to put a bomb inside me. Do you know what I mean?"

Willie looked at her stomach.

Tony, very softly, said, "Boom." And he flinched. She kissed him on the side of the jaw and picked up his right hand, which she squeezed, and then she dropped it and went back to the gray-and-white sofa, where she sat and adjusted her braid so it hung over her shoulder.

It was like the gathering of the actors in a drawing-room play. Mrs. Fevler came in next with a cart on which coffee and a bottle of brandy sat. Someone had used a good deal of deodorant, and the high, sweet, inauthentic odor clashed with the dark smell of the coffee. "I decided that we would need the B&B a lot more than the pie," Mrs. Fevler said. "Is that all right? Would you serve us, Mr. Bernstein?"

"Willie," Willie said. He gave Tony a snifter, and then Mrs. Fevler. He poured himself more than a double, and decided to sit in one of the dark gray upholstered chairs across from the sofa where they sat.

And then, as if the star had arrived, Serge Fevler, in black suit and white shirt and a narrow solid red necktie, entered the room, moved an upholstered chair so that he sat at the head of the room, facing them all, and he pointed, raising his brows, at the glasses. Willie brought him brandy and Fevler smiled. "My good fellow," he said.

He said, "This is the beginning of a series of more subtle announcements. I am going to find them very difficult. I find this one relatively easy, although we are speaking of minute degrees of difference. Willie Bernstein, you are here because it is owed you, and because you have been, unwittingly, a catalyst. You have experienced what I avoided—here, at any rate. At home, in the beginning: another matter."

Pamela Fevler clutched her side, but Willie thought she wanted to hold her stomach. She knew what her husband was about to say. Tony looked lost.

"When I began here," Fevler said, "an immigrant although with excellent English and first-rate degrees, it was a difficult time in the United States. Indeed, in the world. Tolerance was limited, and on campuses like this one even scarcer. It is the tradition, alas. I suppose it will change. But I took a decision then, and I observed it. I often, but hardly always, regretted it, if only because one derives a certain satisfaction from creating one's own identity. A *legend* is what the KGB terms it. Our CIA acquired the term from them. So: the appeal of putting over the fiction. Understandable. It is, after all, the American experience: you give birth to yourself.

"On the other hand, there is the fact of the lie. We would"—he seemed, now, to be addressing Tony—"call it, these days, a failure of nerve. Instead of a sociological ploy, it would be called a moral lapse. It is how the war, wars, perhaps, the Great Patriotic War Number Two, as well as this Vietnam thing, have taught us to regard our actions. Nothing is viewed pragmatically unless one confers with, say, Dean Rusk." He nodded at Willie, who thought that Fevler might wink. He had become paler than usual, paler than his wife, and now his great nose and sallow skin seemed to echo his daughter's. Mrs. Fevler plucked at the sofa or her dress and looked steadily at the floor.

"We speak of the inherent morality of actions instead of their results. Perhaps this will make for a better world. If we all were Isaiah

Berlin, then just possibly. And he, I ought to point out, was of use to the intelligence services. He knew about the undercover life."

Fevler seemed to become disconnected from whatever had provided the great energy with which he had begun.

Pamela Fevler studied her husband and then, in her high Southern whine, she said, "Your father is about to say—"

"No," he said. "Please. Let me."

"Then do it," she said.

He said, "Pamela." Then he fell back into silence.

"Your father," she said, and she offered him a pause. He didn't take the opportunity, and she continued. "Your father would like to announce, darling, that you are a Jew."

Tony looked up quickly, leaned forward as if to stand, then held in place. Her braid moved sideways. She looked not at her father but at Willie. Her expression was confused, and then it grew studious.

Mrs. Fevler said, "Somebody give me more brandy, please. I need to get tight."

Willie watched Tony's eyes as they focused into his. Her face grew, little by little, triumphant, and she very slowly licked her lips. Then she rocked herself forward from the sofa and went to her father.

Pamela Fevler held out her empty glass. "Hey, Willie," Mrs. Fevler said. "Son."

Chimneys

Willie went home at Christmastime although he had thought to stay upstate. He had enjoyed contemplating the long, cold, snowy afternoons spent drinking wine and trying to read *Ulysses* or the stories of John Updike, which always made him wish he could describe what he thought of as his world as well as Updike drew his. He had thought to stay and had told his mother that he would. But, walking across the quadrangle after filing his final grades, appreciating the stone Colonial buildings and envying someone who must know and be enjoyed by the pretty woman in her loden coat throwing snowballs for her large, liver-colored dog to chase, he knew that this place could not be his. He would always, like Professor Fevler, be pursuing an acceptance by the people to whom the place belonged. He would never believe that he deserved it and neither would they. And he would detest himself more, if he stayed and was allowed to stay, than he did at this moment; for he would want to earn their approval. So Willie went home to New York to attend the convention of the Modern Language Association and to court interviews for jobs, like this one, for which he was as unqualified as many other young women and men.

His father was, presumably, at work when Willie arrived. His mother was at the door, and dressed, no doubt in response to his phone call, like the model *bonne femme*. She wore a dark A-line dress from the waist of which a crescent of starched white apron fell. She was in good black stacked heels and dark hose, and her garnet earrings, made from the rings of one of the aunts who had shepherded them to England and then here, gleamed on their gold settings against her almost olive skin. Her eyes looked exhausted, and her lips were pressed in what could have been called a tight smile, though Willie would have called it a grimace. She kissed him on both cheeks, then on the mouth, pushed him away, regarded him, drew him in, kissed the cheeks again, the mouth, then pulled at his bag until he hauled it from her and carried it into the house.

"Sweet boy," she said, leading him into the living room, which was dark but fragrant with a lit fireplace.

They sat on the sofa facing the fireplace and she poured tea from a service for two which she had somehow prepared to be steeped and hot for precisely the time of his arrival. She had smoked a cigarette and lit another by the time he had sugared and sipped at his tea.

"Since when, Mom?"

"Silly thing," she said, "I was smoking *bleus* before we left France."

"And when did you start again?"

"Shall I be dramatic and say?"

Willie shook his head. "A little spying or deceit, and you go up in smoke."

She smiled to applaud his cleverness, but she drew on the cigarette with more interest than she showed in her smile. "There was a woman you alluded to," she said.

"Did I do a lot of alluding?"

His mother shrugged. "She pleased you. She troubled you. Has she left you yet?"

"How did you know?"

"Your letters, infrequent as they were, seemed terribly poetic. A man who writes with such lush imprecision about emotions and landscapes—barren country with snow on top of it, as far as I understand—is either in love or suddenly on the outskirts of that not quite fatal place."

He whistled at his tea. "Who's that you're quoting?"

"Your father."

"Well, that's a relief," Willie said. "I was afraid, for a minute, that we were talking about *me.*"

"Inasmuch as he is your father . . ."

"And you my mother."

"There you are."

"Here I am."

She smoked and Willie watched her. She looked up to catch his eyes, and they both smiled. "I have decided," she said.

He nodded.

"I believe him."

"You do?"

"No. But I have *decided*. That is: I live in the posture of one who believes."

"You pray but know it goes nowhere. Is that the sort of—"

"No, you see, because I surely have belief."

"In Pop."

"In having lived with him as a girl. In having come to love him. In having loved him. In having borne his son, my dear boy. In having escaped with him from the roundup, the train, the camp, the furnace. History, I believe, I could call it."

"History," Willie repeated, almost breathless with admiration, perhaps with envy.

"Not as it is written, you understand. As it is lived. As, one could say, it *itself* lives."

In the dark room, in the slow shadows of the fire, behind the smoke of her cigarettes, he saw his mother's skin grow even darker as a flush came up her neck and cheeks and forehead. He watched her body demonstrate its choice as she called it her mind's own.

"This is terribly painful for you," Willie said, aware as he said it that he sounded like a boy of eighteen inside the body of someone older, a stupidly earnest, somewhat pompous fellow with an overbite that made him look thoughtful when he was merely confused.

His mother laughed a girl's sudden pleasure, stubbed her cigarette out, leaned over and kissed him on the cheek. He was, he knew, ridiculous. And he began to suspect that he would spend his life with women who forgave and found his boyishness endearing, every once in a while.

Willie thought that his father, with whom he dined a day and several hours later, on Ninth Avenue in Manhattan, found him less than endearing. They too were side by side, though in the red leather banquette of the restaurant his father called a bistro. His tall, saturnine father, whose beard never looked well enough shaved, seemed less than pleased with Willie's assessment of international affairs and his pronouncements on domestic politics. He seemed to fall into the residue gesture of his shrug more than Willie remembered, and he seemed to smile less frequently at Willie's cleverness. His father ordered a *sauté de lapin* for himself and suggested the braised beef with olives for Willie. He asked for a bottle of Châteauneuf-du-Pape and more butter. They had an aperitif of Ricard and water, and his father lit a cigarette.

"Since when do you smoke, Pop?"

"I stopped when I was younger than you, Willie, and then—who knows?" He shrugged and left the cigarette in his mouth an instant, a gesture Willie had believed only when seeing it performed by Jean-Paul Belmondo in *Breathless*. His father looked no less authentic. When he said, "You don't mind?" the cigarette wobbled in place, and Willie studied it.

"No, sir. Mom started too, huh?"

"She? She smoked before I did, at home, back then. We are a pair of well-matched chimneys, eh? This I mean as a rather dark irony. I refer to the chimneys of the camps, you understand?"

Willie nodded.

"One comes back to them, as it were, time after time."

"Of course," Willie said, shrugging in imitation of his father.

"And this unhappiness of your mother's, Willie. What do you make of it?"

"She seemed happy enough yesterday and last night. She seemed all right."

"Do you know that is not what I mean?"

"Yes, sir."

"Do you know to what I do refer?"

"Some."

"About *that,* then: what do you think?"

Whenever his father cross-examined him, a part of Willie was pleased to witness the flash of the sword, the athleticism with which his father parried and lunged. A part, too, was intimidated, as he was meant by his father to be. He sipped at his Ricard to give himself time to think, but couldn't manage to think, so opened his mouth and spoke, as interested as his father in what he might say: "She spoke of her love for you."

"Of course," his father said, moving his hand through the air above the table, "we share great experience and admiration, *commitment,* you might call it. We do, naturally, love each other. In the event that anyone must describe us."

"I think you kind of asked me to do that, Pop."

His father smiled in actual pleasure. *"Bien dit,"* he said.

"As for the other parts of it—"

"Which *it,* Willie?"

"The CIA?"

His father put his finger to his lips.

Willie whispered it: "CIA. The control. Danger to her and me. Blackmail. Cuba."

His father nodded at each word. Then he held up his hand. He looked toward the nearest waiter and leaned over the table. "It is true, Willie. The coercion is actual, their requirements demonstrable. I spent most of last week in Milan, did you know that?"

Willie shook his head.

"Upon returning, I was interviewed. That is not the word they use. Briefing."

"Debriefed," Willie said, remembering his senior professors' pride.

"Exactly. In a room in the Department of State. These are serious people," his father whispered. "It is not a work I necessarily mind, because the danger seems only occasional and not that great. One feels useful, if compelled. But the pain for your mother—"

"Pop, how come your control's a Cuban if you're working for them in Europe?"

His father hushed him and looked theatrically about, although his dark leanness gave the gesture a sense of actual urgency. Then he shook his head three times, closing his eyes, and opening them with a fluttering of the lids, as if almost overwhelmed by the power of the truths he knew. He looked at Willie, shook his head again, and finished off his Ricard.

Willie interviewed in narrow rooms and lush suites with committees representing English at Notre Dame, Hamilton, Alfred, and the University of New Mexico. He fancied the Albuquerque job because he liked the idea of the pueblos and prehistoric cliff dwellers and because the three men who interviewed him had attractive tans while everyone else looked pasty and verging on gray. He didn't understand where Alfred was, and when one of the interviewers said, "Near Hornel," his fellow interviewers laughed themselves close to hysteria. He stayed at home for a week, dining most nights with friends at the convention but lunching in the city with his father and escorting his mother on one grand shopping expedition and one day among the art galleries. On Fifty-seventh Street, in one of the large office buildings, at a gallery dedicated to photography, he saw a picture of a woman's pregnant belly, the taut, bright skin expanding toward the camera made into an abstraction of packed ripeness by the shot, and he wondered if it might not be his child in Tony. Standing before the photograph in midtown Manhattan, but seeing (or trying to) their each moment of locked, wet socketing upstate, remembering (or trying to) the method of contraception, he was certain that he had left it, almost always, up to her. Oh, bold adventurer, he thought, to let a damaged woman protect you. He offered himself this, at least: that she was the reason his nose was broken and made him appear quite French. Now the picture looked more like a basketball than part of a woman's body, and he and his mother moved on, to stand before shots of Celtic ruins and Irish fields.

His father discussed the relationship between the Kirkuk oilfield in Iraq and America's import of 30 percent of its petroleum. His mother meditated on her son's removal to Indiana, his return to upstate New York, and what she called, when she spoke of New Mexico, "the moon." Willie learned nothing of their life together, except for his mother's remarking on his father's unaccustomed presence at every evening meal of the week.

At Scribner's, Willie bought a book of poetry by James Wright called *Shall We Gather at the River*. He found himself jealous with a physical sickness that he could not write down important, actual-seeming moments—their smells, their tactile textures—as a charm against what he had come to see as the disappearance of his parents in smoke, and the quick, wasteful passage of his own short days and nights. He wept as the poet called to Jenny, dead under water,

> Come up to me, love,
> Out of the river, or I will
> Come down to you

and he knew that he wept not only for Tony, not only for what she and her husband had taken away, but because he knew that he never would dare the alluvial darkness, or the cold current, to struggle against gravity and his own terror to bring someone precious back up.

Or I Will Come
Down to You

Pine

WILLIE'S MOTHER DIED NEARLY six years after his father left her. They had fled Paris together, with only a haversack and a canvas bag. This time, Etienne Bernstein left with his briefcase and a garment carrier containing the gray-black sharkskin suit he wore when pleading before the Supreme Court of the United States of America. She hadn't shrunk and grown pale and silent. She had smoked more, had consumed more wine and, after a year or two, Scotch whisky. She had traveled for a little more than two weeks shortly after Etienne's departure, and had then, as Willie saw it, begun to stop moving, had begun to melt into the elements comprised by her household; she and the building itself became one, and when she died, he told Miriam Delnegro, he found himself holding his breath and squinting as he returned to unpack her presence from the structure itself. He found himself, he told Miriam, violating his mother's final privacy, and he felt as through he scraped along the soft skin of her upper arms, the secret hollow beneath her pale, sculpted, Gallic chin, as he surrendered to the immense forces arrayed against them all by, finally, giving away most of her clothing, packing most of the papers in cartons to be held in storage, and drinking a very large belt of her cheap Scotch, bottle upturned above his face, before—as he saw it—abandoning her.

Her gestures didn't diminish toward the end, but her activities slowed and then stopped. After her return to Europe, traveling with a widowed friend, after her visit to her old *arrondissement* and her assessment of a few French cities, and after her tour of Italy, she returned to her house and didn't leave except to shop for food and see to the routine inspection of the car Etienne had left behind but which she rarely drove.

She saw her friends, she corresponded and read the newspapers, became addicted to television programs in which couples fought, often physically, as they exposed to several million strangers their corruption, terror, and rage. Willie visited her, traveling from his new jobs—the first at a college in western New York State, and then at a prep school in Columbia County—before he returned to Manhattan to become a rising junior publisher who hadn't started as an editor's assistant, but as a textbook specialist who made the difficult shift to the publication of general trade books.

His mother fell, at night, while drunk, although she claimed that she had suffered dizziness and was on her way to the bathroom for a cold washcloth. She recovered, apparently, from the headache and bruised occiput, and she died two days later when an aneurysm blew up her brain.

He saw her the night before her death, and catalogued the features of her face because he was frightened, each time he left her, that she would die before he returned. He was a lugubrious guest, and she drank and chattered, he later thought, to counteract his dolefulness.

She sat in the club chair in which his father used to sit, and she kept an open book, upside down, on her lap. It was her way of denying that, until he had walked through the door, she had been watching family gang wars on television. Cigarette smoke gathered around the funnel-shaped bridge lamp beside and above her head, and her cup of cold coffee, sweetened, Willie knew, with whisky, was half consumed. He tried to read the title of the book as he bent to kiss her cheek, but all he could see through her fingers was *Night*.

Her dark brown eyes seemed to Willie to gleam, as if with recent tears, and he said, "Mom? You okay?"

"Excellent," she said, smiling like a girl and sitting taller in the chair, pressing at the hem of her dress with the edge of the open book. "Very, very well, thank you. And the job?"

"Sometimes it's a lot of fun," he said. "Nobody works unless they have to—*until* they have to. So it's lots of gossip, too many telephone calls, a little doodling on P&L forms—profit and loss estimates for books we might publish, but we make up most of those figures—and then, all of a sudden, we run and run and sweat and sweat, and we do what we're supposed to. It isn't what you would call a disciplined profession."

He knew that she knew what he meant: *It isn't what Pop would call a disciplined profession.* They looked into each other's eyes, then away. Her eyes still looked damp. Her flesh was a little yellow, he thought, or even orange, but not a reassuring pink. The lines at her eyes and forehead and throat were furrows now, and her smile was a bit of a grimace as well, and Willie, in his stomach and the bottom of his throat, felt pressure; he was like a panicky child in a department store who suddenly looked up from the bin of lead soldiers and could not see the mother he expected he would find.

He hurriedly said, to fill the silence, "I just might be pretty good at it. Which shows you what kind of mettle *I* have."

"Metal?" his mother said. "Explain, if you please."

"Metal. *Oh.* No. Stuff. Substance? As a measure of, ah, character."

"Character," she said. "Then yes, of course."

"Tell me about you, sweetheart," he said. "How—really—have you been?"

"After this time? This many months and years? Still baffled. That it could happen? No. Of course, life is filled with people who change, wander, disappear. I know, as you understand so well, about disappearance. But *him.* That I never knew him. Some of him, I suppose. Perhaps. But all of him? No. So I hardly feel betrayed. Is that what you meant to know? I feel stupid. I feel . . . dull. Disappointing. He is in a new life, and I am left in the old one. It is larger, because he has left so much room behind, and it is chilly. I find that I wear sweaters more often. The sweatshirt you sent me from the school where you—"

"Tony."

"That one, yes. And I feel jealous not of the woman, the Cuban woman who doubtless dances—what do they dance? the rumba, I think—with a ravishing panache." She drank some laced coffee and smiled a guilty conspirator's smile, and he of course smiled back. "I confess, Willie, that I am jealous of *him*. He gets the new life. I get only the old. After all the travels of our years, he has moved and I have stayed in one place. And it is somehow made to be—and by who else but me?—*my fault.*"

"Which, of course," Willie said, "it is not."

His mother drank more coffee. "Of course," she agreed.

And she died that night.

He had, filled with loathing for his inclination to mourn in public, made a grudging pilgrimage to Paris and had paced, nervous about drawing attention to himself, back and forth on a silent, rain-blackened street in what was left of the Marais, where his parents had lived and from which they had fled to England, and where seven of his relatives were rounded up by French police under SS officers to be taken in trucks to Drancy for the train ride ending their lives. He had carried grief—over his mother's death, his father's transformation—and what he knew to be a youthful resentment that his parents had lived their lives, finally, with so little thought of how he might be affected by their decisions; his stomach had ached from his bilious knowledge, and his excellent English shoes had scraped as he paced. He felt nothing he had not felt at home, except a breathlessness which, he realized, had begun in his wondering if someone in the district, peering through old eyes, might not see in his features the family face. He despaired of being recognized. It had been the same, two days before, on a gray street of failing shops off a ring road in Southampton, England, though at least he had left with the pair of new shoes.

After Paris, he had rented a car and driven too long without resting to no place he had heard of, but which Miriam Delnegro had grudgingly told him was handsome country, to the east and south of Bordeaux. Near a little town called Piane-sur-Garonne, he had found a room at the hotel and restaurant of M. Rully, and had eaten until he was ill, drunk until he was stupid and loud, and had slept for a night and much of a day until the chambermaid woke him by opening the door and rattling the latch and asking brightly if monsieur cared to see the *patron* about his *note*.

As Willie later paid the bill, blushing, M. Rully said, in English, "I regret your tragedy."

Willie said, "I regret that I informed you of its presence in my life," speaking his own language as if translating it from his parents', and, as if to comment, M. Rully, burly and bald and smelling of orange water, shrugged as Willie's father always had when he thought language superfluous to the moment. Willie, believing himself haunted, shrugged back, in spite of his wishing very much not to. And his new shoes pinched his feet beneath the ankles and across the toes.

To quote Miriam Delnegro: "You will hate this trip, Willie. You'll get lonely before the first day is over, your clothing will rebel against your body, and you'll eat bad food. Take me with you or pine."

"Pine?"

"As in pine away," Miriam said. She was the managing editor and therefore always moving, for she was in charge of production schedules, and she could not rest. She walked two steps from his desk, then turned like a majorette, her pointed chin high and her dark forehead, as usual, wrinkled over delay, and she walked as if marching to return to his desk. "Die in sickness over love you lost or squandered: pine."

"Are we so shaky together that I'm going to lose you if I go to England and France?"

"Alone?" she asked.

"Let's say, just for argument's sake, alone."

"Then yes," she said, "for argument's sake. I'd definitely say you're running a risk. And Maine, afterwards?"

"Maybe."

"Maybe my Sardinian ass."

"I am enchanted by your Sardinian ass."

"That's why I'm wearing this dress," she said. "Though now I regret it. *You* should be the one parading your ass to change *my* mind."

"I could never fit into that dress," Willie said.

"You wore my underwear," she said, her face turning dark.

"Barely got one thigh through a leghole, and that was because I was crazy with sex."

"And now?"

"Still," he said. "Who wouldn't be? Look at you. Listen to you. I dreamed about finding you in a cupboard, even."

"Eerie," she said, walking away from his desk again. "Icky. Claustrophobic. I'm the skeleton in your closet." She stopped, held up her hand, said, "Never mind. I know. That's your parents' job. So, pine, Willie. Pine."

He flew from Paris to Logan, feeling somehow that he was sneaking into the country he had left at Kennedy in New York, and he stammered when Immigration asked him what he had done in, let's see, England and then France in such a short time.

"Bought a pair of very expensive shoes," Willie said, smiling hollowly and holding up his left leg to display the bright, heavy walker's brogan that pressed too hard at the second joint of his toes.

The pale, weary Immigration officer didn't smile. He looked at a shelf below the counter on which his elbows had been propped, and Willie wondered if his name might be on a watch list because of his protesting the Vietnam War, or perhaps his publication of the seven-year diary of a woman who had fled Princeton for, eventually, Seattle after blowing up a lab and killing two technicians and two chimpanzees. She had, of course, been protesting the cruelties of animal research.

Willie tried again. "I was trying to trace my family. Parents. My parents went from France to England before they came here."

"Some big trace in five days, huh?"

Willie shrugged the shrug. "I don't get that much time away from the office."

"How'd you make out? Besides the smart-ass shoes?"

"I apologize," Willie said. "I didn't really find anything out."

"Lousy vacation, then," the Immigration officer said. "Sorry about that."

"Thanks," Willie said. "Thank you very much."

"And now that you're in Boston?"

"Try a little vacation, I thought. Try to have some fun."

"Nice idea," the officer said. "Welcome home." He stamped the passport and gestured for the next in line as Willie tried to look like something other than an illegal alien while he went to find his duffel bag, slink through customs, and rent a car to drive—where else? he thought, thinking also of Miriam Delnegro, who had as usual read his thoughts—to Maine.

He remembered having been on US 1 as a college sophomore, mildly drunk, high on male friendship and adventure—they had fled New York and preparation for spring semester finals—as he and a schoolmate searched for college girls in sweater sets. The traffic had been sparse and Freeport a little town with a diner, and L. L. Bean had been just a large wooden building, not an institution the size of a college campus in the midst of the longest street of malls he now made the mistake of driving through. Everyone, he speculated, each of them, wearing their bright primary colors or the several shades of luminescent teal, along with floppy shorts and thick, white sneakers, had driven up, all night, to get from the malls in New Jersey to this one. It's a homing instinct among shoppers, he thought.

It's their *life,* Willie thought, and it's honorable enough. But he heard Miriam bubble her breath out and he envisioned her holding her throat as if choking herself to death for having even *heard* such shallow mendacity. Miriam bought her stockings and underwear from catalogues, her clothing over the phone in response to ads in the *Times,* and, because she had elegant taste and was a perfect size 6, she looked as if her clothes were custom-made. Willie bought suits from J. Press because his father had taught him to, and he looked in them as if he had found them on the bargain racks downtown at Mern's. He pictured Miriam's underwear.

Don't Tell Anyone

HE DIDN'T STOP IN Portland, as he'd thought to, but—driving by now on the Maine Turnpike, avoiding the slower traffic on US 1— he drove through the night to get northeast and reach Lubec on the coast, not far from Eastport, which was the end up there of America. A number of people who spoke French lived in and around Lubec, and one of them was Willie Bernstein's father.

At a large white chandler's shop at the Lubec harbor, a corner of which was a short-order kitchen, Willie ordered fried clams and a long ale, which he took outside to a picnic table, where he looked at the chop and the bruised low sky as gulls lined up in the air to lay out on the intermittent winds and cruise him for food. It was the best meal he had eaten since starting his vacation, he thought. But then he thought of Miriam, who might have been sitting beside him with her brown legs tempting his touch. She would have taken a single fried clam from his plate and, with her small white teeth, have worked it over for five bites. He tossed the rest of his food toward the harbor, and the gulls, barking, followed his dinner down.

"Hello, Pop," he said, driving up into the hilly streets that ran from the harbor.

He tried it again: "Hi, Pop."

"Pop, I was in Maine anyway—"

"I need to talk to you, Pop."

"Daddy?" he heard himself say.

He drove past their house and followed streets in town until he had seen a good deal of what there was: handsome houses, shabby houses, shops not faring wonderfully well, a lot of houses for sale, two public laundries, a couple of outfits that hired out for fishing trips, the offices of lawyers, and a bank. He might find more if he looked, but he didn't want to look. He wanted to think of how to address his father, and he wanted equally to drive out of Lubec and back down to South Trescott, then, heading the way he had come, pass the turnoff to the Cutler Naval Station, where he had seen, as he slowed, hundreds of girderlike masts; they weren't dish-shaped for reception, so must serve, he figured, for some kind of transmission. They were so tall that red lights warning off low-flying planes winked from the pinnacle of each. How many coded thoughts to ships with coded names were bouncing around off the coast of Maine? He remembered the time that he and Tony Fevler and her mother had marched with college students to end an undeclared war. How could they have thought to battle so many invisibilities?

And he remembered his certainty that his time with Tony, exquisite and sapping and inspiriting—when he was drunk on the surge in him of sex—had seemed to him to be responsible, somehow, for his mother's sorrows. He wondered if those old pleasures were still a sin to the cruel God of his mother and whether, therefore, he and his lusts had been the cause of her death. Maybe we'll have a little luck, he thought, and there won't be a God.

"What a boy," he said. And then he said, "Hello, Pop," as he parked at Etienne Bernstein, Attorney-at-Law, a small building of yellow brick with opaque glass cobbles where the windows might once have been. He carried with him a bottle of duty-free Cos d'Estournel, which he had fancied they might drink together to salute the woman who had died from them, but only after learning how completely Willie's Pop, tall and slim and elegant, lived his secret life.

There wasn't an anteroom, only the office, a rectangle of cherry furniture, which Willie recognized from his father's New York office, on a long Afghan carpet the design of which was a garden of great delicacy and into which Willie, as a boy who played briefly on the floor when his mother came to see his father at work, had tried to will himself: on the background of maroon and brown the blues of pond or waterfall, the greens of vegetation, the sense of balance, repose, shelter he had always felt more possible within this floor than in the life that sat or strode upon it. The carpet was set on clouded tan linoleum squares, and his father's partners desk, with a fan of three chairs before it, shone, as if it were night, in the light of the yellow ceiling fixture. Off the carpet and along two walls were filing cabinets, the old wooden ones that Willie remembered, and some of olive-drab metal. His father sat smoking behind his desk, and, in one of his visitor's chairs, a big man smoked a bulldog pipe, pressing at the coals in the little bowl and puffing small clouds, his lips pursing as if he wished to imitate a fish.

Willie, finally, called his father nothing. He lifted the bottle of Bordeaux in the air, as if to show that he had returned with it as instructed, and he smiled a smile.

"A pathetically tentative smile, you poor mutt," he thought Miriam might have commented.

"Well," his father said, rising. "Well, well."

The man with the pipe stood too, and Willie, without knowing why, went to shake his hand. The hand was large and loose and dry, the smell of the pipesmoke was heavy and sweet.

"Sidney Bauer," his father said, perhaps reluctantly, Willie thought. "This is my son, Guillaume. William."

"Willie's fine."

"Well, I'm fine, too," Sidney Bauer said, smiling widely around the pipe that sat in his clenched teeth.

"Glad to hear it," Willie said, making a social clown's face. "Pop," he finally said, walking around the desk and embracing his father, who smelled stale and smoky. The blue cloud of cigarette and pipe lay midway to the ceiling fixture that did not illuminate the office so much as it made the furniture look heavy and dark. His father patted his back and stepped away. He leaned forward, then, a Frenchman, and kissed his son on each cheek. Willie closed his eyes each time. He knew that Miriam Delnegro would have noticed.

"So," his father said. "You come all the way up here—"

"Down east," Sidney Bauer said.

"Of course, of course," his father said, nodding. "I cannot remember."

"Don't ever be logical," Sidney Bauer said, "if you want to understand any local geography. Up's down, and that's all she wrote. You're the professor—no: you *were* the professor. Good deal of respect for the teaching profession. You used to be in it. Book-something, now, am I right?"

"Right," Willie said.

"Good for you," Sidney Bauer said. "I always read. History. Coastal water guides. I'm practical, I guess you'd say."

"And you didn't telephone," Willie's father said, as if never interrupted. "What a long journey. What if we had not been home? In the town, that is to say. What if we had made a vacation?"

"I'd have missed you, Pop. But I didn't know I was coming all the way here until I was here."

"Spur of the moment," Sidney Bauer said. "Impulse. Dangerous, those impulses, I'd have said."

"If I had known you, sir, I would have consulted you as soon as I felt the impulse coming on," Willie said, watching his father slowly redden.

"Willie," his father said.

"Point well taken," Sidney Bauer said. "Time to butt back out. Steve," he said to Etienne Bernstein, whom Willie had never heard addressed in a translated nickname; he had always been Etienne or Steven. "I'm off. I'll see you at the mooring, then? Early as hell?"

"Comme d'habitude," his father said.

And Bauer, with an easy, accurate accent, replied, *"À bientôt.* And that goes for you too, Mr. Willie."

He sat now, studying his seated father—the pallor of his face, the gray crescents underneath his eyes, the nicotine stains on his long fingers the nails of which were dirty, as if his father worked on engines instead of briefs. His father turned off a computer notebook and closed its lid with force, as if something were trying to escape. Willie said, "You haven't any pictures on your walls, Pop."

"I have meant to."

"So you're busy, then. That's good."

"I have work to occupy me, but, no, it is the choice."

"Of picture?"

"Of what matters. What matters enough, of all the images in my life, to select and hang here? I find myself . . . stymied."

"Can I help? The one of Mom and you in New York at the Sheep Meadow?"

"I don't think you can, actually, Willie. No. But: my thanks. But no."

"I didn't mean to be making your choice for you."

"You would be entitled to try. It is your right."

And so, because of his deftness, Willie thought, they had slammed against the past so promptly that no further words seemed possible. His father lit another cigarette.

"You don't smoke the *bleus* anymore."

"She requires of me a filter on the end. It doesn't repay the expense of Gauloises. I can smoke the droppings of the horses in the barn with such a filter."

"Did she try to get you to quit?"

"What else? But she is addicted as well. I have said that I await the pleasure of her company in the ecstasies of withdrawal."

"You're a stubborn man, Pop."

"And you, Willie. Are you stubborn as well? Yes. I answer for you. Yes, you are. Tell me what I do not know. Are you, in every way, content?" His father rubbed his eyes and blinked. His shirt looked limp, and he wore, Willie realized, khakis with his necktie and spread collar. He hadn't seen his father in khakis except on weekends. He had always worn expensive suits he bought at J. Press because an Ivy League partner at his first American firm had taught him how to dress. And here he was, in this dusky office, looking ill and wearing the kind of pants you bought at malls. "Willie?"

"Yes," he said. "Sure. Good job, a few friends, a decent place."

"Where is it?" his father asked, and Willie realized that they had exchanged some telephone calls, but never a letter, since his mother had died. He kept his father's address in his phone book, and wasn't surprised that his father never had his.

"Murray Hill," Willie said. "I'm on Thirty-eighth between Third and Lexington. I'll give you the address."

"I have the telephone number," his father said.

Willie nodded. "Great. Pop, how are *you?* You seem tired. Are things okay with, you know—"

"Brenda."

"Yes."

"Yes," his father said.

They sat in the smoke and the silence, and Willie caught himself rubbing his eyes in the manner of his father.

"She asks about you," his father said. "She thinks of your confusion at our—"

Willie nodded. "Sure," he said. "That's great, I really appreciate it. I'm not too terrific at writing to people. I take after you."

"But we think of each other," his father said. "I am always certain of that. Do we not?"

"Lots, Pop."

"Lots. Exactly. It was very dreadful to me to not appear when—"

"I wondered."

"I had betrayed your mother, Willie. How could I, like a genie from a bottle, appear before her to rectify what, as we both know, cannot be made right? All of our . . . amity. All friendship. It seemed to have vanished." He blew out smoke and said, puffing, "Poof. Gone. Goodbye. One becomes desperate at times."

"Were you desperate, Pop?"

"About her death," he said, swiveling his chair and leaning back to look away and up. "About dying."

"Are *you* sick, Pop?"

"Willie, who is well? I wonder, though, if we might declare a moratorium in these discussions of our history."

"History's a lot of what I've got, Pop."

"I understand."

"How about Brenda, then? What's she up to? How's she doing?"

"Everything is well, Willie, and all right. I have fled my life, my former life, the friend I had in New York, and I have come here to Lubec to have a different life. I have done so repeatedly, I fear. So. I am something of a fugitive, then, but perfectly legal. 'Legitimate' as my client, Bauer, might say. I am a legitimate fugitive. I miss you. I lament your mother's death and every fragment of an instant of disquiet I might have caused her. We were children together in a different world. The cloth of one's clothing, then, became wrinkled at once, as soon as one put it on. Antibiotics were not available. One ate sulfa in giant lozenges that tasted execrable. And there was dirt, it seemed, everywhere, once we had survived it and owned our own implement for the manufacture of hot water. Finally: as much hot water as we wished! It was like being married, in our early days, to one's sister as much as the child I had erotically pursued. Do you sense any of what I say? That it was like a betrayal of myself when I lived both with her and another—"

"Brenda," Willie said. He felt as if he balanced a ball on his nose and clapped his flippers.

"Oh, no," his father said, "you must recall, surely. The woman of that time was someone else. She grew weary of my conscience. She felt, she told me, *tainted* by my own feeling of having soiled my life." He smiled and rubbed at the pouch beneath each eye, pushing the tired, gray-brown flesh to and fro. He lit another cigarette. Willie thought he heard his father's lungs squeak as he inhaled. "It was a vile, secret time. I lived inside myself as if inside a room into which no one was permitted."

"I remember some of that," Willie said.

"I regret it."

"You were tough. You were cold."

"I intended to be. I did not wish to be discovered."

"But she did. Mom. Discover you."

His father nodded. "Everyone always discovers," he said. "There are no secrets. You can construct them. You can memorize the false details that make them persuasive, and you lie and lie. But, ultimately, all secrets are told. No. Not told: suspected. One infers, from the lies and the very persuasive details, that something is not being said. It is like the earth above a burial place. You cannot see the corpse but, even after a long time, you can see that something is buried. What might it be? Someone will wonder. Someone will think: Ah! Corpse! This, I think, is how it works, the secret life. You do not wish to tell, so you tiptoe about like a drunk waiter, going from person to person. You whisper into their face, and they smell the wine on your breath. *Don't tell anyone,* you beg them. It doesn't matter that they do not know what not to tell. It is the not telling, of course, that they know, and that is enough.

"Don't tell," his father whispered, shaking his head ferociously, his eyes bulging, his lips compressed, a burlesque and a sorrow at once.

Willie wiped his eyes. His father, noticing, reached into his drawer for a tattered packet of tissues, which he pushed across his desk. Willie shook his head, and his father shrugged. They sat and didn't speak, and Willie began to forget what his father had just told him. He would remember, he knew, on the long drive home. He would remember the pain on his father's face and would regret that he had offered no comfort, whether or not he could imagine—and he could not—what balm was available to give.

"You have to learn," Miriam Delnegro would tell him, "to just stand the hell up and wail with a person. Give up, Willie. Surrender, for heaven's sakes. *That's* what you do. You turn yourself in."

Willie compromised. He reached for the tissues, said, *"Mouchoirs en papier,"* to please his father, and he blew his nose. "Thank you," he said.

His father nodded.

Willie said, at last, "What kind of practice is it, Pop? This." He gestured at the furniture, the walls.

His father shrugged. "Small potatoes, you would say, I suppose. Real estate closings, wills, liability a little—from the fishing accidents, you know: nets and hooks and knives and motors. And some maritime law, of course. And then there is Canada, across the bridge at Campobello, so even some foreign matters, although I seek help from Boston or New York with that. I am a country lawyer who lives at the edge of the sea. I go upon the sea, from time to time. I do not enjoy such errands, but I go."

"Errands? Someone sends you on errands?"

"You see? I am too voluble. That is what emotion does."

"That sounds like a secret, Pop. What you just were talking about."

His father sat silently.

"Is that Mr. Bauer's department? The 'see you at dawn at the mooring'? The French coming out of his pipe or someplace? He *summons* you? Shit, Pop, it's a boat, and there's Canada, and there's FDR's Campobello place, with tourists coming in from every damned country. Or someplace off Eastport? Or sailors coming *into* Eastport? Is he a shady guy, Pop? Are you?"

"Oh, yes," his father said. "You know it already from my life with your mother and you. Oh, yes. Who could be more of a 'shady guy'?"

"That's not what I mean."

"What is it that you mean?"

"I have no idea."

"Good. I sense the commencement of wisdom. Come home with me. We will open this excellent wine and permit Brenda to—ah: the sound of chickens?"

"Cluck."

"Exactly. Cluck."

Tant Pis

"IT'S CALLED FIESTA," Brenda said. "It's an antique. *I'm* an antique." She set down the bright glazed dishes, some orange, some green, and some a shade of yellow that Willie thought of as radioactive. Brenda was taller than his father and slender, with very long arms and legs. Her hair was a shade of red that clashed with the dinnerware, and her lipstick seemed too bright for her hair. She laughed a smoker's hollow, echoing cough that tailed off into a rasp, and she might have been—given Willie's memories of home, kitchen, a woman preparing dinner while his father sat and worked at a wine bottle's cork—in a black-and-white movie into the showing of which he had strayed about twenty minutes late.

"I like to collect," Brenda said. "Whatever. I have Russian matchboxes. I have a basket of nineteenth-century Canadian coins."

"Do you get over there," Willie asked, "to Canada? You're so close."

"No," she said, lighting a filtered cigarette from his father's pack, which sat beneath its brass lighter to the left of his place at the table. She blew out smoke. "No, we don't do a lot of the tourist thing. Antiques are cheaper over here, and the food's better, so you don't mind its being more expensive. Your dad gets over quite a bit, of course, with his practice and everything."

Your dad, he thought. It was a different language.

"That's where Mr. Sidney Bauer comes in, I imagine."

His father looked up and shrugged. "I cannot persuade Willie that I am not part of a smuggling circle."

"Ring," Willie said.

"Of course," his father said. "Smuggling ring. He sees in Sidney something . . . shady. And he cannot be deterred." The cork gently lifted out, and, saying *"Tant pis"* to him, staring up through half-lidded eyes, his father sniffed at the air above the bottle's mouth. "I expect pleasure from this," he said, "and I offer many thanks."

"De rien," Willie said, offering the French because he would not, as his father said, be deterred.

"That's very imaginative," Brenda said. "Of course, in your line of work you need that kind of imagination, don't you? Does it happen very often that you give the authors their ideas? Or do they come to you with the story pretty much in mind?"

"It's all them," Willie said. "I just try to help them say what they wanted to in the first place. If I help them at all."

"Aren't you the modest one," Brenda said. "Is brisket of beef going to be all right with you, Willie? And Moroccan carrots? And just a salad with a little sorrel in it, a balsamic vinegar dressing? You know, your father and I are law-abiding citizens, I promise you."

"And gourmets," Willie said.

Brenda beamed and nodded agreement. His father had left the room, and now he returned with two hardware-store wineglasses, small and heavy-looking. He held them up to the light and then filled each halfway. "We'll sample it together," he said, passing one along the oilcloth cover of the kitchen table.

"Brenda?" Willie suggested.

"I never drink now, hon. I did that once for too many years, and enough got to be enough. I'll enjoy your enjoying it. But thank you," she said, turning back to the stove.

Willie raised his glass in the narrow, bright kitchen. The little TV set on the counter, the sets of pottery canisters in graduated sizes, the hanging Revere Ware pots on their hooks, the yellow-and-red wall-paper showing children splashing in puddles, ducks observing them, little clouds, a smiling sun: he toasted it all, his father's new life, and he thought of his mother. "Climb into the oven, why don't you," Miriam Delnegro would have said. "Get yourself into a kettle and roast, while basting well for years and years, until done. Prick with a fork. Prick with a *wineglass,*" she'd have said. "Then serve yourself up."

He nodded to his father. *"A ta santé,* Pop."

"Et à la tienne, Willie." He drank. "It's exceptional. It is like black-berries and blood."

"That good, huh?" Brenda laughed her long and wheezy laugh.

Willie looked down—he realized that he'd been staring at the slightly sagging ceiling, as if someone resided there to whom he had to pay attention—and he found his father contemplating him. He raised his brows, and his father did the same, smiling the old, gallant, charming smile in the older, maybe less healthy, face surrounded by its new life.

"Pop," Willie said, "hello." He found himself unable to speak and ready to cry. His father nodded, as if he knew.

So they ate the brisket in what Willie thought was a barbecue sauce, and they drank the bottle of wine while Brenda served, eating little but smoking several cigarettes, and drinking what looked like tomato juice, leaving red stains on the filters she stubbed out in a wide ashtray that was shaped like a ring cut from a birch tree. Willie told them a little about Miriam Delnegro before he knew that he would, and his father spoke of some eccentrics who summered out-side of Lubec with half a dozen Jack Russell terriers.

Brenda said, as if to her plate, "This was a good thing to do, Willie. I really appreciate it that you came to see us. Don't you imagine how much your father does too."

"The past keeps waking up and biting me," Willie said.

She said, "It's never been over is why."

Willie nodded. "Never," he said. "I wonder if that's good."

"Well, sweet boy, we don't have any *choice.* Why worry?"

"You and Miriam would get along," he heard himself say fatu-ously.

"Of course we would," she said. "Bring her to us, one of these days."

As he knew she would, after they had eaten pie and ice cream, Brenda sent Willie and his father into the living room—its braided rugs, its reclining blue cloth chair, its matching sofa, the end tables and coffee table with brass fixtures matching one another, a stack of magazines and local papers in a basket next to the chair—and they sat, his father in the chair and Willie in the sofa's corner, in the silence between them to which Willie was accustomed.

The photo, not hung but propped on the closed keyboard of an upright piano, took a while for Willie to notice. He knew it, of course. It had hung in their house through his boyhood: his parents, younger than Willie was now, wearing sweaters and tweed knickers, looking as ever like siblings instead of man and wife, sitting on a picnic table outside a country pub in what Willie knew to be Hampshire, their knapsacks at their feet, a pint of ale in his father's hand and a half of shandy in his mother's, the light causing them to squint or wince but to anyway smile. He saw his mother's welcome of the social moment, his father's reserve, and the life before the life he knew, which would funnel down into this small house above the coast of Maine, with all the pulse of that early, that ancient, moment—had they then walked up the gentle hills and found a place to make love? had they talked through dusk and into evening with strangers who savored her Gallic intensity and forgave his father's inwardness?—gone.

"Ah, Willie," his father whispered across the living room. "You begin to understand."

"Will you tell me *what*, Pop?"

"We—that is to say, people, we included—will always be strangers. We should nevertheless try always to be friends."

"That's so, difficult," he said. He felt as though he'd whined it. "One always wants more," he said to his father.

As he expected, his father shrugged. "Of course."

"*Tant pis,* then," Willie said. "Is that right?"

"I cannot think of anything much that is available to us, my Willie, except what we already know. You will of course be staying the night."

He had of course intended to leave. He could not contemplate a night of confinement in the kitsch embodiment of someone else's dream. And he could not bear, even now, before he had to say it, a farewell to his father. For the longer he was with him, the more he missed him. The more he was moved, the more he was cowed. Seeing him, he saw that his father was right: they would not know each other, ever.

Willie didn't hear the phone ring. Brenda, half-bowing, as if to apologize for what Willie thought of, later, as the end, said from the doorway, "Sidney Bauer, hon. Emergency, it sounds like."

"More monkey business, eh, Willie," his father said, rising. "I am on retainer. He is a fisherman. He has a little fleet of fishermen. It is not Wall Street, and they are redolent of cod, but he and his fellows are my practice. My hanky-panky, you would wish to say."

"What kind of emergency, Pop?"

His father shrugged. "It matters little. Someone's arm is torn away in the gears that pull the nets in. Someone has fallen overboard and drowned. Or, of course, the usual matter of Sidney Bauer and Etienne Bernstein smuggling heroin from couriers sent to Canada from where? Cambodia? From Turkey, perhaps." His father was in the foyer, and Willie was behind him. From a peg on the wall, his father took a yellow rain jacket. Willie took the one beside it. "This is not for you," his father said. "They are crude men."

"You aren't," Willie said.

His father leaned an arm on each of Willie's shoulders. Willie could smell soap on the skin of his face and wine on his breath. He was reminded of sitting, as a boy, on his father's lap in the club chair in the living room as his father, after dinner, read to him, in French, from Babar stories. The liquid murmur of the language, and his father's scent, the hard, reassuring muscles of his thighs and his soft, relaxed stomach, had hypnotized Willie and sent him to sleep, but always with a sense, underneath every other sensation, of the familiarly alien; his comfort in his father had always, he realized, been tinctured with a thrill of something like fear.

"You are a good fellow, Willie. You became a good man. I am happy that you are my son. I am happy that you sought me."

"Would you have come after *me,* Pop, one of these days, if I hadn't shown up?"

After a few seconds, his father blinked, and blinked again, and leaned in to kiss him on each cheek. "Like your mother," he said, "you have always sought a little more. *Salut,* Willie."

As if they held glasses, Willie said, *"Salut."*

The Law of Violated Flesh

THEY LEFT WILLIE'S CAR in the public parking lot and thumped along the boards of the narrow jetty to the U-shaped rubber dinghy that waited, its motor gurgling, its tubular sides bending in the active seas that beat against the dock. A very small man with wide, gloved hands helped them in, and then, without comment, he coiled the line that Willie, at his instructions, untied from a cleat, and he made for the harbor's mouth in three snarling increments of speed that had them wet with foam in a minute. The fishing boat was lighted, and so was the dock, but in between darkness glistened and writhed.

His father shouted, over the noise of the engine and the slap of the boat against the sea, "This is LaVerne Autry. The sailors call him Gene. As in the cowboy."

Willie shouted, "Hi, Gene."

The man nodded and pulled at his watch cap.

"Gene says that the Coast Guard has already responded with first aid."

"So not such a bad emergency," Willie called.

His father shook his head. "The first aid was too late, apparently. First became last. Apparently, the man is dead."

Willie had expected a wooden vessel some thirty or forty feet long. The rusted white hull, pitted and gouged and flecked, seemed as high as a house, and the narrow metal ladder they climbed was icy under his hands. Seawater soaked his feet and legs up to the knee before he was out of the rubber boat and making his way, leaning against the sway of the ship, toward a very distant rail. His father, ahead of him, climbed like a boy. Autry waited below.

The deck was slippery, and Willie learned to seize a handhold before he moved his feet. Sidney Bauer, bulky in a red-and-black-checked shirtjacket and wearing a dark peaked hat, waited for them in the cockpit, drinking from a tall can of Australian beer and grimacing after each sip.

"Steve," Bauer said. "And son. Anybody want a beer?"

The cabin lights gave a soft, unfocused look to charts, manuals, paper tacked and taped to bulkheads and tables. A man who looked like Sidney Bauer, but whose shoulders were more rounded and whose neck seemed shorter, and who wore an air of sorrow that Willie thought genuine, walked across the cabin to shake his father's hand and nod to Willie. He wore black-rimmed glasses and Sidney Bauer didn't, but they looked almost identical.

Sidney Bauer, looking at Willie, said, "That's my cousin, Herm. Herm, you met Steve's son just now. He's from New York."

"New York," Herm said, in a high, gentle voice, pronouncing it as Noo Yawk.

"But I'm originally from Mars," Willie said, and Herm laughed a long, cackling laugh, and Sidney Bauer smiled.

"So," his father said. "The crisis?"

"Stanley Emerson, who only shipped with me for thirteen years, during which time the worst thing he ever did was lie about being drunk when we sneaked in some fishing off Prince Edward Island"—Sidney Bauer turned to tell Willie, "A virgin caught in the men's locker room ain't half as touchy as Canada on fishing rights," and he nodded solemnly, because, Willie guessed, fishing rights were money and money was sacred—"Stanley took it upon himself to beat to death a half-weasel, half-man by the name of Louis Alporto. Launched himself off at him carrying a hell of a heavy wrench, and he just pounded shit out of him until his face looked like that toothpaste used to have stripes in it from mouthwash?"

"You knew he was dead," Herm said, "before it was over. Nothing in the joints after the first few blows. You know, knees and elbows. It was like a prizefight. The head's still up in the air, and the soles of the feet ain't showing yet, but the rest is real loose. Here's the Coast Guard back.

"No, I lied. It's more Coast Guard, an officer, I would wager, plus it looks like too many police in one place."

"Before we speak with them," Willie's father said, "and before I call a criminal specialist in Augusta—I can do a contract, and I can do a broken contract, but I cannot do a *murdered* contract, Sidney—tell me, merely to satisfy my curiosity and that of Willie, why. That is: why did Emerson kill what was his name?"

"Alporto," Sidney Bauer said. "Some variety of spice, maybe Portuguese, I think. They're a hard-ass bunch, and they sneak around some."

"I have known valorous Portuguese," Willie's father said.

"Well, then, this was a fella you didn't ever know," Herm said. "He was as much of a snake as cobras get to be."

"A weasel and a snake," his father said. "And the offense he committed against Mr. Emerson?"

"Touched his daughter," Herm said.

"Touched."

"Felt her up, according to Stanley, in the place she waits table. She's a schoolgirl. Say, eleventh grade."

His father looked at him and Willie said, "Around sixteen or seventeen years old."

"What part of the body? Was that a decisive factor?" his father asked.

"There," Sidney Bauer said. Herm nodded. Sidney Bauer said, "You know. There."

His father looked to Willie, who could only shake his head.

"Under the belly," Sidney Bauer said.

Herm said, "He went for her crotch. Then he said, 'Whoops,' and he laughed. She dropped the food she was carrying. They docked her pay for that. I wonder if Stanley wasn't as furious over the money she lost as the face."

"Crotch is face, but a dollar's still a dollar," Sidney Bauer said.

Willie's father looked at the compass on the bulkhead, then he looked at Willie. "They did not prepare me in the school of law, Willie, for the law of violated flesh. I will now speak, unprepared, with the authorities. A moment, little more. I must ask about bail, which will not be permitted, and then I must use the telephone to waken the expert in Augusta. A moment, then?"

It was an hour and a half. Willie, very cold, even in the zippered rain jacket with its hood drawn over his head, stayed outside, pacing the deck along the railing, not looking over at the gleam of the sea as it shoved against the fisherman, hauling the hull up and down, and causing Willie to lurch as he walked. The ship throbbed, lights glowed everywhere, as if they made ready for a voyage. He thought of his parents on the boats that took them from Le Havre across the English Channel and around Spithead to Northampton, and later from the Thames out past Margate to New York Harbor and the North River and New York. How young they'd been, he thought, how alone together in the vast, dangerous world. Shaking with cold, he thought, then, of how his father had voyaged to the edge of his new country, at the outer edge of his life, to live with Brenda and her cough and canisters and wallpaper as a new man. How American his father's story was! How pinched and provincial his own had had become. Then the engines stopped, and so did Willie, caught in his orbit around and around the cockpit and cabin and the two holds, a net boom amidships, another at the stern, and the silence from the interior of the ship where his father and the owners and the Coast Guard and police discussed the next twenty or thirty years in the life of a man named Emerson, and probably mentioned only incidentally Louis Alporto's stopped life. And Willie wondered whether the woman from Cuba could really have been, after all, CIA, and what it meant that she permitted his father to come up here to live with Brenda and the teeming possibilities in this part of Maine for border crimes.

It was midnight when they stood at the docks, the two Bauers, the two Bernsteins. The fisherman was closed down, with only Autry on board, and Emerson had been taken away to begin his long wait. Next to last to leave the vessel was Alporto, brought on deck after storage in one of the holds, zipped into a body bag and spinning slowly in his death, lighted from above by the helicopter's warning beacon, flashing halfway red as he was hauled through the dark air toward his own long wait.

They stood beside Willie's rental car, talking about murder, about life insurance, contracts, and cod. When they paused, and when each of them exhaled as if at the prompting of the other, and when all acknowledged their fatigue, Willie's father said, "Sidney, will you drive me home? I think Willie is on his way. I know when he is staying and when not, and I believe that he is on the verge. Are you on the verge, Willie?"

"Pop, it beats a slow goodbye."

"I agree," his father said. "Goodbye is sufficiently difficult. Saying it over an evening and a breakfast: intolerable. I want to hear from you, Willie. *D'accord?*"

"You too, Pop. Love to Brenda. Many thanks to Brenda. And you too, all right?"

His father kissed him on each cheek. "We are French, you know," he said to the Bauers. "This is a ceremony of ours."

"You go right ahead," Sidney Bauer said.

"Bye, Pop."

"Willie, *à bientôt.*"

Willie climbed in to drive away as smoothly, with as calm an appearance, as he could muster. He honked once, to signify one more farewell to his father and his father's life, and then he found his way to 191, which would take him back along the coast.

The Bracelet on the Bone

HE MIGHT HAVE STOPPED anyplace along the narrow, sand-bordered, potholed road just because of his fatigue, but it was the lights that he saw, approaching the turnoff to the Cutler Naval Station, that led him to the sandy soil at the side, where he opened his window, cut his lights, and turned off his engine. He could see the dozens upon dozens of high girderlike antennas, each topped with blinking red lights. He thought of the blinking light that flashed upon the shrouded corpse of Louis Alporto as the military helicopter ferried it ashore. He stared at the lighted antennas and found himself wondering at the coded messages that floated from them along the air and into and out of his rented car, his body, his brain.

He closed his eyes and listened to the distant ocean and, underneath its rhythms, the pumping low surge of generators from the vicinity of the masts. "We use *in* the vicinity," he heard Miriam Delnegro say. "Otherwise, we make changes, and we try to be more precise. It's in the *Handbook*. Bad language is in effect a lie. At this house, we do not buy lies." He saw her in his office as she held up the stapled pages of her *Handbook for Style,* which was sent to authors when they read and worked at the copyedited manuscript pages turned in to Miriam and passed along by her to editors in the house who sent them back to their authors. It instructed them in the house style— please use *all right* instead of *alright;* never use a dependent clause following a semicolon; there is no need to employ a capital initial after a colon or em-dash. "Baby," Miriam would have told him, "you knew the rules. You know them now. Live the situation, please."

As he thought of her, he watched the approach of a short, wide man in a sailor's white uniform. He wasn't armed, except with the very large and alert Rottweiler beside him on a thin chain. Willie blinked into the glare of the sentry's flashlight.

"You all right, sir?"

"I was resting," Willie said.

"Can't let you rest around here," the sentry said. "Can you move along, sir?" He wasn't as young as he'd looked, nor was his dog as uninterested as he had seemed, and Willie reached for the ignition key. "Hold it!" the sentry said, and the dog stiffened, began to make deep noises in his throat.

"Ignition," Willie said.

"Roger that," the man said. He reminded Willie, but only with his unblinking stare, which matched his dog's, of Tony Fevler's husband, who had returned from Vietnam to find his wife and to break Willie's nose.

"Turning it," Willie said. "Sorry."

The sentry nodded. His dog looked ready to tear a tire from the car.

Willie drove slowly because his hands seemed uncertain, his vision a little blurred, and he left the lighted masts and their sentry behind as he drove north on 191 before turning toward Dogtown and East Machias. He cursed himself for a melancholy wanderer, a man too old to feel this young. He thought of Miriam Delgado with a comfortable mixture of apprehension, awe, and desire. But that was his cover story, he scolded himself. Miriam was Miriam, and there would be much of her and him when he returned, he hoped. But now, for tonight, she was the legend—the plausible story that he spun to persuade those he spied upon that he was anything else but a thief of their secret truths. He was wielding Miriam, whose buttocks he bit at, whose slender strong throat he loved to touch, as a cover for Tony Fevler, who returned to him as he contemplated Coast Guard helicopters ferrying the dead, and U.S. Navy broadcasts from the edge of the country out to sea. He remembered them, carrying their lies and silences and—yes, damn it—love, as they marched to protest all of the Pentagon, each armed service, every bomb dropped and mine triggered and cartridge fired. They had never discussed how outnumbered they were. They had blindly, stupidly, even courageously marched.

He remembered, as he drove, how fifty or so had gathered to see their students off to die in the war, over now for nearly ten years. Their purpose was to demonstrate their outrage at educating boys over four years and watching them die for the sake of the careers of politicians. They assembled below the faculty club—Oh, Jesus, he thought: *Tunk!*—and there were women with strollers and carriages, faculty and students in rented black academic regalia. They carried signs denouncing all violence and they made speeches to each other, and then they set off. They strolled, a little self-consciously, down the library walk that went to the town's main street, lined here by fraternity houses. It was early upstate May, and the boys who sat on lawn chairs or leaned against the outside of the second story on top of the flat roof of the first fraternity in the row wore varsity jackets or college sweatshirts such, he remembered, as his mother had taken to wearing. They drank beer in the pale sunshine of forenoon, and, it was clear, they'd been drinking beer since the sun had first struck the roof.

"Queers," one of them called.

"Pinko dipshits," a fraternity brother said.

"Bunch of Commie assholes," called a third, bridging them into the chorus, which was whinnied by all the kids on the roof: "Ass-holes."

He imagined, as he drove toward East Machias, how he might tell this story to Miriam. Even as he did, he apologized to her for employing the clean, taut angles of her face, the depth of her angry brown eyes, the apprehension always lining her forehead. Because it was Tony's lighter hair and larger head, and Tony's lusher, looser, somehow more available body he could almost feel now, and even taste and smell.

Someone threw an egg from one of the houses, and then many eggs came. A short woman wearing black tights under black shorts, who clearly was experienced at such parades, unfurled an umbrella and held it over her baby and herself. She could not keep off the flashlight batteries that followed the eggs, however, and she broke to the right to get onto the sidewalk across from the fraternity houses so she could follow the march in safety. They swatted some of the missiles away by using the posters stapled onto sticks. Several of the marchers wept, and Willie made himself walk, he remembered, with his head held high, so that no one would suspect him of considering the effect of a second broken nose. They were joined by the boy who had played the blues at the campus demonstration in the fall. Willie had forgotten his name. He carried an acoustic guitar at which he played, and they began to sing Joan Baez songs.

Then Tony fell in—she was very pregnant, and she waddled—and she was joined by her mother. Willie remembered watching as Mrs. Fevler took the arm of one of the graduating boys and walked beside him. Tony did her best to keep up. Willie stayed behind her. He thought of the photos he'd seen of the laborers' parades in the Marais. He heard his mother's voice grow flatter and lower over the months as she reported on his father and the Cuban control who ran his *sub rosa* work. Some townspeople were at the sidewalk now, and their faces were grim. A recent high school graduate had died in combat, the first local kid, and it seemed that he could only be honored if the war's opponents were scorned. His stomach ached during the march, he remembered, recalling how it had ached in Paris as well.

They turned to the right, circling back onto the campus, walking down between a line of elm trees, most of which were dying, all of which were drastically pruned. From behind one of them, against the background of a long campus lawn, Professor—Willie clenched his teeth and sought to remember his name. He could see his face, behind his movie camera, which whirred as Professor, yes, Clendinnin recorded their faces as he slowly, lovingly, hatefully panned.

Pam Fevler, he remembered, had shouted at him: "You ought to be ashamed, Hal Clendinnin!"

"No, ma'am," he said in his surprisingly deep voice. *"You* all should be ashamed. And you will be. This film goes directly to the FBI. They ought to know who our enemies are."

Six or seven marchers at once spoke the Pogo line about meeting the enemy and they is us as Clendinnin backed away from them, still filming, capturing face after face. Willie remembered thinking that he would always be there, watching the thickened body of Tony Fevler as she always walked away from him. The students, who would have left there to die or be wounded by snakebite or land mine or madness or slow infection, would also always be there, entire. In some brittle copy of the film, perhaps in Clendinnin's cellar or inside a cupboard of the Federal Bureau of Investigation, Willie thought, he would keep marching, even after the march's end, in protest against the war, against his own eradication in it, holding his broken nose and his version of his undercover father's chin raised high against the pallid sunlight of a chilly upstate spring. He would forever be subversive as he followed the lost lover of his fantasies and maybe the weapon against her of his mother's restive God. And, if Clendinnin had caught his face right, Willie thought, driving away from what was left of his family now on Route 1 toward Machias, someone in some future day—this one, for instance, he thought—someone stumbling upon that moment might notice how carefully Willie Bernstein studied her, and how always he seemed to adjust the pace of his progress to the slowswinging drift and catch and lift and drift again of her sad, defiant bright braid.

For Jane Pinchin

Don't Tell Anyone

Anyone

FREDERICK BUSCH

A Reader's Guide

A Conversation with Frederick Busch

KN: You are acclaimed both as a novelist and as a short-story writer. Do certain themes lend themselves better to one or the other?

FB: No, I don't write about "themes." I find that I write about characters. They occur to me, or even haunt me. They come about as I try to answer a question that occurs to me: Why is that small child standing outside in the winter, waiting alone for a school bus, wearing only an insufficient sweater? What could it be like to be those two women, living here in the country in a dilapidated house, working every day—at the labor associated with men—to bring it back from ruin? What happens if you're a kid and your parents love each other more than they love you? And so on. I try to answer those questions about people, in terms of the people, as I make them up; you can get the truth from that sort of making up. And some people—some answers—take the long course of many hours, days, years; they become characters in a novel. Some exist in—and for—a moment: all of their lives may be concentrated in that moment, or it may be the most important event in their lives that the moment expresses. They, of course, become characters in a story. The writer brings them through the story to that culminating moment and then seals them up in amber; they're preserved forever in the instant of hearing, of knowing, of feeling, of sensing—or of willfully turning away from—what will prove, all their lives, to have been the crucial instant of every other moment they go on to live.

KN: Do you prefer one form to the other?

FB: I'm a failed poet, and the story is closer to the poem I wish I could write. The novel examines people as time roars through them like a great river. The novel, alas, takes forever to write. And you're responsible for so much when you write it, and therefore the novelist, it seems to me—if that writer is honest and really wants to make art—is always dissatisfied, cranky, worried that he or she has failed the characters. If you fail your characters, then you fail your readers, and of course you then fail yourself.

KN: **One more quick question about form: Is the novella a long short story, a short novel, or a hybrid of some sort?**

FB: The novella is a hybrid, I believe; longer (and, most importantly, thicker and broader) than a story, with room for several characters and the strand of story that each carries, it permits a multiplicity of concerns that the story tends not to support, but it focuses more narrowly than—what I think of as—the novel. The novella is a delight to write because you can do so much in it, yet can avoid the responsibilities that are incumbent on the novelist. And you get to finish it! While the novel, as you write it, seems to go on and on, requiring ever more—weather, details of history, ancillary or supporting characters who must be served as fully as major characters. For the reader, it's a fuller experience, perhaps less dramatically emphatic as to the moment of realization, the sense of a crux having been reached and failed or survived, as in the case of a short story, but still offering a sense of both drama and more conscious thought about a matter (as well as a moment) than the story.

KN: **One of the sections in the novella, *A Handbook for Spies*, is titled "A Father Stolen or Strayed." Those words lend a sense of what is at work in this collection of stories as a whole, and several of the stories seem almost preparation for the novella that closes *Don't Tell Anyone*. Could you comment on the design of the collection and why you chose to include these pieces?**

FB: The stories are about people whose lives are fraught. They need to tell their story (as, most obviously, in "The Talking Cure," the title of which comes from the description by an early psychoanalytic patient about her experience in therapy). They also fear to tell their story. If they don't tell it, they sicken, their lives are unhealthy; if they do tell it, they might feel relieved, yet they might also feel exposed—emotionally naked. The book, for me, is "about" the story: how well we tell it about ourselves and others, the various ways in which we tell, the ways we seek not to tell. As for "A Father Stolen or Strayed," that title for a section of the novella is an echo of one of the concerns I believe I, and some readers, find in my work: the fractured family, the family as it frays, the way we function or fail to as a unit of parents and children who are dependent upon each other yet, sometimes, inimical to each other. That image of Hansel and Gretel being led into the dark woods by their parents, who will leave them to be eaten by forest creatures so that the parents have enough food—a family "where," as I've written elsewhere, "hunger comes first"—is a motivating and haunting vision that drives a good deal of my work, I think. Of course, I'm seeking a paradisal opposite to that situation. And, once in a while—in the case, say, of Catherine and her children in my novel *Harry and Catherine*, Rochelle and her children in *Closing Arguments*, Chun Ho and William Bartholomew and Chun Ho's kids in *The Night Inspector*, as well as some of the parents and some of the children in these stories—I feel lucky to find some families in which generosity prevails.

KN: **In "Bob's Your Uncle," the character of Jillie, deeply wounded by a double betrayal, asks her husband, "What did you think was coming to you that you deserved so much?" That question appears in different ways throughout the collection. Is it that "wanting more" that makes the American family so tenuous?**

FB: Not what I was thinking of, although you're right about Americans in general—the world's middle class in general: Appetite leads us to devour our lives without tasting them, and we expect what we might not earn. But, no, I was thinking of matters that are more individual: How so many of us, individually, think that we've a right to satisfaction. People complain that they're not fulfilled, that they're denied, that the world does not give them what they hunger for. The husband in "Bob's Your Uncle" thought he had a right to that splendid woman because he wanted, even needed, her. I pray for, wish for, believe in, hope to have, more discipline than that. Be brave. Keep your clothing on. Help someone else. Stop whining. This is a time of everyone writing memoirs about their deprivations—soft-core psychological pornography, a lot of it—and of people telling us what they need and need and need. And I keep thinking: Do go ahead and make somebody ELSE glow with satisfaction. I guess it's the Boy Scout in me.

KN: **Near the end of the novella, Willie's father says, "We—that is to say, people, we included—will always be strangers. We should nevertheless try always to be friends." Is that a response to the hurting children in these stories?**

FB: It's a response to the wounded children and the wounded everyone-else in the stories. But it's my sad, sad conclusion. I think of watching my children, when they were infants, as they slept. I think of watching my wife, Judy, now, when she sleeps. I watch those eyelids pulse with their inner life—dreams, neurons randomly firing in their nervous system, or the muttering to itself of the deep subconscious: Who knows? And who knows what thoughts, dreams, visions, terrors, or mundane concerns are racing to and fro in there, under their eyelids, inside the secrecy of their skulls? I don't know. I cannot know. I never will know, for they probably don't—in a conscious way—know either. So they, whom I love more than myself, beyond all others, remain unknown to me. They are, in that way, lost to me. And, while celebrating their gloriousness, I find myself mourning at the same time. It's like the past: always tickling, or even grinding, us in the present; never vanished, yet not apprehensible—except through art. In my work, I think I am seeking or celebrating or, least useful of all, mourning that unknown territory of those I love and those whom, on my behalf, my characters love, and the vast, subconscious continent between them and me, between them and themselves.

KN: **Unfair question: Do you have any particular favorites among these stories?**

FB: I like "Joy of Cooking" because it was rejected by every glossy magazine in America, and by many of the literary quarterlies, and yet it is a story that readers of the book mention very frequently as a favorite of theirs. "Domicile" steals its little trailer, and the building of walls, but not the emotional truths, from the life of one of our sons. "A Handbook for Spies" took me thirty years to get right; I've been working on the Vietnam era and some of those social matters—including the anti-Semitism and the chanting of the names of the dead, including the disappearing father—since the late 1960s or early 1970s. But all these stories are my children, and I care about them as I do for our sons, Ben and Nick: with a father's total love for each.

Karen Novak is a writer and teacher living in Mason, Ohio with her husband and their two daughters. Her first novel, Five Mile House, *was published in October 2000. She's currently at work on her second novel.*

Reading Group Questions and Topics for Discussion

1. In "Machias," the old man, Charley, tells the young couple a story of improbable heroism. Their response disappoints him, and they belatedly interpret the story as a test they have failed. What exactly is the test? Why did they fail? What point is the father trying to convey to his soon-to-marry son in relating the incident and admitting the failure? Does Charley's "test" tell you anything about how to approach stories in general?

2. Ghosts, of one sort or another, figure prominently throughout the collection. Identify the different "hauntings" in the stories. Through these various apparitions, what is Busch suggesting about the way the past works in present lives?

3. Who is the little boy in "Domicile"? Where do you think he came from? Where and why did he disappear? Can you sense his presence in any of the other stories?

4. What is the significance of the pocket knife in "Heads"? Given the history of the knife, what do you make of Alec's use of it? Does her choice of weapon affect your response to her or her actions?

5. The daughter meeting her estranged father in "The Ninth, in E Minor," realizes that "the man I had thought of as my father, looking like himself was no longer available. He was several new selves, and I would have to think of him that way." How does this understanding inform Busch's depiction of the parent-child relationships in these stories?

6. Myrna, the narrator of "Vespers," recounts an afternoon's excursion into the time-altered terrain of her childhood. She is in the company of her brother, Ira, and her lover, Bert Wagg Jr.

What is the purpose of the outing? What do you make of Myrna's relationships with both men? What about how the men respond to one another in the story's beginning and then at its end? How might the story change if Ira or Bert were narrating? What has happened for Myrna by the story's conclusion?

7. Busch uses music to deepen our intuitive experience of a character's emotional state. This is especially true in "Joy of Cooking," in which two popular and happy songs—of very different origins—are sung in moments of dawning heartbreak. Think about other choices the author might have made. Why are the one he uses so effective?

8. Along the same lines, consider the choices Busch makes in other sensory details: the "cold smell of old fires" in the smokehouse in "Malvasia"; the "hot, flavorless tea" during the dinner in "Passengers"; the "little brass screw" that breaks on the eyeglasses in "Debriefing." How do these specific observations guide your experience of the story? Find other examples of the *telling* detail and discuss how description can serve as more than just the backdrop to narrative action.

9. Kevin, the unnerving boy who arrives unannounced on the threshold in "Bob's Your Uncle," is greeted by the said Uncle Bob with a set of polarized descriptions. In the first, Kevin is a handsome, elegantly dressed young man, but as he moves past Bob, farther into the house, those details degrade. How does Bob's reversal in perception prepare you for what is to follow? Are there other such reversals for the characters or for you, the reader? How do these help you decipher the probable content of Jillie and Deborah's unheard phone conversation?

10. "Timberline" and "Still the Same Old Story" appear physically connected. Back-to-back in the collection, both close with the

narrating characters' comments on being in a story. In the first, Hank thinks, his thoughts sounding in his wife's voice, *"If you don't have a story, there isn't an end. You don't get punctuation."* In the second, Sharon says, "Once you are in a story, you must live forever. You must choose again and again. You always do it the same." Discuss the implications of these ideas in terms of how they reflect upon each other; what does Sharon's reasoning say for Hank's story and vice versa?

11. The novella, *A Handbook for Spies*, is divided into two sections, each titled from the final lines of James Wright's "To the Muse." What is accomplished by dividing the narrative and yet, bridging the division with these lines from the poem?

12. Poetry, both the subject and the form, surfaces in several places throughout the work. Given that context, what becomes of the anti-war demonstrators' reading of the names of the dead?

13. The narrative concerns, in part, the characters' differing, pragmatic strategies of getting what they need by pretending to be something they are not. Consider each of these characters and strategies in turn. Would you include Willie among them? Why or why not?

14. When Tony's husband, a Vietnam vet, assaults Willie in his campus office, it is with a rage fueled by more than sexual jealousy and humiliation. Consider the scene in the faculty club that takes place immediately before the attack. Upon leaving the club, Willie spots the ex-husband watching him. What exactly is happening in the build up to the assault? Why do the memories of his father's "just in case" chocolates and Tony's admonition to "stay away from the wine" hold importance here?

15. The next chapter, "I'll Be Home for Christmas," is almost a mirror image of the assault in several ways: Professor Wherry's pres-

ence at the faculty club, Tony's husband's concrete declaration of his claim of her body, another powerful revelation of the entrenchment of anti-Semitism. What does Busch accomplish in the dovetailing of these two scenes in this fashion? What is behind Tony's smile of triumph? How is Willie changed by the juxtaposition of these two events?

16. In the novella's second half, in the section from which the collection takes its title *Don't Tell Anyone*, Willie confronts his father with the fact that his attempts at a secret life failed; his mother had discovered the affair the father was trying to hide behind the lie of being a CIA operative. "His father nodded. 'Everyone always discovers,' he said. 'There are no secrets…. ultimately, all secrets are told. No. Not told: suspected.' " What then do you suspect is Willie's secret? What is "The Bracelet on the Bone"? How does the novella's final scene echo the imagery of the James Wright poem?

17. And finally, to return to the stories, "The Talking Cure" begins: "Love is unspeakable." Consider the shades of meaning in that statement. How do you reconcile what cannot be spoken with what dare not be told? Does the struggle to effect that reconciliation, in the end, give us any insight into what exactly "literary art" might be?